I0717023

GAYLE AND STEPHEN
PORTER

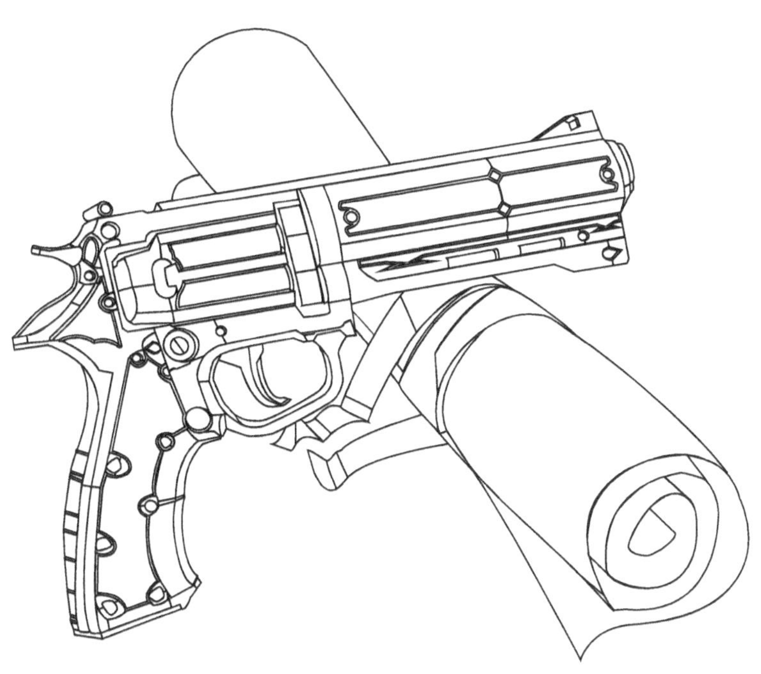

EX LIBRUM

DIKAIÓ: Book II

ISBN: 978-1-957907-10-9 (Paperback)
ISBN: 978-1-957907-11-6 (Hardcover)
ISBN: 978-1-957907-12-3 (Ebook)

Library of Congress Control Number: 2023951691

Any references to historical events, real people, or real places are used fictitiously. Names, characters, and places are products of the authors' imagination.

Book design by Stephen Porter.

First printing edition 2023. Printed in the United States of America.

Porter Creative
3647 Oviedo
Brownsville TX 78520

www.portercreatives.com

To our wonderful readers,

The first book was for our kids.

This installment is for all of you that demanded a sequel.

Guess that cliffhanger worked out in the end.

The Library
Aiworth Bridge

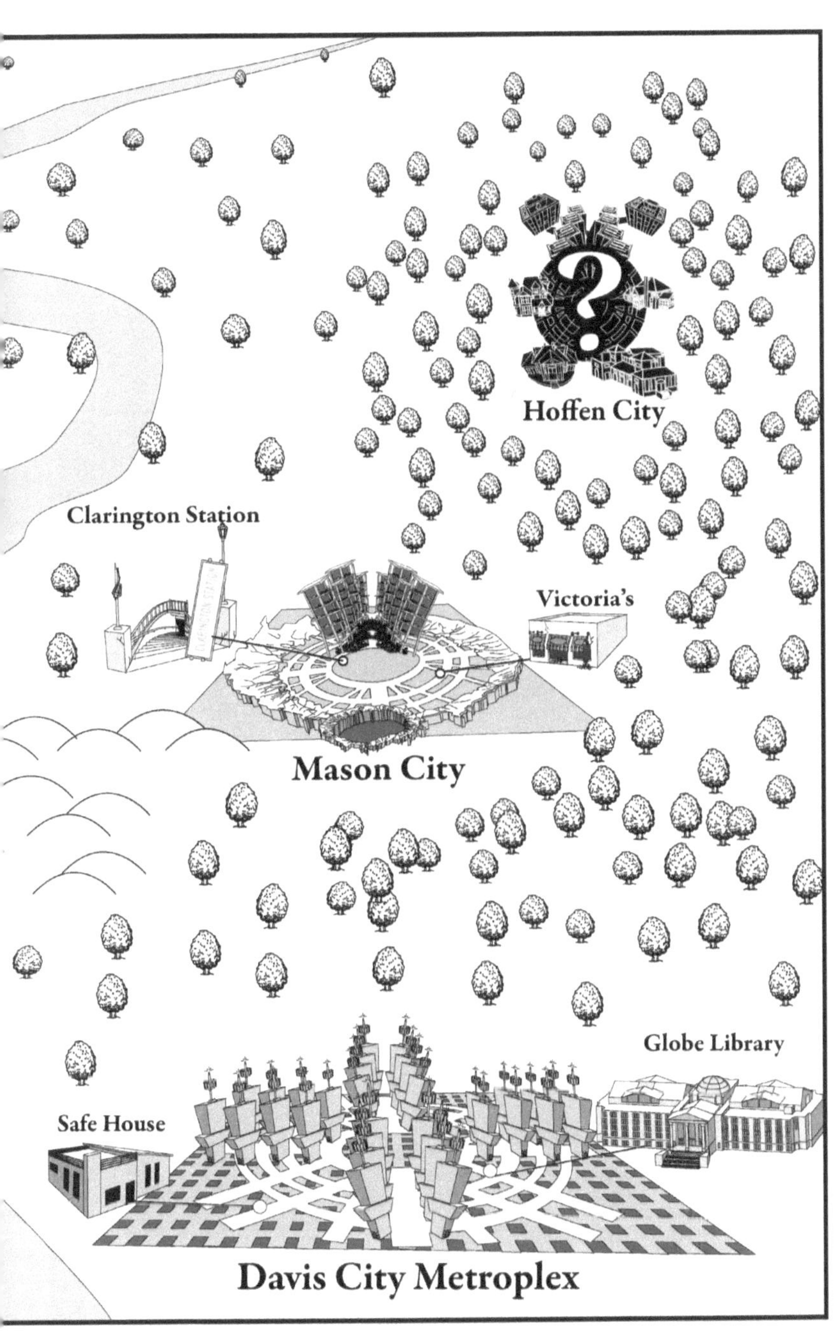

Hoffen City
Clarington Station
Victoria's
Mason City
Globe Library
Safe House
Davis City Metroplex

CONTENTS

Plosing her eyes did little to block out the light. There was no escaping it. The brilliance emanated from rows of tiny white bulbs lining the ceiling, walls, even the door, which were all coated with stainless steel and buffed to mirror-like reflectivity. The light shone endlessly around the tiny, three-feet-by-three-feet space. At first, with the lights so near her body, she expected the room to get hot like a sauna, but instead, the room was freezing, and the lights were oddly cool to the touch. A vent in the ceiling above her was pumping cold air into the room, and with only the white shorts and white spaghetti strap top they had given her to wear, her body was racked with constant, uncontrollable shivers. She was tired too. Time had ceased to exist in the little room, but she guessed days, maybe weeks, had passed since she had been able to sleep. Even with the light, the cold, and the lack of space to lie down, she probably could have leaned against a wall and dozed if it were not for the noise. Music blared continually from unseen speakers somewhere in the room. A discordant cacophony of wailing screams and electric string instruments. She wasn't sure if the electric gypsy was using a real language or if the lyrics were intended to be incoherent, but she feared the screeching lunacy was driving her mad.

She tried to focus on her next steps. Her captors had questioned her for hours in another tiny room with mirror-like walls, though this one was big enough to also hold a table and a chair. Iron shackles were welded to both pieces of furniture. Her wrists and ankles were still chafed from their chains, though those wounds were slight compared to the battering her captors had inflicted. They were unrelenting with both their questions and their fists. The mirrored walls of her cell displayed an endless gallery showcasing their work: a kaleidoscope of purple bruises and eyes nearly swollen shut. The worst piece in the exhibit was the parade of broken noses. She had lost consciousness from that blow, and she flinched with the fresh pain the memory brought to her face. The room swam slightly, and she put her hand out to steady herself. Her fingers brushed against a brown smear on the wall, a paint flourish of dried blood she had spilled after the last interrogation, just one more piece in the installation of pain. In retrospect, she should have been grateful for that final blow; the bit of unconsciousness it provided was the most rest that she had experienced since she had knocked on the gates of the citadel.

She looked the room and the motion reflected in the mirrors made her nauseous. Her eyes closed involuntarily to block out the swirling woman in bloody white, and fresh pain spread across her face. She kept her eyes closed anyway—if only she could sleep or wake from this nightmare. Of course, it was not a nightmare. She was really there, and it was her own foolishness that had put her in this position. She was not sure what she should have expected; it was a fool's gambit, but she was so tired of the never-ending war: her parents' parents' parents had been fighting it long before she was born, and her children's children's children would be fighting it unless someone did something brave. Something that would at least save a modicum of her society. They had been so close to losing everything so many times. An entire generation had been lost in defending Hoffen City, and now, the new Governor wanted to repeat the same mistakes.

When she was younger, she had championed the advancements in weaponry and defenses, but now that she had her own children, the thought of them dying with all the rest that had gone before in the endless war was just too much to bear. She was going to end it. She had waited to make the journey until the new moon was in the sky, and the clouds were thick enough to hide her in shadows. Her husband barely stirred when she slipped out of bed. Her sons—Josiah, six and Harris, ten—smiled in their sleep as she brushed their foreheads with light kisses. They were so young, and yet their father was already teaching them to fight, showing them how to handle the magistrates' weapons. Harris was deadly accurate: one of the best marksmen in their compound. But what good was a bullet against the silvered steel of a sprite? They came in all shapes and sizes with any number of wicked weapons: whips, blades, saws, fire, acid, light beams, electricity. The enemy no longer came out to fight. Instead, they sent never-ending legions of sprites to rain down death and destruction on every human being they could find. That is why that night, she took a small pack of food and other supplies she had loaded days earlier and walked out on her family. Someone had to end the war before they were all dead.

The journey to the citadel was dark, and there was no path to mark the way. When the enemy came out of the citadels, they did not travel by road; rather, they rode the skies on flying silver sprites: mythical gods on winged horses. At least those were the stories her parents had told her as a girl. As an adult, she had seen their cities and knew they were not gods, but they liked to think of themselves that way. Her compound regularly ran reconnaissance missions to report the sprites' movements to the Governor and the people's army. It was harder to navigate the brush in the dark, and she heard the wilding wolves hunting in the distance. She had to move quickly before any of the nocturnal pack caught scent of her.

It took the better part of the night, but soon she was standing on a rocky outcropping overlooking a tall black tower jutting out of the dark horizon. A red light blinked on and off near the top of the building, and she could vaguely make out sentinel sprites flying around the top. In the dark, they looked like dragons with triangular wings and long necks extending from their bodies, but she knew that those necks were actually heavy guns that projected bits of molten steel with deadly accuracy. The sprites detected them by their heat, so the night would offer little protection from this point forward. She pulled a heavy silver blanket from her pack. The insulation would make her invisible to the flying sprites. The threat she really needed to worry about were the bands of silver-steeled culture sprites in the fields below that led up to the citadel. They mostly just took care of the enemies' crops, but their arms were equipped with blades and could extend to long, steel whips in an instant. She had seen them slice through wolves—and at times her people—like butter. The culture sprites were hard to see in the darkness of night, but she had spent hours in this very spot, recording their movements and noting patterns for the people's army. She did not need to see them to know where they were, and if she timed it right and moved with surety, she could navigate the patterns of the fields and reach the gates before she was detected.

She threw the insulated blanket over her, and tied it securely around her neck, forming a cowl that covered her head and body. Then she began the slow climb down the craggy face of the cliff into the enemy's fields below. She had lived a hard life like all her people, and her hands were nearly as calloused and hard as the rocks she gripped. No one had ever gone down this cliff into the fields, but she had climbed enough rocks and mountains to descend with speed and stealth. Not one pebble was loosed to alert the enemy's sprites before her deft feet touched the soft soil at the bottom. She turned, hunched low, and waited, silently counting the seconds in her mind: " . . . twenty-seven seconds, twenty-eight seconds, twenty-nine seconds, thirty seconds." Her body tensed at thirty as, right on cue, a culture sprite buzzed through the rows of corn ahead of her. She waited five more seconds then sprinted into the maize.

Her counting changed as soon as she crossed the threshold of the enemies' fields. Now, she was counting in musical time; her feet pounding rhythm on 16th notes: "one e and a two e and a three e and a . . .." The words to one of the old hymns played along in her head, and when she hit the third measure, she quickly turned right and ran forward for four measures, then turned back toward the gate and ran that way. The hymn hit a double rest, and she dropped flat to the ground. Two culture sprites floated past her: one behind and one in front. The double rest ended, and she popped up running straight ahead again. By the time the hymn reached the chorus, she was within a few feet of the gate. The temptation to make a break for it beat hard in her chest, but she forced herself down flat again, waiting for another culture sprite to go by, and then she ran with all her might to the gate.

There was nowhere to hide now. If the enemy's sprites swooped in on her, she would die. She made it to the dark gate and began to pound on its iron surface and call out for someone to answer. Within a fraction of a second, bright white lights sprang up all around her, and she was blinded.

A loud siren blared an alarm, and though she could not see them, she could feel the attention of all the enemy's sprites behind her turn in her direction. She pounded the door all the harder and screamed for someone to give her an audience. She had come too far to die without one.

A dark shadow moved somewhere around her. Her eyes still had not completely adjusted to the bright lights, and then something had a hold of her hair. It yanked hard, and she found herself temporarily weightless as it pulled her off her feet, and then she hit the ground with a hard thud. Her scalp burned as the unseen thing dragged her by her hair across the ground. She thought for a moment one of the sprites had hold of her, but the bright white lights were replaced by simpler electric lights on paneled walls, and she could see glimpses of feet walking in front of her. The enemy had taken her into the citadel. This was her chance.

"Please!" she screamed. "I'm here to talk—to end the war."

The enemy did not break pace—just continued dragging her like a sack of potatoes down the hall. She switched tactics and began to squirm. She tried to employ the warrior training she had received from her parents. She engaged her core and windmilled her legs, trying to pull loose from the enemy's grip and get to her feet. The enemy did not acknowledge her movements, barely breaking pace with her shift in movement. She kept windmilling: one way and then another.

Finally, the enemy growled a gravelly frustration: "Enough!" The boot moved almost too fast to track. Her ears whined, and her eyes swam an instant before the pain nerves triggered through her skull. She had never felt such pain as the enemy's kick. She tried to pull herself to her knees, but her disorientation had not even registered that she was being dragged by her hair again. She was thrown like a child's toy into the mirrored room, and here she had spent most of her time in the citadel with the rare exceptions of the brutal interrogations.

They wanted to know where Hoffen City was. An answer she could not give them. It was the lost city; they could not find it if they wanted to. She had come to offer them something else: a way to end the war, but they were not interested in her suggestions. Instead, her every insistence that she did not know the location of Hoffen City was met with the crack of a fist, or a boot, or a stick. They brought in sprites with wicked-looking instruments—scalpels, saws, pincers—to torture her, but she could not give the enemy what she did not have. When she could physically take no more, she found herself back in the endless lighted mirrors of this little room. Then a terrible thought crossed her mind, and she wondered if this cell would be her tomb.

Suddenly, the lights went dark.

She pressed herself up against the back wall, and the cold of the room was replaced with an icy terror. A silver slit appeared in front of her as the door unsealed and began to swing open. They had come for her again.

The bronze sprite's long tentacle-like arms whipped wildly, whizzing so near Mallory's face that blood sprayed her cheek as it let loose from the copper-tinted metal. She had been standing in its path just a moment before, and if Caleb had not pulled her back against the rock outcropping, the strange little sprite that had found them in the woods would have split her in two. Her heart raced wildly, urging her to run from the sprite's deadly melee. But she was frozen: breath caught in her chest, fingernails digging harshly into her husband's hand. Even in the midst of their present danger, she thought it strange to think of her childhood friend as her husband. Their wedding had been anything but traditional. Her mother performed the ceremony and then stripped them of their titles, exiling them from the city. Their names had been printed on a monument as fallen among the dead. She had many regrets about the events that led up to that moment. Being married to Caleb was not one of them. She stole a glance at her beloved. His face was agony. He was staring down at the hand she was gouging with her nails. She relaxed her grip, smiled, and would have probably laughed under different circumstances.

The sprite's long arm sprang back then, smashing hard against the rocks above them. A shower of tiny stones fell on their heads, and Mallory tried to pull away from the wall to avoid being hit. Caleb's free hand pushed her back against it, hard. "It's not done," he shouted, "There are more coming from both sides and above!"

Mallory looked up. They were in a shallow gorge, barely wide enough for a person to squeeze through, and the walls were about twenty feet high. She saw the dark hairy forms of the four-legged forest beasts running above them. Their eyes glinted green as they ran, and the whites of their fangs dripped drool. They barked and yipped as if they were making battle plans to secure their dinner below. She and Caleb had first encountered the beasts months ago in the pastureland when the things had attacked a cow; the beasts were what had convinced Caleb that they should repair the old fire sprites to protect the city, but fire was so much more dangerous than the forest beasts. It was a fool's errand to think they could control the fire sprites, and they had all learned just how dangerous sprites could be.

Now they were witnessing the danger of this new

clockwork sprite. It was unlike any other sprite Mallory had ever seen, almost an amalgamation of many sprites. Their bronze escort looked like a culture sprite, one of the farming sprites that cared for the city's farms and animals, but it was not silver and sleek like the city sprites or even the fire sprites. It certainly had not been forged in the fires of the Sprite Rookery; rather, it looked like it had been cobbled together from spare parts of different machines. When repairing the fire sprites, Mallory had studied the inner workings of many different kinds of sprites, and this one had some features she had not seen in the sprites book. Its hull was bronze colored and looked like it had been carefully hammered into shape rather than molded from liquid steel. There were gaps in its hull like the fire sprites she had repaired and unwittingly unleashed on the city, and she could see gears ticking and whirring in its chest. Its eyes were like reflective discs, and it could turn the light behind them up painfully bright or turn them off at a whim. It could also speak and seemed to be able to reason like the medic sprites at the hospital. However, with everything that was unfamiliar about the sprite, there were parts that were terrifyingly familiar; its arms were the silver-steel arms of a culture sprite, and they were currently extended into deadly accurate whips. The culture sprites in the city could extend their arms in a similar fashion, and also like those sprites, she had seen this clockwork sprite cut down multiple forest beasts with just a flip of its steel wrists.

The sprite's wrists flicked out again, and whips whizzed past them. A forest beast that had pushed past its fallen companions winced as the whip tore its skin, but it did not fall. Caleb let loose of her chest and pivoted with the sword his father had given him. He caught the beast on its tip and threw it to the ground. Then he leapt back to avoid the sprite's retracting whips, as it prepared for another swing. The effectiveness of its whips was severely limited in the close-quarter battle. If it used full force, it ran the risk of harming its charges, namely the three teens journeying with it. "Alex!" Mallory thought in panic. She looked past the clockwork sprite and saw the silhouette of her best friend Alex in a wide stance behind it. She was wielding two magistrate weapons, firing into more beasts running from that side. The beasts dropped before each volley, and their bodies were beginning to pile up. Alex was the only one in their party that had been trained with the magistrate weapons before they were exiled, so Caleb and Mallory—who could not aim the things anyway—had given Alex the weapons they had received as they left the city. She had two of the holstered belts criss-crossed over her chest, and the third around her waist, and she was rotating the weapons, loading them faster than Mallory thought was possible.

Alex had been in line to succeed her father as the Chief Magistrate; a position that Mallory's father took when the City Council voted to exile the teens. Mallory never did get a chance to ask her father why he left the Order of the Magistrates. She did not even know he had been a member until the day he fought Alex's father and won. His promotion to Chief Magistrate would have been a glorious event if the circumstances surrounding it had not been the death of Alex's grandfather in the fires of the sprites. Alex's grandfather was the Administrator of the city, and he was an evil old man. He had planned to use the magistrates and their weapons to take over the city, which was another reason the three of them had built the fire sprites to thwart his coup d'état, but in the end, he gave his life for his people, and that was at least somewhat commendable.

Alex looked back over her shoulder, her black bobbed hair bouncing lightly as she turned, and paused when she saw Mallory watching her. Alex grinned widely and lifted up the two magistrate weapons; raising her eyebrows, she looked from one arm-length gloved hand to the other; there was a crazed glee in her eyes. Was she having fun? Mallory shivered at the thought. Alex had been through a lot more than Mallory or Caleb leading up to their exile. Those gloves covered a hideously scarred arm from when she had been caught in a fire at City Hall. Mallory had tried to rescue her, but Alex's arm was trapped under a burning beam. Then she had to betray her family to protect the city, and in the end of it all, she was still exiled. And now she was a third wheel to a married couple about to be eaten by carnivorous monsters at the bottom of a gorge. If Alex was losing her mind, who could blame her?

However, helping Alex with her psychopathic break-down would have to wait; right now, Mallory was mentally measuring the bodies that were piling up on both sides of the gorge. She felt anxious seeing their exits being barricaded with forest beasts. It was possible they could climb over the beasts, but she did not imagine a pile of furry carcasses would be very stable, and if and if they fell when there were more beasts waiting on the other side of the pile, they would be quickly overwhelmed. The other option was to climb the walls of the gorge, and they would have to deal with being overwhelmed at the top or having the creatures jump down on them while they climbed. She bit her lip, and the world slowed down while she ran through the scenarios in her head.

"Sprite?" Mallory yelled.

"Yes, Chorus." The sprite answered while winding up its whips for another swing.

"Can you get to the top of the ridge?" Mallory pointed up.

It let loose its whips and replied, "Yes, but leaving you here unprotected would almost certainly result in your deaths."

Mallory shook her head. "We need to get out of this gorge, or we'll die anyway. You'll have more room up there to use those things properly." She pointed at its whips. "If you clear the top quickly, we can climb up."

The sprite seemed to consider her logic, and then it tilted itself to an angle, and whatever force caused it to float fired in a blast of air lifting it off the ground. It flew diagonally into one side of the gorge, and as it hit the wall, it pushed off at the opposite angle, firing the blast of air again into the wall Mallory and Caleb were pressed up against. Small rocks fell down on them again, but they barely had time to register the downpour of earth before the sprite was on the opposite wall. It zig-zagged its way up the face of the gorge in just a few seconds and landed at the top, spinning its torso in fast circles, causing its whips to whirl like a buzzsaw. Two bodies of forest beasts flew into the gorge from above, knocking over one of the piles blocking the exit.

Alex and Caleb yelled her name simultaneously, and Mallory's gaze dropped from the sprite to her husband and then quickly to her friend. They must have been watching the sprite leave too, and the beasts had taken advantage of the distraction. There were two bearing down on Caleb and three on Alex. Mallory drew her own sword in one hand and the small knife in the other. She followed the sprite's lead and took a running leap toward the far wall, pulling her legs into tight coils, she kicked hard off the wall, spinning with both blades extended toward the beasts on Alex's side of the gorge. Just as Alex fired shots into two of the beasts, Mallory's sword lodged hard in the chest of the other one; its jaws snapped shut and just missed her face as it fell, but Mallory did not take time to see if her strike had been lethal. Instead she let the jerk of her impact spin her slightly in the other direction, and as she spun, she lifted Alex's spare magistrate weapon from its holster and landed facing Caleb's attackers.

He had plunged his blade through one, but the other was in the air about to clamp down on his shoulder. Mallory lifted her weapon and fired. The projectile moved across the space faster than her eye could track and hit Caleb in the back. His body flew forward just out of the reach of the beast's teeth. Mallory screamed. She just could not get the hang of these blasted weapons, and now she had killed her husband to save him. She re-cocked the weapon and aimed again at the beast now standing between her and Caleb's body, but before she could fire, a silver lightning bolt fell from the sky and cut the beast in half.

The clockwork sprite called from above, "The upper ground is clear, Chorus. You may ascend. I will keep your way clear."

Mallory ran to Caleb's side. Blood had started to spread through his white shirt on his right shoulder, but he was breathing. She wanted desperately to see his face, but all she could see was the overgrown blond hair on the back of his head—it had been a long time since any of them had a haircut. She knelt down and tried to roll him over. The man weighed a ton. She was never going to get him moved, but then his arm muscles clenched, and he pressed himself off the ground and rolled over all on his own. His blue eyes shimmered with tears. "You shot me!"

"Oh, Caleb!" She screamed and fell on him, hugging him tight.

"Ow!" He screamed in her embrace.

Alex had edged nearer to them. "We don't have time for this, you two! Are we going up then?" She nodded toward the top of the gorge and the waiting sprite that was sending its whips down like spears into the beasts still trying to advance on them in the gorge.

Mallory nodded and then turned to Caleb. "Can you climb?"

Caleb shrugged and winced. "Doesn't matter. I'm going to have to. Let's get out of here while we can." He picked himself up and gripped a handhold on the sheer rock wall. He shifted his weight and tried to pull himself up with the handhold. The blood on his shoulder bubbled a little, and his shirt grew redder. Caleb slipped off the wall and fell backward to the ground. His eyes rolled in his head, and he moaned.

Mallory shook her head as she bent down and checked his shoulder. "He's never going to be able to climb out of here like this."

Caleb tried to sit up. "No. No, I can do it."

Mallory shook her head again. "It's okay, Caleb. We'll figure it out."

He laid back and said, "Good. There's no way I'm climbing that wall." He looked pleadingly at Alex. "My wife shot me, Alex! Can you believe it?"

Alex shrugged and fired two shots toward some beasts that were poking their heads over the barricade of furry bodies; she hit one, but the other ducked back too quickly. "To be honest, I'm surprised she didn't kill you." She fired another shot in the other direction at a beast's ear that appeared over the other pile. It vanished in a puff of hair, and the unseen beast winced and howled. She smiled at her marksmanship, but then grew solemn. "How are we going to get out, then?" She slowly reloaded her weapons.

Mallory bit her lip and cocked her head thoughtfully. The sun glinted off the sprite's whips as they flew into separate sides of the gorge. The clockwork sprite was covering a range of at least twenty feet in each direction with its whips, and she wondered how long its arms could get, and whether they were totally flaccid, or if they could be held in a continuous shape. "Alex, you climb up. Ask the sprite if it can hold a shape with its arms." She curled her pointer finger: "Like a hook that we could lay Caleb over. Oh! And ask it how much it can lift."

Alex's eyes lit up, and she nodded, holstering her weapons. She nimbly scaled the rock face and disappeared over the edge. Mallory looked to the left and the right. For now, the onslaught of the forest beasts had ebbed, but she could hear their yips and howls on both sides of the gorge. Their teeth gnashed and scraped, and she could hear the pad-falls of their paws moving back and forth as they were pacing. They seemed to be having trouble scaling the piles of their fallen comrades, but Mallory knew it was only a matter of time before they figured out a solution to the problem. They were remarkably smart creatures. Even their trek into this gorge seemed to be orchestrated by the beasts as an elaborate trap.

Just a day ago, Mallory woke up in the makeshift tent they had erected in a clearing in the dark forest. They had used a sheet set that Mallory had packed and strung it up with the rope the Sprite Master, Reddy Lamarr, had given them when they were exiled. Mallory hated that rope. Well, not so much the rope, but the giver. Reddy LaMarr was younger than most of the others on the City Council—at least she looked younger—Mallory did not know her exact age. Whatever her true age, she was older than Caleb, and she was too friendly with him in Mallory's book. Caleb thought it was funny that Mallory was jealous—especially considering she had married Caleb, and they were never allowed to return to the city. Maybe it was, but that did not mean Mallory had to like the Sprite Master's stupid rope. Alex's smaller tent was tied onto their larger one with the same rope, as a sort of guest room. Caleb slept on the opposite wall from Alex's tent, and he was still sound asleep, exhausted from the events of the night.

He had been on watch, keeping the fire burning, which seemed to be the only thing that kept the forest beasts away from them in the night, and he had drifted off and so did the fire. Mallory and Alex woke up to his calls for help and an armada of forest beasts in their campsite. They fought as hard as they could and would have been easily overwhelmed if the clockwork sprite and not appeared seemingly out of nowhere and dispatched the enemy from their midst. Then when it saw the insignia of their families on their broaches, it said, "The Dikaió Archivist requests the city leaders to send a Chorus, that they may study the ancient ways," and they agreed to follow the thing to a place called the Library.

As Mallory blinked in the early morning light, she half wondered if it all had been a dream. It felt like a dream. She sat up and peeked out into the camp. The clockwork sprite was floating near the burned-out fire, its unblinking eyes scanning the forest for any sign of threat. The air was chilly, and Mallory grabbed her coat before exiting the tent. "Good morning," she called to the sprite.

"It is morning," the sprite answered. "Whether it is good or not is outside my parameters to judge, Chorus."

"Well, it's a better morning than it would have been if you had not shown up last night." Mallory knelt down and pulled Caleb's fire striker from his pack. She heaped some sticks into the pile where they had built their last fire and began to scrape sparks onto the pile.

The sprite watched her silently, not responding to her

previous comments. After some time of her scraping, it said, "You do not know how to start a fire, Chorus."

Mallory's jaw dropped open. She folded her arms incredulously. "I'll have you know I very nearly burned down our whole city. Don't tell me I don't know how to start fires." She went back to scraping and muttered under her breath, "I can't start a fire? Dumb old sprite, let's see you start a fire."

The sprite hovered over to the pile of sticks. A tiny spout slowly protruded from the sprite's hull, and Mallory heard the familiar sound of metal scraping on metal that the fire sprites made before unleashing their flames of death, though the sound was much smaller. Then, a small stream of liquid fire emitted from the spout and splashed onto the pile of wood. Within a few seconds, the fire was roaring. Mallory wondered where this little patchwork sprite had come from and how its maker knew so much about how sprites worked.

"Well sure, if I had an internal striker and paraffin tanks, I could do that too." She crossed her arms and pouted in the heat.

"Paraffin would be far too unstable to carry in a sprite's tanks." The clockwork sprite intoned. "Butane is a much more stable fluid while still being highly combustible."

"I've never heard of butane," Mallory marveled. "Is it something the Dikaió Archivist will teach us about?"

"Your question is outside my parameters to answer," the sprite replied. "The Archivist knows many things."

"Did she birth you?" Mallory wondered.

"Yes, the Archivist is my maker," it affirmed.

Mallory felt thrilled. She wondered what all they could

learn from the Archivist. Before she could ask any more questions, she heard a deep-throated roar bellow out of her tent.
Caleb was waking up and stretching.

Then a higher-pitched but equally scary voice yelled from
the smaller tent, "C'mon, Caleb! I nearly jumped out of my
skin. Why do you have to do that every morning?" The tents
shook violently several times. Alex was kicking the walls
again in irritation.

Caleb and Alex emerged from their respective tents at the
same time: Caleb with a big sheepish grin, and Alex scowling
while pulling on her gloves.

"What's for breakfast?" Caleb asked jovially.

"Same as always," Mallory replied and pulled some nuts
and berries from her pack. She looked at the few that were
left and said, "though I don't know how much longer they'll
last."

Caleb walked over to the fire and warmed his hands. "It's
okay! We have a sprite now. Go round us up some breakfast,
sprite!"

The clockwork sprite floated unmoving, staring at them
without replying. Alex shook her head. "Apparently, one
needs the Dikaió to command wild sprites too."

Caleb sighed and thrust his hand out to Mallory for some
nuts and berries. Alex came and squatted by the fire, and she
took some breakfast from Mallory as well. Then Alex spoke,
"Well, sprite? What next?"

The clockwork sprite turned toward her and said, "We
need to leave within the hour. If we traveled at a human's
maximum speed with minimal stops for rest and refueling, we

could reach the Library in four days."

Mallory's draw dropped. "Did you say four days?" None of them had ever travelled anywhere that took longer than two hours. She did not know how far they were from the city, having lost their bearings before finding the clearing and making camp, but it could not have been much farther than walking from one end of the city to the other. And they had not gone anywhere since then. Weeks had passed without wandering further from the city. Traveling straight for four days? How much world was there?

"Yes, assuming we do not encounter any difficulties along the way." The sprite floated, staring at them.

Caleb threw all of his breakfast in his mouth at once and spoke around bites: "Welp! There's no time like the present. Let's get things packed up, ladies." He walked to the tree that their tent was tied to and reached for the knot.

"Wait!" Mallory yelled, but it was too late. Caleb tugged the bit of rope, and the knot came loose. The tent fell with a plume of fabric.

"Why?" Caleb asked, brushing his hands past one another, as if shaking off dust after completing a hard job.

Alex shook her head. "It would have been nice to get our stuff out before the tents came down." As the sheets settled, the lumps of all their belongings could clearly be seen below the fabric folds.

"Oops!" Caleb rubbed a hand through his hair and chuckled.

The sprite's eyes glowed, and its head turned quickly to the right. "We do not have much time. The smell of death has drawn more predators, and they are congregating not far from here. If too many come, I may not be able to protect you all."

Mallory, Caleb, and Alex went silent and began quickly rolling the sheet up and packing their belongings in the backpacks they had been given when they left the city. The work seemed to take too long, and Mallory felt as if every leaf of every plant was watching her, waiting for the chance to be knocked out of the way of a charging forest-beast's attack. As she pulled on her backpack, she made sure that both her blades were within easy reach, and she saw Caleb do the same. Alex strapped on her magistrate weapons and loaded extra ammunition in the loops of the holster belts. Mallory had no concept of war, but the three youngsters were preparing for one.

The sprite wasted no time once the camp was packed and set off into the thick undergrowth of the forest. It floated above the scattered sticks and stones of the forest floor, and branches and brush parted before it like bread before a blade. The three companions had trouble keeping up. They had to climb and clamber over the forest debris, and the branches and brush scraped and scratched while they passed. At times the forest fauna was so thick, they had to use their blades to blaze the trail. More than once they lost track of the sprite and found themselves going the wrong direction. For its part, the sprite never seemed to lose track of them, and when they wandered, it would appear and redirect their course, but the trip was exhausting.

Caleb finally collapsed onto his knees. "I can go no further," he moaned. "I'm famished."

Mallory smiled. "It does seem like a good time to break for lunch. Alex?"

Alex nodded and yelled, "Sprite!? We need to rest." Then she knelt down and started to pull her backpack off with the other two.

Soon the three of them had pulled some nuts and dried berries from their stores and were quietly chewing. "You know," Caleb mused, "I could really go for some real food. Meat! Bread! At this point, I'd settle for hot vegetables."

Alex held up a dried berry between her gloved forefinger and thumb. "Yeah, for once I agree with the big oaf. This nuts-and-berries diet is starting to wear on me."

Mallory shoved a small cluster of nuts in her mouth and laughed. "Look, I'm a squirrel!" She crossed her eyes and pulled up her lip, exposing her two big upper teeth. Then she scrunched up her nose as if she was wiggling it. Caleb smirked and pulled back his arm like he was going to throw his pile of nuts and berries at her. But then he paused, looked at his hand, bobbed his head as if considering his actions, and shoved the whole pile in his mouth. The girls burst into peals of laughter.

Suddenly, a blast of leaves and twigs burst in on them in a blur of copper metal. The clockwork sprite spun around the circle. "Choruses, follow me now!"

The companions did not even have time to react before they heard howling coming from all around them. Mallory's heart jumped, and she threw what was left of her lunch in her mouth and hurriedly pulled on her pack. Alex and Caleb followed suit, and then they were racing through the forest again. This time Mallory barely registered the cuts and scrapes of the branches and debris on the forest floor; she was too desperate to keep up with the sprite and not get left behind in the midst of the forest beasts.

Every two-hundred yards or so, the clockwork sprite would pause, and its eyes would pulsate as it looked around the trees. All Mallory could see was an endless expanse of tree trunks and other plants. Nothing looked familiar, but it all looked the same. Then seemingly without rhyme or reason, the sprite would pivot and start leading them another direction. Intermittently, Mallory would catch glimpses among the trees of green glowing eyes. They were hard to spot and vanished nearly as soon as she saw them, but the forest beasts seemed to be everywhere. Mallory could not help but wonder where all these beasts came from. There were endless numbers of them roaming in the forest, and they were relentless in their pursuit. As the pattern of pausing and mad dashing continued, Mallory began to suspect that the sprite was not making its decisions about which direction to turn based on their destination but rather on avoiding the forest beasts that were chasing them.

"They're herding us," she yelled as they ran.

"What?" Alex yelled back.

"They're herding us somewhere!"

The sprite paused, scanning the forest, and the three companions clustered together for a moment. Caleb grabbed Mallory's shoulders, "What do you mean, Mal? Explain it to us."

Mallory pointed at the sprite. "It can see them out there."

She waved at the forest around them. "And it's trying to keep us away from them, but we're moving in one direction in a weaving pattern." She waved her hand like a fish in water. "They want us to go somewhere, and we're blindly following them."

Alex shook her head. "They're just animals, Mal. They don't think like that. Not like a person."

The sprite interrupted, "The Chorus is correct. We are being herded toward the ruins of Mason City, and it will be difficult to escape them there, but there are too many to confront here. Come!" The sprite burst away into the forest again, and the companions had no choice but to follow it.

Before long, the trees began to thin, and then they emerged into an open terrain. Mallory inhaled sharply. They were standing on a ridge of a cliff, and before them in an immense valley stood giant skyscrapers, five times the size of those in the city. Countless buildings and houses spread out in every direction as far as the eye could see. They were staring at a city so large that their own city would not have filled a tenth of it. This city was dead though. There were no signs that anyone had lived here in ages. A crater was carved into the outer edge of the metropolis—roughly where City Hall would have stood in Mallory's city—and large cracks in the land emanated out from it like lightning, zig-zagging this way and that. What had happened there? Where were all the people? Mallory wanted to stay, studying the city, but the sprite was already rushing along a path down the cliff, and the companions hurried after it. At the bottom, the path led into one of the cracks from the crater, which from the ground looked like a narrow gorge with walls roughly twenty feet high—and that was where the forest beasts had them trapped.

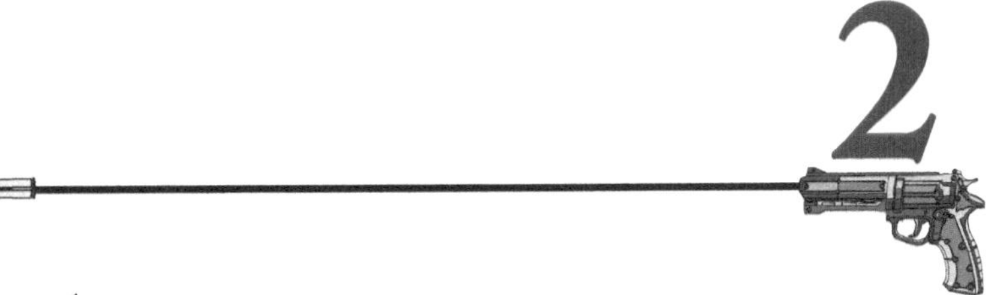

Alex handed Mallory two of her magistrate weapons. "You'll need these more than me."

Caleb groaned. "Alex, don't leave me with her." And then he pointed at the weapons in Mallory's hands. "She shot me."

"Shut up, Caleb," Alex ordered. "This isn't the time for your jokes. We need to get out of here." Then she turned to the rock face and began to climb.

Caleb looked hurt, and not just because his shoulder was bleeding out. "No one's on my side, but you still think I'm funny—right, Mal?"

Mallory was holding the two weapons, facing toward the two animal-carcass bulwarks on either side of them, praying that nothing scaled the ramparts or breached the walls. "Of course, dear," she comforted. "Now be quiet, so we can get out of here."

Caleb closed his eyes. "Maybe I'll just take a nap then. I'm so tired."

Mallory's eyes widened, and she nudged him with her knee. "Stay awake, Caleb. You'll go into shock."

"Shock?" He smiled. "I'm already in shock that you shot me."

Suddenly, Alex floated down beside them. She was standing on a silver hook: one of the sprite's tentacles. She stepped deftly off the tentacle and gingerly took the magistrate weapons from Mallory, being careful to keep their barrels pointed safely away from anyone. "It says it should be able to pull him up—but just him."

Alex and Mallory helped Caleb sit on the crux of the clockwork sprite's long arm, and he wrapped his hands around the tendril and grimaced when his shoulder rubbed up against it. The sprite started to retract its arm, pulling him carefully up the face of the wall. The angle of its trajectory was not quite right, and Caleb bounced against the wall, scraping his good shoulder and corresponding hip over and over again as he ascended. Mallory and Alex climbed up beside him, grasping handholds and footholds as they went. When they were about halfway up, Mallory heard yipping and snarling below them. She looked down and saw that the forests beasts had broken through the barriers and were prancing around below, clearly irritated that their dinner had escaped again. Mallory looked up and kept climbing. Now was not the time to stop paying attention to what she was doing and fall back into the swarming mass of deadly teeth below. Finally, she reached the top and swung her legs up onto the ridge and rolled over, breathing hard.

"No time to rest, Mallory. I'm going to need help getting this big lug up." Alex called.

Mallory rolled onto her belly and looked toward her husband and friend. Caleb was clinging to the sprite's arm and trying to swing his leg up while Alex pulled on his good shoulder. Every time he tried to pull himself up, another part of him fell back. If they kept going the way they were, Caleb was likely to drag the whole lot of them—Caleb, Alex, and the sprite—down into the abyss of swirling beasts below. Mallory could see how to get him up, but it was not going to be an easy job: Caleb weighed as much as the two girls did combined. She slowly raised herself up off the ground and said, "Caleb, I'm going to have to grab your hurt shoulder to pull you up."

Caleb nodded and gritted his teeth, but he still yelped when she wrapped both hands under his armpit near his wound. Mallory bent her legs and looked at Alex. "On three?"

Alex bent down like Mallory and started counting: "One. Two. Three!"

The girls straightened their legs and arched their backs, pulling Caleb up over the ridge. He scrambled his legs trying to help but only made the trio wobble uncertainly. The wide stances the girls had taken absorbed the movement somewhat, but Mallory was certain they were all going to end up in a heap on the ground—or over the edge—before they got her husband to his feet. Fresh blood was bubbling under his shirt and coating Mallory's hands, making her grip slip, and Caleb started wheeling his arms to gain his balance. She clenched her hands tighter, and Caleb moaned but kept wiggling his arms and legs, trying to reach a standing position. Just when it seemed that all their efforts would fail, the clockwork sprite floated up and gently pressed upward on Caleb's backpack. Stabilized: Caleb stood up straight. The girls let go of him and stepped back, but as soon as they did, Caleb's eyes rolled in his head, and he started to swoon. Mallory jumped forward and put her shoulder under his arm. His weight pressed down hard on her, and she knew she was not going to be able to hold him up forever. Alex jumped in under Caleb's other arm, which helped a little, but Caleb was never going to be able to walk like this.

The clockwork sprite spoke, "He needs to be treated, or he will not be able to continue. Please take his covering off." A small compartment opened on its chest and a bottle extended. Mallory recognized it as the same spray bottle the culture sprites had used to treat the cattle back in the city when they were injured. When the forest beasts had first arrived and attacked a cow, they had sprayed it with whatever was in the bottle. The cow had been in much worse shape than Caleb, but after being sprayed, it had recovered and then returned to the herd.

Mallory said, "We need to take his shirt off, Alex. The sprite can help with the wound." They took turns taking the brunt of his weight and unbuckled his backpack, letting it fall heavily to the ground. Alex and Mallory pivoted as best they could and tried to pull Caleb's shirt up, but they could only get it to his armpit. If they raised his arms and took away their support from under them, he would slide down between them like a slippery bar of soap. Mallory yelled, "Caleb!"

His eyes rolled slowly in her direction and then away again.

"Caleb, I need you to pull it together long enough to get your shirt off." She slapped him hard in the face.

Caleb looked at her in shock, blinking his eyes in disbelief. His legs straightened, holding his weight, and he shook off the girls. "I can't believe I married you," he said shaking his head. "You shoot me; you slap me. If this is what love is, who needs it?"

Mallory's eyes narrowed. "Shut up, and let's get your shirt off before you pass out."

"Oh well, in that case. I take it all back. She finds me irresistible even now." He smirked but caught a glimpse of Alex's grimace and shrugged with a sheepish grin. "Ow." He reached toward the wound on his back and stumbled sideways a little.

"Caleb?!" Mallory grabbed his arm, trying to steady him.

"I'm fine. I'm fine." Caleb straightened. He tried to pull his shirt up, but he could not quite lift his arm on the wounded side high enough to pull it out of the sleeve. Mallory stepped up and gingerly helped lift the shirt over his wound. As soon as the wound was exposed, the sprite moved forward and began to spray it down. White bubbles fizzed on Caleb's back, and his muscles rippled as he tensed. "Ow, that really stings." He tried to squirm away from the spray.

"Caleb, hold still!" Mallory shouted.

He stopped squirming and clenched his eyes closed.

The sprite continued to spray the wound, and then another compartment opened, and a needleless syringe extended. It squeezed the contents directly into the hole in Caleb's shoulder, and soon a pinkish gray foam began to bubble out of the wound. Then a blackish bulb appeared in the center of the foam. It wiggled around and around and seemed to grow in size, but Mallory realized it was not growing, it was extruding out of Caleb's back until it fell out. It was the projectile from the magistrate weapon! It had been lodged in his back, and the sprite's foam had extracted it. The foam hardened into a rubbery gel. Caleb wiggled and flexed his back. "Huh. That feels weird, but it doesn't hurt so much anymore."

"The nano-sprites inject a local anesthetic that should mask the pain, and they will help your wound heal. You should not do any heavy lifting, and we should replenish your stores and water for energy and healing," the clockwork sprite said. "However, we cannot stay here to do it." It motioned toward the side of the gorge. "Their tactics are shifting."

Mallory stepped to the edge and looked over it. Some of the forest beasts were still yipping and howling while trying to scale the walls after them, but their paws were clearly not meant for climbing. Most of them were running back along the canyon floor toward the city. She held her hand up to her eyes and peered into the distance. After several twists and turns, there looked to be a slight inclination in the land that the beasts could use to exit the gorge. Next to the entranceway, there was a large black slab of what used to be the street, cracked and jagged and pointing up into the sky. Mallory looked along the gorge again and noted that there were pieces of street everywhere. The gorge seemed to be what was left of a sewer system. An explosion had blown apart the streets above the subterranean tunnels. Black blotches of carbon scarring were everywhere in the canyon, and she noted the same scarring was on most of the husks of what buildings remained standing in the city. There was very little vegetation anywhere that she could make out. Whatever had destroyed this city had also left the land barren. She also found it odd that she had not seen any other animals other than the forest beasts since they had left their living city: no birds, no rabbits, nothing.

Mallory nearly got lost in the mystery of it all, but the howls of the beasts below drew her back to the immediate problem. Since the beasts could not climb, the incline out of the gorge appeared to be their only means of escape without going back to the forest entrance. If that bit of destroyed street were collapsed, the incline would be sealed. The beasts would have to go all the way back, giving the teens a substantial head start in evading their pursuers. Together, she, Caleb and Alex might be able to push over the concrete obtrusion. However, she was not certain they could outrun the beasts below. If the beasts gained the surface before they did, they would be no better off than before.

The clockwork sprite was fast enough to outrun the beasts though. She pointed toward the entranceway. "Sprite, do you have the strength to push over that large section of street and seal off their escape?"

The clockwork sprite's eyes moved in the direction of her extended finger. Its eyes undulated and flashed, calculating the task Mallory was asking of it. Then a burst of wind nearly knocked Mallory off her feet, as the clockwork sprite blasted away.

Alex stepped up beside Mallory. "Are we going to help it?"

"We would never get there in time," Caleb said from behind them. "We should move toward the high ground."

Mallory looked back at him and saw that he was pointing toward the abandoned skyscrapers in the city. She nodded. "Yes, we'll have the advantage there if the sprite fails." She paused and looked at Caleb. "Can you make it?"

"The Sprite's right. I'm super hungry and thirsty, but my back feels better." He wiggled his arm and shrugged his shoulder. "It's really amazing. The hospital back in the city could really use this stuff."

Mallory smiled. Even in exile, with the threat of death if he returned, her beloved was still thinking like a Governor and trying to improve the lives of his people. "Maybe someday we'll be able to go back. For now, let's focus on surviving."

Alex picked up Caleb's backpack and started off without them. "C'mon, you two. I gave my word to protect you, and I intend to keep it. Let's move!"

They were nearly to the building when an earthquake shook the ground below them. They turned to see the clockwork sprite hovering in a dust plume. It had succeeded in trapping the beasts in the gorge. Then another sound, nearly as loud as the falling chunk of concrete, erupted over the tops of the buildings. It was different though, more like a grumbling whine, and it was growing louder. Whatever it was, it was coming closer. The three companions started to walk away from the ruined skyscraper to see if they could spot what was in the sky coming toward them. Suddenly, a wind blew past them, and Mallory nearly fell forward from its velocity. Her curly brown hair slapped about her face haphazardly, and she closed her eyes to keep the hair out.

Alex's voice sounded in the darkness behind her closed eyes. "What are you doing? What's the rush?"

Mallory opened her eyes to see the clockwork sprite pulling Alex, dragging her toward the skyscraper in which they had intended to take refuge. Mallory shouted too, "What's wrong? The beasts are trapped in the hole."

"No time, Chorus! Run!" The clockwork sprite continued to pull Alex.

Caleb looked at Mallory, and they both started sprinting after the sprite. Mallory had never seen a sprite exhibit any sort of emotion, ever—but the clockwork sprite seemed desperate to get them into the building. If she did not know better, she would say it was afraid. When they got to the doors of the skyscraper, they found the metal frames rusted, mangled, and bent, completely blocking the entrance to the building. Mallory mused; they were in the same position as the beasts in the gorge. The path to their desired prize blocked by whatever destruction had come to this city. But their path was not closed for long; the clockwork sprite grabbed hold of the mangled doors and peeled them off the entranceway like paper. The small band ran inside.

The sprite led them deep inside the building to a door with a sign above it marked "STAIRS," which was just past a pair of rusted sliding elevator doors. Whether the hinges of the stairwell door even worked anymore did not mattered; the sprite pulled the door off the wall and tossed it down the hall. The only light in the building was what was coming from the open doorway, and the cave of the stairwell was pitch black. The clockwork sprites' eyes illuminated and lit up the darkness inside. "Come," it motioned. "Quickly."

The companions followed the sprite into the stairwell, and they climbed up three floors before the sprite knocked off another door. "The structure of this building will not safely support further ascension. We will shelter here." They exited the stairwell into a large room with an open floorplan. There were desks and knocked over cubicles sprawled throughout the room, and ancient papers and leaves blew about aimlessly in a breeze circulating through the space. Mallory noted that this room used to have windows, but if there was any glass left, it remained only as sharp, craggy fragments in the rotting window frames. Her curiosity mounted. What was this place? Who used to sit at these desks? And what was on these papers floating around?

As enticing as these questions were, there was a bigger question that needed to be answered. The roaring whine outside was now directly over the building they were in, and Mallory desperately wished she could see what it was.

"What is that?" she whispered to Caleb.

The clockwork sprite whirled around on her and whispered as best it could in its metallic voice, "The Ex Natu. Be silent. We must not be seen."

And then Mallory could see it out the window: It looked like a man riding a flying sprite. The sprite was bent like an L and had arms spread out on either side. The man sat on the sprite like a child might sit on a chair backwards with his legs straddling the seat. He manipulated the sprite's arms in front of him to indicate the direction he wanted to fly. The man had no hair, he was not wearing a shirt, and his body was thin and wiry. Scars nearly covered his body.

Mallory looked at Alex and saw that she was looking at her arm. Alex whispered, "His skin looks like my arm."

The clockwork sprite whispered in response, "The markings are not scars. They are tattoos."

"Tattoos?" Caleb asked.

"A drawing under the subdermal layer of the skin," the sprite clarified.

The human companions stared at the rider in awe. "Why would someone do that?" Mallory asked.

"Your question is outside my parameters to answer," the sprite replied.

The rider circled above the gorge with the trapped forest beasts like a vulture watching a dying animal. Then another rider flew into view atop a similar sprite: This one appeared female, though at this distance Mallory could not quite make that distinction. Their figures were both very slight and thin. However, the new rider was wearing a shirt and jacket, so it seemed likely. Similar to her companion, she had tattoos on the sides of her neck, extending up to the base of her skull, which was completely free of hair as well. While Mallory was trying to figure out the new rider, two more flew into view, and they were also tattooed and bald. They joined the same flight path, circling the canyon. The first raised his fist, and the other riders broke from the circle, all flying off toward the West, away from the canyon and the skyscraper in which they were hiding. The riders were slowly shifting their path in an arc toward the North. Then they were out of view.

Caleb turned to the sprite. "Well, what was that all about?"

Mallory shook her head. "They're not gone. They're circling around. Listen!"

The group held their breath and listened. The whining roar of the flying sprites was getting louder, but they still could not see the riders out of the windows. When the roar seemed almost overhead, Mallory started walking toward the windows; she wanted to know what was going on, but Caleb grabbed her arm and held her back. "Wait, Mal. We don't know—"

WIK-SHAW!

The whole room was bathed in white light, and a shock-wave rocked the building before he could finish his thought. Mallory was on the floor. She did not remember exactly how she ended up there, but her vision was swimming, and her ears were whining as she tried to gain her bearings. She pulled herself into a sitting position and looked around. The abandoned room was starting to come back into focus, and then another bright flash followed by another shockwave put her back on the floor again. This time she curled into a fetal position and stayed down. Whatever was happening out there, more than one rider was doing it, so she figured there could be at least two more explosions. It would be better to stay curled up than get flattened again. Another shockwave confirmed her suspicions, and Mallory was pleased to find that if she closed her eyes and covered her ears with her hands that the disorienting effects of the explosions were somewhat muted.

After the fourth shockwave rocked the building, Mallory opened her eyes and tried getting up again. Dust and debris were swirling in the old building like a storm, but she squinted to make out what had happened outside. The canyon they had just escaped from was now a roiling river of fire. The riders had eviscerated the forest beasts trapped there. Her ears were still ringing, but she was pretty sure that the roaring whine of the flying sprites was gone now, so she started heading toward the window to get a better look. She half expected Caleb to grab her arm again to stop her, but when she turned to see if her husband was going to say anything, she saw both Caleb and Alex sitting on the floor looking dazed. Caleb had a finger in his ear jiggling it wildly—no doubt, trying to clear away the ringing. Alex was rolling over and starting to push herself up off the ground. The clockwork sprite was laid out on the floor as well, but it was moving and seemed relatively undamaged. Seeing that her compatriots were all alive and well but also incapable of stopping her, Mallory turned back and made a sprint to the window.

She leaned out of the rotted wooden frame to survey what the sprite riders had done. The fire glowed orange and rolled like water about three feet above the edge of the gorge, though it did not seem to be spilling out. The smell of the fire in the canyon was different than any she had encountered before. It smelled musty and tart at the same time, almost like soap mixed with paraffin. There was also the distinct smell of burning hair, and all of that was mixed with the smell of cooking meat. That last thought made her stomach growl, but the thought of what was behind the enticing smell turned the hunger pangs into nausea. Mallory backed away from the window trying not to retch. The sprite riders were gone, and her curiosity was more than sated. She went to check on her friends.

Caleb was standing now, still wiggling his finger in his ear. "What was that?" He yelled.

"What?!" Alex yelled back. "Why are you mumbling? You sound like you're underwater."

Mallory thought their voices were muffled as well, but she could make out what they were saying. Clearly, they had not covered their ears after the first shockwave, and their hearing had not recovered yet. She pointed at her ears and then expanded her fingers out and wiggled them to make them look like little explosions.

Caleb nodded at her and yelled, "Yeah, I can barely hear anything either. Are they gone?"

Mallory nodded, yes.

The clockwork sprite had righted itself and zoomed to the window; its eyes flickering, extending and retracting as it surveyed the gorge. Its metallic voice sounded from across the room. "The Ex Natu have left the area. We should make haste to leave the open city before they return."

"Would they do that to us?" Alex asked, her voice already down a few decibels indicating her hearing was returning.

The clockwork sprite replied, "No."

"Well, that's good." Caleb chuckled and absently picked up the backpack Alex had been carrying for him because of his wounded arm and then he winced in pain, dropping the bag again.

The clockwork sprite floated toward the door. "We should go before they come back to make sure all the wolves are dead."

"Wolves?" Alex asked.

"The creatures they bombed," the sprite responded.

"Wol-ves," Mallory mouthed the word. It did not feel sinister enough for what those beasts were.

"Come, let us depart." The sprite headed out the door and toward the stairs.

Alex picked up Caleb's backpack, and Caleb said, "I can carry it."

Alex shook her head. "You couldn't even pick it up just now. When your shoulder heals, you can carry both of ours to pay me back." Then she headed out the door, following the sprite.

Mallory and Caleb turned to each other. "You, okay?" Caleb touched her cheek tenderly.

"Better than you!" Mallory chuckled, playfully punching his hurt shoulder.

"Ow! You're so mean!" Caleb winced.

Mallory smiled widely. "And that's why you love me. C'mon, we better go."

The pair ran out after Alex and the sprite. When the group made it to the street, waves of heat from the canyon were washing across the city. Mallory thought for sure she should be sweating, but she realized it had been hours since any of them had had anything to eat or drink, and they had been on the run that whole time. Her body was conserving all the liquid it could. She ran her tongue across her lips; they were dry and chapped, just as she suspected. She could tell that the clockwork sprite was not going to let them stop and rest, as it was quickly moving North on what was left of the broken street, while the human companions ran hurriedly after it.

Abruptly, the sprite angled to the right and started heading toward two rusty metal poles on the side of the road. A large square of rusted metal was swinging off the side of one of the poles, and Mallory could barely make out some writing on it: "Clarington Station." Between the poles were a set of stairs that descended into darkness below the city. The sprite passed the poles and floated down the stairs into the blackness of Clarington Station, whatever that was. Mallory, Caleb, and Alex paused and looked fearfully down into the darkness.

Mallory was the first to speak. "I don't want to go down there."

Alex signaled agreement, "Me neither."

Caleb smiled bravely. "Well, I better stay here with you girls for protection."

Mallory and Alex both gave him their best mom-glares, but neither changed their minds about descending into whatever was in that blackness below.

Before long, light began to shine in the darkness, and then the clockwork sprite appeared and floated up the stairs. "Choruses, please follow me. We must hurry."

Mallory shook her head, "We took a vote. We don't want to go down there."

The sprite replied, "The Ex Natu do not travel underground. It is the safest path."

Caleb shrugged. "I thought you said the Ex Natu wouldn't hurt us."

The sprite turned to him; its eyes fluttering light. "I have no record of saying this."

Alex crossed her arms. "I asked if they would do that to us." She pointed at the fiery canyon. "And you said, 'No.'"

The sprite's eyes glowed brighter. "That is correct. The Ex Natu would not bomb you as they did the wolves. Your fate would be much worse."

Mallory froze. Caleb and Alex did too. Somewhere above the tall ruins of the ancient city, a distant roaring whine sent a warning that echoed down the abandoned streets. The Ex Natu were returning. The clockwork sprite did not have to say anything more to cajole the girls down the stairs into the cave of Clarington Station. Mallory started descending first, and Alex quickly followed. The clockwork sprite's eyes increased their brightness as it followed the girls. Caleb waited, bouncing from foot to foot and looking around for the source of the sound, but soon Mallory poked her head back out of the darkness below and hissed at him to hurry up. Caleb looked at the skies once more and then headed down after the rest.

The staircase led into a cavernous room. Light from the streets above sifted down in swirling dusty shafts, and Mallory could see that the room was covered from floor to ceiling in what looked like ceramic tile. It had once been white, but now it was covered in black carbon residue, as if a fire had once filled the entirety of the space, just as it had filled the cavern with the burning wolves. The clockwork sprite was moving toward a row of rusty rectangular boxes that stood roughly waist-high. Some of them had three metal bars extending out from them, but the others had rusted off over time, and they lay in scattered piles of decay on the ground. The sprite casually broke through some of the remaining bars, and the broken metal clanged to the floor, echoing around the silent room. The three young people froze in fear at the noise, and then they ran as fast as they could to keep close to the sprite, clambering awkwardly around and over the metal boxes. Alex, who was carrying two packs, had a particularly hard time getting around the boxes, and ended up falling on her rear-end with a thump. She did not stay down long though, scrambling to her feet. The farther away from the stairs they got, the less light there was in Clarington Station. Soon, there was nothing but the sprite's eye-lights, picking out an illuminated tunnel in the black cavern.

The darkness of Clarington Station was unlike anything Mallory had ever experienced; it hung around them like a cold, wet fog. The air was stale and dusty. The farther into the station they walked, the heavier Mallory's chest and limbs felt. Bits of trash and clumps of dirt were scattered everywhere, and while Mallory could see them coming by the sprite's light, by the time the debris was underfoot, it was hard to distinguish and avoid. They were all stumbling blindly behind the sprite and falling farther and farther behind the floating lights. Soon, the sprite's eye-lights were just pinpricks of hope, and Mallory felt that old claustrophobic terror straining at the nerve endings in her chest, pulling it tight and making it hard to breathe. Then the sprite's lights vanished. It had gone around a corner or into another room. Her muscles froze. She did not know how long she stood there, but she could sense that Alex and Caleb were no longer beside her. On the other hand, she did not feel completely alone either. There was water dripping somewhere in the huge room, but there were other sounds too. Scampering noises. Squeaks. Hisses.

Something brushed past her ankle, and she screamed, "Caleb!"

"Mallory?" Her husband's voice was distant and alarmed.

There was more movement around her now. Small, eager motions in the darkness. Mallory's throat caught, and she called, "help," or at least she thought she called.

Caleb had not heard her: "Mallory, where are you?" He yelled, panic raising the tenor of his voice. "Sprite! We need your light here! Please, come back!"

Mallory tried to will herself to move toward his voice, to answer him; even though she could not really say where she was. She could unfortunately say that she was definitely not alone: She felt more movement brush past her legs. The air stirred with the motion, and a musty smell like wet fur wafted about in the darkness. Whatever was scurrying about her, there was more than one of them. Terror began to pull her down into herself like quicksand. The more she struggled against it, the more she sunk. For the first time since leaving the city in exile, Mallory desperately wanted to crawl into her mother's and father's laps and curl up into their protective arms. The thought of her parents gave her a nudge of courage, and she shuffled a foot forward. It pressed up against something small, solid, and moving. The small animal squeaked and hissed at her.

Then she saw a dim light in the distance: A light that was rapidly making its way toward her. As it drew nearer, it became two dim lights. It was the clockwork sprite's eye-lights. Caleb and Alex were with it. Mallory looked gratefully at her friends. She blinked and felt a drop trickle down her cheek. She had been crying in the dark. She quickly reached up and brushed away the tears, not wanting to appear the baby she felt she was. The room illuminated around her, and Mallory kept her eyes solidly fixed on her approaching friends and the sprite. She did not want to see what was climbing over her feet and brushing against her legs.

When her rescuers were about twenty feet away, Caleb and Alex froze. Alex raised the back of her gloved fist to her mouth and bit her knuckles. Caleb's eyes were wide, and his mouth twisted in disgust. The sprite kept coming toward her, and the compartment in its chest that housed the butane lighter began to open. Mallory's heart started to thump rapidly, and she looked down at her feet. Swarms of small, black-furred animals with long pink tails that looked like twisted yarn flowed over her feet and around her legs. Some paused and looked up at her with eyes that glowed red in the sprite's light, and then they looked down and made another lap around her legs. The sound of metal scraping on metal sounded in the dark chamber.

Mallory knew what was coming next, and the claustrophobic fear that had caused her to freeze in place gave way to the fear of fire. She leapt out of the river of small animals. Her feet kicked them as she leapt, and she landed squarely on at least one of their bodies, nearly losing her footing. The creatures screeched in pain, and then all of them began to screech. Mallory felt tiny claws prick at the back of her calves and then her thighs. They were climbing up her, squeaking and screeching as they did. A stream of fire lit up the chamber, as the sprite's small fire nozzle began to spray liquid butane into the swarm. Mallory spun and kicked the animals climbing on her legs into the streams of fire. Then Caleb was beside her brushing the remaining little creatures off. The animals twisted and turned under the sprite's flames, and though it only directly hit a few of them, the swarm was so thick that soon they were setting each other on fire. The creatures that were aflame screeched even louder, and the ones that were not burning began to run in panic back toward the exit of Clarington station. The flaming creatures ran after them, seeking the solace of their companions and casting the huge, empty room in fiery shadows as they went.

Mallory turned around and threw herself into the arms of her husband, "Oh, Caleb!" She sobbed. Part of her hated her weakness in this moment. Her whole life had been a string of courageous solutions to impossible problems, but put her in a dark enclosed space, and she became a weak, sobbing wreck of a woman, incapable of saving herself, much less anyone else.

She appreciated that Caleb did not try to console her or give her some trite platitude like "Everything's okay now" or "There, there, I'll protect you." Instead, he just stood there quietly holding her protectively in the wall of his strong arms, while she clung desperately to his shoulder.

His injured shoulder!

She let go and stepped back in concern. "Oh, Caleb! Your shoulder! I'm so sorry! Are you okay?"

He did not let go of her, and his arms pulled her back. "I'm okay. I'm just glad you're okay."

Mallory winced. He had not even offered a wisecrack about how her hug had not hurt as bad as when she shot him. He was genuinely concerned about her this time. He was the only one who had ever seen her claustrophobia surface back when she had been stuck in the herd of cows in the city. A sprite had saved her that time as well.

Mallory felt a surge of adrenaline. She was tired of being weak, and she was tired of needing to be saved by man or sprite. She grabbed hold of Caleb's collar and twisted it around her hand, pulling him closer. He jerked in surprise, but then she made her intentions known by looking at his lips and pursing her own. He smiled and leaned in to meet her lips with his own.

"Oh yuck!" Alex yelled. "It stinks so much!"

Mallory, her lips just millimeters from Caleb's, inhaled sharply, and the smell of burning fur registered in her nose.

Caleb's mouth curled in disgust, as he smelled it too. With the moment destroyed by the acrid smell, they both stepped back from each other's embrace and waved their hands in front of their noses. "It's awful," Caleb moaned and kicked at one of the dead, blazing animals nearby.

The clockwork sprite motioned for them to follow. "The rats will return to eat their dead. You must not be here when they do. They will be much harder to dissuade from attacking now that they know what to expect."

"Rats." Alex mused. "What other terrible animals will we discover down here?"

"The world used to be full of millions of species," the sprite intoned. "Few are left. Let us continue."

Millions. Mallory lingered on that thought. She had a vague concept of the word 'million,' but she could not think of anything in the city that had ever been counted to a million. There was not a lot of time to ponder the idea because the sprite was on the move again—and this time Mallory intended to not get left behind even if she had to run to keep up.

The corner that the sprite had taken earlier led to a long hallway of empty stalls with large glass display windows, most of which were broken. The sprite's eye-lights revealed very little as they walked through the dark hallway, but Mallory could see that signs still hung on many of the stalls, and while they were somewhat faded by time, the lack of sunlight had preserved most of them. There was a bakery, a grocery mart, a pharmacy—Mallory's eyes widened; this was an ancient underground marketplace, just like the farmer's market in their city. She wondered why the people of this city held their market underground. She tried to imagine how hard it must have been for the farmers lugging all their wares down here to sell. On the other hand, unlike the market stalls in their city that were only set up once a week on Main Street, these stalls seem to be permanent. There would have been a lot less work carrying things up and down the stairs if the stall owners could just leave them here. Soon they passed what looked to be an elevator shaft; the doors had been pulled off and lost to history. Well, an elevator certainly would have made it easier to transport goods down here. Mallory paused a moment and looked closer at the elevator. It did not just go up. It looked like it went further down as well. She could not give that idea much thought because the clockwork sprite was still moving down the hallway and taking its eye-lights with it. Mallory ran to keep up.

After a few minutes of quietly walking down the long hallway, Caleb spoke, "I'm starving! Let's take a break and eat something." Apparently, he had been thinking along the same lines as Mallory, and the memories of the market had made him hungry.

Mallory's stomach rumbled in agreement. "What do you think, sprite? Can we stop and refuel?"

The clockwork sprite stopped and hovered silently in place, signaling agreement to the proposition.

The three young people dropped their bags and began to dig through them for food. Mallory found a little less than a handful of nuts and berries left in her sack of rations. Alex had a bit more, and Caleb had considerably less. They divided up the piles equally amongst themselves and ate slowly. In the sprite's light, Mallory could see the worried looks on her husband's and friend's gaunt faces. This was the end of their food supplies. Mallory wanted to say something: the could make a plan for getting more, but it felt like giving this problem a voice would make it real and where were they going to find food down here? They were tens of feet underground. Unless they were willing to start eating the rats, they were going to go hungry for a while. She wondered what the rats ate down here to stay alive. For that matter, what did the wolves eat? She had seen very little edible vegetation or animals in either the forest or the abandoned city—at least not any kind of food with which she was familiar. Still, they had to eat something.

And with that thought, Mallory plucked the last dried berry from her palm, and she mentally prepped herself for the hunger that was going to inevitably come. That was a mistake; just the thought of going hungry made her stomach rumble again. "I just fed you," she mentally chided it, but the stomach answered with a dissatisfied turn.

"How long until we reach the Library?" Caleb asked, while slowly chewing his last nut.

The sprite's eyes dimmed and lit while it calculated, making the shadows in the underground hallway undulate eerily. "We have not completed one day's journey, Chorus. There are still approximately three and one-half days until we reach the Library."

Caleb leaned back against the wall of one of the empty stalls and groaned loudly. "It's taking forever!"

Mallory laughed. "We haven't even slept one night since the sprite told us how long it was going to take this morning."

Alex shrugged and looked around. "How are we going to know when night is down here?"

The clockwork sprite answered, "The sun sets in approximately one hour."

"Are we going back up to the surface before then?" Mallory asked hopefully.

"No."

The sprite did not elaborate further, so Mallory pressed it for more information. "How long will we be underground?"

"The old subway lines run sixteen miles outside the city to the Aiworth bridge."

"Aiworth?" Caleb perked up. "That's my name."

"The Aiworths have been a powerful family in the world for generations," the clockwork sprite whirred and clicked; its eyes flickering. "The Aiworth bridge was completed 408 years ago, before the Great War."

"Great War?" Alex asked.

"Wait, wait!" Mallory called over the questions and the answers of the others. "You said sixteen miles. How far is that, and how long will it take us to travel the distance? I want to get back up to the surface as soon as possible."

The sprite turned toward Mallory. "Without any foreseeable delay, it will take us the entirety of tomorrow to travel the distance, and perhaps part of the next day."

"What are the chances we'll find some food while we're down here?" Caleb's stomach growled while he spoke.

Mallory was not the only one still hungry after their meager lunch.

"Unlikely," the sprite returned.

"So, no food until tomorrow or the next day?" Alex seemed to have forgotten her question about the Great War now that their immediate situation had become clearer.

The sprite now turned toward Alex. "The Library's stores are more than sufficient to provide for your dietary needs."

"But that's three days away," Caleb moaned.

"And a whole day underground!" Mallory added.

"And we're hungry, now!" Caleb continued his complaints.

"And underground!" Mallory reiterated.

They both looked at Alex, waiting for her to add a complaint to their list. She shrugged. "What? Do you really want me to say what I'm thinking?"

They waited.

Alex shook her head. "Fine. Let's not forget about wolves and rats in the dark while we sleep."

Caleb stood up, eyes wide. "Well, let's get going. We need to find a place in these tunnels that will be secure enough to defend."

The sprite's eyes brightened. "Follow me, and I will show you where you can rest in safety for the night."

The three human companions stood and followed quickly after the sprite. Soon, they left the rows of empty market stands and reached another set of stairs that led further down into the dark. At the bottom of those stairs was another large open room with several evenly spaced, square, tiled pillars. The tops were hard to make out in the dark, but they appeared to meet the ceiling in gentle arches. Tiny pairs of red eyes glinted in the sprite's eye-lights amongst the crevices of the arches. "Rats." Alex whispered.

"Bats." The sprite corrected.

"Bats?" Mallory asked following Alex's gaze toward the ceiling.

"Yes. Mammals of the order *Chiroptera*. After rodents like the rats, bats are the most numerous mammals on the planet." The sprite moved further into the room, and the three young people stayed close to it eyeing the ceiling warily.

"So, they're like rats?" Mallory asked cautiously.

"Similar, but with wings."

"Wings?" Squeaked Caleb.

"Please, watch your step." The sprite cautioned, and the three companions looked down at it. The sprite was floating downward away from them into what appeared to be a ten-foot-deep chasm that opened in the middle of the room. There were two strips of rusty metal running down the center of the chasm, and the sprite's eye-lights illuminated a dark tunnel that the metal strips descended into and disappeared.

Mallory shivered. She would rather take her chances with the bats than go into that tunnel, but Caleb was already scrambling over the edge. She called to him softly, "Caleb, no!" But it was too late. He had clearly forgotten about his hurt shoulder again, as he tried to lower himself down by arm strength alone. As soon as all of his weight was on his arms, his face contorted in pain, and his strength gave out. He dropped, vanishing into the chasm. "Caleb!" Mallory called louder, and she was answered by a thousand squeaks above her and the thunder of flapping wings.

Alex threw Caleb's pack into the chasm, but neither Mallory nor Alex took the time to look up and see what horrors were swooping down on them. They both sat down on the edge and quickly twisted and lowered themselves down. Caleb was sitting on the ground, rubbing his head and looking up at the ceiling in wonder. Mallory followed his gaze and gasped. A black storm swirled in the tiled skies above them. The sound of wings echoed around the chamber like quiet thunder, and red eyes, reflecting the sprite's light, streaked about like intra-cloud lightning. Then the storm calmed, and the bats all settled back in their perches, hanging upside down, pairs of red dots appearing and vanishing in the darkness as they blinked down irritably at the traveling companions.

"Let's get out of here." Caleb whispered as he climbed to his feet and started wandering into the entrance way of one of the tunnels.

The sprite headed the opposite direction into the other tunnel, and Mallory hissed, "Caleb! This way!"

Caleb ran back out of the tunnel and soon they were all back in blackness. The walls of the tunnels were much closer than the ones in the great room and the underground marketplace. Mallory could not quite reach out and touch both sides of it, but it sure felt as if they were going to close in on her and crush her in the darkness. She tried to keep her breathing regular and not hyperventilate, but the farther into the tunnel they went, the shallower her breaths became. Still, she did not get behind the others this time, mostly because

Alex was in front of her, and Caleb had taken up the rear. They were herding her forward and keeping track of her at the same time.

After several minutes or hours of walking (it was impossible to tell how time was moving underground), the clockwork sprite stopped and turned toward the wall. There was a rusted door set in the side of the tunnel. The sprite inserted the tips of its arms into the cracks of the door and worked its way around the perimeter, breaking loose the rust between the door and the frame. Then it locked its arms tight and pulled the door off the wall with a screeching yank. It carefully set the door against the wall, and then floated to the side to let the young companions enter. Inside the door was a small room with a desk and opposite that, a wall with several small boxes that had broken glass in them. Mallory thought they looked somewhat like fish tanks, but she was not sure what the small buttons on the side of the tank would have been for, and there were deteriorated rubber wires leading to and from the inside of the boxes. The wires looked very similar to the Dikaió sprite boxes inside the heart of a sprite. She had birthed three fire sprites with similar wiring, and nearly destroyed her city. Were these fish-tank sprites? There did not seem to be any fish remains or a source of water.

The walls were peeling paint, and there seemed to be a slight draft coming from the direction of the wall across from the door, though the dimness of the room made it very hard to tell if it was coming from the top or the bottom of the wall. Mallory could make out a symbol engraved in the front of the desk. It looked like a heater shield: almost like the city's Sprite Master Reddy Lamarr's family crest. Her crest had not been the same crest that the ancient fire sprites used. They had a crest that was more like a crescent moon with stars. She had been amused that the sprite master's family did not have a long lineage as sprite masters. But Mallory wondered why Lamarr's crest would be here in this ancient room hidden underground. She walked to the desk and bent over to investigate it further.

CRASH!

Mallory jumped away from her curious exploration and spun around toward the entranceway. The sprite had replaced the metal door, essentially sealing them into the tiny room. "What are you doing?" Mallory demanded.

The light in the sprite's eyes fluctuated slightly, causing the shadows in the room to flicker eerily like campfire. "You will be safe here for the night. There is no way into this room other than the door, even for something as small as a rat or a bat. Rest now. We have a long way to go tomorrow."

Mallory pushed past the sprite and tried the door. It was sealed tight. Tight enough that only the sprite would be able to let them out. She was suddenly very worried that it would not. Her breaths turned ragged, and she felt panic rising in her chest, but then Caleb had his arms around her. "Mal?" He said her name with such tenderness that her breathing calmed a little. "I need you to be strong. We're going to get out of here real soon, okay?"

She nodded, but she still felt like she needed to get out of this room and run back into the open air or die trying. She bit her lip and cocked her head to the side. It was time to retreat into the rational side of her mind and reason out a solution for her fear. Caleb and Alex were pulling the sheets out of the packs. There was not room to set up the tents in here, but if the desk were pushed up against the wall, there would be space on the floor for them to all lay down and sleep. As Caleb and Alex laid out the sheets, Mallory positioned their packs to act as makeshift pillows. Before laying down, she opened hers and pulled out her water bottle. It was about half full. She took a big gulp of water, and then stopped, careful not to spill a drop. Mallory swung around to the sprite. "Is there water down here somewhere?"

The clockwork sprite buzzed and whirred for a moment and then answered: "No, the nearest source of water is at the end of our journey: Where the subway meets the bridge."

"And we'll get there sometime tomorrow or the next day?"

"Correct," the sprite affirmed.

Caleb and Alex both pulled their water bottles out and took a drink from them as well, but their drinks were much smaller than the one Mallory had just taken. When the City Council was exiling them, Jacob Carpenter, the Manager of City Services, had provided them with bottles that could filter out impurities and bacteria, but they could not produce water out of nothing. They were going to be in real trouble when their water ran out, so they were going to need to ration liquid very carefully over the next day.

After they had stowed their bottles, Caleb laid down on his pack, and Mallory laid down beside him with her head resting on his shoulder. Alex lay opposite the married couple with her head at their feet. Mallory thought how difficult it would be if their roles were reversed. What if Alex had been married, and Mallory was tagging along like a third wheel. It must be very lonely being Alex right now. Yet Alex never complained—well except for hemming and hawing if they got too romantic in front of her. Still, she took her oath to protect them—and one day their children—very seriously, and Mallory was surprised at how good of a protector she was. She had gotten glimpses of Alex's skill as a magistrate back in the city, but out here in the wild, all of those training exercises—so out of place in a peaceful society—made a lot of sense. For whatever it was worth, she was thankful that Alex was with them. She only wished she knew how Alex felt about it. Her thoughts were soon interrupted again, this time by a deep, deep sleep, which came faster than she thought it would. She could not have imagined sleeping while trapped in a small box underground bathed in the light of a clockwork sprite's eyes. But that is how exhaustion works sometimes.

Mallory woke to the sound of the sprite's voice. "It is time to continue our journey."

Caleb rolled over and said, "It's still dark. Can't we wait until morning."

The sprite replied, "It is well past—"

"C'mon you big lug," Alex interrupted the sprite and kicked Caleb's boot. "It's always dark down here. How would you know if it was morning, noon, or night, anyway?"

"Five more minutes, Mom!" Caleb tried to snuggle his face further into his pack.

Mallory tried a more delicate approach. "The sooner we

go; the sooner we'll find something to eat."

Caleb's eyes sprang open, and he jumped up from the floor, dusting himself off. "C'mon, you bunch of lazy do-nothings. Let's get going. Stop wasting the day."

Mallory laughed and began folding the sheets and putting them into their packs. It occurred to her that she was not petrified about being in a small space this morning. It was still unnerving, but she seemed to be acclimating somewhat. Alex folded her smaller sheet and stowed it away in her pack, strapping it on her back. Then she grabbed Caleb's pack from the floor.

"What do you think, big guy? Healed up enough to carry your own pack this morning?"

Caleb rolled his injured shoulder and stretched. "Yeah, it's hardly noticeable."

Mallory touched his back. "How? That should have taken a couple of weeks at least to heal all the way."

The sprite buzzed and whirred. "The nano-sprites rapidly build a cellular matrix in a wound that facilitates faster healing than a body is normally able to manage. As they learn the Chorus's unique composition, healing will occur even more rapidly."

"Imagine that!" Caleb grabbed his pack and slung it over his shoulders. "Yeah, I think I can carry my own pack now. Should we go?"

The sprite turned and pushed open the metal door to the room with a riotous screech. It held the door until the group was out of the room and then loudly pushed it back into place. Mallory bit her lip and wondered why it had shut the room back up again. Was it planning on keeping the room clear and safe for someone else in the future? Why not just throw the door open and be done with it? Whatever the case, as soon as the door was in place, the clockwork sprite was on the move down the dark tunnel.

The tunnel was never changing, and the group did very little talking. Every attempt at conversation was met with dry lips and throats. Mallory was trying her best to focus on breathing through her nose to keep moisture in her mouth, trying to avoid the need for another drink of water. There was no point in stopping for breakfast, lunch, or dinner because they did not have any food to eat anyway. Water breaks were used sparingly, and restroom breaks were almost non-existent because they had nothing in their bodies to waste. It was a miserable walk to nowhere, and the only interesting part was that the tunnel seemed to be ascending at a gradual upward slope, but it was so minuscule a change that Mallory often wondered if her mind was playing tricks on her. Eventually, she decided it must just be wishful thinking that they were going up, as the scenery of the endless black tunnel never changed. Mallory could not count the times she thought it would be better to just lay down here in the tunnel and let the rats have her than to continue to walk, dehydrated and hungry. Still, she put one foot in front of the other and kept moving.

After an eternity in the darkness, she saw a light shimmering in the distance. It was faint, barely distinguishable from the rest of the tunnel, but even in the monotony of the sprite's eye-lights, she could see it. It looked like water reflected on the walls. Soon she could see it more clearly, and the others could see it too. They ran past the clockwork sprite, sprinting as fast as their weak legs would carry them. They had reached the end of the tunnel and could see the moon and stars in the wide expanse of the night sky, but when they got to the opening, they all halted at the edge of the tunnel in uncertainty. The opening was a hundred feet above a steep decline that ended in what appeared to be rushing water. A long bridge stretched over the water, the end of which they could not see in the darkness of the night. But away in the blackness, a blinking red light pulsed against the night sky.

"What is that?" Mallory pointed. Caleb and Alex offered no ideas about what the light could be, but Mallory was immediately reminded of the red light that had begun blinking in the heart of the fire sprite that they found in the woods. She shuddered. "It looks alive."

The sprite caught up with the traveling companions, and Caleb looked down at it. "What is that blinking light in the distance?"

The sprite's eyes dimmed as it looked in the direction of Caleb's index finger. It rolled slowly back into the mouth of the tunnel as if the red light might notice it from so far away. "That is an Ex Natu citadel."

The clockwork sprite backed further into the cave. "We must be very careful as we travel near the tower. The Ex Natu have become less watchful after the Great War, but we must not rouse them again. You will rest here in the tunnel tonight because crossing the Aiworth bridge is dangerous for humans, and far too dangerous to do so at night."

"Because of the Ex Natu?" Alex asked.

"No, because it is dark, and human eyes do not work well at night." The sprite answered matter-of-factly.

Caleb laughed. "Well, that makes sense."

Alex did not drop the topic that easily. "Who are the Ex Natu? Why do we need to avoid them? How dangerous are they? We need some real answers here."

The clockwork sprite buzzed and whirred, and its eyes dimmed and brightened for a few moments before answering. "The cost in time to adequately answering your questions would be too great and not allow you sufficient rest for the next stage of our journey. It is best to sleep now and wait for the Dikaió Archivist to answer your questions."

Alex stamped her foot. "So, you are refusing to tell us what the danger is?"

The sprite whirred, "The danger-level of the Ex Natu is quite high. They should be avoided."

Alex stammered, "That's not what I meant." She threw up her hands in frustration.

Mallory put her hand on Alex's shoulder. "We're all curious, Alex. Let's just wait and ask the Archivist. It's just a sprite, after all."

Alex's hands dropped to the butts of her weapons. "How can I be a protector if I don't know what I'm protecting you from?"

Caleb smiled, "Well, we wouldn't have made it this far without you, Alex. I think you're doing a great job for what it's worth."

Alex's eyes narrowed, and she exhaled in frustration, knocking Mallory's hand off her shoulder. "You both act so innocent and childlike. It drives me crazy! It's always driven me crazy! And we're in real trouble here. We've been in real trouble since that night in Book Club when we read the words to fix Mallory's Dikaió and destroyed magic in the city. I just wish you would care about it all as much as I do."

Mallory felt indignant. Alex had run away and hidden

below City Hall the night she read the words in the Administrator's attic. Mallory had been left to face the ire of the city alone and was nearly executed for the crime. If not for Caleb and the fire sprites, she would be dead now—though she did not like to think about how many others died because of that gambit. Still, Alex suggesting that she was the mature one in the group who had it all together just because she could aim her magistrate weapons was enough to make Mallory's blood boil. Mallory drew her shoulders back and stood taller. She was about to unleash a tongue lashing on Alex when Caleb spoke softly.

"Look, Alex. We're all scared, and we all deal with it in different ways. I make jokes. Mallory makes elaborate plans. And you shoot stuff." He made a magistrate weapon with his thumb and forefinger and a popping noise with his lips for emphasis. "But in the end, we're all in this together. You were sworn to protect us, but we're going to protect you too. This," he moved his hand in a circle, motioning around at the three of them, "is our family now. We're going to look out for each other, no matter what dangers are out there." He pointed toward the blinking red light in the distance. "Whatever they are. Whatever vicious creatures we encounter. Whatever the Dikaió Archivist or the Library are—we'll face them together. Understand?"

Alex's eyes glinted in the soft light of the clockwork sprite's eyes. Mallory thought she was about to cry, but instead her nose twitched slightly, and she gave a stiff nod. Mallory turned and looked at her husband with awe. She knew he had a way with people, but she had never really understood why until this moment. Somehow, he knew that Alex's bravado just now was fear. She was ready to draw her proverbial sword and engage in the fight Alex was asking for, but Caleb parried Alex's blow and struck the heart of her need without even hesitating or thinking about it. Mallory wished she had a notebook, so she could write down everything that had just happened. She wanted to remember every detail and figure out what he had seen or heard that she had missed.

But instead, she helped her companions pull out their sleeping gear from their packs. There was still no way to set up the tent system they had worked out in the forest, but they made do sleeping on the ground of the tunnel with their backpacks as pillows. Mallory felt very little fear of wolves, rats, or bats here. She actually felt pretty worry-free in the fresh air at the end of the tunnel despite the blinking light in the distance. She imagined that even though she had buried her claustrophobia in the tunnels to make it through, it was still there lurking in the background the whole time and getting out of the tunnel had finally given her some relief. Without even thinking, she pulled out her water bottle, took a huge gulp, and finished it. Alex and Caleb looked at her in horror.

"Mallory!" Caleb said. "That's all the water you had."

Mallory looked at him in surprise, and then she turned her gaze thoughtfully towards the clockwork sprite. "Sprite? Is there any way you could get me some more water?" She motioned out toward the river below.

The clockwork sprite buzzed and whirred and then

rushed forward, collecting her bottle. Caleb and Alex quickly finished theirs as well and offered their empty bottles to the sprite. The sprite collected them and exited the tunnel into the night. Suddenly, the three of them were alone with only the luminescence of a cloudy night sky and a blinking red light in the distance to push back the darkness of the tunnel. Mallory noticed for the first time that the outside air was slightly chillier than the inside of the tunnel. She was not sure exactly how long it had been since they had been exiled from the city, but they had left at the end of summer, shortly after her birthday, which meant that they were somewhere in autumn. Winter would follow soon after. She had not considered what living in tents in the winter would be like, but she was suddenly very happy that they were on their way to an enclosed space to keep out the cold. She laid down and cozied up against Caleb to keep warm. Soon, the sprite would return with fresh water, and life was looking pretty good. Caleb's belly rumbled under her hand, angry for having been starved all day, and Mallory's stomach answered its call. Well, life was looking somewhat better anyway. She closed her eyes and tried to think of ways to get something to eat, but all she could do was imagine sitting at her family's long table and eating breakfast with her mother and father. Above her rumbling stomach, her heart began to ache, and then she was asleep.

When Mallory woke up, the sun was still below the horizon, but the sky was starting to brighten. Her stomach rumbled more, still angry from the night before. Hunger had a way of shortening sleep. She sat up and found her filtered bottle sitting beside her backpack. It was full of crisp, clean water, and she silently thanked the City Services Manager for his gift and felt grateful for the sprite collecting the water. With the sound of the rushing river outside the tunnel, Mallory threw frugality to the wind and finished the entire bottle. The rumbling in her stomach subsided under the onslaught of liquid, but Mallory knew from experience the relief would be short-lived once her body realized the trick she had played.

Soon, light began to stream through the tunnel opening. Day had dawned. Alex and Caleb both stirred in the warmth and brightness of daylight. Caleb knocked over his bottle as he stretched, and while the cap kept the liquid inside from spilling out, the sloshing noise it made while it rolled away from him made his eyes go wide. He quickly grabbed the bottle and drank the entire contents in what seemed like one gulp. "Ahhh!" He sighed, and then looked up at Mallory with a glint in his eye. "Hey beautiful, wife of mine. What's for breakfast?"

"You drank it." Mallory shrugged.

Caleb's face fell. He looked at the empty bottle he was holding and turned his nose up at it. "This measly draught? I was hoping for bacon and eggs."

Alex had already strapped on her magistrate weapons and backpack. "Well, the sooner we get going, the sooner we eat."

Caleb pushed up from the ground with determination. "Then what are we waiting for?"

Mallory looked around the tunnel. "We're waiting for the sprite. Where did it go?"

"It's out on the bridge, coming this way." Alex pointed toward the entranceway, and Caleb and Mallory looked out into the brightening day.

The clockwork sprite was rushing across the bridge toward the tunnel, flashing golden rays as the sun reflected off its coppered hull. However, its normally smooth movements were halting and erratic, though still quite fast. The bridge did not have a solid bottom. Wooden tracks ran across metal beams, but there were large gaps between the wooden pieces. The sprite was leaning forward at a forty-five-degree angle by using its propulsion to pulse along the bridge, adding thrust when it achieved the right angle on the tracks to leap over the gaps and not fall through to the river below. Mallory was amazed at how quickly it could calculate just the right moment to add the burst of speed, but the thing that really caught her eye was the river itself. She stepped curiously toward the entranceway to get a better view of the water. Now that the sun was rising, she could finally see the scenery that had been cloaked in darkness in the night. A massive amount of water flowed below the bridge; blue tints zigged and zagged down its center, but as it got closer to the land, the water churned brown waves crested with white foam. Trees and rocks lined both sides of the banks, and on the companions' side, the bank ran steeply up a sheer cliff into which the tunnel where they were standing had been carved. Mallory figured they were up at least as high as the roofs of the skyscrapers in their city, though not as high as some of those in the abandoned city this tunnel led to. With her head outside the entranceway, her curls whipped wildly in the current of air flowing along the top of the river below, but when she stepped back from the entrance, the wind was gone; it flowed past the opening like water around a stone.

The sprite burst through the opening and came to an abrupt stop. "Choruses, we should go now. The weather may not hold, and it would be better to not be on the bridge when it is raining."

Mallory looked up at the sky. It was cloudy, chilly, and there was a red haze on the horizon that traced upward, painting the clouds with pink light—it was a perfectly decent morning. "Seems okay to me, but we're ready."

Alex stepped past Mallory and folded her arms in front of the sprite. "Where did you go last night?" Caleb and Mallory both looked at Alex in surprise. The sprite's eyes blinked and processed the question, but it could not answer before Alex threw out another question. "Did you go to the Ex Natu?" She pointed at the citadel in the distance, which Mallory noted looked far less intimidating in the daylight than it did at night as a mysterious flashing red light. It was just a tiny spindly spire that was far enough away to appear blurry against the trees in the foreground.

The sprite edged back somewhat from Alex and answered her. "The subway and its bridge were abandoned when the city was lost. There were many points of disrepair along the way that needed to be reinforced to support the weight of three choruses. I enacted temporary repairs that should see you safely across."

Alex narrowed her eyes and then quickly glanced at the tower in the distance. "Okay, I believe you. Let's go," she said motioning toward the bridge. "The sooner we're out from that thing's shadow, the better."

The clockwork sprite floated out onto the first track of the bridge, and Mallory noted that the wind that had flicked her hair seem to float over the sprite just like it did the entrance to the tunnel, so she assumed that it must have been a gust that hit her earlier. That assumption was wrong. When the trio stepped out of the tunnel onto the bridge, a gale force nearly knocked them over. The bridge suddenly seemed alive and bucking under their feet. Mallory could not get over the illusion of a perfectly still bridge ahead of her, contrasting the wobbly swaying bridge under her feet. She grabbed hold of one of the steel cables that ran along the length of the bridge, and rusty metal splinters poked at her hands. The wind jerked her handhold, slashing at her palms. Caleb and Alex seemed to be having the same issue, though Alex was better able to hold onto the cable with her gloved hands than Mallory or Caleb could.

"We need to protect our hands!" Mallory yelled.

Caleb looked at her inquisitively. "What!?" he responded.

In addition to its intention to kill them by throwing them from the bridge, the wind was also stealing away their voices in its deafening roar. Mallory backed up off the bridge and walked back into the tunnel. Caleb followed after her. Alex hesitated, clearly wanting to keep walking across the bridge, but soon she walked back into the tunnel as well. When the wind was out of their ears, Alex yelled, "What? Let's go!"

Mallory held up her hand, covered in tiny cuts and trickling tiny streamlets of blood. "We need to protect our hands like yours, or we'll never get across."

Alex looked at her leather magistrate gloves and tilted her head to the side. "Wow! First time I was happy to have these."

Mallory pulled off her backpack and started digging through it. There were some cloth gloves to keep their hands warm, but the metal splinters would tear through them as readily as it was tearing through their skin. She pulled out the rope that they used to put up their tents and started to wrap it around one of her hands. She figured it would take about three feet to properly protect her palm. Together, that would be nearly twelve feet that would have to be cut off for her and Caleb, which meant they would be unable to put up one of their tents, and the three of them would have to share one space until they reached the Library. She looked at Caleb sadly, and he seemed to catch what she was thinking and whispered close to her ear, so only she could hear, "Privacy isn't as important as staying alive, Mal."

She nodded and started to cut the lengths of rope with her knife. It was not as easy as it should have been. Once she got through the outer fibers, she found the rope was reinforced with what seemed to be thin metal strands. When she touched the metal with her knife, it got warm and made the muscles in her fingers and forearm twitch slightly. She cursed Reddy Lamarr and her stupid rope under her breath. She had to use the serrated side of the knife to get through the metal. Once she did, the weird tingling sensation went away. Eventually, she managed to cut four three-foot strips of the blasted stuff. The couple helped each other wrap their hands in rope gloves, and when they were ready, they all headed back out onto the bridge. The bridge was about two-hundred yards across, and the clockwork sprite was nearly on the other side already. Alex led the way, grabbing hold of the frayed metal cable, stepping out onto the first rail. Caleb followed her, and Mallory followed him. The space between rails was about two feet, which was not a long step, but every time Mallory crossed between the rails, she looked down into the waters raging below her. She had never been all that afraid of heights. Even when they were fighting the fire sprites atop the skyscrapers, she had been more afraid of failing than falling. The bridge over the water was different. Looking down into the water gave her the same feeling as being stuck in an enclosed space. Her heart felt like it was permanently lodged in her throat. She could not quite put her finger on what the difference was. Maybe it was the bucking bridge, maybe it was the fact that she had never seen so much water in her life, or maybe it was that there was no clever invention that she could just throw together if something went wrong out there—suspended on air. Whatever the case, terror whipped about her insides while the wind whipped about her body.

Despite all that, the rope gloves were working pretty well at keeping her hands safe. She could not grip the cables as tightly as she would like, but her grip was tight enough to keep her from blowing off. The only downside was that the metal slivers in the cable kept sticking to the loose threads in the rope, and at times, she had to use a bit of force to get her hand off the cable, which also meant shifting her body weight. Whenever that happened, she closed her eyes tightly and imagined spiraling down into the water below, and she fell another step behind the others. The farther behind she fell, the more furious with herself she became. All of her life, everyone around her had used the Dikaió to accomplish anything they wanted, and she had never been as good at anything because of it. After they accidentally destroyed the Dikaió, she was suddenly able to do everything better than everyone around her, especially Alex and Caleb. But they had adapted so quickly. They fought off vicious wolves with ease, walked through the tunnels without the slightest qualm, and now here they were crossing a bridge suspended above certain death as if they had been doing things like this all their lives, and once again, she was straggling behind them. The irritation caused her to pick up speed, and she started leaping from rail to rail, trying to catch up to Caleb. When her rope glove got caught, she ripped it off the wire quickly, pushing forward harder and faster. This was no longer a journey across a suspended bridge; it was a challenge that she intended to win.

Mallory leapt from rail to rail until she was right behind Caleb. All she had to do was let go of the cable and take three jumps, and she could pass him. Mallory's muscles tensed as she prepared to make her move, but her foot landed on the edge of the rail she was aiming for, and her boot slipped into the empty air between the rails. Her body over-compensated for the error and leaned backwards. The weight of her backpack pulled her further than she had intended, and then her other foot slipped off the backside of the rail on which it was resting. Suddenly, she found her legs spreading out between the two rails into the splits. Luckily, she had not yet let go of the cable to make her move, but her grip was not as tight as it should have been. The only thing that kept her from falling to her death in the river below is that the rope gloves wrapped around her hands had snagged on the loose cable's slivers of metal, which gave her just an extra instant to tighten her grip. The abductor muscles on the inside of her legs screamed in agony as they were stretched farther and farther into the splits. She tightened her biceps and pulled herself slowly up—using just her arms until she was able to squirm one of her feet up onto a rail. Then she pushed herself up to a standing position. She looked over to see if anyone had noticed her slip. No one had. They were all several steps ahead of her again, keeping the same steady pace, looking straight ahead. Then she looked down at the flowing water far below and let out the breath she did not even know she was holding.

She was standing over the darkest, bluest part of the river, a little over one-half of the way across. The water looked deep and foreboding. Her gaze travelled along the water's path up toward the horizon, and then she saw the Ex Natu's citadel. The tree line on the bank of the river opened up somewhat, and she could see a lot more details than she could in the subway tunnel. The tower was dark stone and rusted iron. Mallory typically loved architecture, even though many building techniques had been lost in her city over time, she was still fascinated by the choices ancient architects and builders made to create a building aesthetically pleasing. The Ex Natu's tower had none of those features. If it had been ugly, it might still have been interesting, but it was not even that. The building was drab. It was as if children had stacked blocks on top of one another and glued them together: utterly unremarkable other than that it had been stacked up in a rather scenic environment amidst some fields, in a forest, near a river.

Mallory paused and looked again. The tower was rising out of what looked to be fields of crops. She knew it was autumn, but not this late in the season. The crops in the field looked harvest-ready. There was food not far from them! They would be able to eat tonight. She started to run toward her companions to tell them the news, but then remembered where she was, and instead began to work her way carefully across the rest of the bridge. The slow endeavor nearly drove her mad, and she was even more put out when she looked up at about the three-quarter mark and saw Caleb and Alex standing on the other side with their arms crossed, looking impatient. Gah! How were they so much better at everything than she was?

Slowly, Mallory finished crossing the last quarter of the bridge, and then leapt off the last rail onto solid ground. Her fingers were raw and bleeding. The rope gloves had done a pretty good job at protecting her palms, but the tips of her fingers had rubbed against the wire splinters quite a bit. Caleb hugged her, and then called, "Sprite, can you spray Mal's fingers, too?"

The clockwork sprite dutifully hovered over to Mallory and sprayed her fingers with antiseptic spray. Mallory squeaked as the spray coated the tiny gashes, and sharp stabbing stings throbbed in her fingers like a thousand tine paper cuts. She blew on her hands and soon the sting began to abate. "Great, will they heal quickly now like Caleb's back?"

The sprite's eyes fluctuated slightly, and it said, "My compliment of nano-sprites was used to save the male Chorus. However, this spray will prevent infections."

"Great," Mallory shook her head. "Miles from home, and I'm still getting my mother's painful infection treatment." Then she remembered what she saw on the bridge. "Did you guys see the tower?" She pointed in its general direction, though the forest obscured it now that they were off the bridge.

Alex shook her head, "No, I was focused on getting to the other side, not site-seeing."

Caleb signaled agreement. "Yep, me too. No wonder it took you so long, Mal."

"Took me …?" Mallory stumbled over her words. "I nearly fell to my death, and the two of you were so focused on getting across, you didn't even notice … Took me so long?" She began unwrapping the rope on her hands and talking to herself. "I have half a mind to keep all the food for myself. That would show you … took me so long?"

"Food?" Caleb at least caught that part of Mallory's diatribe.

"Food?" Mallory sarcastically mimicked him.

Alex sighed and said dryly, "Okay, Mallory. We're all hungry. What are you talking about?"

"Fine," Mallory stuffed the rope from her hands into her backpack. "There are fields full of ripe crops just past those trees." She pointed toward the citadel.

The clockwork sprite whirred and spoke hurriedly: "Those are the crops of the Ex Natu. The danger in obtaining them far outweighs the nourishment you might receive. There are ample stores at the Library. I suggest we make haste on our journey."

Mallory hesitated. "But it's not far. Just past these trees, there's a clearing. We can go in and grab some and be out before anyone notices."

Alex answered this time. "It's too dangerous, Mallory. Let's just cover as much ground as we can before nightfall."

Mallory bit her lip and cocked her head to the side, trying to think of a solution to the resistance she was getting toward gathering food. She looked toward her hungry husband for support. "Caleb?"

"Ah, Mal!" He shuffled. "You know I love to eat, but I love you more. Let's not risk it. Okay?"

Mallory's shoulders slumped. "Fine," she capitulated in defeat. She wagged her hands toward the sprite. "Lead on!" As the party began its hike through the forest, Mallory muttered to herself, "Too slow, too hungry, too dangerous—too cowardly more like it—could be eating now instead of walking around mumbling to myself . . ."

"Mal?" Caleb touched her arm. "We're going to be fine, okay?"

Mallory nodded, but she could not seem to think about anything but food. Maybe it was just the denial of harvesting some crops when they were so close, but she felt like she had never been so ravenous in her life.

The woods on this side of the river looked exactly the same as the dark woods around their city. Before the protective light fell when they destroyed the Dikaió, Mallory had never seen a forest before. What they called a forest in the city was more of a park or a garden compared to the endless armies of trees they were walking through now. Rivulets of light that looked like arteries streamed through the canopies above them. The leaves and branches of each tree moved gently in the wind but never touched. Mallory wondered if they did not touch because they crashed into each other when the wind blew, and friction broke parts off, or if the trees were aware of one another and just stopped growing branches when they sensed another tree nearby. The mess of branches on the forest floor suggested the former, but the ominous presence of the trees felt as if it was the latter.

The canopy kept out a lot of the light and heat of the sun, and they walked in perpetual shade, but the day was still warm, and soon Mallory was thirsty from all the walking. She reached behind her for her filtered bottle, but when she touched it, she could feel that it was too light. They had forgotten to ask the sprite to refill their bottles for the journey. Now she was hungry and thirsty. Her limbs began to ache with tiredness. "Sprite," she called. "Is there any water nearby? We forgot to fill our bottles."

The sprite kept moving forward while it spoke. "We have been walking parallel to a stream for the last two miles. It's just to the east of this line of trees. A break to refresh is allowable." It shifted direction to what was apparently the East, though it was impossible to tell in the midst of the forest and soon they were standing beside a small trickle of water that was running along the base of the forest. Large mossy rocks sat by the stream's banks, and the three companions sat down and refilled their filtered water bottles. As they sat and drank, Mallory kept thinking about the fields that had been so close, and her stomach rumbled. Alex and Caleb were looking very thin as well. They had lived on nuts and berries for weeks, and even before they were exiled, the city was having a food crisis. She remembered walking through the lethargic crowds of starving people. They had had a strange rancid, almost metallic smell about them. Then just like that, she could smell the odd smell in the air. She sniffed again just to be sure, and it was there, but faint. As she exhaled, it got stronger. She cupped her hand over her mouth and let out a long exhale. The smell filled the cup of her hand. It was her breath.

She stood up and walked over to Caleb. "Take a deep breath," she ordered.

He looked up at her puzzled, and then after they stood in awkward silence for a while, he acquiesced and breathed in deeply.

Mallory nodded, "Now, let it out."

Caleb exhaled, and Mallory leaned in close, smelling his breath. It was tinged with starvation as well. Mallory bit her lip and tilted her head, trying to understand what it was about hunger that affected the smell of one's breath. There were so many things in the world she wanted to understand, and she wondered if it was even possible to live long enough to figure them all out.

Caleb sat wide-eyed with Mallory inches from his face. Finally, he shouted, "What!? Why are you sniffing my mouth like that?"

Mallory rocked back and said matter-of-factly, "You're hungry."

Caleb nearly fell off the rock on which he was perched. "I'm hungry? Of course, I'm hungry, Mal!"

"Yes, but now you smell hungry." Mallory motioned a hand in circles by her mouth, simulating breath to help him understand.

"You're so weird!" He yelled. "And that's why I love you."

Alex stood up then. "Okay, I think we're ready to get moving. Let's go, sprite."

Mallory looked back at Alex and felt a bit perturbed. She again thought it must be hard to be the third wheel in the group, but she was starting to wonder if was not harder to have a third wheel and guard her mouth when she wanted to flirt with her husband. She wished they were at the Library already, just so that she and Caleb could be alone for at least a little while.

Caleb grabbed her hand and winked at her, as if reading her mind. "Let's get going, Mal. The sooner we get there, the sooner we can eat."

Well, he almost read her mind anyway. She smiled back and jumped into the stream, following after the sprite. The water was not deep, but it was higher than her boot. First, she felt her pant legs and then her socks fill with water. "Ugh!" She moaned and climbed out to the other side. Alex and Caleb had much the same experience as they crossed the stream, and the rest of the day was spent squishing through the forest behind the sprite. As the sun began to set, they entered a small clearing, and the sprite stopped.

"This will be a good place for you to rest tonight, Choruses," it said, and then moved to the edge of the clearing and hovered quietly.

The three traveling companions pulled off their backpacks and began to set up the one tent they were going to have to share that night. When the tent was pitched, Alex once again laid her pack down at the opposite end from Caleb and Mallory's, so that she would sleep with her head at their feet. Mallory knew that Alex was probably being considerate, but she could not help but feel that Alex was making a quiet protest about being stuck with the married people again. Then Mallory wondered if all of her irritation was legitimate or just her hunger talking.

Either way, Mallory had had enough water to replenish her body's needs, and maybe a little more since she suddenly, urgently needed to relieve herself. "I'll be right back. Nature calls," she said and then walked a little way out of the clearing into the woods. When she had finished, she started to head back to the clearing, but then something caught her eye. Rising just above the tree canopy, she saw the Ex Natu's citadel. It looked just as near as it was that morning. She walked through the trees toward the tower, and the trees thinned out as she did. She found herself standing in a field of crops, and there in the middle of the field was the citadel. Just past the tower she could see more trees, and what looked like some bluffs rising above them. She could not see it from here, but she assumed that below those bluffs was a river, and it could be crossed on a bridge leading to the abandoned subway tunnel. They had spent the entire day taking a wide track around to the other side of the Ex Natu citadel. A straight line might have taken them a half hour.

She was furious at the sprite. What a waste of their time and their day!

On the other hand, here she was standing amongst a treasure trove of food. There were melons, strawberries, carrots, beans, corn stalks, all planted in nice, neat rows. She took off her jacket and folded up the corners of it to make a knapsack of sorts and then began to load as many fruits and vegetables into it as she could manage. As she was on her hands and knees plucking strawberries and dropping them into her jacket-knapsack, the hairs on her neck stood on end. Her muscles tensed, and she felt like something was watching her. She rocked back on the balls of her feet and looked around.

Her heart stopped.

A silver-steeled culture sprite floated not ten feet away from her, its hull reflecting the red and purple sky of the setting sun. It did not have eyes, but Mallory could tell it was looking right at her. She scrambled to her feet, clutching her jacket full of Ex Natu contraband. The sprite arms slowly began lengthening into deadly whips, and Mallory screamed.

Mallory's eyes flashed left and right. She was still screaming, but she was not screaming from panic; rather she was screaming in the hopes that the clockwork sprite would hear her and come to her aid. And if that did not work, she was checking her surroundings to find a way to get around or past the silver-steeled culture sprite and its lethal whips. The setting sun made it harder to make out her options. The dark outline of the forest was fifty yards behind her, and in every other direction there were only various shadows of crops that would offer very little protection against sprite steel. She could make a run for the woods, and the cover of thick trunks of the trees, but she knew that she could never hope to outrun the thing; she had seen too many wolves fall using that tactic. The culture sprite's whips were fully extended now, and it was pulling them back. Mallory stopped screaming and bit her lip. Her head tilted slightly to the side as the culture sprite cocked its whip ready to strike. Mallory bent her knees and began to sprint as fast as she could straight at the culture sprite. It swung both whips at her.

CRACK!

The whips supersonic tips tore the air where Mallory used to be standing, but Mallory was still running directly toward the sprite. The whips had struck her—one on each shoulder. But only the middle section of the whips had connected. She had remembered that the clockwork sprite had not been able to cut down wolves in close quarters. Since it was the tip of the whip that seemed to make the crack, she figured the middles would be safer, and she was mostly right. The impact of the whips had not been lethal, but it was certainly painful, and she felt thick rivulets of blood begin to flow down her arms as she ran. She was not sure exactly what she would do when she reached the culture sprite, but she could not let it expand the gap and use its whips effectively, or she would not survive.

The culture sprite seemed to understand her tactic and began to retreat from her advance. It was moving at four times her speed, quickly moving to a range where its whips would strike their target. Mallory changed tactics. She slowed her pace. As soon as the sprite began to retract its whips, and she judged that it was far enough away to kill her, she stopped, turned, and ran as fast as she could the other direction. A crack sounded behind her, and she felt hot wind puff against her back, but the culture sprite had missed. That was the last of her tricks though; the sprite was not going to be fooled by either again. She kept running: a break for the woods. Those trees would give her a better chance of close-quartered survival than these crop fields ever would. She was sure that she would not make it, but she intended to try.

CRACK! CLANG!

A bright light accompanied the crack of the sprite's whips, and Mallory felt herself falling weightlessly through the air. "So, this is what death feels like," she thought, and found herself curiously looking forward to discovering what the life after life held. Would she soon fade from existence into an eternal sleep? Would she float around this world forever haunting the sprite that killed her? Would she go to another world and see her loved ones again? Would she get to talk to her grandmother again? That thought filled her with a feeling of tranquility, but that tranquility was quickly replaced with dark pain, as she hit the ground with a thud and squeezed her eyes shut.

Mallory lay there on the cold sod for a moment and smelled the earthiness of the dirt. "I'm still alive," she whispered. Her eyes fluttered open, and the world was lighter than it had been when she first encountered the sprite.

CRACK! CLANG!

The sound of sprite whips snapping sounded somewhere near her, but they weren't striking flesh. She was in one piece.

CRACK! CLANG!

They were hitting metal. Mallory sat up. A flash of

copper circled a flash of silver, metal tentacles wiggling wildly around the flashes. The clockwork sprite spun backward and unleashed its whips.

CRACK! CLANG!

The whips sang amidst bright amber sparks. Part of the culture sprite's steel flew off, and Mallory could see the familiar interior she had become acquainted with while rebuilding the fire sprites. There inside the shadows a red light blinked: the sprite's heart. Mallory knew that the red light was affixed to a Dikaió box that had small tentacles with heart shaped tips, which connected to all the major appendages of the sprite. When she had connected the tentacles on the fire sprites that had come loose, their red light had started blinking, and the fire sprites were birthed back to life. She wondered if she could stop the Ex Natu's culture sprite by disconnecting those wires.

CRACK! CLANG!

The culture sprite took a piece of copper hull off the clockwork sprite, and it was significantly greater than the damage the clockwork sprite was inflicting. If Mallory did not do something, they would lose their guide and be stranded here below the Ex Natu citadel. And then what? Keep stealing crops until the sprites killed them or worse?

She pushed herself to her feet and started running toward the culture sprite. She thought she heard Caleb and Alex's voices behind her calling for her to stop, but it was too late. She was in action. She was a little worried that the culture sprite would turn on her and end her before she could get close to it, but she figured the clockwork sprite would seem like the bigger threat, and it would be too occupied to worry about her. Her gambit was correct, as the culture sprite never acknowledged her approach, keeping its attention trained on its assailant. Mallory dove for the culture sprite and thrust her arm through the hole the clockwork sprite had opened. She grabbed a handful of the tentacles attached to the Dikaió box.

At first, she worried that she was not going to get them loose. She had had to use a screwdriver to push in the tips with the fire sprites, but that was when she wanted to disconnect them without breaking them. This time, she did not care if they broke. She spun her whole torso around as she pulled, ripping the heart from the sprite. The culture sprite, which had been floating about a foot off the ground, fell to the earth with a dull thud—its long arms laying limply in the dirt. Mallory stood over the motionless sprite, holding the box. She looked at the clockwork sprite with a grin and held up the culture sprite's heart. Caleb and Alex came to a running stop behind her, and she showed them the heart too. Her grin growing broader, excitement brimming over the rim of enthusiasm.

"You killed it, Mal!" Caleb laughed.

"Yeah, yeah I did," Mallory gasped.

"Well, it almost killed you! What do you think you were doing?" Alex chided.

"Getting food, Alex." Mallory pointed at her knapsack jacket laying a few feet from where she had dropped it. "We need to eat, Alex!"

"We need to stay alive, Mallory! You're going to get us all killed pulling stunts like this." Alex waved her hands incredulously in the air, and then pointed at the clockwork sprite. "The sprite said it was too dangerous. You should have listened."

Mallory crossed her arms and rolled her eyes. "You sound like my Moth—"

An eerie wailing filled the air, cutting off Mallory's statement.

The clockwork sprite floated up to them, holding the piece of copper that the culture sprite had cut off. "The Ex Natu have been alerted to the breech of their fields. We have very little time to escape."

Their eyes grew wide. They ran back to the campground, and Alex and Mallory began to quickly untie the tent as Caleb was haphazardly stuffing things into packs. The clockwork sprite stood at the edge of the campsite, its eyes focusing and unfocusing at the trees around them.

Suddenly, it spun and rushed across the site into the forest. "They are coming. This way, quickly!"

Her heart pounding in her ears, Mallory began to run. The sun was not quite set, but it was nearly night, and the forest's shadows were deep and getting deeper. The trees were smaller here than the ones in the dark forest they had crossed at the beginning of their journey. The trunks were not as wide, and the canopy not quite as high. This forest was younger, but that also made the foliage denser, and it was harder to see what was ahead. She was following the lights of the sprite's eyes, which was working pretty well, but out of the corner of her eye, she saw four more pairs of lights heading toward them: The Ex Natu sprites were in the forest. Suddenly the clockwork sprite's eyes went dark, and Mallory found herself running in blackness again. She could hear the movement of Caleb and Alex nearby her, but it was difficult to make them out among the foliage and the trees.

Something grabbed hold of her shirt and pulled her down to the ground. Thorns and thistles in the undergrowth clawed at her, as Mallory tried to scramble away from her assailant. She was just about to yell for help, when Alex landed with a thud beside her, and then Caleb. "Shhh" a muffled sound emitted from the undergrowth, "There's a small passage here. We will escape the Ex Natu underground."

Mallory's eyes strained in the dark, and she could barely make out what had hold of her. It was one of the clockwork sprite's whips, wrapped firmly around her arm. It quickly unraveled, and she saw some rustling in the bushes behind her.

A dark form that was so large it could only be Caleb dove into the bushes and whispered urgently, "C'mon!"

Alex followed quickly after Caleb.

Mallory sighed heavily. She did not want to go back underground. She peeked up and saw that the Ex Natu sprites were drawing nearer. She did not want to be caught by the Ex Natu either. She sighed again, and then dove into the bushes where the rest of her party had disappeared. The ground gave way beneath her, and she fell hard on her backside into a squishy cushion of mud. Then she began to slide down an incline. She twisted and turned trying to find a handhold to slow her descent, but all she managed to grab was wet silt and empty air. Darkness rushed by and then abruptly she stopped. She lay there for a moment trying to catch her breath. Cold water slowly began to seep into her pants, and she spun over and tried to push herself off the ground, but her perch was wet, and she slipped. She fell into about an inch of stagnant water on the ground, which was now soaking through her shirt as well. A bit had splashed in her mouth, and she spit, hoping she had not swallowed any of the foul liquid. Slowly and carefully, she used her core and legs to rise to a kneeling position. Looking around, Mallory noted that it was dark, but there seemed to be enough light to make out a tunnel of sorts. It was similar to the subway tunnel, except that this one was much smaller. Away in the distance, two dim lights hovered a little off the ground, and they were getting smaller and dimmer. Her heart quickened; the clockwork sprite was not waiting for her.

She tried to stand, but the weight of her backpack pulled her off balance, and her feet slipped out from under her again. She rolled over in the dank water and cursed under her breath. Then a hand was hovering above her in the shadows. "C'mon, Mal. We have to go!" Caleb hissed.

Mallory reached up and grabbed his hand, and Caleb pulled her to her feet. She looked over his shoulder and could see that the sprite had now stopped and was waiting. Alex's shadow was dimly illuminated halfway between them and the sprite; she had her arms crossed and was fidgeting irritably. Mallory's molars ground. She wanted to shout at the magistrate, but instead she just huffed air out her nose. Caleb smiled at her and tousled her wet hair. "Let's go!" He said with too much enthusiasm and began to run down the small tunnel toward the sprite.

Mallory sighed heavily. Then she looked around herself again, and that old familiar foe, claustrophobia knocked on the door of her mind. The walls shrunk even smaller, and the tunnel seemed to extend even longer. How long were they going to be in this tight, enclosed space? She shook her head. "No, there's no time for that," she chided herself. Besides, she did not want to get left behind like in the subway tunnel, so she picked up her heavy feet and chased after her companions.

Once again it was impossible to tell time in the darkness, but Mallory's burning legs and lungs swore that they had been running for hours. The stagnant water they had landed in was getting deeper as they ran, and Mallory worried that they were going deeper underground. She checked behind them every few feet, but none of the Ex Natu's sprites were in the tunnel behind them. The clockwork sprite had been insistent that the Ex Natu would not travel underground, and it seemed that their sprites would not either—or perhaps the sprites just never found the tunnel. They certainly knew that someone had visited their crop fields. There was no way they would find the sprite husk and think that it had all been a false alarm. She felt the sprite heart bouncing against her back while she ran and wondered if it had been a mistake to bring it with her, but she wanted to take it apart, and maybe the Archivist would know how it worked with the Dikaió to bring a sprite to life.

"Mal?" Caleb called.

Mallory stopped. Caleb's voice was behind her somehow.

When she turned around, she saw the sprite pulling itself up a ladder that was about ten feet high, and Caleb and Alex were both staring at her. She had been so lost in her thoughts, she had not noticed them and had walked right past them. "We're going up?" she asked hopefully.

Caleb nodded. "The sprite is going up first to see if it's safe."

Mallory smiled. "Makes sense."

CRACK!

A loud noise at the top of the ladder made them all step back uncertainly. Then a half crescent of nearly imperceptible light formed in the darkness, as the sprite opened a circular hatch and ascended out of the tunnel. It was night, and Mallory could vaguely see the dimly illuminated outlines of trees and brush in the sprite's eye-lights above. When the sprite was gone, darkness returned. The tunnel was not completely black thanks to the circle of night sky at the top of the ladder, but Mallory thought comparing the circle with the tunnel around them was a lot more like comparing shades of darkness than any sort of light coming into the tunnel. Still, she stood there staring at the lighter shade of blackness until her neck began to ache. "Raaa!" She hissed to no one in particular. "The sprite is taking forever up there!"

Alex hissed back at her, "Be quiet! If there is someone or something up there, they'll hear you!"

Mallory crossed her arms and looked disdainfully in the direction of Alex's voice and then stuck out her tongue at her friend. It was childish, but no one could see her, and it made her feel better.

"Grow up, Mallory!" Alex whispered irritably.

Mallory sucked her tongue back inside her mouth and she peered deep into the darkness. "You saw me?" Surprise amplified her voice beyond a whisper.

"You're not invisible, Mallory. Now, be quiet!" Alex's voice came back urgently.

"Girls!" Caleb chirped at them both and then whispered, "Both of you need to shut up."

The trio went silent, and Mallory stared in Alex's general direction. She was trying to make out anything other than the amorphous black blob of shadow in front of her. It was impossible. How could Alex have seen her without any light? Was her vision also better than hers in addition to everything else? She opened her eyes as wide as she could, and she thought that she could see the whites of Alex's eyes.

Suddenly, she was blinded by light. She stumbled backwards blinking uncontrollably. Caleb caught her hand before she fell. "It's just the sprite, Mal. It's all clear up top. Let's go."

Mallory shook loose from her husband. In her head she screamed at him, "Stop saving me!" But out loud she murmured a quick "okay" and began to climb the ladder. The climb was long and slow, and the night seemed bright even though the moon was barely shining through the canopy of trees above. Mallory looked around her and could see that they were in a small clearing. The soil was very rocky, and she kicked at the dark pebbles under her feet. Her shoes squished as she walked. Since crossing the stream earlier in the day, her pants and feet had not been dry, and now, the underground cave water had added even more to the dampness. She desperately wanted to get her shoes and pants off and hang them above a fire to dry out.

"Are we making camp here?" She asked the sprite, which was still spinning slowly in circles scanning the forest with its eye-lights.

The sprite replied without looking at her: "That would be unwise, Sprite Slayer."

Mallory's eyes went wide. Sprite Slayer? What happened to Chorus? Was the sprite afraid of her after she tore the Ex Natu sprite's heart out? Were sprites capable of fear? She decided to press the advantage and stood up taller. "I think we should make camp here, sprite."

Alex spoke then. "The Ex Natu know we're nearby. Their sprites are going to keep looking for us. Setting up camp just increases the chances that they'll find us. We need to keep moving."

The clockwork sprite turned to look at them. "The Chorus is correct. We must flee."

Mallory bit her lip and tilted her head.

"Mal," Caleb leaned in close to her ear. "Let's just go. We can try to figure this all out when we get to the Library."

Mallory pushed her foot deeper into her water-logged boot and felt the uncomfortable cold liquid ooze between her toes. Her nose scrunched up in disgust, and she looked hard at Caleb. Her eyes had adjusted to the outdoor lighting, and even though it was hard to make out details in the dark, she could see the concern on his face. She softened. "Fine! Lead on, sprite," she said and flicked her wrist in the sprite's general direction.

Once again, the companions were running through a forest in the dark, trying hard to keep up with the clockwork sprite. Their only point of navigation was the dual pinpoints of light from the clockwork sprite's eyes. Mallory's eyes burned, desperate to close and sleep, and her stomach burned and gurgled, having gone without a morsel of nourishment for over a day now. She decided that she would not think about her stomach and tried to think about something else. She wondered what her parents were doing right now. Sleeping. Obviously, it was the middle of the night. She wondered what they would do tomorrow morning, and then she wondered what they would eat for breakfast. Eggs? Juice? Fruit? Her stomach lurched so violently that she almost stumbled and fell. Thinking about something else was not working. Maybe she would try thinking about nothing for a while. She focused her vision on the sprite's eye-lights and tried to let her mind go blank.

It worked for a time, but then she began to think about the figures they had seen riding the sprites in the abandoned city. Who were the Ex Natu? A fuzzy idea about their identity was floating just out of reach, but when she tried to focus in on it, her thoughts turned toward her grandmother. Her mind's eye drifted back to the stain-glass dragonfly window in her room, under which her grandmother had told Mallory the story of the city's last Chorus. She had told her that the Chorus's parents had left the city and not returned, and her curiosity had been piqued. The light that protected the city kept anything from passing it, either in or out, so how could the Chorus's parents have left? Her grandmother had explained that "before the city's light was stoked to protect it, people could leave whenever they wished, but that also meant that things in the wild beyond the borders could come in."

Caleb had been convinced that the fire sprites and the light were meant to keep the dark woods and the wolves from harming the city, but what if they were to keep out the Ex Natu? Then another idea struck her. What if the light prevented citizens from returning to the city? What if the Ex Natu were the descendants of the Chorus's parents that had been trapped outside the city, separated from their child? She considered that prospect. Without the community of the city to help raise them and teach them what is important, what would children become as adults? Could they become the savage things they saw destroy the wolves in the abandoned city: the creatures the clockwork sprite seemed to fear so much? For all she knew, the Ex Natu could be distant relatives that had been forced to grow up in these woods without access to the rooftop gardens, the joy of the musicians, or the beauty of having an extended family. Fear gave way to pity.

The woods were growing lighter now. Dawn was upon them; they had been running all night. As the day grew brighter, the sun swallowed up the clockwork sprite's eye-lights, and just when Mallory feared the lights would be lost among the trees, the trees began to thin out. And then, they were walking on the edge of an endless prairie. Five-foot high grass moved like waves on a golden sea in the breeze. Spotted here and there within the prairie sea were islands of trees and piles of rocks, but for the most part there was only grass. The clockwork sprite stopped and waited for them to catch up. "From here there will be very little cover. Try to keep up."

Caleb sat down hard on the ground. "We need rest, sprite. We're not made for this."

Alex sat down across from him. "Agreed. I'm exhausted."

The occupation of her thoughts had kept her mind off her body's protest, but when her husband and friend collapsed, Mallory felt all the energy drain from her limbs, and she dropped down next to Caleb. "Go on without us, sprite." She dismissed the clockwork sprite with a wave of her hand. "Let us die here."

The clockwork sprite's eyes wobbled and whirred with distress. "That is an unacceptable course of action, Sprite Slayer. I must deliver a Chorus to the library."

Mallory sighed and her stomach rumbled. "I wish I hadn't left all the food back with the Ex Natu."

"What are you talking about?" Caleb asked, though his voice was muffled somehow as if his mouth was full.

Mallory's eyes shot quickly in his direction, and she was astonished to see his face covered in sticky strawberry juice. In his lap lay her jacket, and it was full of her spoils from the Ex Natu's field. Caleb was scooping up handfuls of fruits and vegetables and shoving them into his goofily grinning mouth. Mallory and Alex both tumbled over themselves to get to the food, and Caleb roared with laughter. "You didn't really think I'd leave the food behind did you?"

Mallory shoved a handful of strawberries in her mouth. Normally, she would have taken the time to pluck off the green leaves, but all she wanted to do was push down as much food into her belly as it could hold, and then a little bit more. The sweet juice of the strawberries poured down her throat, and the rush of sugar hit her brain with a flood of daylight. Her eyes dilated maddeningly, and she began to work on pulling the husk off a cob of corn.

The clockwork sprite hovered back and forth, watching the humans wildly devour the food. "Grains should not be consumed raw, Sprite Slayer. The human digestive system is not adapted to . . ."

Mallory gave it a hard stare, and then began gnawing kernels of the corn off before it completed its sentence. The corn certainly did not taste as good as when it was boiled or roasted, but it tasted infinitely better than starving in the woods. After the corn, she ate a melon, celery stalks, and carrots. By the time she got to the rainbow chard, her stomach signaled that it needed a break, which was just as well, as she was not a huge fan of the fibrous plant anyway. She used the back of her hand to wipe sticky saliva and fruit juice off her chin and smiled broadly. "That was amazing! Caleb Aiworth, I could marry you."

Caleb stopped chewing and looked at her mischievously. "Sorry, pretty lady. I'm taken."

Even Alex laughed at their flirtatious antics. "Of all the people I could get banished with, it had to be you two!" She flicked a strawberry at Caleb, and he deftly caught it in his mouth.

"You're lucky," Caleb chewed. "You could have been exiled with that dumpy old Smith Guild leader." He stood up, hunched his back, and bent his knees to make an arch of his legs. Then he pretended to tuck one hand in his shirt and danced around like a monkey. "Jingle, jangle, I'm covered in jewels and metal. Jingle, jangle."

Mallory laughed hysterically, and then she stopped and touched the jeweled dragonfly pinned to her lapel. For all his faults, the Smith Guild leader had given them each a reminder of their houses and the connection they had to the city. Alex had also stopped laughing and was fingering the scroll of law on her own shirt, clearly thinking along the same lines as Mallory. Soon Caleb sat back down next to Mallory again; the mirth of the moment lost in a bout of somber homesickness. Mallory thought then that this was the first time they had even spoken of the city since they had been exiled, and the thought sapped every ounce of energy from her body. She wanted nothing more than to curl up in the soft grass and sleep. Her eyes began to slowly close; a night without sleep and a full belly had caught up with her.

WHOOSH!

A loud roar rushed by somewhere, and Mallory's eyes popped open. The clockwork sprite dashed toward them and said, "Quick, back to the cover of the trees!"

Mallory looked up in the air and saw a sprite flying over the prairies. She expected to see an Ex Natu rider on it, but this sprite was riderless. Still, she stumbled over herself, pushed up off the ground, and ran quickly back to the tree line. She crouched down behind a large oak trunk and looked out toward the prairie. The flying sprite flew in a line toward the horizon, and then slowly began to turn. She watched as it made a large sweeping circle over the tall grass, and then after what seemed like hours, but was probably only a few minutes, it flew back over the forest.

The clockwork sprite floated out toward the prairie again. "There is no time to rest, Choruses. The Ex Natu sprites will conduct hourly surveillance of this area. We can be outside the range that they are likely to check if we leave now." It did not wait for an affirmation and started out of the tree cover.

"Wait!" Mallory yelled.

The sprite slowed and turned, floating backward toward the prairie. "There is no time for argument, Sprite Slayer. We must go, now."

Mallory pointed at the fields of grass. "We'll never be able to see you in all that. Give us a point to aim for if we lose track of you."

The sprite's eyes fluttered. "There is a pile of boulders two miles sixty degrees Northeast of this point. I will meet you there if you cannot find me." And then it disappeared into the grass.

Mallory hesitated and looked at Alex and Caleb. She indicated with her head toward the prairie. "That's Northeast, but what's sixty degrees?"

Alex's eyes went wide. "The compass the Science Guild gave me 'to find our way.' It has number marks on it." She set down her backpack and unzipped a pocket. "I've been checking the compass whenever I can, and we've been generally heading North since we left the city, which is easy enough to tell with the great big N, here, but I've been wondering what these numbers and hash marks were. I guess they're degrees?"

Caleb started walking toward the prairie. "Let's hope so, ladies. The sprite is almost out of view already.

Alex shouldered her backpack, held her compass out in front of her, and followed after him.

Taking one last look at the forest, Mallory followed Alex into the wide-open fields of the prairie.

6

The three companions had to move fast, but running in the prairie was impossible. It was too easy to get separated. Mallory's head barely reached over the tall grass, and at times, she found herself walking on tiptoes trying to see Caleb, who could see over the stalks. He and Alex had switched places after she kept yelling at him that he was going the wrong direction. She was holding the compass after all, so she should be leading. So now Caleb was following Alex, who short frame was nearly engulfed by the grass and solely navigating her way by looking at her compass. Caleb was navigating by tracking Alex's black bobbed hair and every once in awhile turning around to make sure that Mallory was following behind him. Mallory knew this because every ten minutes or so, she would walk on tiptoes and call, "Can you still see her, Caleb?"

"I see her, Mal!" he would call back to her. "And I see you, too. We're doing fine."

"What about the sprite? Can you see it?"

"I think so, but it's pretty far up ahead of us. It's hard to tell."

Mallory would sigh heavily and keep walking in the vague direction of the last time she saw Caleb.

The grass was mesmerizing in front of her, the wind's rustling touch made it wave back and forth like the golden hands of a watch, ticking time lazily. As the stalks rubbed against each other, they whispered music like the wordless hymns her mother used to hum when she was little, lying below her covers in her cozy, comfortable mattress. Her eyes grew heavier and heavier, transported off to dreamland in the music. She stumbled and nearly fell, and her eyes shot back open. She was sleep-walking. She stood up on tiptoes and saw that she had veered off course quite a bit to the West. Caleb's head was now visible about one-hundred yards to the East. She wondered how long she had been walking with her eyes closed. She thought about calling out, but she knew he would just stop and wait for her, and the clockwork sprite said that they had precious little time to get outside the range of the Ex Natu sprites, so she corrected course and started heading in a diagonal to intercept Caleb.

She walked on the tips of her toes like a ballerina to keep Caleb in sight, and it reminded her of having to wear heels to the fancy city events when the Matriarch's family was required to attend. She hated wearing heels because they made her calves and ankles burn. Her mother wore heels pretty much constantly, always the epitome of proper governance. She even had managed to continually keep her naturally curly hair in a tight bun without a strand out of place. As Mallory walked through the uneven prairie on her toes, her ankles and calves began to burn, and the wind whipped her wildly curly hair in different directions leaving no strand in place. She had never been much like her mother. In fact, her mother often told her that she was a lot like her grandmother. When Mallory was younger, that felt like an awful insult. What child would ever feel good when a parent tells them that they are nothing like them? If a child cannot be like their parent, to whom would they belong? Being an individual without history to anchor onto was a lot like being adrift in this prairie sea without a target destination. Mallory had tried hard to change and be more like her mother, but after her grandmother passed into the life after life, Mallory had begun to embrace the insult and model her life and personality after her more free-wheeling grandmother.

Of course, that had not paid off spectacularly well. She would not be out here with Alex and Caleb if not for her free-wheeling choices. Mallory knew that she could not blame herself completely for the decisions of the other two, but she also knew that things would have gone differently if she could have just accepted her magic-free existence, instead of trying to fix things.

Eventually, she intercepted Caleb and dropped the soles of her feet back to the ground. Her calves screamed in relief, and she called out: "Can you still see, Alex?"

"What?" Caleb called back.

"Alex?" Mallory yelled louder.

"Yeah?" Alex called from somewhere to Mallory's left though her voice was distant in the tall grass.

Caleb stopped moving, and Mallory ran into him. "Oof!" She stammered and stumbled backward. "Can you see her or not?"

"I guess I lost track of her. Must have been dozing. Hey, Alex, raise a hand, so we can find you." He started walking forward again. "Oh look, I found her!"

Mallory rolled her eyes but said nothing. Soon they were back in the slow single-file line walking through the tall, hypnotic grass. Mallory felt her eyes growing heavy again, and every step took herculean effort. It had been so long since they had slept.

WHOOSH!

The sound of a distant flying Ex Natu sprite snapped Mallory out of another daze. She stood on tiptoes to make sure she had not lost Caleb again. His head was right in front of her where she hoped to see it. He was scanning the sky, looking for the sprite.

Then Alex shouted, "I see the rocks and the clockwork sprite. C'mon!"

The three companions began to run and soon they came to a large stack of boulders where the clockwork sprite hovered patiently. "Quick, Choruses. This boulder marks the border of the Ex Natu's citadel. The flying sprites will not search for you beyond it."

"Great!" Caleb dropped down to the ground. "We need to sleep."

Alex addressed the sprite. "Can we sleep here?"

The clockwork sprite's eyes bibbed-and-bobbed. "There is a tree two-hundred yards from here, which would offer better protection from the sun's intensity and would not be so near to the flying sprites' search path."

Caleb sighed loudly and rolled on the ground in protest. "C'mon. C'mon. Let's just sleep here. I'm tired."

Mallory laughed and joked, "C'mon yourself, big man. I know I didn't marry a giant child."

Alex did not laugh but said, "I've always thought he was a giant child."

Caleb sat up and then pushed himself off the ground, looking at them somberly. "We were all children just a short time ago; we never had to worry about any of this."

The clockwork sprite began to fidget. "The Ex Natu's patrol is coming closer. Perhaps the Choruses could reminiscence about their childhood after we have reached safety?"

As if to emphasize the sprite's point, another whooshing noise sounded somewhere in the distance above the trees. Caleb jumped ahead of the girls as adrenaline surged through the trio. The clockwork sprite moved into the tall grass, and they followed it at a quick gallop.

Mallory yelled in between breaths: "How long will they keep looking for us?

The sprite called back from the front of the line. "The Ex Natu will continue to look for you until you are found. Their motivation is never exhausted."

Alex called, "Then they'll probably widen the search?"

The clockwork sprite replied, "The Ex Natu are very patient. They will ensure that you are not within the first perimeter before sending scout sprites beyond it."

"Is that what the flying sprites are called? A scout sprite?" Mallory wondered.

"No, Sprite Slayer," the clockwork sprite answered. "The scout sprites cannot fly, but they can travel farther than the flying sprites. Flying requires much more energy and frequent refueling. The scout sprites have very little energy consumption."

Soon the tree that the clockwork sprite had selected came into view. It was a large willow tree, and Mallory was amazed that such a large tree could grow all alone in a huge prairie like this. Usually, willows needed a source of water to get so big, but as near as she could tell, there was not any water around. Perhaps there was some underground source that was nourishing it. The tree really was massive, though. She doubted that the three of them together would have been able to join hands and reach all the way around its trunk. The shade beneath its drooping branches was cool, and the grass had not grown quite so tall beneath it either—it was roughly ankle deep. The clockwork sprite moved slowly beneath its branches, and its eyes began to glow. "This is a safe place to rest, Choruses."

Caleb dove under the tree and took off his pack, quickly placing it under his head. He was apparently not going to wait for the clockwork sprite to change its mind. Mallory marveled that within seconds of his eyes closing, he began to softly snore. The man had a knack for sleeping and eating, and she loved him for it.

Alex was more ritualistic in getting ready to rest. She pulled her boots off and rolled off her wet socks. "Sprite," she called. "Can you dry these out? We don't want our feet staying wet while we walk."

The clockwork sprite hovered over to her and took out its small torch: "There is very little butane remaining. It would be best to dry all of your footwear at once, Chorus."

Mallory kicked off her boots and pulled her socks off too, handing them to Alex. The grass was cool and soft between her toes, but her feet immediately felt better without the soggy footwear covering them. Then she turned to Caleb's massive feet. She knew that it would be nearly impossible to wake him, so she unlaced his boots and struggled to pull them off his giant feet. She had to stand bow-legged and lean backwards, leveraging her entire body weight as a counter against the soggy footwear. Caleb's wet socks created even more friction, and her attempts to pull the man's boots off failed. Finally, Alex walked over and together they managed to wrestle one of the shoes off. When they started working on the other one, Caleb snorted and kicked. The girls fell over each other, trying to clear out of the path of his flying foot. Luckily, it did not connect with either of them. They went back to work and finally got the second boot loose. Mallory took his socks off by herself, while Alex lined up their shoes in a row. Caleb's socks smelled like old cheese, and she wished they could wash them before drying them out, but she knew they should not waste their water, and there was no time to figure out where the willow's source was. The sprite passed its torch quickly back and forth over the boots and the socks. The old cheese smell intensified.

"Oh! Why?" Alex, who was downwind from the drying footwear, made retching motions and moved to the other side of the tree, coughing and hacking.

Mallory joined her, and the two situated their backpacks as pillows on that side of the tree. Mallory was careful to hide the sprite heart from Alex. She could only imagine what her protector would have to say about that. But then Alex shot up and said, "What's that?"

Mallory's cheeks flushed. "What?"

Alex grabbed her arm. "You're bleeding, Mallory."

"What?" Mallory said again, sitting up too. She was genuinely surprised.

"Your shirt is torn, and your arm is bleeding. Sprite?" Alex called.

The clockwork sprite stopped blowtorching their footwear and hovered around the tree. "Yes, Chorus?"

Alex pointed. "Mallory's arm is bleeding, and it's covered with mud. Do you have any antiseptic spray left?"

Mallory shook her head, not wanting to get sprayed with that painful stuff again. "I can hardly feel it. It's not necessary. It's just a scratch from the culture sprite in the fields."

The sprite's antiseptic bottle popped out. "Infections can occur without initial pain, Sprite Slayer."

Mallory squeezed her eyes shut as stinging pain shot through her tricep.

"Oh, it looks like the other one got a lashing too," Alex

said matter-of-factly.

Mallory's eyes sprang open. "You snitch!" She hissed at Alex, and then she squeaked when the spray hit her other wound.

"It's for your own good, Mallory." Alex smirked laying down. "I'm sworn to protect you against every threat, even infections."

"A scratch is hardly a threat, Alex!" Mallory laid beside her friend roughly and propped her head up on her backpack. Alex did not respond, and the two girls lay there in silence for a time, side by side. The willow tree branches danced like nymphs in the late morning light. They were enthralling as they flitted and sashayed above them. Mallory could feel sleep tug at her eyelids watching the hypnotic performance, but she wanted to ask Alex something before they fell asleep. She turned to her best friend and said, "Alex?"

"Mm-hmm?" Alex answered, nearly asleep.

"Do you regret what happened in the city? Do you regret being my friend?"

Alex did not open her eyes. "What good would that do? It wouldn't change anything, would it? Now, go to sleep, Mallory. We've got a lot farther to go."

Mallory rolled over and stared up into the drooping yellow branches above her. Regret would not change anything. Alex had always been wiser than her age. Caleb said that Alex was afraid, and Mallory had seen that bear out more than once. Alex tended to worry about the future, which is essentially what fear is, but she also never really looked back. Caleb, on the other hand, was a lot like his father, the

Governor—an infernal optimist when it came to the future, he loved the traditions of the past but never really thought through his actions in the present. Mallory thought about how she approached the past, present, and future, and the world began to fade into sleep. She was a dreamer. Nothing was ever set in stone or resolved: past, present, future, dreams, sleep, it was all the same. Whatever moment of time she thought about brimmed with mysteries needing to be solved. She smiled at that insight into her character; it made her feel safe to know who she was. Her muscles relaxed then, and she fell asleep in the cool shadow of the willow's whisper.

"Choruses!" The clockwork sprite's voice broke in on Mallory's dreamless rest.

She moaned and rolled over on her side and buried her face into the rough burlap of her backpack, but there was no way to drown the metallic voice out.

"Choruses!" There was more urgency in its voice.

Mallory opened one eye. The world was dark, but not the darkness of night. It looked as if the sun had been muted somehow. With trepidation, she pulled herself up and stretched. Alex was already on her feet, pulling on her pack. Mallory noted that she also had her shoes and socks on and that her own footwear was sitting next to her. She started to pull on her socks; they were completely dry and even still a little warm from the sprite's fire. They felt exquisite.

"What's going on?" she asked.

Caleb walked around the tree already prepared to go just like Alex. How long had the clockwork sprite been calling them? How long had she ignored its calls? Caleb picked up

Mallory's backpack and helped her put it on. His eyebrows were set in his serious mode, and Mallory resisted the urge to pinch his nose to make him lighten up. He nodded toward the sky. "The storm the sprite predicted yesterday is coming."

"You cannot stay under this tree in a storm," the sprite cautioned.

"Will the Ex Natu find us?" Alex asked.

The sprite's eyes grew brighter and fluctuated slightly. "If lightning strikes, you will not survive."

Mallory thought about City Hall, and the lightning strike that had set the building on fire during a rainstorm as she tried to move her fingers more quickly while buckling her pack. The sprite headed out into the tall prairie grass. "We will continue Northeast at forty degrees for ten miles. There is a small cave that will shelter us from the storm, and you can rest there for the night." Then it was gone in a rustle of waving grass.

Alex pulled out her compass and set the marker at forty degrees. Her hand extended toward the grass. "This way," she said.

Caleb followed after her, and Mallory pulled up the rear. At first, the rest under the willow tree seemed to have done the trick in keeping Mallory from falling back under the spell of the waving grass, but it definitely had not been enough sleep. Soon, she felt her eyelids drooping heavily and sleep was beckoning. She really needed to splash cold water on her face to stay awake. As if sensing her need for a refreshing splash, the skies opened and began to pour rain in large, relentless drops. That did the trick. Mallory's eyes opened, now alert, and all the travelers hunched their shoulders up against the cold, hurpling in single file toward the promise of a dry rest somewhere far away in the distance.

BOOM!

The world grew instantly brighter, and thunder shook the ground under them. Mallory swung her head around, shocked by the sound. The willow tree was ablaze. She grabbed Caleb's arm, and when he turned, his mouth dropped open. Alex walked past them toward the tree. She was absently rubbing her right arm—the one the burning debris in City Hall had left scarred forever: a reminder of her great sin in trying to undo Mallory's curse. Alex kept walking, spellbound by the fire rapidly consuming the tree, a beacon of dancing light in the dark of the storm.

Mallory ran up and caught her good arm. "Alex!" She had to yell because the rain was so loud.

Alex turned toward her, fire dancing in her dark eyes. As soon as the tree was outside of her vision, she shook loose from its fiery spell and pulled away from Mallory. She said nothing but held her compass in front of her and once again began to lead the party through the tall grass.

One benefit of the rain that Mallory found was that it was weighing down the grass enough that she could easily see both Caleb and Alex in front of her. The downside was that the ground below their feet was quickly turning to marsh, as the dirt struggled to absorb the downpour. Trudging through the mud drudged her mind through memories of that terrible night at City Hall. While she did not have such extensive scarring as Alex did, Mallory did have some tiny scars here and there from the burns she had received when she ran into the building to get Alex out. Lightning had caused that fire, too. Usually, the city's light deflected lightning away from the city, but when she and Alex had destroyed the Dikaió, something had happened to the light. She still was not entirely sure what it was, but when the light went down, rain and lightning poured through freely. A single bolt had lit up City Hall like a box of matches. Mallory tried not to think about what would have happened if they had still been under the tree when lightning struck it.

Then she wondered if the Ex Natu would come and inspect the blaze. Surely every sign that they had been there was gone now that the tree was burning. Still, sprites were not like humans. They had a tendency to uncover the smallest detail. Would they find their footsteps in the muddy ground below the grass, or would the water wash it all away? She honestly could not answer those questions, and she again found herself wondering if the Archivist would be able to answer them. Whoever the Archivist was, they had built the clockwork sprite, so they certainly knew how sprites worked—and who knew what else? So much of the city's history and knowledge had been lost when the last Chorus died in the fire sprite attack. And then when the city leaders discovered the boys that built the fire sprite had learned from an ancient book, they had all the books in the city destroyed. Mallory glanced back at the willow tree. It had stopped burning now. While the topmost part of the tree was black and smoking, much of the tree remained unscathed; it would probably survive and heal. And Mallory thought about her own life and that of Caleb and Alex. So much of their world had been destroyed by fire, and yet here they were, scarred but still surviving, walking through a world that six months ago, they had not even known existed.

The rain let up after an hour of walking, and without it, they probably could have covered ten miles in less than three hours, but the initial hurdle of the storm meant that it took nearly four hours to cover the distance. Of course, they had no way to track their mileage—or time, for that matter—all they could do was keep walking in the direction the sprite had indicated. The sun had set long ago, and they were walking in the dark without the sprite's eye-lights. Clouds blotted out the moonlight, and Mallory had begun to wonder if Alex could even see the compass anymore in the darkness. She was just about to ask when a flickering light in the distance caught her attention.

The light was coming from a small rocky opening in a hill. The clockwork sprite hovered at the entrance in front of a fire, and Mallory shivered. She had not really considered her own condition in the long, tired walk. She was wet, she was cold, she had only slept a couple of hours, and she had been walking for days. She wanted so much to get to the cave, get warm, get dry, and get to sleep. Her tired legs began to pump, and she sprinted past Alex and Caleb toward the cave. Soon both of her companions were running past her. They seemed to have the same idea as she did, and she did not even care that they were both faster runners than her.

The clockwork sprite moved to the side like a door opening as the three young people blew through the entrance.

They plopped down around the fire. Mallory and Caleb crouched on their knees and held their hands toward the fire to warm their chilled digits. Alex sat with her gloved hands folded in her crossed legs. She closed her eyes and let the fire come to her. Mallory looked at her friend thoughtfully. "Alex? We don't mind. You can warm your hands over the fire if you want."

Alex opened one eye inquisitively. "Why would you mind?"

Mallory squirmed. "I just thought you were self-conscious about your scars."

Alex closed her inquisitive eye. "You've seen my scars before. What would I care if you saw them again?"

"It's just that you're always wearing your gloves." Mallory stood up and began to warm her backside over the fire. "It seems uncomfortable."

Caleb laughed. "C'mon Mal, you know that magistrates like wearing gloves. It makes them look intimidating."

Alex opened her inquisitive eye again. "Are you intimidated by my gloves, Caleb Aiworth?"

Caleb threw his head back and chortled heartily, and Mallory snorted and then burst into a fit of laughter, nearly setting her rear-end on fire. Caleb stood up and joined Mallory, roasting his backside over the fire. "How's this for intimidated?" He shook his rump at Alex mockingly.

Alex plucked a brand from the flames with her gloved hand and waved it up toward Caleb's pants. He jumped away and yelled, "Hey!"

Alex dropped the brand back into the fire. She wiggled

her gloved fingers. "They're fireproof too. Now, are you intimidated?"

"A little." Caleb pretended to mope.

Alex started laughing now too. "Ha, ha, ha! You should be . . . You should be!"

"Why didn't we get fireproof gloves?" Caleb looked inquisitively at Mallory and stuck out his bottom lip like a pouting toddler.

Mallory laughed. "We've got all the fire we need; we've got each other." She leapt on top of him and tackled him to the ground.

Caleb chirped like a bird as he fell on the cave floor. Mallory pinned his arms down and wrapped her thighs around his stomach. Caleb squirmed playfully below her curly, wet locks that were licking his cheeks, and then a look of concern passed across his face. He bucked her off and rolled out from under her quickly, looking in Alex's direction. Mallory followed his gaze. Alex was no longer sitting at the fire. She had crossed the cave and was standing with her arms crossed behind the clockwork sprite, looking out into the blackness of the night.

Mallory sighed.

Caleb looked into her eyes with deep intention and gave her a sideways head bob. She knew she was supposed to know what his motions meant, but she had no idea. She had read an entire book on body language once, and there was nothing in there about what it means when a husband bobs his head like an embarrassed chicken. She looked at Alex again and figured he was trying to communicate that they should save that sort of physical contact for when they were alone. But when had they ever been alone? At some point, married people did married-people things whether their bodyguard was around or not. They had had so little time for married-people things before the wolves and the clockwork sprite came, back when Alex had her own tent. Mallory stuck her chin out and held her hands up in a "What do you want from me?" sort of way.

Caleb nodded toward Alex, confirming Mallory's interpretation of his impression of a disconcerted chicken.

She reiterated her previous gesture.

Caleb rolled his eyes, stood up, and grabbed his backpack. That, she understood; it was body language for "I'm done talking about this." Mallory leapt up after him and stamped her foot in frustration.

He shrugged and walked away from her.

The fight ended, and they had not even said a word.

Caleb pulled the rope out of his backpack and found a couple of places to secure it on both sides of the cave. Then he pulled out a change of clothes. Mallory got his drift immediately and followed suit. The backpacks were waterproof, and their supplies inside were perfectly dry. Soon the couple's wet clothes were hanging on a line over the fire, and they were sitting in nice dry ones again. "Alex!" Mallory called. "You should dry your clothes."

Alex turned around and saw the setup. She nodded and walked over to her backpack, pulled her change of clothes from the pack, and walked behind the hanging clothes to change. Caleb moved over to the sprite, where Alex had been standing, and looked out at the night to give some privacy. Mallory watched them dancing around each other like square dancers and found herself again hoping that the Library offered better living conditions than their current situation. As Alex changed, Mallory could not help but note that her rib cage was horribly pronounced, as if her skin had gotten too tight over her bones. Mallory looked down at her new wardrobe, and her eyes widened. Her belt was on its last notch and still it was feeling pretty loose. Caleb, standing in the doorway, was still large in his shoulders, but his muscular build had diminished quite a bit as well. Mallory glanced at her hands and opened her palms, bouncing them up and down like her father used to when he was weighing his options. Would she rather the Library offered privacy or food? Her stomach rumbled its answer below her too-thin skin.

Alex ducked under the hanging clothes and added her wet garments to the rope then whistled. Caleb turned and smiled. He bounded over to Mallory and kicked his backpack into place beside hers. The group of compatriots settled in their usual fashion around the fire: Mallory curled up next to Caleb and Alex with her head at their feet, and the sprite standing guard at the door for the night. Mallory's eyes grew heavier as the fire danced about, gyrating with the shadows about the cave in an exotic, hypnotic tango. Their stomachs and yawns kept beat with the crackling music of the flames and soon exhaustion caught up with them. Mallory's eyes slid closed just as she thought she saw a beam of light in the night sky over the clockwork sprite's head. It was impossible to tell if it was real or an insomnia-laced dream, a threat or a friend, but she found that she cared very little to find out.

Sleep trumped self-preservation.

A chill woke Mallory out of a dreamless sleep. She slowly opened her eyes and saw that the morning's light was just beginning to creep past the clockwork sprite where it sat defending them at the cave's mouth. The glorious fire from last night was a cold pile of half-burned logs. Ash was scattered about it like it had been put out in a hurry. Mallory's bare feet were exceptionally cold, and her socks were hanging on the rope that stretched across the cave. The socks were probably too cold to alleviate any of her discomfort. However, there was some warmth emanating near her: Caleb lay breathing slowly on her left. She gently touched his back, and his warmth reached out from his shirt and took her hand in its embrace. She rolled over to face him and added a second hand to his shirt. He did not even stir while she warmed her hands on him, which were slowly turning from blue to pink. However, her feet were still quite cold. She turned her head and bit her lip and slowly contracted her core, bending her legs and bringing her feet up toward Caleb's back. Just as they were about halfway up, Mallory noticed that her husband's shirt was untucked. If the heat from over his shirt had warmed her hands so well, she wondered what it would be like if she tucked her feet under his shirt closer to the skin. Would it be like being under a warm blanket?

"AAaarrgghhh!!!!"

Caleb's shrill scream reverberated through the cave, as he squirmed and bucked trying to free himself from attack. Alex shot up off her backpack, drawing her magistrate weapons in a flash. The clockwork sprite's whips swung and cracked against the cave walls. Both of them ready to ward off whatever it was that was attacking Caleb. Mallory did not care. She kept her cold feet firmly pressed against Caleb's warm back, tucked under his shirt. She giggled while he tried to buck her loose, swishing himself around on the cave floor like a mop cleaning up a spill. Eventually, he began to spin, and Mallory had to pull her feet loose or risk getting them snapped off.

Caleb shivered, finally free from the frozen feet, and leapt up. "Ugh!" He looked down at his wife with daggers in his eyes. "Why would you do that, Mallory!?"

Mallory stuck out her bottom lip and looked up at him with puppy-dog eyes. "I'm so, so cold." Then she smiled wickedly, "And you're so hot."

Caleb's look of horror melted into a sheepish grin, and he shrugged. "Well, you know . . .," he said, running a hand through his overgrown blond hair. "I try."

Alex holstered her weapons and groaned.

The clockwork sprite spun back and forth, looking from Alex to the couple; its whips hanging limply on the rocky cave floor. "Is the danger past?" it asked, confused.

Alex answered, "I'm afraid the danger will never be over with these two."

The sprite's eyes clicked and clacked more rapidly than Mallory had ever seen them move before. She was afraid that it might break itself trying to figure out what was going on, so she clarified, "It's a joke. The danger has passed; well except for this blasted cold. Where's the fire?"

The sprite stopped calculating and began to reel in its whips. "Humor is beyond my parameters, Sprite Slayer. The Ex Natu expanded their search in the night. The fire needed to be extinguished."

Mallory remembered the flash of light she saw in the night just before falling asleep. "Are they out there right now?"

The sprite turned to the door. "Most likely, but if we leave soon, we will reach the Library midday. You will be safe there." The sprite waited for its human companions to follow.

The three teens jumped up, and they pulled their clothing off the rope hanging across the cave. Mallory was disappointed that it was still a little damp without the fire, but she figured they could finish drying it when they reached the Library; maybe, they'd even be able to wash their clothing, too.

When they were packed, Mallory looked around and asked, "Do we have any of that Ex Natu produce left over?"

Caleb's eyes turned hopeful, but Alex shook her head. "We ate it all yesterday."

Caleb shrugged, "Well, we'll be at the Library soon enough, and the sprite says there's food there. Might as well get going."

They lined up behind the sprite, and Mallory said, "We're ready, sprite. Lead on!"

"Very well, Sprite Slayer." It turned its eyes toward the horizon. "The Library is twenty-one miles, fifty-six degrees northeast."

Alex pulled out her compass and set the dial, and then she pulled a pencil from her pocket and quickly wrote something on a scrap piece of paper before tucking it back into her pocket. Mallory wondered if Alex had been keeping track of all the sprite's directions. Why would she want to know how to get back here? Was it in case there was not food at the Library? The Ex Natu's crops did sound pretty good. Her stomach rumbled its agreement, and she pulled her water bottle out and tried to douse the emptiness with a bit of liquid to little effect.

Then, they were on the move. The storm had blown in a cold autumn air, so the morning chill did not abate even as the sun rose. Mallory looked back toward the forest. It was a long way off, but the prairies were so flat, she could see the trees ten miles out, and from this distance they looked like they were on fire just as the willow had been last night.

Nearly a quarter of the trees seemed to have turned orange, yellow, and red overnight. The tall grass had also lost some of its green; it looked yellow like wheat nearly ready for harvest. It was still wet and hanging limply after the deluge yesterday, which made it easier to follow each other—but it also meant that soon Mallory's clothes were soaked through. She was wet and cold again, and she had not fully warmed up after the night's chill in the cave.

After a long time, the ground began to rise and fall in shallow inclines, and these steadily grew higher and deeper, until they found themselves walking through hills and valleys. Trees began to grow more regularly as the hills increased. It was not really a forest, but the hill country was definitely not as sparse as the plains, and Mallory noted that the grass started to grow shorter in the hills. She wondered what the mechanism was that changed the topography of the land and the plants that grew on it so dramatically? Was it the wind, or was it something else? When they crested the next hill, Mallory gasped.

Stretched out to the east of them was a large lake. Like the river they had crossed, none of them had ever seen so much water collected in one place. The path the clockwork sprite was leading them on came within a few feet of the lake's banks, so as they got closer, all three of them guzzled the water in their filtered bottles and ran down to the shores of the lake to refill them. The clockwork sprite did not stop and wait for them. It just kept moving forward, always forward, relentless in its task to deliver a Chorus to the Library. Mallory wanted to yell at the thing, but she knew that it would never understand why she was upset. So why waste the breath on such a trivial and worthless endeavor, except that it might make her feel better to let it know how she felt. "The Sprite Slayer is tired of being herded like cattle, you ungrateful hunk of tin!" She thought. Then her stomach rumbled. She took in a deep breath and let it slowly exhale. Better not let the hanger drive her emotions or her words.

They finished filling their bottles with the lake's cool water and returned to the trail. The sun was high in the sky, so it must have been close to midday—which meant the Library was not far now. Butterflies began to spin in Mallory's stomach, chased by the hunger pangs. The nearer to the Library they got, the more she felt like she was going to be sick: a nervous nausea rolling up in her. She suddenly wished that they did not have to go to this new place, no matter what mysteries it held. She wanted to go home and be with her parents, move into the apprentice quarters of the Governor's house with Caleb and live the life they were supposed to have. She wondered how long it would be before her sister was born, or if she had been born already. Would her mother ask her to babysit? Mallory wished she could meet her. No. Mallory shook her head to clear away those thoughts too. Being a dreamer had its own downsides. Escapism led to all sorts of regrets and unfulfilled fantasies. She needed to focus on the problem at hand, which was making it to the Library and starting whatever new life awaited them there.

She started trying to imagine what that new life would look like, but her thoughts were interrupted when the clockwork sprite floated up another foot off the ground, and without a word of warning or explanation, shot forward with incredible speed. A moment later a small sonic boom reached the traveling companions. They paused and watched it go, disappearing into valleys, and then quickly scaling the hills, only to dip down and disappear again. Its shiny copper hull reflecting the autumn sun soon became a bright glint in the distance, until they could not see it anymore.

"Now what?" Caleb asked.

Mallory just stood there with her mouth agape.

Alex held up her compass and said, "it's heading exactly fifty-six degrees northeast. I say we follow it. There's no point in changing the plan."

"But why did it just take off like that?" Caleb wondered.

Mallory shrugged again. "Maybe it's excited to get home?"

Alex raised an eyebrow. "Do sprites get excited?"

Caleb ran a hand through his hair. "Maybe it's hungry?" He grinned.

Mallory laughed. "Sprites can't be excited, but they can be hungry?"

Caleb's smile broadened. "Who isn't excited about food?"

Alex shook her head and started walking in the same direction as the clockwork sprite.

"What?" Caleb shouted after her.

Mallory walked around Caleb, following Alex. Behind her, she heard Caleb mutter dejectedly under his breath: "Well, I'm excited about food."

The three companions continued to follow with Alex diligently marking the direction indicated on her compass. They plodded up and down the hills. There had been an incline going up Main Street in the city, and Mallory had always enjoyed racing down it as a child; gravity pulling her faster than she could run of her own accord, but these hills were another beast altogether. The incline was twice what Main Street was, which made going uphill an incredible chore, and her thigh muscles and calves burned long before they reached the top. But going downhill felt like flying. The extra weight from their loaded backpacks made the trip down even faster and more exhilarating. By mid-descent, they were running so fast that Mallory knew that even trying to stop or slow down would result in a terrible crash, and they would be rolling the rest of the way down the hill. She just focused on picking her feet up to keep from tripping and let gravity do the rest. Somewhere in her mind, she thought that it might be fun rolling down the hill, but she would have to take the backpack off, or she would roll like a stick with a knobby knothole protruding out of it: bump, roll, bump, roll, bump.

After ten hills went by, they were standing in a valley looking up at the next one, and Caleb said, "I need to take a break!"

Alex shook her head. "We need to keep going. It's got to be close. The sprite wouldn't have just run off like that if it wasn't. Besides, on the top of the last hill, I saw a group of trees not far ahead."

"So what?" Mallory already had her backpack off and was getting ready to lie down and rest.

"So what? What if those trees are where the Library is?"

"And what if it's not, Alex?" Caleb plopped down on the ground yawning. "We're well passed midday now." He pointed up at the sun, which was about a quarter past the midpoint of the sky, heading west. "I'm dying here. I just need a quick breather."

Alex sighed heavily, "Fine! I'm going up to the top of this hill to look around. You lay there like the lazy slugs you are."

Mallory and Caleb nodded and then got comfortable, nestling their heads on their packs. Mallory yawned, "just a few minutes, Alex, and then we'll be right up."

Her eyes had barely blinked when Alex started screaming their names: "Mallory! Caleb!"

Mallory opened her eyes fully intending on telling Alex to shut up, but Alex was not there anymore. She was standing at the top of the next hill, screaming down at them. "Now, how did Alex get way up there," she wondered before realizing that her blink must have been a nap after all. That was a disappointing revelation as she did not feel at all rested.

Alex yelled down again, "Mallory! Caleb! Come on!"

"What?" Mallory called back. "What do you want?"

Caleb stirred now, having been obliviously asleep even through the shouting. "Go back to sleep; it's too early," he murmured.

"C'mon, you two! They're coming!" Alex screamed down.

Mallory shrugged. Was it someone benign like the clockwork sprite and the Archivist, or was it one of the threats they had already faced: wolves, rats, bats, flying sprites, culture sprites, scout sprites, the Ex Natu? Whatever it was, Alex seemed to think that getting to the top of the hill was vitally important.

Mallory stood up and kicked her husband in his rear end.

He spun around and pouted, "What?!"

"Something's coming. We have to go!" Mallory pulled on her backpack.

He sat up concerned. "Wolves? Ex Natu?"

"I don't know. Alex sees something. C'mon!" Mallory fumbled with the straps of her backpack trying to cinch it tighter while quickly climbing the hill.

Caleb climbed up beside her, his backpack already secured, constantly looking back over his shoulder as they climbed. Soon they were standing beside Alex. She had her eyes trained on the hills behind them. Caleb scratched his head, "I don't see anything."

"Just wait. It's about four hills back." Alex stood stock still.

Mallory stepped back behind Alex and tried to point her eyes in the same direction as Alex's. She could not see it either, but then a glint of light flashed on the top of the fourth hill. She could not make out what it was, but it was something metal, and it was moving fast.

"It's a sprite!" Caleb yelled. "Run!"

Alex flew down the hill, running in what Mallory hoped was the direction the clockwork sprite had disappeared earlier, but at least in the direction of some tree cover that was not too far ahead, about two hills' distance. Maybe they would be able to hide in their shade from whatever sprite was behind them. Caleb flew after her, and Mallory after him. Her heavy pack pushed her down the steep track, faster and faster. At the top of the next hill, Mallory risked looking back; she could not see it at first, and then it crested a hilltop: The sprite had closed the distance by two hills to their one. If they could not hide in the trees on the next hilltop, it would overtake them in just a few minutes. Mallory wished the clockwork sprite was there to protect them. She was sure that they had passed the point where it had disappeared, but there was still no sign of it. Why had it just run off and left them behind?

Breathing hard, the trio began the fast descent into the next valley. There was not much wind right now, but when they were running down these hills, their speed created its own wind. Mallory nearly grinned as her curly locks flapped out behind her, momentarily giving her some respite from the curse of having curly hair and making her head feel perpetually hot and heavy. The artificial breeze was at least keeping her head cool, even if the rest of her was a sweaty mess.

She was lost in these thoughts when Caleb fell.

Mallory's world seemed to slow down, and she watched in horror as his ankle rolled below him, his knee buckled, and then his backpack pushed him off his feet into the ground. Caleb fell like a rag doll; his pack's momentum dragging him down the hill, rolling, spinning, bouncing, and even flying at times. Caleb bounced past Alex, and her run slowed slightly as his flailing body whirled by. Then he hit the bottom of the hill with a dull thud and lay moaning until the two girls were standing over him in the grass. His ankle and arm both looked funny, like they had been put on wrong. Blood was everywhere, oozing from cuts on his head and face, as well as through torn sections of his clothing. Mallory dropped to her knees, yelling his name, "Caleb! Caleb! Are you okay?"

He moaned, and then through gritted teeth said, "help me up. We need to get to the tree cover."

Mallory shook her head in reply, but Alex was already grabbing the obviously broken arm and dragging him up. Caleb groaned but pushed with his legs trying to get himself up. The one with the foot that was twisted, twisted further. It was not going to support his weight, and he nearly took Alex down with him as he buckled.

"C'mon, Mallory! You have to help me!" Alex hissed. "The sprite is going to catch us if we don't hurry!"

Mallory wiggled herself under Caleb's side opposite Alex. With Caleb supported by the two girls and hopping on one foot, the trio began to climb the next hill. It was very slow going. There was no way to look back while supporting the giant, hopping along like they were in a three-legged race. Still, Mallory could almost feel the sprite behind them drawing ever nearer. Her legs burned, but still she pushed harder. Gravity pulled heavily on Caleb, and then suddenly, he was walking. Just a hobble, but walking. Mallory looked down at his leg, and the odd angle of his ankle had straightened out.

"Caleb?" she asked, still looking at his ankle.

He looked down. "It still hurts, but I think I can walk on my own."

Alex asked, "the nano sprites?"

He shrugged. "I guess. C'mon, we're getting close." He pulled his arms off the girls and then started limping quickly up the incline.

The trees were some ways beyond the top of the hill, and the ground seemed to level out for a distance. There were not enough trees to make a forest like the ones Mallory had become used to, but there was still more than their park back home. She glanced behind her. The sprite was now just one hill back, and if it had seen them, it sure was not in any hurry to catch up with them. Sprites could move at incredible speed. If the thing saw them and wanted to, it could overtake them in seconds. Maybe it was not an Ex Natu sprite? Maybe it did not mean them any harm? Mallory had no desire to answer those questions—at least not in the open. The trees of the wooded area at the top of the hill would at least make it hard for the sprite to use whips if it had them, which was more hope than they had here.

The three companions walked quickly toward the trees, and by the time they reached them, Caleb was moving faster than the two girls with no discernible limp whatsoever. His broken arm pumped as he ran, as if it had not just been twisted and broken even worse than Mallory's after the City Hall fire. Mallory marveled that even the cuts and bruises on his face were completely healed. What a wonder the nano sprites were! Mallory wondered if the Archivist had more. There would not even be a need for the Hospital back home. The city might even lift their exile if they brought home a miracle like nano sprites. She imagined the heroes' welcome they would receive, and then she imagined what would happen if their parents did not welcome them back. Their return was death. The magistrates would execute them… if they could. The repairs to this last set of injuries went so much faster than the wound she had given him in the ravine. Why was that? The sprite said the nano sprites would get better at repairing his body the longer they remained in his system. She wondered if Caleb had become immortal, and then she wondered what else the little sprites were doing inside her husband.

She was so lost in thought that she nearly walked into a tree. Caleb signaled to be quiet and pointed at the hill behind them. The sprite was just coming over the ridge. Not moving any faster but still gaining ground. Mallory ducked into the woods, and she felt the temperature drop several degrees in the shade. She shivered, as she crouched behind a tall gray trunk and looked out toward the open hill. The tree's bark was rough against her face, but its solid frame felt very comforting. Her breathing slowed, and her hands stopped shaking. Mallory smiled as she thought back to their discovery of the Dark Forest surrounding the city. Trees like the one she was hiding behind had terrified her then, and now, she was rubbing up against it like a cat trying to get dinner.

Suddenly, there was a flash of silver beyond the border of the wooded area. The sprite paused and turned toward the trees. It was smaller than the culture sprites, and slightly more cube-ish than oblong. Two panel lids opened on its sides, and five cylindrical tubes extruded through each opening. The cylinders were arranged in a cluster, like a metal stool turned on its side, and they slowly began to lower and angle toward them. Tiny copper pieces of metal tinkled in rows of chains dangled from the tops of the tubes. The copper pieces almost looked like magistrate ammunition. The tubes began to spin.

"Get down!" screamed Alex.

WHHIRRR! . . . CRAKETY-CRACK-CRACK!!!

Slivers of wood and shredded leaves filled the air. Mallory ducked behind the solid trunk, wrapping her arms around her knees and pulling them up to her chest. She could see Alex a few trees over, hiding behind a similar gray tree. And she could see Caleb's legs ahead behind another. It seemed like an eternity passed with pieces of wood flying around her, and then the cracking noises stopped, but the whirring continued.

Mallory saw Alex, weapons primed, poke her head around her tree. The whirring noise began to slow and then stopped. Alex rolled to her feet, fired two shots at the sprite, and yelled, "Move!!!"

Mallory did not hesitate, nor look back at the sprite with the spinning magistrate weapons outside the woods. She jumped to her feet and started running after Alex. Caleb was up and running too. They weaved in and out of the trees trying to make hard targets for the sprite to hit with its spin-ning tube weapons. Then, Mallory heard the whirring noise begin again. Alex dove behind a tree—again yelling, "Get down!" Mallory landed behind a tree next to Alex's. Caleb was just a couple of trees over.

WHHIRRR! . . . CRAKETY-CRACK-CRACK!!!

It was hard to hear anything over the weapons' fire, but Mallory could barely make out Alex yelling, "It's in the woods and coming closer."

Mallory listened, and it did sound like the whirring sound was getting closer, though she could not be sure amidst all the mini explosions of the trees being shredded around her. When the next pause in firing came, Mallory looked out from behind her tree. The sprite was barely ten feet from her. It was boxy and had no semblance of humanity like some sprites did. There was no face, just a silver frame with a black horizontal slash on the front, toward the top. The slash swiveled toward her, and the tube-like clusters pumped furiously. Empty chains fell to the ground, and small pincer-like arms emerged from inside the sprite, hauling new chains loaded with ammo. The pincers began spooling them into the clusters.

Alex was already running and screaming, "Run, Mallory, run!"

Mallory shoved up from the ground and hustled from tree to tree. There was a very large oak tree, one of those too big to fit all their arms around varieties, and Mallory headed for it. There was no way the sprite's projectiles would penetrate its trunk. Apparently, Caleb and Alex had the same idea because when Mallory came around the trunk of the tree, they both came around the other side. There was a loud snap followed by a twang.

Suddenly, the ground of the wooded area sprang up around the three of them. Dried leaves and sticks flew about them like confetti, and Mallory felt herself soar up into the sky. It all seemed to happen in slow motion, but then she was tumbling over Alex and Caleb, squirming around inside a very unstable cloth-like bag. It was a net! They were all dangling in a net several feet off the ground. Caleb's boot pushed on her ear, and Alex's backpack was pressing uncomfortably up against her chest. None of that bothered Mallory nearly as much as when she looked through the net and saw the boxy little sprite with the magistrate tubes come around the trunk. It paused, and then the black slit on its front angled itself upward at them. The tube-clusters began to turn slowly, and then they began to whirr. Mallory closed her eyes and waited for death.

ZIP-KABOOM!

A wave of heat flushed over her, and she was surprised at how undramatic death felt—just a bit of heat. She expected it to involve more pain and discomfort, and there was none of that—well, except for the discomfort of Caleb's boot squishing her cheek against her teeth. That did not seem right. Mallory opened her eyes and saw the boxy sprite below them was several feet away from where it had been standing, in several directions. There were bits of it everywhere, and they were all on fire.

She wanted to know what happened, but she was pretty much pinned where she was with Caleb on top of her, and Alex below her. Caleb began moving his boot, probably trying to maneuver himself to see what was going on and scraped the heel of it against her face over and over. She yelled, "Stop it, Caleb! You're kicking me in the face!"

"I am?" he asked innocently. "Sorry. What's going on down there?"

"Silence!" An unfamiliar voice yelled. It sounded old and female. "I'll ask the questions, Ex Natu!"

"We are not Ex Natu." Alex said defiantly. With her backpack pressing in her chest, Mallory realized Alex was facing down and could probably see who she was talking to. "We're traveling at request of the Archivist."

"The Archivist?" The old voice responded.

"Yes, these are the Choruses I informed you of," a familiar metallic voice sounded from below.

"Is that our sprite?" Caleb called down.

"Your sprite?" the old woman's voice asked. "No, that's my sprite. Now, be silent. How do you know they're not Ex Natu?"

"Observe." The clockwork sprite said.

Alex began to squirm, and Mallory winced as her backpack rubbed her chest raw. "Hey," Alex yelled. "Stop!"

"I see," said the old woman's voice. "Very well. Cut them loose."

Suddenly Mallory was falling. Then a powerful thud took her breath away as they hit the ground, but none of them took the time to lay and recover. They began to scramble and roll about trying to disentangle themselves both from the net and each other. Caleb kicked at Mallory's head, Alex kicked at her shins, and Mallory kicked and clawed at both of them trying to get up. Just when she thought she had her footing, she tripped over the nylon strands and fell into Alex, tangling them both in the netting again.

"Ha ha ha ha," the old woman cackled as the teenagers fumbled about.

Mallory had at least been able to catch a glimpse of her as she swam through the netting. The old woman was nothing like what she had expected. In her mind's eye, she had conjured a vision of a hobbling woman dressed in a shambled, patchwork dress with straggly white hair, several missing teeth, and leaning heavily on a gnarled wooden cane. She wasn't sure where the idea had come from, but that's what her imagination had come up with. The real-life figure laughing at them looked a lot more like her grandmother; except somehow younger and more vivacious than her grandmother had ever been, which was saying a lot. She had very few wrinkles, and Mallory could not help but make a comparison to Reddy Lamarr: an old woman in a young woman's body. She had darker skin, and short-cropped white hair. The woman looked thin and athletic, but it was hard to tell as her body was obscured in loose fitting silk clothes that shimmered about her in the breeze. It seemed that the outfit was mostly construed of primary colors: red, blue, and yellow. But as the breeze blew, the somewhat see-through layers would overlap into a myriad of secondary colors: green, indigo, and orange appeared and disappeared. She looked like light shone through a prism.

In one hand, the old woman held one of Alex's long gloves. In the other, she held a long tube over her shoulder, that had a trigger on it similar to Alex's magistrate weapons. She had one foot up on a fallen log and was leaning over slightly with her elbow resting on her bent leg, and she was still laughing at them. The clockwork sprite watched them unblinking beside her.

Alex managed to get clear of the netting first. She stood up, straightened out her navy-blue clothing, and marched over to the old woman, who stopped laughing and straightened defensively. Mallory knew how scary Alex could look when she was mad. She wanted to call out to Alex to stop, but before she could tell her not to do whatever she was thinking about doing, she fell back into the net's grip. Alex simply reached out and deftly snatched her glove from the old woman's grasp. As she fit it back over her scarred hand with her bottom lip slightly protruding, the old woman nearly fell over from the fit of laughter that racked her.

"Oh, the indignation of youth!" she hooted, breathing hard. "It's been so long!" She turned to the clockwork sprite. "Go fetch that last one out, or we'll be here all day, and I doubt these two little ones have learned any sort of patience."

Last one? Mallory looked up from the new tangle she found herself in and saw Caleb free of the net and dusting himself off. She gritted her teeth and started dragging herself toward the edge of the pile of netting around her. Just when she thought she was going to get clear of it without help, she felt a tendril of a sprite whip slip around her waist and lift her neatly into the air. She nearly spat with frustration. The sprite set her down by Alex, and the two of them were a mirror image of one another with their bottom lips thrust out in indignation.

The old woman screamed with laughter. "Oh! Ho! This is the most fun I've had in years. Come on! Come on!" She waved her hand in a circle. "Let's get you all to the Library!" She started to walk deeper into the woods.

Caleb held up a hand. "Wait just a moment, ma'am. We've only just met and haven't introduced ourselves. We don't even know who you are."

"Nonsense!" The old woman called back. "You know

precisely who I am, and you wouldn't have traveled all this way if you weren't here to meet me and go to the Library. Now, Chorus, pick up your feet. There's still a ways to walk, and I'd like to get back to the Library's safety. The Ex Natu will send more scout sprites when this one doesn't return, and the wilding wolves lurk even in these woods."

But Caleb was not so easily deterred. "I am Caleb Aiworth, heir of the Governor," he said.

The old woman froze. "The Governor? A Dikaió Athenó?" She spun on the clockwork sprite. "You told me they were all Choruses."

Mallory said, "Well, I was the only one christened a Chorus, but there was an accident—"

Alex interrupted, "It was no accident, Mallory. We destroyed the Dikaió."

The old woman's eyes went wide. "Destroyed the—" She stopped short and shook her head, holding up a hand. "There will be time enough for stories when we reach the Library. Now, come!"

"Are you the Archivist then?" Caleb asked still making no move to follow the old woman.

The old woman's brows furrowed. "Am I . . . am I the Archivist? You're not all that bright, are you? All brawn, no brains?" She motioned to Alex for confirmation.

Mallory's blood boiled and stepped in between the two women and pulled herself up to the old woman's height by standing on her tiptoes. "I'll have you know Caleb is quite intelligent!"

The Archivist's eyebrows raised in surprise.

Alex shrugged and said, "they're married" as if that explained everything.

"Ahhh . . .," the Archivist nodded as if it really did.

Mallory stamped her foot, and Caleb threw his head back in laughter. Mallory turned and glared at him. "Are you just going to let them insult you like that?"

Caleb took her hand tenderly. "I'm smart enough not to pick a fight with our host who we've come all this way to see." He winked at the Archivist, satisfied now that they had been properly introduced. "Alright, lead on, Archivist."

The Archivist turned without another word and headed deeper into the forest, and the three companions followed after her.

Mallory had changed her mind about the trees again. She did not like walking through woods. Sure, the trees may have just saved her life from the scout sprite, but she found that the inability to see more than a few feet in front of her nagged at her claustrophobia. It was not quite the same as being enclosed in a small space in terms of inducing paralytic panic, but it felt similar. Following the Archivist did not help matters one bit. She moved through them as if she were half her age and in way better shape than the teens: crouching and leaping over fallen trees and brush, more like an animal than a person. Not even Alex and Caleb could keep up with her, and more than once they lost sight of her in the maze of trees.

And then, as they came through a particularly thick patch of woods, they saw her standing still, waiting for them. The trees acted as a windbreak, and the air was still. In the darkness of this patch of trees, her colorful clothes hung around her, less like a bright prism of color and more like the dim robes of a solemn priestess. The clockwork sprite hovered beside her, its eyes bright and emotionless. Mallory's stomach twisted. Something was off about the forest. It wavered and moved unnaturally. The air around her seemed almost electric. She thought of the stories her parents had told her of all the dangers outside the city's light, how generations had been lost outside its protection, lured to their doom by unnatural beings that appeared human. She had originally thought the Archivist might have been one of those citizens that had left the city like the old Chorus's parents, but now she wondered if the old woman might be one of the dangers that stopped them from returning. Her stomach turned again, and it felt like the forest was closing in on her.

Then the Archivist pulled her hand close to her mouth, and her sleeve revealed a silver bracelet with a small square box on it. It looked like a watch, but instead of a face with hands ticking time, there was a glowing panel that bathed the Archivist's face in an eerie blue light. "Dikaió, open," she spoke into the box, and suddenly, the forest behind her vanished.

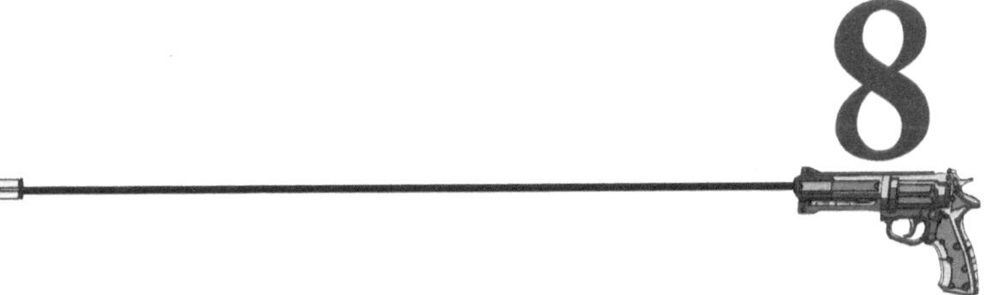

8

Mallory, Caleb, and Alex stood staring with their mouths hanging open at the sight that appeared before them. Where the trees of the dark wooded area had just been, a beautiful, flowered garden spread out for hundreds of yards, and instead of brush and branches, the garden was carpeted with lush, well-manicured grass. There were some medium-sized trees, but above the scene was a bright blue sky with lazy clouds floating by. Birds, squirrels, and other small animals busied themselves bounding this way and that in the garden. A family of deer drank from a small stream, which ran beside a cobblestone path. Cows and goats munched on grass in penned areas, and across from them, several rows of crops grew in a well-tended garden, very similar to the Ex

Natu fields they had just raided. Mallory could see the silver glint of at least three culture sprites working the fields, and she shuddered a little.

However, Mallory did not wait for an invitation to walk into the Archivist's hidden wonderland; because as incredible as the garden and fields were, at the end of the cobblestone path and across a stone bridge, sat a building that made their former City Hall look like a peasant's home. A gothic palace rose six stories off ground-level with red brick, cobblestone, and green iodized-copper accoutrements. Round turrets were interspersed around the building connected by long colonnades, tastefully overgrown in ivy. A fountain, similar to the one in the city park, stood in the building's courtyard. The part that drew Mallory's attention the most was the gigantic stained glass window above the entranceway, emblazoned with Dikaió lights from the inside out, depicting identical images to those that stood in the foyer of the Governor's house: a Governor holding a sword and shield on the left; an Administrator holding a projectile weapon and the scroll of law on the right; and in the center, holding a bowl full of water being poured over a child while dragonflies flew over her head in a wreath was a Matriarch clothed in a blue gown.

"Welcome to the Library," the Archivist said, and as soon as the group had crossed onto the cobblestone path, she once again raised her arm near her mouth and said, "Dikaió, close."

The dark forest that they had just entered through vanished and was replaced with flowered gardens as far as Mallory could see. Caleb started to raise his hand as if to touch the space they had just walked through.

"You don't want to do that," the Archivist said and bent down to pick up a small twig that they had tracked in from the forest floor. She tossed it past Caleb's head, and the twig vaporized in a pink sizzle.

"You have a light, too!" Alex marveled.

"A light? I suppose you could call it that. It's a holographic plasma field—gas and light as it were." The Archivist wiggled her fingers on one hand and opened and closed the fingers on her other hand, while she made O shapes with her mouth.

Mallory looked at Caleb and Alex, and the wide-eyed, open-mouthed perplexion looked almost as silly as the Archivist and her attempt to explain the light to them with body gestures. Mallory started to laugh hysterically. "You all look like a bunch of fish out of water."

Caleb and Alex looked at each other and started giggling too.

A look of indignation passed over the Archivist's face, and then she shrugged and smiled. "It's been some time since I've had anyone but a sprite to talk to; it's quite possible my interpersonal skills with human beings are in need of some polishing."

Caleb started making Os with his mouth and wiggling his fingers.

"You're not doing it right," Alex said. She did the same but added the opening and closing hand.

The Archivist narrowed her eyes then burst out laughing. "That's a good impression of a holographic plasma field—or a fish out of water. Quite astute. Quite astute." She turned and started walking along the cobblestone path toward the Library. "Now, come. Let's get you showered. You all smell terrible."

Mallory nearly cried. "A shower?! It's been so long."

The Archivist answered, "Yes, I just said that. You stink." She shook her head at the clockwork sprite. "This is quite the handful of Choruses you've brought me to train, and one of them a Dikaióless heir to the governorship, no less."

"And the Matriarchy and the Administration," Mallory added.

The Archivist looked back at her with her eyebrows raised, shook her head, and kept walking toward the Library. "Showers first, then stories."

"And dinner?" Caleb asked hopefully.

Mallory felt her stomach rumble, mirroring Caleb's hope. She had forgotten about food in all the excitement, but its mention and proximal existence suddenly made its possibility the only thing she could think of, so it was like a kick to the stomach when the Archivist answered: "Dinner? This early?" she shook her head in disbelief. "And they're savages too," she said confidentially to the clockwork sprite. "Couldn't you find anyone else?"

"I have been searching for many years, Archivist. These are the only Choruses I have ever found, and they are malnourished by every indication," the sprite replied.

The Archivist sighed heavily. "Fine, showers, then stories, AND dinner."

The Library was much farther away than it appeared at first. Mallory had thought that the cobblestone path was a hundred yards give or take, but it was at least triple that. The deception in her perception was due to the size of the Library: it was even bigger up close. The double doors of the entrance were nearly twice as tall as Caleb, and the triad in the stained glass staring down at them were giants who could have held any one of them in their hands. The light shining through the glass illuminating their images was almost too bright to look at, so it was shocking to enter a dimly lit ante-chamber when the Archivist opened the doors to the Library and stepped to the side to let them in. The ceiling was so high that Mallory had to strain her eyes to make out the curved beams leading up to its zenith. The stained glass windows were dimly illuminated on this side with the natural light of the sun shining through them. She bumped into Caleb trying to get back outside to look at them on the other side of the wall again.

"Mal!" He exclaimed.

"But how?" She queried, trying to get past his bulking frame to see the windows on the other side.

"Shower first! There's plenty of time to discover the secrets of the Library, Chorus," the Archivist called. "Come on, now!"

Mallory turned around to follow the Archivist again and had her breath sucked out of her once more. The set up inside was again very similar to the Governor's house, but much, much bigger, and instead of the symmetric staircases on each side of the foyer just leading up to a balcony, two symmetrical spiral staircases ascended the left and right sides of the room, up six stories, and each floor was lined with bookshelves as far as she could see. She thought back to the meager collection of books the three of them had assembled in Alex's grandfather's attic; all the known books in the city that had not been destroyed in the reading purge long before she was born. They had been thrilled with their little assortment of contraband, and now they stood in the halls of Shangri-La.

"What do I have to do to get the three of you clean?" the Archivist yelled. "Bring buckets here and scrub you down in the doorway? Stop gawking and go get that smell washed off. You're assaulting all sense of decency as guests in my home!"

Mallory blushed, as did Caleb and Alex. They followed sheepishly behind the Archivist, trying to keep their heads down and not stare at the marvels around them.

She led them up the staircase on the right, and on the second floor, she went through double mahogany doors, which led down a hallway with plush red carpet lit by golden Dikaió light sconces. It had been so long since Mallory had been inside a building at all, she could not help but visually explore the intricate geometric designs in the carpet and how they were mirrored in the wall sconces and the wooden trim in the base boards and the ceiling molding. It seemed like the patterns were moving, flowing down the hallway with them. When she tried to focus on a section to understand the optical illusion, her eyes widened. It was no illusion. The hallway was alive. She traced a triangle as it crawled along the molding. It was moving beside the Archivist. She looked across the hall, and noticed a triangle directly opposite, also keeping pace with the Archivist. The baseboards, and even the carpet, were tracking her with triangles as well. Then she noticed that there were squares traveling alongside Caleb, and Alex had circles. She looked around her and found stars tracking her motions.

Just to see what would happen, she stopped. The stars stopped as well. They really were following her. The other shapes kept moving ahead with the group. As she stood in the hallway studying the fluid decorations, three lines appeared in front of her stars. Shapes appeared at the tips of each line: a triangle, a circle, and a star. They were arrows pointing toward the location of her companions and the Archivist.

"How do they know where we are?" Mallory called to the Archivist.

The Archivist stopped, and Caleb and Alex nearly ran into her. "What's that?"

"The shapes in the walls. How do they know where we are?"

A flash of irritation passed quickly over the Archivist's face, but it was replaced by a smile just as quickly. "My, you are an observant one, aren't you? The Library is a very large place." She opened her arms wide and made a half turn. "One could literally get lost in the books. So, the Library's Dikaió keeps track of the patrons in the building."

"The Library's Dikaió?" Alex asked. "How does a building have its own Dikaió?"

The Archivist's eyebrows arched quizzically. "I don't understand the question."

Caleb said, "Isn't the Dikaió for a person—given during someone's christening?"

The Archivist shook her head in disbelief. "Are you sure you're from Hoffen City?

Caleb replied, "It's like we told the sprite. We're from the city, but we've never heard of Hoffen City."

The Archivist's eyes squinted slightly, but then she shrugged. "Wherever you're from, you still stink." She turned and continued down the hallway.

"But how do the symbols work?" Mallory called, irritated that her line of questioning had been so easily usurped.

"Later!" the Archivist called back, but she did not stop until she had them in the rooms they would be staying in while they were at the Library.

Mallory and Caleb's room was huge. There was a King-sized bed buried in throw pillows. A huge picture window looked out onto the flower gardens outside. The wallpaper was light blue with golden filigree repeating in patterns that resembled a lattice. The plush carpet was light yellow, and there were golden Dikaió light sconces like the ones in the hallway. Mallory noted that her star and Caleb's circle were hovering over the inside of the door, but the triangle and square were not visible inside the room. She dropped her backpack in a corner, knelt down, and started unlacing her boots. Their muddy exterior contrasted horribly with the speckless carpet. She looked behind her and was horrified to see footprints on the beautiful textile.

Caleb, on the other hand, tossed his backpack in the middle of the room, kicked off his shoes, and jumped into the bed laughing. "Now, this is the life, Mal!"

"Caleb!" She stood up and yelled.

His eyes went wide and his muscles tensed. He tried to leap off the bed, but it was so soft, it was like trying to climb over a giant bowl of gelatin. "What is it? What's wrong?"

"You're filthy," Mallory whined. "We have to sleep there tonight."

Caleb froze, then he burst into fits of laughter. He fell back onto the pillows, knocking several onto the floor. "We've been sleeping in the dirt for weeks, Mal! What's a little more going to hurt?"

Mallory huffed. "I'm going to get cleaned up."

She stepped into the bathroom. It was as luxurious as the bedroom was. The sink had a bronze faucet and bronze handles. The basin was clear glass with polished stone pebbles at the bottom. A row of Dikaió lights marched along the top of the mirror. The shower did not have a tub, but it did have a bench where you could sit while showering. The tiles on the floor and wall reminded Mallory of the tiles they had seen in Clarington Station in the abandoned city, but these were polished a gleaming white rather than being covered in carbon stains There were two fluffy white towels hanging on a rack on the wall, and two equally fluffy white robes hanging on the door. She felt the urge to bury her face in them to see if they were as soft as they looked, but she caught a glimpse of herself in the mirror and decided against it. She was filthy: head-to-toe filthy.

It had been weeks since Mallory had showered, and warm water and soap on her skin felt glorious. But the cleaner she got, the more her thoughts turned toward what was outside their bedroom. She wanted to explore the Library and uncover all its secrets. There were too many books to read for her to waste all this time worrying about hygiene. Yet, when she looked down at the floor of the shower, she was aghast to find a pile of dirt and debris pooling at her feet. She had been so filthy, the drain was clogging as she rinsed off. Her fingers snagged in her matted curly hair when she tried to wash it, and it took several passes with her comb in the shower to remove the tangles. When she finally felt clean, she stepped out of the shower, and used a towel to wipe the condensation off the mirror, so she could see. She curled up her lips and was horrified to see clumps of yellow and brown coating her teeth. There were two toothbrushes sealed inside clear plastic wrap in a cup beside the sink. Toothpaste was on the opposite side of the sink with a stick of deodorant. Shaving cream and a razor sat on a small porcelain shelf just above these items. She thought back to the day she had packed for their impending exile. She had not thought to pack any of these items.

Mallory finished grooming and slipped into the white robe hanging on the door. The fluffiness enveloped her in a cloud of luxury. For a moment, thoughts of the library's secrets vanished, and she let the coziness take over. The comfort made her yawn, and she thought of the bed waiting on the other side of the door. She walked out of the bathroom. All the throw pillows had been tossed on the floor. Caleb was stretched out on the bed, snoring slightly with drool running down his bearded face, pooling on the pillow under his head. Mallory tried to remember what he looked like without a beard and couldn't quite picture him. She

thought she liked him better with the beard, but it was difficult to feel any sort of attraction now that she was clean, and
he was not. He smelled so bad; she felt like throwing up.

"Caleb!" She shouted.

He startled awake and started rolling around on the bed
trying to get up and come to her rescue, but the bed's softness
had him trapped again. "I'm coming, Mal!" He murmured,
and then finally lay back, defeated. "Ugh! Sorry, Mal, I tried,"
he sighed and fell back to sleep.

"My hero," Mallory said to herself and then walked over
to the bed and yelled louder, "Caleb, get up!"

His eyes shot open and looked her over. A sly smile
slowly spread across his face. "You clean up nice, Mrs.
Aiworth." He rolled over and reached for her.

She jumped back. "Oh, no! You need to get cleaned up.
The shower's open."

His smile faded a little, but then it returned. "And then?"

"And then dinner," Mallory smiled back.

Caleb clapped his hands. "Exactly what I was hoping you
would say! I'll hurry!" He still couldn't quite pull himself off
the bed, so he just rolled off the edge and then sprang up and
ran into the bathroom, closing the door.

"Leave the beard!" Mallory yelled to the closed door. "I
like it!"

Mallory did not know if he heard her and was going
to repeat herself, but suddenly a small door opened in the
wall. Three house sprites filed in. Two of them were carrying
folded clothes, and the third was carrying a stack of linens.
The one with the linens began stripping the dirty sheets and

pillowcases off the bed and replacing them. The other two left the folded clothes on the mahogany dresser. When they had dropped off the clothing, one of them went to work on the carpet, vacuuming and shampooing it back to its pristine condition. The other went to work on their boots, scrubbing and polishing them back to almost new. A small canister of spray deodorizer appeared from a compartment on the sprite and sprayed the inside of their boots, and gave a couple of courtesy sprays in the room too. When their work was finished, the sprites retreated back into the wall from which they came.

Mallory walked over to the stack of clothes and found an outfit that looked very similar to the one the Archivist had been wearing, but this one was all blue. She shed the robe and tried on the clothes the house sprites had just delivered. There were three full-length mirrors hanging on the wall, and she examined herself in the new clothes. The blue silk outfit was huge. The arms hung past her hands by almost an inch. The pant legs were also draping on the floor by nearly the same ratio. Clearly it had been made for a much larger woman, but then the clothing began to move of its own accord. The sleeves and pant legs bunched up and folded themselves then strings of fabric unraveled and sewed new seams. Whole strips of extra fabric separated off the clothing and fell to the floor, and when the process finished, the clothing fit her perfectly and was incredibly comfortable to boot. The silk shimmered in the mirror as Mallory spun around admiring herself.

"Wow!" Caleb appeared in the mirror behind her.

"Looking good, Mal!"

Caleb had left the beard, and he smelled better too, but he was wearing the other robe, which was way too small for him. The robe clearly did not have the same Dikaió tailoring magic the clothes did. The sleeves showed off two inches of his forearms, and the bottom of the robe was so high up his legs, he looked like he was wearing a mini-skirt: one wrong step and there would be nothing left to the imagination. Mallory smiled at him. "You're looking pretty good yourself, Mister Aiworth."

Caleb looked at himself in the mirror and roared with laughter. "I am, aren't I?"

Mallory grabbed the other set of clothing and threw them at Caleb. The outfit was almost exactly the same as the one Mallory was wearing, but it was red, and Caleb was a lot taller than her. It was short on him, not quite as bad as the robe had been. "I'm not so sure, Mal," he laughed.

Then the fabric began to move. The blue pieces on the floor from Mallory's outfit shimmied up Caleb's legs and began to sew themselves into what he was wearing. Caleb squirmed and danced around the room, "Ahhh! It tickles."

Mallory laughed. "It doesn't take long. Hold still."

Caleb tried to stand still, but he trembled as the fabric tailored itself around him. When it was finished, he walked to the mirror next to Mallory. "Well, it fits, but it's not as nice as yours."

Mallory nodded. The blue fabric had worked itself into the new clothes at all kinds of different points to make the clothes fit Caleb, but it looked a bit like a patchwork quilt now. "It is kind of awful looking," Mallory agreed.

Then the dye in the blue fabric began to seep into the rest of the outfit, and the red began to seep into the blue sections. Slowly, the outfit's color completely homogenized. There wasn't enough blue to change it purple, but it was definitely a deeper shade of red than it had been. Caleb nodded. "This is nice. Way nicer than anything we had in the city."

Mallory nodded, "I wonder what other marvels we'll find with all the books here. I can't wait to get started reading."

Caleb shook his head. "You promised me dinner, Mal. Dinner."

Mallory's stomach growled. "Good idea. Let's go!"

They ran to the door and opened it. Outside on the ground were two pairs of sandals. Mallory put her feet into one pair, and they Dikaió cobbled themselves into the right size, leaving bits of material on the floor, which then incorporated themselves into Caleb's pair when he slipped them on. "Amazing," Mallory said. She looked up at the symbols on the wall; the triangle and the circle had arrows pointing to the left. "I guess we go this way to find dinner." Mallory pointed toward the arrow, and the young couple ran down the hall in the direction the Library told them to go.

They found the smells long before they found the dining room. Mallory tried to catalogue everything she was smelling: black pepper, chili powder, cumin, thyme, bread, peaches—her mouth watered in anticipation. Caleb was not even looking at the shapes on the wall to guide him through the halls of the library, he would just sniff the air and say excitedly, "This way, this way!"

Finally, the hallway rounded a corner, and they found a staircase leading down to two massive oak doors. Mallory noted that the doors were covered with carved, scenic reliefs, picturing people doing heroic things like fighting sprites and wolves, everyday things like gardening and building, but mostly the motifs were full of women and children doing familial things: mothers holding babies, mothers watching over toddlers, mothers teaching adolescents. Most of these motifs included the symbols of her city's triad of government, but there were other unfamiliar symbols too. One symbol appeared prominently in the relief, and she froze. It was a heater shield. The same one that she had seen in the room they had spent the night in underground. It was the family crest of the Sprite Master Reddy Lamarr. She reached out and ran her hand over the shield. It had been odd to see it in the underground room, but it was even stranger to see it here.

She was broken out of her thoughts as the door swung away from her field of vision when Caleb pushed through. She almost waited for the door to close to keep looking at the crest, but she caught sight of what was waiting beyond them. A long oak table ran the length of a large, high-ceilinged dining room. On the table were several steaming dishes; their aromas drew her into the room, saliva pooling over her tongue. Alex was already seated at the table, and she had not waited for them to start eating. She held a chicken drumstick in one gloved hand, and a hunk of bread in the other, and was alternating bites between the two. The Archivist was sitting at the head of the table in the host's seat, watching her with amusement.

Alex looked up at Caleb and Mallory when they walked in, her eyes went wide, and both her hands dropped to the table.

"What are the two of you wearing?" She laughed.

"My dinner clothes," Caleb laughed back as he pulled up a seat and began to fill his plate.

Mallory sat next to him and began to do the same. There was roasted chicken, mashed potatoes corn, bread rolls, salad, and what tasted like lemonade to drink. It may have been the single greatest meal she had ever eaten. "Why are you wearing your old clothes? Didn't you shower?" Mallory asked Alex as she shoved an entire bread roll in her mouth, making herself look like a chubby-cheeked chipmunk.

The Archivist threw her arms up. "Thank you! She demanded that her old, dirty clothes get washed immediately. She wouldn't wear the ones I had provided. You both look great, by the way."

"Thanks," tiny bits of food sprayed out of Caleb's mouth as he spoke. "They're super comfortable too."

The Archivist shook her head and scowled, "Did no one teach you manners in this city you came from?"

Caleb looked down, brow-beaten. He finished chewing and then said, "Sorry, ma'am. It's been a while."

Alex chimed in then: "I don't need to be comfortable. Besides those don't come with gloves." She waved one of her gloved hands to demonstrate.

"Well, anyway," the Archivist shrugged, "I had a sprite clean her clothes and return them to her. She still beat the two of you down here. What were you doing?" She paused, and Mallory was about to answer, but the Archivist cut her off, "No. Never mind. I don't want to know."

Mallory gave her a scowl but did not stop eating to offer any more information. Caleb just smirked and grabbed another piece of chicken.

The Archivist sat quietly while the three young people ate. Mallory was vaguely aware of her staring at them, but the food made it too hard to pay the old stranger much notice. Alex had stopped eating about halfway through her plate. Mallory figured their stomachs had shrunk considerably, but Caleb had already made it through his first plate of food and was on to his second. His stomach may have shrunken, too, but Mallory wasn't sure what to call a shrunken bottomless pit. What was half of infinity? She managed to clean her own plate as well, and she found herself filling up a second plate, too. She was mostly craving the chicken, but the buttered potatoes were also really hitting the spot. She and Caleb finished their second plate at about the same time. There was one chicken leg left, and they both reached for it.

Caleb looked up at Mallory in surprise, holding his hand over hers. She quickly snatched away the piece of chicken and smiled demurely at him. "You don't mind, do you, handsome?"

"I...I guess not," he stammered. "But what am I going to eat?" He blinked at the empty chicken plate and scratched his head.

The Archivist slapped the table and stood up. "What are you going to eat? Do you eat like this all the time?"

Alex nodded, "all the time. Well, him anyway. For her," she pointed at Mallory, "she's usually a little more reserved."

The Archivist threw her hands in the air. "Well, only one of them will be eating me out of house and home then."

Mallory tore some meat off the bone with her teeth, and then spoke with the chicken stuffed in her cheek. "The sprite said you had plenty of food here at the Library."

The Archivist nodded a little too enthusiastically and laughed. "For normal people, yes."

Caleb smiled and spread his arms wide, leaning back in his chair. "I am quite extraordinary."

The Archivist smiled and laughed too. "A joke? Sprite, how long has it been since I've heard a joke?"

The clockwork sprite's eyes dimmed and blinked. "I have no record of there ever being a joke told in the Library."

The Archivist's humored elation darkened. She sat down and looked far away past her guests. "Not since my husband and my boys died then."

"I'm sorry." Caleb offered, looking at her with genuine empathy.

The Archivist nodded and continued. "It was a long time ago. That's why I've been looking for a Chorus to train as an Archivist, but now I have you; and a married couple to produce a line of heirs, too."

"What happened to your family?" Mallory asked, pushing away her plate.

Tears formed in the corner of the Archivist's eyes. "The Ex Natu happened." She looked past the three of them into a past that none of them could see and moved her hand in a wide circle around the room.

"There were not many of us left after years of fighting.

Our triad had fallen. Our children were starving. There was only a handful, laying low, trying to build the only successful defense we knew: what you call the light. Our ancestors built the one in Hoffen City, and it was impenetrable even by the Ex Natu. But they were on the wrong side of it when it was activated, and all of the plans for its construction were locked inside when it covered the city. We knew the basic principles of how to create a holographic plasma field, but the calculations required to calibrate the magnetic field were difficult to reproduce from scratch. The crater of Mason City is all the proof you need of that." She interlaced her fingers, and then pulled them apart quickly, making a small explosive noise with her lips.

The three teens looked at each other. Mallory could only assume that Mason City was the abandoned city they had wandered through on the way to the Library.

"It took years to get it right. I was the one that figured out how to use the Dikaió to modulate the currents, simulating the high voltage of a super-conductive substrate with a regulator cap on the generators; it turned out to be a simple fix using the Dikaió to emulate the settings at Hoffen City, adjusted for size of course. Even though we weren't there, the Dikaió was."

The three teens looked at her perplexed, but she didn't seem to notice. The tears began to flow more. "But it was too late; we didn't have time to get it up. They hunted us with their sprites night and day. They made me watch—." She shook her head, as if trying to ward off the memories the story was dredging to the surface of her mind.

But then she continued anyway: "We were building this space; this Library was going to be a fortress: built to protect us and our families. We worked in shifts, and never stayed here, so our true numbers would never be known. Instead, we lived in caves. Every trip to work on the fortress risked being found out. The plasma field would have meant we could stay here without fear—we were so close, but no one wanted another Mason City." She got up from the table and walked to a window. "I mean, look at it. If we had just turned it on, we would have all been saved."

The Archivist touched the window and went silent. The trio waited for her to continue, but she did not.

Finally, Caleb broke the silence. "The Ex Natu tracked you down?"

The Archivist spun around. "Tracked us down? No! We were betrayed by one of our own. She led them to us—she was afraid. Afraid the plasma field wouldn't be enough. Afraid the war would either continue for generations, or we'd all be killed. So, she tried to end the war all on her own: thought she could reason with the enemy. The diplomatic fool.

"They came in the night with scout sprites at every cave exit. Men, women, children: the Ex Natu slaughtered them indiscriminately. Some made it out and ran for the fortress here. We had stockpiles of food and weapons here, but she brought them here, too. The skies filled with Ex Natu sprites, and napalm rained down. When the fires went out, they encircled the place with scout sprites and fire sprites to finish off stragglers. We were all going to die anyway, so I ran to the generators and turned on the plasma shield. If it were a

Mason City bomb, at least it would take them all with us—but it wasn't. The magnetic field contained the plasma dome just like it had been designed. Most of the Ex Natu and their sprites were stuck outside, but not all of them.

"My husband died just over there," she pointed toward a corner of the dining room. "He was standing over my two sons, and they gunned all three of them down while I watched—."

The Archivist stopped. "That's all the stories for tonight." She turned away and walked abruptly out of the double doors. The clockwork sprite following after her.

Mallory realized she had been clutching Caleb's arm, digging her fingernails in. He didn't even notice as she released her grip. Alex flicked at the fork on her plate. Mallory broke the silence, "I guess she must have cleared out the Ex Natu after that?"

Caleb shrugged. "Apparently, but at least we know what happened to the old Chorus's parents."

Mallory nodded. "Trapped outside the city's light. Stuck in a war with the Ex Natu." She looked out the window at the crackling light surrounding the Library grounds. "At least we're safe inside the Library with its light working."

Alex threw her fork across the table and yelled, "Yeah, we're safe, but what about our city? What about our families? We destroyed their light. Remember? What's to stop the Ex Natu from bringing war to them?

$\mathbf{M}$allory breathed in deeply and had difficulty letting the air back out. She had considered the danger the city was in due to the wilding wolves, but she had not connected the danger that they faced due to the Ex Natu. What if these beings that killed the Archivists' family found the city? Would the ancient war lead to an attack on the peaceful people there? They had a hard enough time fighting off three barely functioning fire sprites; if the Ex Natu brought an army, would anyone survive? All the old feelings of guilt and regret swirled about in her mind. She had once again gripped Caleb's arm, and he still seemed not to notice. "We have to do something," Mallory whispered through clenched teeth.

"What would we do?" Caleb asked. "We can't go home, or

they'll kill us. We don't know what the Ex Natu are. We don't know what they're capable of or what our ancestors' war was all about. And we certainly don't know how to build a hollo-plasmic-what's-it." He motioned his arms toward the window dramatically, emphasizing the point he could not pronounce.

"No," Alex said. "But she does." She pointed toward the double doors. "She knows a lot more than she's letting on." She stood up. "Plus, she's doing a lot more than any one Dikaió christening ought to be able to. There's something about that bracelet on her arm."

Mallory tilted her head and bit her lip. "What do you mean?"

"I don't know. Maybe as an Archivist the Dikaió just works differently for her, but that bracelet does something. It at least controls the light. You saw it. And if there's a way we can use it to save the city and restore its protection, we should find it." Alex folded her arms. "Whatever it takes."

Caleb stood up now. "We've been invited here as guests. We need to respect our host. Besides the Council, including our own families, banished us on the pain of death if we return. We should respect the rule of law and their wishes. Why not embrace our new life here?"

Mallory recoiled from her husband. "Caleb, they're our families. I don't want my parents to die if there's any chance we could stop it. My sister might be born now. She's just a baby. How can we leave them defenseless like that?"

Caleb's shoulders slumped. "You're right. I'm sorry. But what can we do? We're so far out of our depth here."

Mallory and Alex looked at each other, and something

unspoken passed between them. Alex started, "You're right; we don't know enough."

Mallory nodded, "But we're in a building full of books, and our host has already offered to teach us how to be an Archivist."

Alex walked around the table to them. "And she wanted Choruses. That must mean she knows how to change our christening and let us use the Dikaió again the way she does."

"And if that's the case, then we could bring back the Dikaió to the city." Mallory swiveled in her chair and pointed out the window. "Plus, she knows how to build the light. If we learned how to do that, we could protect the city."

Caleb shifted his weight uncomfortably. "We nearly died getting here. The Archivist said the light is the only thing that can stop the Ex Natu. They know we exist. They know approximately where we are. If we go back, what's to say we don't lead them straight to the city and put everyone in danger?"

Mallory stood up then, too. "Well, my guess is that the fire sprites in the dark woods circling our city are theirs, because as soon as they had any sort of energy, they attacked us. The question isn't *if* they know where it is, it's whether they know that the light is down."

"So, we're working against the clock then." Alex's arms dropped to her sides, and she started walking toward the double doors.

"Where are you going?" Caleb asked.

"I'm going to find the Archivist and start my training," she said without looking back.

Mallory and Caleb scrambled after her. They got to the double doors and saw their symbols on the wall and floor. To the right of the staircase there was a large wooden doorway, and above it was a triangle with an arrow pointing forward. The three of them walked through the doorway and froze. They found themselves among rows of shelves stacked to the brim with books. There were more books on the shelf right in front of them than existed in the entirety of the city since the written word had been all but purged. The Library's books looked very well cared for. Mallory reached out and ran her finger over a leather-bound volume, and there was not a speck of dust on the book. She looked down the row and saw a housekeeping sprite atop extended legs, cleaning books on the top shelves. Then she noticed that along the top molding of the bookshelves, the tracking symbols showed that the Archivist was somewhere to the left of them. "This way," she said and ran down the length of the row.

They passed a gap in the shelves, and the triangle's arrow changed direction. Mallory stopped and Caleb and Alex nearly ran her over. "Go back." She said, and the group turned around.

Now, Alex was leading the search party. She turned into the gap, and they found themselves in a tight aisle running between the rows. Small signs with letters and numbers were attached to each row, and Mallory wondered what they meant—just another item on a growing list of questions she wanted to ask the Archivist. There were so many at this point, she barely remembered them all.

Mallory could not see much in front of her except Caleb's

red-silk covered back. She marveled at how much bulk the man had lost. She doubted he would have even fit in this thin space six months ago. He'd dropped a lot of muscle as well as fat during their banishment. Of course, she and Alex were pretty thin at this point as well, and she wondered how long it would take them to get back to health now that they had a place to stay and food to eat. She did not want to go hungry again for the rest of her life if she could avoid it. And then she thought about the journey back to the city they would have to traverse. That route would likely involve hunger. And it would involve being stuck in small spaces like the underground tunnels, except there would not be a sprite there to open the door to sleep in the small room or save them from the bats and the rats or to provide light with its eyes. They would be on their own in the dark—and hungry too.

Suddenly, she did not want to follow through with this plan. Caleb was right. They could have a good life here. Their children could have a good life here. She imagined children running through these aisles: laughing, playing, reading. It was a paradise, and they were about to sacrifice it all to save a city that had turned against them, parents that had counted them as dead, and threats on their lives if they ever returned. She slowed down, as the thrill of the chase passed. The rows of books felt like they were starting to close in on her. Sweat bubbled out of her forehead as goose bumps prickled along her arms. Her breathing became shallow and quick.

Her vision began to blur along the edges, but as Caleb and Alex moved ahead, and she could finally see more than Caleb's golden mop of hair, she saw that the ceiling ended just a little farther ahead, and that where it ended, a bright light shone down from somewhere above it. The claustrophobic anxiety attack abated, replaced with a feeling Mallory found much more compelling: curiosity. She started running to her husband and friend and caught up with them just as they exited the aisle into an open space. Twenty aisles emptied into the space, like spokes connected to a hub in a huge wheel. Six floors full of rows of books rose above them, all the aisles meeting in this same hub, creating an inner chamber in the center of the Library. Above it all, a giant stained glass dome lit up from behind by what could only be Dikaió lights this late in the afternoon.

The image in the stained glass was of a man that could have been an identical twin of the City Service's Manager, and two boys that could have been his sons. Mallory pointed up and whispered, "It looks just like Jake Carpenter."

"Probably a relative. He was also a Carpenter," a voice answered.

Mallory startled. She almost tripped over the Archivist who was sitting in a leather-upholstered wingback chair just inside the circular inner chamber. Caleb and Alex swirled around coming quickly to Mallory's aid.

The Archivist looked unsurprised to see that the group had followed her. She slowly rose but did not look at them. "He was my husband, and those were my sons. It's just more evidence that your city is Hoffen City; your Jake is my husband's distant cousin, no doubt." She paused and turned toward them. "I've become accustomed to being alone; it was rude of me to run off, especially since you're all so young and in a new place. You'll have to give me some time to adjust."

Alex smiled, and Mallory winced at how awkward and insincere it looked, but the Archivist did not seem to notice. Alex said, "We understand. Maybe if we got started training." She paused and rotated around slowly with her arms out. "Reading even. We could give you the space you would like."

Caleb shook his head. "I can't believe I'm saying it, but we're asking for homework."

The Archivist's head tilted slightly to the side, and she blinked her eyes. "That's reasonable. Tell me some of the books you've read, and we'll go from there."

Mallory spoke. "Well, there aren't many books left in the city after the purge—"

"The what?" The Archivist interrupted.

"The book purge. Most of the books in the city were burned," Mallory clarified.

"Burned?" The Archivist looked like she was about to faint. "What about the Hoffen City Library?"

Caleb shrugged. "There's no library in our city. We had about thirty or forty books hidden away in Alex's attic, but nothing like this." He waved his hand at the rows of books around them.

Alex nodded. "We called our little stash The Book Club, but if my grandfather had ever found out about it, all of the books would have been burned."

Mallory jumped in then too. "Because he built a fire sprite using a book and burned down houses and killed people."

"Madness!" The Archivist whispered in unbelief.

Caleb responded. "We used the same book to rebuild

three fire sprites, and nearly burned down the whole city and killed dozens of people. It's not that crazy to see books as dangerous."

"But a fire sprite is a weapon of war. What did you expect it to do?" The Archivist asked.

Mallory answered this time. "We don't even know what war is. The city was peaceful before—"

Alex cut her off. "Before my grandfather, the Administrator, tried to take over."

"The one who burns the books?" The Administrator clarified.

"Well, all of our grandparents were the ones who purged the books. Alex's family was just tasked with enforcement of the ban," Caleb answered.

"Classic totalitarians: control the information, control the people," the Archivist mused and then took a step back. "Have you come here to burn my books then?"

"Oh, no!" Mallory stepped toward her. "I love books. Without the Dikaió, books have been the only way I've ever known to navigate the world. I was—I mean—we were exiled because of my passion for reading."

The Archivist relaxed a little. "What do you mean without the Dikaió?"

"Before I was born, my grandmother had a dream that she would christen me a Dikaió Chorus and that I would save the city. There weren't any Choruses left at that point, and no one was entirely sure what the christening would do."

The Archivist began to pace. "Not any Choruses left? What's the point of that? The Dikaió was made to serve the

Choruses."

Mallory continued. "My grandmother said the last Chorus said something like that too before he died. No one understood it."

The Archivist rolled her eyes. "What's there to understand? Everyone can't be a baker, who would buy the bread?"

Alex just stood there, that fake smile still holding on her face. "We're all Choruses, now, at any rate. And books are what got us banished from the city."

The Archivist stopped pacing and said, "That and you apparently tried to burn the place down."

"Yes, that too." Caleb chuckled uncomfortably.

The Archivist shook her head and then shrugged her shoulders. "Well, you're what I've got either way. You all know how to read then, I assume?"

"Clearly," Mallory answered. "They taught the Council and the heirs how to read. There was still city business that required reading and writing. Everyone else was forbidden."

"Is there an oral tradition?" The Archivist asked. "You don't know about the war. How far back does your history go?"

Mallory answered. "My grandmother spoke to the last Chorus when she was a child. He told her at some point before the light, his parents left and never came back."

Caleb said, "And we have the traditions of our people. The Triad of Government, the guilds, the City Council, and of course the christening of the Dikaió. The Governor runs the day-to-day life, manages the guilds, that sort of thing."

Alex offered, "And the Administrator enforces the laws as

set down by the Council and the Triad, using the magistrates, who were trained to fight—but we mostly just helped with civil disputes."

"And the Matriarch christens children with their Dikaió, so they know what they're meant to do in life," Mallory said.

The Archivist continued shaking her head. "And that's all you know about the Triad of government and your history?"

The three young people looked at each other and nodded.

"Well, then we'll start your training there. Grab a seat." The Archivist turned around and pointed toward the middle of the room where there was a round table with chairs. The three young people sat around the table as instructed. The Archivist raised her bracelet close to her mouth and said, "Dikaió, bring all three volumes of *The History of the Triadic Government*." She lowered her arm. "You can't very well learn to be an Archivist if you don't know who you are."

A house sprite entered the inner chamber carrying three large leather-bound books and placed them on the table. "Ah, excellent!" the Archivist exclaimed. She picked up the first volume. "First, the Administrator—I assume that's our magistrate here." She handed the large book to Alex. She picked up the next book. "Then the Governor because I doubt very much you would be a Matriarch." She handed the book to Caleb. "And finally, the Matriarch," the Archivist said.

Mallory took the book, and her fingers traced over an embossed dragonfly that looked almost exactly like the stained glass dragonfly in her room. Alex and Caleb already had their books open, and Mallory could see the familiar emblems of their offices on the covers: the scrolls of law and a magistrate's weapon on Alex's, and a sword and shield on Caleb's. "Why is the Matriarch's emblem a dragonfly?" Mallory asked the Archivist.

The old woman sighed heavily. "There are many answers in those volumes of our history and others, young one. What fun would it be if I just told you everything? Read. Read."

"Where should we start?" Alex said flipping through pages.

The Archivist shrugged. "Well, Alice, 'start at the beginning, and when you come to the end, stop.'"

"My name is Alex, and that's hardly helpful. There are a thousand pages here with multiple columns and tiny print."

"Welcome to Wonderland, child. Most of the story is yet to be told. Besides, if you're busy reading, I won't have to worry about the three of you starting fires." The Archivist spun around on pointed toes like a ballerina, and then chasséd down one of the aisles. The house sprite followed quickly behind her.

"She should not be able to move like that at her age," Alex mused.

"Maybe she has nano sprites like Caleb that repair her," Mallory offered. "To keep her young, as it were."

"How old do you think she is?" Caleb asked.

Mallory shrugged. "If old age is just the body wearing down and being unable to repair itself, there's no telling."

Caleb sat back in his chair and looked at his hand, which he was clenching and unclenching. "What does that mean for me?"

Mallory shook her head and shrugged. "Maybe we'll learn

something from the histories?"

The three young people looked at their books. Mallory struggled to get comfortable at the table and soon moved to the wing-backed chair the Archivist had been sitting in. There, she opened the thick tome and began reading:

The Chronicles of Humanities' Matriarchs

I have been asked to begin this record of Matriarchs, a living document to be passed through the ages, though I am no writer, nor am I an Archivist. When I asked what I should write in the record, I was told to tell my story, so future generations, should any survive this war, would not forget our history; maybe they will understand why we made the choices we did, maybe they will avoid the mistakes we made. My hope, our hope, is that they will continue to live in the way we have lived for millennium, and to that end, I will begin these chronicles not at the beginning of 'my' story, but at the beginning of 'our' story.

My name is Eva Knenne, first Matriarch of the new age. It is an odd turn of phrase to refer to oneself as a Matriarch, yet this is the nomenclature the Council settled on, and because of our family's role in the resistance, I was appointed to this position of leadership. I argued that my husband Colonel Kirk Knenne should be the one appointed to leadership, not me, but the Council maintained that his experience was needed with the fighting forces and not in politics. I understand the need, but I feel there are many more qualified to fill this role than me, and yet it is hard to deny the part I played in starting the resistance to begin with.

It was a cool autumn night, and my husband Kirk had just called me saying he was on his way home from the front lines. The war with the southeastern islands was brutal and long. Kirk had been away for three years, but it was finally over. The war started because the islanders had opposed the Ex Natu's orders to abide by the Population Accords. Children were an ancient point of pride in their culture; more children meant more honor for the men, but the Accords were dictated as a planet-wide measure for allocating a limited number of resources within a rapidly growing number of humans. The environmentalism worries of the 21st century had proven largely unfounded as the Earth could easily supply enough food and space for an almost unlimited population, and nearly unlimited energy sources that did not pollute the atmosphere were discovered in subatomic research, but a new biologic technology had drastically decreased the death rate and increased lifepan for an indeterminate time: nano sprites unlocked the secret of near immortality.

The Ex Natu, who controlled the supply of nano sprites, said that there were, and always would be, a limited number available; they claimed that there were not enough rare-earth materials to supply them to every person: the population was just too large. The announcement led to world-wide rioting, as people clamored to get access to the lifesaving technology. In an attempt to restore peace and order, the Ex Natu invited the leaders of the world to what they called the Population Accords. They proposed to peacefully reduce the number of people on the planet by limiting reproduction without a permit, and letting older generations pass away naturally. At some point, everyone alive would have the nano sprites. They offered the promise of immortality for the human race, and the only catch was giving up the hope of ever having a family. All the leaders signed the Accords happily, receiving their nano sprites upon the day of their signing. And just like that, all the nations of the world were Ex Natu nations. But some nations rose up against their leaders, refusing the mandate. Most of those that refused were undeveloped people groups, and they chose to continue having children unabated. Studies showed that after a generation passed, the population in the nations that rebelled and opposed the Accords would outnumber the Ex Natu two to one. The Ex Natu declared that their continued procreation was a threat to the future. The non-member nations were declared enemies of the United World, and that's when the wars started.

Kirk was drafted into the United World's armies, and with his previous military experience, he was awarded the rank of Colonel. While he was away, we spoke almost everyday. The things he told me that he did in the name of a better future for us—they were atrocious. They made me hate him. Men, women, children: their lives snuffed out for the immortal promise of the Ex Natu. I pointed out that even if all of the non-conformers were wiped away, there would still be too many of us left to all receive nano sprites. He waved off my anxieties. "I'm a Colonel in the United World's armies, on track for a promotion. We'll be high up on the wait list, Eva," he assured me.

I knew it was not true.

Not because his rank did not call for it, but because I had

kept a secret from him during the time he was away: A secret that would not only jeopardize his career and our chance at immortality, but our chance of surviving at all. And now he was on his way home. There would be no more hiding. I was not sure how he would react. Would he denounce me and turn me over to the Ex Natu as duty demanded, even if it meant forfeiting his own life too? Would he shun me and turn me out quietly? I hoped he would see the beauty in what I had done—what we had done. However, as his arrival drew nearer, I panicked. I pulled the battered old green suitcases out from under our bed, dusted them off and began to pack. I did not have time to pack neatly, throwing our clothes in without even bothering to fold them. I scooped up toiletries and added them indiscriminately. We did not have much loose money—most of our funds were tied up in electronic currency, which would have been too easily traced, but I scrounged up what paper money and coinage we had available. It would have to do. This plan I had for my husband was not going to work, and I had put us in unnecessary danger.

It did not matter. Long before I was ready to leave, the front door opened, and my husband who I had not seen in person in three years rushed in, calling my name, "Eva? Eva? I'm home."

I stepped out of the bedroom. It was hard not to love him in that moment. He was tall, lean and muscular; he had the body of a perfectly fit soldier. His skin was deep olive brown like bronze and that made his gray eyes and white teeth almost shine when he smiled. I wanted to spend forever with him, but I knew I could not. His joyous expression faded into one of concern. "Eva? What's wrong?"

I caught a glimpse of myself in the mirror. My appearance was curly hair was disheveled: My shirt was half tucked in, my pants were stained, but more telling was the terror that clung to my face like a shroud. "Oh, Kirk!" My voice squeaked out just before I sank to my knees and began to sob.

He rushed to me; concern written all over him, and that's when he saw her. My sweet Mari. Our sweet Mari. His face contorted.

I started to babble, "I didn't know I was pregnant when you left, and maybe I should have gone to the authorities to abort her, but feeling her grow inside me was like having you here with me: a piece of you anyway. I didn't want them to take her away. I didn't want them to kill her, Kirk. I hid her away here in our house—kept her quiet, so the neighbors wouldn't find out. You have to see how beautiful she is."

He looked down at me with betrayal and disgust, and I looked away crying. Mari ran to my defense. She looked up at her father with the sort of courage and fire only a two-year old has and shouted, "Don't hurt my momma, Daddy."

"Daddy?" The word rolled slowly around his mouth, muffled like he had been drinking. He stumbled backward out of the doorway of our bedroom. His jaw worked open and closed, and then his expression softened. He dropped to one knee. "I'm not going to hurt your momma, Sweetie. Come here and let your daddy see you."

Mari looked at me for permission, and I wanted to say no. I knew what he had done: the monster the Ex Natu had made him. I was afraid of what he might do to our little girl.

That softened expression. That luring, caring face. How many people had been lured to their death by those same tactics in the wars? I knew he could kill us both in a moment. I also knew I still had a chance to stop him, but if my plan was to work, I had to risk both our lives. I hugged Mari goodbye, and then nodded toward her father. She walked to him, and then leapt into his arms with a joyful shout, "Daddy!"

I closed my eyes and waited for the worst.

Whatever becomes of this new society we are creating, what happened next will always be the cornerstone of its existence: A child transformed a monster into a father.

"What's your name?" he asked softly.

"Mari. And yours is Daddy. Momma talks about you. I am a lovely secret, but my name means "bitter 'bellion."

Kirk laughed out loud. "Bitter Rebellion?" He looked at me and smiled. "Your mother has always had a way with words."

"Yeah, she talks a lot." Mari kissed his cheek. "But you're home. Now, we can talk about other stuff."

"What would you like to talk about?" He smiled.

"Mostly, I'd like a puppy." Mari pulled away.

I pulled myself up. "Come now, Mari. It's time for bed."

"No! Daddy's home. I need to stay up!" The girl crossed her arms in defiance.

Kirk stood up as well. "What if I tell you a bedtime story?"

Mari took the bait and ran to the little space I had made for her in the spare room. I had to keep it from looking like a child's room. She slept on a loveseat and used a throw pillow and a tablecloth for bed sheets. There were no toys, no children's books, nothing that would give her existence away. Kirk sat down with her and told her a story that his father used to tell him when he was a child, and then he hummed a song that his mother used to sing to him until his daughter fell asleep. We moved to the dining room table and sat down to talk.

Kirk started, "I always imagined being a father. My father was an amazing man, and my childhood was wonderful, but I never thought I would have a child of my own. I thought the age of children was over, and I told myself that I was okay with that." He turned away and started to cry. "I took so many others' children away, Eva." He held out his hands and looked at them in horror. "I don't deserve to have my own child after everything I've done."

I stood up and walked over to him. I pushed him upright and sat down on his lap, burying my face in the nape of his neck and whispered into his ear. "Deserve it or not, Kirk. She's here. She's ours. Part of you and part of me."

He moved his head to the side away from me; his voice hardened. "And now I have to watch someone like me come and take her away." He shifted in his chair indicating I should get off.

I clung to him, as if I were in a sea storm clinging to a rock for life. "There's another option, Kirk. We're not alone."

He froze. "What are you saying?"

I released my grip on his neck but did not get off of his lap. "Do you really think the human race is going to be so quick to give up *family*?"

"The Ex Natu are stamping out anyone that opposes them. I just got home from a war for this very thing." He shook his head.

"You got done fighting a war with undeveloped nations that couldn't fight back. I'm asking you if you really believe everyone in our nation, in the developed world, is willing to give up their ability to have families? Do you think you're the only soldier that dreamed of having a child?" Now, I did stand up. "The Ex Natu are immortal, not invulnerable. Just yesterday, on the news, one of them died in a train accident. The nano sprites could not save her."

Kirk looked at me as though he were looking at a stranger. "What are you saying, Eva?"

I narrowed my eyes and spoke low and evenly, "I'm going to fight for her, Kirk. I'm going to fight to have more children. I'm going to fight, not just for our family, but for every family, and I am not alone."

"Not alone?" He stammered.

"There are hundreds and thousands of us. Millions maybe. In the governments, in the militaries, across the world. There's a man known as Omaha. He's created a new technology that will give us the upper hand against the Ex Natu." This was the moment of truth; Kirk would see the vision and become a leader in our resistance or end me and our daughter now. I stretched out my hands toward the kitchen and called, "Dikaió, bring me two glasses of water." Kirk looked confused as the glasses filled themselves with water and floated to my hands. I handed him a glass of water and raised an eyebrow.

"So, you intend to defeat the Ex Natu with a parlor trick?"

He shook his head. "I've been on the battlefield, Eva." He drank his water in one gulp and held up the glass. "This isn't going to do it."

I knew my husband well enough to know that this would be his logical response, and I was prepared. "Dikaió, defend me," I yelled. Suddenly our home was alive. Sprites loaded to the hilt with guns, knives, and even a couple with rocket launchers for dramatic effect, came swarming out of the closets and cupboards. The sprites set up a defensive perimeter around me, leveling all of their impressive firepower at Kirk.

His eyes narrowed. "This was your plan if I did not fall for the 'you're a father' routine?"

I shook my head. "No. A family is all of us. A mother, a child, and a father; there was no alternative. If you weren't with us, what would I be fighting for? What would we be fighting for?" I waved my hands and softly said, "Dikaió, cease." The sprites all holstered their weapons and returned to their various hiding places. "But you can see what I'm getting at. One soldier with this tech can become one hundred. We can fight back and win."

My husband stood up and began to pace. "I'm tired of war, Eva. I'd hoped to come home to a quiet life."

"A quiet life of what, Kirk? Immortal boredom? What will we do one-hundred years from now when the world isn't new and exciting anymore? Two-hundred years from now? A thousand? Did you see the joy that little girl had meeting her father for the first time? Can't you remember the joys in your childhood when you learned new things? When your father and mother taught you new things about the world? I've spent the last two years with that girl in there. I've taught her to walk. I've taught her to speak. I know what happiness is, Kirk, and what the Ex Natu are selling isn't it."

He held up his hands. "Fine. I get what you're saying. What do you want me to do?"

And now we had come to the rub of it: the ask. "I want you to lead our forces against the Ex Natu."

"Lead our forces? Our forces? Eva, how can you make a decision like that? Who are you?" Kirk's eyes were narrowed again.

"You've been away awhile, Kirk. I had to do something to keep busy." I smiled and winked at him, hoping to break the tension.

He chuckled and smiled back. "So, you formed an armed resistance against the Ex Natu?"

"A global armed resistance against the Ex Natu," I corrected.

"And you're willing to give up immortality for it?" He asked.

"Sickness? Old age? Death? Which of them could outweigh love, Kirk? I'd die tomorrow for Mari: for our family."

He walked quickly across the room and grabbed me in his arms, and just before he kissed me, he whispered, "Me, too."

10

The Library

Mallory looked up from her book and saw Alex and Caleb sitting at the table absorbed in their histories. She wanted to get up and tell them about what she had already learned, even if she did not completely understand all of the historical references; for example, what was an island? And how far away was it that a woman would not see her husband for three years? She did not quite understand the Ex Natu's hatred of families either, but she had read enough to fear it. Killing the Archivist's children seemed right in line with their *modus operandi*, but if the nano sprites were what made someone an Ex Natu, how did the clockwork sprite come to have them in its syringe? And did that mean that Caleb was now an Ex Natu? She could tell by the looks on her companions' faces that they were probably learning some of the same things about the Ex Natu that she was. Caleb's hand was on his forehead, and his mouth was hanging open. Alex looked angry. She kept reaching for her weapon holsters, but she was not wearing them. Mallory decided that they were all going to need to debrief about what they had read. Maybe it would be best to keep going, so she would have more to talk about when the others were ready. She turned the page:

The Chronicles of Humanity's Matriarchs

Omaha was hesitant to meet with Kirk—and for good reason. Kirk was a ranking officer in the Ex Natu's military. There were many enlisted men and women that had secretly joined the resistance, but none of them were so high up the ranks as a colonel on track to being a general—he had received an official letter informing him that his record was being reviewed for accommodation and promotion. Kirk and I had also been informed that our place in the queue for nano sprites was reserved for an injection only six months from when he returned home from duty. Omaha worried that Kirk might cave to the lure of immortality. However, I believed his immediate love for his daughter was sincere. I knew Kirk's parents. They had raised him to be a man of character, and I believed he would be an excellent and faithful father, who would not only fight for his family, but would win. Of course, I was biased. This was the man I loved that I was trying to sell to the leaders of the resistance. It was understandable that they were suspicious.

They wanted me to bring Kirk to meet them personally. To this point in the resistance, we had built the movement electronically via clandestine back channels in the Ex Natu's internet. Their hubris was their greatest weakness. They never even expected we would use their own systems. However, the next step was going to require physical contact, which presented a bit of an issue for our family, seeing since we would have no one to care for Mari, and we could not very well bring her with us. The law said that all children were required to travel with a permit, and as far as anyone knew, it had been more than a decade since any permits had been issued. A two-year old would certainly turn heads. The resistance was sympathetic but unwavering. In the end, we compromised a solution. We had four house sprites that had all been revamped with Omaha's Dikaió programming, and he patched in a domestic babysitting protocol. We watched them for a couple of days to see what the new program would be like, and to be fair, the sprites made Mari breakfast, lunch, and dinner; helped her go to the bathroom; gave her baths; put her to bed; they even let her draw faces on them with my makeup and played with her.

Honestly, I might have gone with the idea except for that last part; watching the sprites play princess-make-believe with my little girl knowing that below the sprite steel there was enough artillery to take down an army platoon was terrifying. When the time came to leave, I felt like I was having a panic attack. We walked out the door and closed it behind us. "I can't. I just can't leave her." I did not even make it one block before I turned back toward our home.

"We have to if we want to keep her, Eva." Kirk caught my arm.

I shook him loose. "She's too little. I can't."

"We have to trust that the sprites will take care of her." He spoke quietly.

"You barely know her," I hissed at him. "I had to give birth to her all alone. I spent two years hiding her and keeping her alive. Don't tell me what I have to do!"

"Eva, be quiet. Someone will hear." He spun around checking the perimeter for danger in the way only a soldier knows how.

I stepped back toward him and lowered my voice to a whisper. "If you think I'm going to leave her with a bunch of sprites to die, you and all the rest have lost your minds. None of you know anything about raising kids."

"Eva, it's the only way they'll meet with me," he implored.

"I guess the resistance dies then. Mari isn't going to." I walked back to the house and shut the door on Kirk. Mari was squatting in a corner of the living room, shaking with fear and crying. The sprites were around her, making electronic cooing noises, but they might just as well have been a pack of wolves howling and circling the little girl. Before I could run to her, Kirk burst through the door, brushed past me, and picked up his little girl, who wrapped her arms tightly around him.

"I don't want to be a sprite, Daddy!" She sobbed.

"What, baby?" Kirk cooed.

"I don't want to have a sprite mommy and daddy. They'll make me a sprite like them," Mari pointed at the silver sprites now circling Kirks legs, cooing up at the little girl. It looked like some kind of absurd tribal ritual.

Kirk looked at me and said, "Okay, Eva. Let's call him."

Even in retrospect, after years of war against the Ex Natu, I still maintain that the level of paranoia Omaha and the other leaders exhibited was ridiculous. The signal for a video call moved through six Virtual Private Networks, parsed between a random combination of sixteen orbital satellites, and I'm pretty sure it was then bounced off a lone mule with a small receiving dish on its back in the Andes Mountains before the parties' connection was made. Then there were a series of passwords and challenge questions that had to be answered. If you got one wrong, the mule died, and the call was disconnected. And I've killed hundreds of mules. Of course, I'm being sarcastic, I have no idea how it all worked. Technology was never my strong suit. After a few failed attempts, we finally made contact, and Omaha's face appeared on the screen. He had dark skin and black hair, which made his light blue eyes stand out in contrast. His nose and mouth were covered by a mask to keep him from being identified should these calls get intercepted. "Eva, your train leaves in twenty-three minutes; you have two minutes to leave, or you will miss it." Omaha was never one to waste time with pleasantries, and empathy was not his strong suit either. He did not even notice that there were tears in my eyes.

That lack of observational skill was precisely the reason he could not lead the resistance. But brilliant strategist that he was, he was able to recognize the areas of leadership he lacked, which is why he agreed to meet with Kirk in the first place. In retrospect, I suspect that he planned to recruit Kirk before he contacted me, but you would never guess it by the precautions he took. How he found out about Mari is still a mystery. I remember the moment his masked face appeared on my screen, and he said, "Eva Knenne, we know you've had a child." I thought he was with the Ex Natu, and I almost fainted in fear, and that jerk did not lead me to believe differently at first. After some time of interrogation over video, he explained that I had two choices: join the resistance or be reported. It was not a hard choice to make.

However, this plan of leaving my daughter home alone with sprite nannies was too much to ask. Let him report me. I didn't care, and I was about to tell him so, when Kirk stepped forward still holding a sobbing Mari. "Look, we're not comfortable leaving our daughter home alone. She's too little. If something goes wrong, we can't trust the sprites to help her. I'm sorry; you'll have to find another way."

Omaha did not blink. "You have passed the first test, Colonel Knenne. Family is the reason for the resistance, not the other way around." There was a knock at the door then, and we both nearly jumped out of our skin. Omaha said, "Open the door. It's my wife."

I walked to the door and cracked it open. A tall blond woman was standing outside. She was wearing a thick coat even though it was not cold outside and looking around somewhat fearfully. "Eva?" she asked hopefully.

"Yes," I said and waved her in.

"Thank, God!" She slid in the door and pulled off her heavy coat. "I'm dying here." And no wonder she was feeling uncomfortable: the woman was clearly several months pregnant, and her clothes were coated in sweat.

"Hi, Beautiful," Omaha said. "I'm so glad you made it okay."

"Yes, I made it. Dikaió, water," she commanded, and my cupboard sprang open, and a glass jumped out, filled itself with water, and floated to her hand. "I hope you don't mind," she said before downing the glass.

"No, of course," I said.

Kirk said, "Well, um, welcome to our home, Mrs. Omaha."

She laughed and half curtsied, "It's Melody."

We both nodded, and then looked at Omaha on the screen. I asked, "You don't trust my husband, and yet you sent your wife and unborn child to our home?"

Omaha's head bobbed slightly. "If he had left your daughter callously behind, Melody would not have come. A good father would never sacrifice his children. It would have been clear that he was not part of our resistance. How could he fight for others' families if he wouldn't fight for his own?" He paused, "Now, I've sent my family to care for yours. Our bonds are forged. But the rest of the resistance still wants to question you in person, Colonel Knenne. Will you allow my wife to care for your daughter while you travel?"

That was certainly a better option than an army of sprite babysitters, but still, I was hesitant. Kirk knelt down and gently pulled Mari loose from his neck. "Mari, my girl. Your mamma and I have to go meet, Mr. Omaha," he pointed at the screen. Mari looked at the screen suspiciously, and then back to her father. "Mrs. Omaha is here to take care of you instead of the sprites. You don't have to be afraid anymore, okay?"

"I don't wanna be a Omaha, neither," Mari stuck out her bottom lip and looked set to cry.

I knelt down with her too, "You'll always be Mari Knenne, and we'll always be your mamma and daddy. But do you know what?"

Tears were bubbling up in my girl's eyes and were about to spill out, but she asked, "What?"

"Mrs. Omaha has a baby in her belly," I answered.

"A baby?" Mari blinked away her tears as her eyes lit up.

Melody laughed, "Yes, and he's waking up. Want to feel him kick?"

Mari leaned to the side to look past us at Melody's protruding belly. Then she looked at us questioningly. I laughed, "Go ahead."

Mari walked timidly over to Melody, who took our little girl's hand and placed it on her belly. "Right here. Feel him?"

Mari pulled her hand away quickly. "Oh! He kicked me!"

"Yes, he's very active after his long trip," Melody nodded.

Mari put her hand back on Melody's belly. "Do it again!" she commanded Baby Omaha.

Kirk shuffled around on his knees to Mari's side. "Would it be okay if Mrs. Omaha watches you while we go see Mr. Omaha?"

"Will the baby come out to play?" Mari asked in earnest.

Melody laughed, "Well, he's not due for a couple of months, but one never knows."

"A baby's better than a puppy," Mari nodded at the adults knowingly, and they were all startled by a loud laugh that filled the room.

It was Omaha on the living room screen. I was shocked. The man was an enigma; enigmas don't laugh. "Kids say the darnedest things," he said and laughed again. "I can't wait to hear what my boy comes up with when he's that age."

And that was that. Our families were bonded forever in the forges of a war to have the right to hear our children say dumb things. I hope that some future generation is reading these words and says to themselves; "that's a foolish reason to start a war"—because that will mean we won. Omaha rescheduled our train for the next day, and we spent the evening getting to know Melody Omaha. It turns out that Omaha was just a code name that her husband made up, but she enjoyed Mari calling her "Mrs. Maha" so much that she refused to tell us what their real last name was. To this day, I still do not know. They are the 'Mahas, and if I have anything to say about it, that is the way history will always remember them.

The next day, we caught our train on time, and though there was still a deep pit of longing in my stomach that only Mari could fill, I felt better about leaving her with Mrs. Omaha then with the militarized sprites. Omaha told us to go to Victoria's, an Italian restaurant in Mason City, and order one glass of sparkling water, one glass of regular water, an antipasto sampler, and ask for a bottle of ketchup. Kirk ordered, and the waiter, who was actually Italian, looked at him in disgust and mumbled under his breath as he walked away, "Americans and their ketchup."

When our food arrived, it was a different staff member who brought it. He handed the ketchup bottle to me and said, "Sorry, it's an off-label brand," and then he walked away quickly. I looked down at the bottle and felt perplexed. It was not an off brand at all, though the label was slightly askew and peeling off. I could not help myself and pulled at the corner of the label. It came off easily. On the reverse side was a small holographic image, though I could not quite make out what the image was.

I showed it to Kirk, and he nodded. "We used these in reconnaissance missions during the war. You have to complete the circuit. There's just enough electricity to watch the message and then it self-destructs." He dabbed his napkin in the regular ice water and squeezed out a few drops onto the image. There was a puff of pink smoke, and then the holographic image began to move like a movie playing on a screen. The video was of Clarington station. The same place we had just arrived at. Words accompanied the camera, as it followed a man who jumped down onto the tracks and walked into the tunnel. "At 2:30, the East tracks en route to Kennedy City will be closed for maintenance. Follow them for two miles. Knock four times on a maintenance door." Then the video vanished as the paper label dissolved into tiny strands.

Kirk looked at his watch. "Hmm…we have an hour. Might as well enjoy our lunch." He started eating the antipasto sampler and browsing the menu. I ordered a salad, and Kirk ordered a medium fire-roasted pizza. When we paid the tab, all that was left on the table was a barely touched salad. I was too nervous to eat.

At Clarington station, we followed the signs to Kennedy City and took the stairs down to the East tracks. The entire section, including the waiting platform, was empty, and no one seemed to notice when we ducked under the chain with the yellow maintenance sign hanging on it. Kirk jumped down onto the track with little effort, and he helped me down carefully. The tunnel was dark, though there were lights spaced out about 100 yards from each other, so it was not pitch black. I'll be honest; I have never been fond of tight spaces, and I felt a little claustrophobic—even with the lights. I swear I could hear dripping water somewhere, but the dirt beside the tracks was dry. Trains were still running in other tunnels, so at times we would hear them coming. They were so loud, I felt like my heart was going to beat out of my chest. What if there was a train on the tracks after all? Where would we go? What if this was all an Ex Natu trick, and we had left Mari in danger? Kirk seemed to sense my unease in those moments, and he would reach back and take my hand, squeezing it for assurance. The trip took much longer than I expected a two-mile walk would, though I did not have a watch like Kirk. It also felt like we were walking up hill, but it was impossible to tell since we were completely enclosed in a cement tunnel. Or maybe it was just that the anticipation made time move slower? Whatever the case, we finally found the maintenance door.

Kirk knocked three times. I elbowed him and held up four fingers. He shrugged and knocked once more.

No one answered. "You did the knock wrong," I accused.

"How do you do a knock wrong?" Kirk laughed then shook his head. "This cloak and dagger stuff isn't at all how it works. I feel like I'm stuck in a bad comic book."

"That's why we need you, Kirk. Knock again." I pointed at the door.

He shrugged and raised his fist to knock again, but the door swung open. A small rectangular sprite, with long belts full of ammunition draped over its back, aimed the multi-barreled muzzles of two gatling guns at us. "You have three seconds to provide the password," the sprite said.

Password? Omaha had not given us a password. "Kirk?" I clung to my husband in terror.

"Omaha, are you in there?" Kirk yelled.

"You have two seconds," the sprite said.

Kirk pushed me backwards behind him and pulled two knives from his jacket that I did not even know he had.

"You have one second," the sprite said. The muzzles began to spin. It was going to gun us down.

Kirk flashed forward and sliced quickly through the belts; bullets tinkled to the ground. He kicked the sprite at a its bottom corner, knocking it off kilter, and then Kirk's other foot left the ground, pushing himself up off the door jamb, spinning into the air just as the sprite said, "your time has expired," Kirk landed on it hard, straddling it from above. His body weight tipped the already off-balanced sprite forward. It began to fire the bullets that were already loaded in the multi-chambers. The spinning of the turrets stuttered and stopped as the cut belts twisted into the gears of the sprite.

When the shooting stopped; my eyes were squeezed shut. I had thought for sure I was going to die, but I was not even wounded. I opened my eyes and saw Kirk prying a panel off the sprite's side. He shoved one of his knives inside and severed a handful of wires. The sprite went dark.

"That was unnecessary," a voice called from inside the door.

Kirk stood up and sheathed his knives. "Because it was firing blanks?" He stepped over to me, looked me over, then pulled me into his embrace. My heart was firing nearly as fast as the stupid sprite's guns had been.

"If you knew, why did you have to destroy it?" Omaha stepped out of the room and bent down to look over his sprite. He was not wearing his mask, and the corners of his mouth were turned down in disappointment.

Kirk held me tight. "My wife didn't know, and frankly, I'm tired of playing spies." He pushed me behind him again and had a knife in his hand faster than I thought possible. "If someone with real training wanted you dead," the knife was at Omaha's throat before the man knew what was happening, "you'd be dead."

Omaha's eyes were wild. He started to call for help from his sprites, "Dikaió—"

He couldn't get the words out because Kirk's other hand snaked out and caught hold of his tongue. "Your tech isn't going to save you from someone like me."

"Kirk!" I screamed.

My husband looked back at me. His face was an expressionless terror: more robot than a sprite ever was. Then he let go of Omaha's tongue and pulled the knife away from his throat. Omaha fell backwards and scrambled back into the room on his hands and knees; his hand touching at his throat to make sure he was not cut. Kirk walked back to me, and then turned to the terrified man on the ground. "So, did we pass your little test?"

Omaha's eyes blinked rapidly, "I don't…maybe I shouldn't have…"

"Life is full of miscalculations," Kirk shrugged. "You make one in a war and you're dead. And that is what you're proposing isn't it? War with the Ex Natu? If you want to win—this," Kirk held up his knife, "is what you need."

Omaha slowly stood up and nodded. "Come with me."

We walked into a room full of monitor screens. Computer code was streaming across some of them; others were tuned into global news about the Ex Natu. I assumed this must be Omaha's workstation, as there was an old metal office desk off to one side. Another man I had never met sat at a keyboard there, typing furiously; his eyes flashing over all of the screens. He didn't even notice us, until he realized I was standing in front of one of the rows of machines. "Do you mind?" he called. I moved out of the way. Omaha crossed in front of him quickly and pulled on one of the light sconces on the opposite wall. A door in the wall slid open, and on the other side was a large underground room. There were at least a hundred people walking around inside.

Kirk laughed. "All that security for that door," he pointed at the one we had just entered, "and this one is just a pull on the light?"

Omaha looked over his shoulder at us and shrugged then he turned and handed Kirk a Dikaió command bracelet. "You'll need this until we christen you into the system. It will allow you access to the Dikaió."

"So, anyone with one of these bracelets can use your weapons?" Kirk asked.

"For now. It's a system in progress," Omaha answered.

"Does anyone outside this room have access to these?" Kirk held up the bracelet.

"I've only made four, and they are all here. They were designed for training purposes during development, but with the new christening protocols, they're really close to being obsolete." Omaha motioned excitedly. "It's all based on verbal recognition, predictability programs, and genetic encoding: real next-gen stuff, you know?"

Kirk shook his head and put on the bracelet. "Is that how my wife can use it without a bracelet?"

"Yes, she was a beta tester. We were able to use the christening protocol long distance; it was a momentous breakthrough." Omaha was getting more excited about his work.

"Are there different levels of 'christening?' Kirk continued his interrogation.

"We can give each person different permissions within the Dikaió, if that's what you mean." Omaha led them to a conference room.

"Individualizing permissions for an army isn't going to work. We'll need to sit down and plan out what ranks have access to which features." Kirk took a seat at the conference table without being asked. I sat next to him.

Omaha nodded absently, "Of course. That makes sense." He paused, and his eyes widened. He got excited thinking about the idea. "That could work for other things too! Dikaió, make a note," he called into the air. "We need ranks of Dikaió christenings." He sat at the head of the table and pressed a red button on an intercom. "Send in the other leaders, please. It's time to begin."

In short order, the eight other chairs were filled with men and women. They all looked at each other with a mix of suspicion and wonder. Omaha stood up and said, "Dikaió, close the doors and engage silent mode." The doors closed, the windows turned opaque, and all the background noise of the underground facility vanished. "I know that you all have not met before, but you all are in the same position. *We* are all in the same position. We have non-permitted families, and we want to keep them. We've chosen to let our genes live forever through our lineage like human beings were created to do, and we're willing to fight for our families."

A tall man in an expensive suit with slicked back hair and a curled mustache interrupted. "Your Dikaió sprites are impressive, Omaha, but do you think they're enough to take down the Ex Natu? They pretty much rule the world at this point."

"They are not enough," Kirk responded. "We'll need real soldiers. Far more than are in this room or this building. The Ex Natu are millions strong. Do we have those numbers?"

Omaha smiled. "You all act as though I'm calling for an attack on the Ex Natu tomorrow. Colonel Knenne, you served in the Ex Natu military. Where do they see their greatest threats coming from?"

Kirk thought for a while. "Now that the Southeast Asia Islands are subdued, there are no credible threats to the Ex Natu."

Omaha turned to a blond-haired man dressed in blue slacks and a white buttoned-down shirt. "Representative Aiworth, you're a leader in the global legislature. Where are the Ex Natu looking for families that are defying the ban on children?"

The man shook his head. "As far as I know, no such searches exist."

Omaha nodded. "The Ex Natu can't imagine anyone in the developed world would give up immortality for the chance to have children. For the last forty years, all we've heard is the messaging that having children will mess up our future, and they think we've bought into it—but there are many who have not. Maybe we are not millions strong like the Ex Natu armies, but if our goal isn't to destroy them today, if we can hide for now, our numbers will naturally grow, while their numbers will inevitably diminish. That's their plan, right? Stop reproduction and let the current generations die out, so there won't be so many people."

Kirk slapped the table. "Your plan is to hide and breed? That's the stupidest thing I've ever heard. That's exactly where the Southeast Asian Islands failed. Why bring me here if you don't want to fight the Ex Natu?"

Omaha held up his hands. "I do want to fight the Ex Natu. I want you to fight them on two fronts: number one, defending our families, teaching each new generation of children we bear to be soldiers, and number two, thinning out the Ex Natu. Remember the Ex Natu that died in the train accident? The Dikaió can be executed in just about everything from household items to entire buildings. I'm imagining a world where everything is a weapon, and every casualty is an accident. When our populations are better adjusted, we can bring the war public."

"You want me to be a terrorist? An assassin?" Kirk scoffed. "There's no honor in that."

Omaha shot back. "Was there any honor in what the Ex Natu did in the Southeast Asian Islands? We are fighting for the survival of our way of life!"

My husband looked down at his hands, darkness shrouding his eyes in shame for the part he had played in the war.

Omaha pressed the point. "If our children and children's children are to survive, the Dikaió must be used to thin the Ex Natu's numbers."

"No!" A woman with red hair and a white blazer shouted. "I'll not be a party to murder. I will fight for my family with an enemy that's fighting back, but I'll not be a murderer."

Omaha sat down in a huff. "In that case, the Colonel is probably right. We don't currently have the numbers to beat the Ex Natu, and we may never have them."

Representative Aiworth spoke then, "I've seen the projected population counts. They won't have a fighting force in fifty years. If we could lull them into believing that there is no resistance, their numbers will thin naturally without us having to murder anyone."

Omaha leaned back in his chair and sighed. "If that's true, there may be a way we could keep the children hidden and secret while training them to fight. I've been working on a kind of cloaking shield. I'm working on calibrating it to hide smaller cities."

"Even from satellites?" Kirk asked.

"Yes. At smaller scales, it's been able to cloak all detection," Omaha nodded.

Kirk leaned forward. "That's something the Southeast Islands didn't have. Maybe then, in a few generations, we would have the forces we need."

I interjected, "But continuing to secretly infuse the Dikaió into everything would give us a decent defense if we needed it, right?"

A larger man who was bald with out-of-control facial hair smiled and spoke over me, taking my comment as his own, "Yes, let's focus on preparing the next generation and spreading the Dikaió through the world in case we need it for self-defense."

Kirk rapped the table with his knuckles and rolled his eyes at the large man. I loved him for it and touched his arm. His cheek twitched a barely noticeable wink in my direction. Then he turned to Omaha. "Can you make it so that no one with nano sprites in their body can use the Dikaió? We don't want this power you've created to fall into the wrong hands."

Omaha thought for a moment and nodded. "I think so. Yes, I think so." He stood up and began to pace in excitement. "Yes, I think the bio-electric feedback from the nano-sprites could be used as a signal to send a no-write message to the christening program."

Kirk nodded. "Look, I'm not going to be a terrorist, an assassin, or a murderer—but I had a dream of putting war behind me when I came home. If you can hide us, I would be happy to adopt that dream to raise a family and live a quiet life. It sounds ideal. However, if the Ex Natu find out about us, and we're not ready for them, all this goes away. Our first steps need to focus on your strategic camouflage, hiding our families, so no one finds them. Until your city camouflage is ready, we can never show our elderly or our children before we're ready."

Omaha nodded, "I've started working on a prototype under the Capitol Building downtown, and there are others in undisclosed locations."

Kirk shook his head. "Mason City is an Ex Natu city. It's too dangerous."

Omaha raised his hands in frustration. "There's nothing I can do. In order to requisition the parts I need from the Ex Natu, the project has to be run through a government grant. It's not like tankers of xenon gas are just lying around for the taking. I'm ordering more than I need for the other locations, but you might have to consider taking this city in a few years, Colonel."

"Do the Ex Natu know what you're building?" Kirk's voice became menacing.

"Of course not," Omaha shook his head. "They think it's a new environmentally friendly energy source."

Kirk mused. "The Ex Natu can never know the secret of what you're building, no matter what."

The Library

Mallory froze. Colonel Knenne was talking about the Mason City light. Was he going to sabotage it? Is that why the calibration was off? She could not read anymore, knowing what was coming. She closed the book and sighed. Alex was nodding off but trying to keep reading. Caleb was on the floor snoring. He had propped about six books under his head and was drooling down the covers. She stood up and stretched. It was time to go back to her room and crawl into that cozy bed. She looked around the inner chamber and realized she had no idea which row to walk down to find her room, and she had no desire to get lost in these tiny aisles. Mallory looked down at Caleb and wondered if that's why her big lug of a man had laid down here. She shrugged and laid down next to him, curling up and using his shoulder as a pillow. Then she fell fast asleep.

"What are you doing?!" a voice screamed.

Mallory jolted out of her sleep as she was violently bucked off Caleb's shoulder. Caleb was squirming and yelling, "Ow! Ow!" Mallory rolled to her right and shifted onto her hands and knees. She was not sure what she was going to use to fight off their attacker, but she was ready. Then she started to laugh.

The Archivist was smacking Caleb in the face with a large fluffy pillow. "Those books are over five hundred years old, and you're drooling all over them! Sound the alarm! The barbarians are at the gates! Get off! Get off!"

Caleb rolled Mallory's way, and the Archivist knelt gently down and retrieved the books from the floor. "How will I ever find John Updike replacements? Do you have any idea what you've done?"

Caleb sat on the floor at Mallory's feet blinking up at the old woman. "I was tired," he said matter-of-factly, as he used the back of his hand to clean the spittle off his beard.

The Archivist threw the pillow at him. "I thought you might be when I saw your room was empty. That's why I brought some pillows down, but to find you like this—with my books—it's unbearable."

Caleb reached for one of the books. "Did I really ruin them?"

The Archivist jumped back, cradling the books in her arms. "Don't touch them! Don't you dare touch them!" She scrutinized the covers and then sighed. "They're not irreparable—thanks be."

Mallory looked around the chamber then. Alex was not there, but the Administrator's history book was on the table. "Where's Alex?"

"Sleeping in her room like a human being. The two of you seem to be taking some time to house train, but at least that one understands what a bed is for," the Archivist turned around. "Breakfast will be in the dining room in one hour." And with that she walked down one of the aisles and disappeared.

"Easy enough for her to say. How do we get out of this maze?" Caleb waved his hands at all the rows of books.

Mallory scanned the tops of the cases until she found Alex's circle and pointed at it. "Well, Alex is in her room." The two of them headed down the aisle where the circle appeared with Mallory leading the way, but then Mallory paused. She read the little metal plaque on the shelves out loud, "fat-gut 700-702." She laughed.

Caleb tried to look around her. "What? What's funny?"

She pointed at the sign. "Fat-Gut shouldn't be too hard to remember next time we want to get to bed."

Caleb laughed too. "Hey, it's my lifelong ambition."

"Getting to bed?" Mallory arched an eyebrow and smirked.

"No, getting a fat gut." Caleb tried to stick out his stomach, but it was too thin to amount to much.

"You've got a long way to go to rival the Smith Guild leader," Mallory giggled.

"And I can't wait to get started on the challenge! Maybe we should go straight to the dining room?" He began to look at the tops of the shelves. "I bet that's where the Archivist went."

Mallory grabbed his arm. "Let's figure out how to get to our room first—then we'll get food."

Caleb looked down at her and draped his arm over her shoulders. "Mrs. Aiworth, we really do need to work on your priorities." He sighed and extended his palm outward. "Lead on, lovely lady. Lead on."

It only took a few moments to find the door to the stairwell that led to the hallway with their rooms, and soon, the couple found their suite. Mallory yawned when she saw the bed. She had not even had a chance to lay down in it yet. She leapt onto the snow-white comforter and was immediately enveloped in a cloud of coziness. The bed was cool to the touch, but her body heat was soon reflected back to her, and she warmed up fast.

"Mallory! Mallory!" Caleb's voice sounded concerned.

"What is it!" Mallory tried to leap from the bed, but just like her husband the day before, she had been swallowed by its softness. It was like fighting against quicksand to get out of the thing. Finally, she remembered how Caleb managed it and rolled off onto the floor. The carpet was thick and soft, and she landed gently. She pushed herself up quickly and spun around, crouched low and ready for danger. "What is it!" she yelled again.

"You fell asleep," Caleb said. "We're going to miss breakfast." He danced impatiently from foot to foot.

Mallory relaxed a little and ran a hand through her hair. It was going to take time to stop living like they were being hunted. "How long was I out for?"

"I don't know. Maybe ten seconds." Caleb shrugged.

"Ten seconds?!" Mallory howled. "I closed my eyes for ten seconds, and you woke me up?"

Caleb ran a hand through his bushy yellow hair and smiled, "It's breakfast, Mal. Breakfast."

She crouched back into her attack position. "I'm going to kill you." She leapt at him, tackling him to the ground. She poked at his ribs playfully, and he squirmed below her.

"No, no!" he yelled. "You know I'm ticklish."

"Oh, for pity's sake!" Alex's voice sounded from the open doorway. "You all have a door now. Use it!"

Mallory looked over her shoulder laughing, "Good morning, Alex!"

"It was until I got woken up by you two." Alex blew hair out of her eye and stormed back out of the room, slamming their door closed behind her, followed by the softer slam of her own door across the hall.

"Breakfast is going to be ready in a few minutes, Alex!" Caleb called after her, though it was unlikely she heard him.

Mallory's brow furrowed. "I'm going to take your breakfast and make you—" she paused, trying to think of a better way to end the idiom.

"Eat it?" Caleb laughed and finished the phrase for her.

Mallory growled, "That's it, buster!" She started poking at his ribs again, and the man squealed like a girl while he bucked, trying to get away from his wife's attack.

When he finally grew tired of her poking, he wrapped his arms around her and flipped the two of them over, so that he was on top of her. "Okay, Mrs. Aiworth. Now, it's my turn!"

Mallory narrowed her eyes and smiled. "Oh?" She looked at his lips and then back to his eyes.

He mirrored her smile, but just as he leaned in close to kiss her, a small house sprite appeared through one of the panels in the wall. It was carrying a rectangular screen on a silver tray. The screen lit up, and the Archivist's face appeared. She looked them over and said, "Oops! Well, this is embarrassing."

Caleb rolled over and let Mallory up. "I hope you're calling about breakfast," he fumed.

The Archivist's eyes narrowed. "Look, after what you did to my books—and this is my Library, you're just a guest—and furthermore, well…" She blinked and tilted her head then she softened a bit. "I'll have the sprites knock from now on."

Caleb smiled, "It's okay, ma'am. We've only been here one day. We'll get used to each other, and I'll learn the rules."

The Archivist shook her head and wagged a finger on the little screen. "Don't try to use your smooth political training on me, kid. There's nothing you were taught about reading and manipulating people that I don't know ten times more about."

Caleb smiled more broadly, "I'm excited to learn everything you have to teach us, ma'am. Would you like us to come for breakfast now?"

The Archivist reached toward the screen. "Only if you want to eat," she said abruptly, and the screen went blank. The sprite shuffled back into the wall.

Caleb roared with laughter. "She's crotchety, but I like her."

Mallory stuck out her bottom lip. "What is it with you and older women? First, Reddy Lamarr and now the Archivist."

Caleb looked at her and touched her cheek tenderly. "My! You're cute when you're jealous. But Reddy wasn't old—at least she didn't look it. I can at least understand why you were jealous of her. She was kind of cute, in a mature sort of way," he smirked.

Mallory growled and grabbed hold of his ears playfully. "She was ancient!"

"Owww!" Caleb squirmed and laughed. "Come on, Mal. She couldn't have been more than ten years older than us."

"I can't remember a time when she wasn't Sprite Master.

Can you?" Mallory reasoned.

"Well, maybe a little more than ten years older than us," Caleb allotted.

"She was an old crone!" Mallory accused, and then pulled his head down to kiss her. "We're finally alone now. You and your YOUNG wife."

Caleb smiled mischievously. "We are, aren't we?"

"Uh-huh!"

"There's just one problem," Caleb leaned in close.

"What's that?" Mallory smiled up at her handsome husband.

"I'm starving!" Caleb leapt off the floor and ran to the door.

Mallory growled again, rolling over and wrapping herself around his leg. Caleb got the door open and dragged her out into the hallway.

Alex was coming out of her door at the same time, and when she saw the two of them, she rolled her eyes. "Oh! C'mon, you guys! Can we just focus on what we're here to do? Enough with the shenanigans!"

Mallory let go of Caleb's leg and pushed herself back on her knees then stood up. "Oh, Alex. We're just having some fun."

"Yeah!" Caleb agreed. "You know, being chased for days by wolves and nearly killed by the Ex Natu has really changed you!"

Alex's eyes narrowed. "You forgot being burned in a fire, nearly killed by a fire sprite, and being banished from our city, which is now in mortal danger from a mistake I made."

Caleb spread his hands out with the palms up as if to say, "You see what I mean?"

Alex huffed and stormed down the hall toward the dining room. "It's time to grow up," she called behind her.

The married couple watched her go and then looked at each other solemnly. Slowly they began to grin in concert, and then they both burst into laughter. Mallory grabbed her husband's hand and whispered in his ear, "Please let breakfast wait just a few more minutes."

He looked down into her eyes, grinned broadly, and followed her back into their room, closing the door behind him.

Several minutes later, Mallory and Caleb entered the dining room giggling like children who had gotten away with some innocent mischief and took their place at the table. Alex rolled her eyes and nibbled at a slice of toast. The Archivist looked at them soberly, seemingly irritated with their noisy intrusion, but Mallory could not help but notice that Caleb had a double portion of eggs, bacon, toast and fruit on his plate, compared to what she and Alex had. She snaked out a hand and grabbed one of Caleb's strips of bacon. "You don't mind, do you?" She giggled and shoved the whole strip in her mouth.

"Hey!" He yelled, covering his plate protectively with his arm and angling his back away from his wife.

Alex sighed heavily, but her eyes kept dropping to the Archivist's wrist.

Mallory followed her gaze and asked, "Hey, is that one of the early Dikaió bracelets? The ones the first Matriarch wrote about in the Chronicles? The ones they used before we had the christening?"

Alex glared at her and then looked furiously at her plate.

The Archivist did not notice Alex's behavior but self-consciously covered the bracelet and nodded. "Yes, it is."

"Don't you have a christening?" Caleb said after swallowing his bite.

The Archivist sighed. "Of course, I have a christening. I was christened a Dikaió Archivist as a child, but there's only so much an Archivist can do with the Dikaió: more than a Chorus, but not much more. Every other person with a different christening that I knew is gone," she paused and looked around the Library. "Without access to all of the Dikaió, I could have never built and maintained this Library, the grounds it sits on, or the light that protects it." She held up the bracelet. "This bracelet helps me do all of that."

Alex spoke then, "Are there more? Or is that the only one?"

Mallory answered, "Omaha made four, right?"

The Archivist nodded and fidgeted in her chair. She was clearly uncomfortable with this conversation. "There were four originally, but that was nearly three centuries ago. If the other three still exist, they have been lost to time."

Alex asked, "Can it work like a Syntec and give us new christenings?"

The old woman looked relieved. She stood up from the table. "Yes, but not until you're ready. I never did buy into that whole christening a toddler thing. You should understand your role before you're given the power to just say whatever you want." A kitchen sprite sped around her and grabbed her empty plate. "Keep reading the histories, and by the end of your training, you'll know what you're getting into. Who knows? By the time you're done, you may not even want to get the Dikaió back. It's a curse really." And with that the old woman walked out of the room.

"A curse?" Alex asked no one in particular. "Life without the Dikaió is a curse, not the other way around." She turned to Mallory. "I know from the *Administrators' Chronicles* that the Omahas had two of the Dikaió Dominus bracelets, but they were lost in the Mason City accident. The Dominus bracelet she's wearing can't be theirs."

"Dominus?" Mallory wondered. "Mine mentioned the bracelets, but not what they were called. I haven't got to the Mason City accident yet, though there was a mention of the light being built below the city." She shuddered remembering the ruins they had traveled through.

Caleb interrupted. "Clearly our books were written by different people at different times. Mine starts long after the Mason City explosion with the founding of Hoffen City and the appointment of the Dikaió Athenos as Governor. The christenings and their abilities in the Dikaió were recorded in a book called *The Dikaió Librum.* There's no mention of any bracelets in my version of the *Chronicles* at all, so far."

Mallory was about to suggest that they should debrief and go through what they had learned so far, but her fork suddenly scraped bare plate. She could not believe her food was gone. Her stomach still felt empty. Caleb's was empty as well, but Alex still had some eggs and bacon left on hers. "Are you going to eat that, Alex?" she asked.

Alex pushed her plate across the table to Mallory.

Caleb looked sideways at his wife. He reached for a piece of Alex's bacon in front of her, but Mallory stabbed at his hand with her fork. "Mine!" she yelled and growled at him.

He pulled away quickly. "Yikes!"

Mallory shrugged as she stuffed all the bacon into her mouth. "I'm sorry, but I'm starving," she mumbled as she threw in the rest of the eggs too.

Alex laughed. "If you two ever do have children, and they eat like you, you'll never be able to afford to keep them."

Caleb smiled. "I'm sure Mallory will sacrifice and share her food with them."

"Me?" Mallory protested. "Why can't you sacrifice and share YOUR food with them?" Alex's plate was now empty too.

Caleb stood up and stuck out his stomach, there was a little lump where breakfast had yet to digest, but otherwise he was still quite skinny. "I can't do that. How will I ever get as big around as the Smith Guild leader?"

Alex groaned. "Okay, okay. Enough. Mallory, it sounds like your book starts earliest. Tell us what you know so far."

Mallory nodded and recounted the story of Kirk, Eva, and Mari Knenne; the Ex Natu; the Omahas; the Dikaió; and the beginning of the resistance. "And that's where I couldn't keep my eyes open anymore."

Alex started recounting her section of the history, "The first entries in the Administrators' book were written by Mari Nelson: General Knenne and the Matriarch's daughter."

Mallory leaned forward. "What? Mari was the first Administrator? How is that?"

Alex flexed her gloved hands and began to tell the story:

The Chronicles of Humanity's Administrators

My name is Mari Nelson, christened first Administrator out of necessity rather than desire. I begin this record with a hurting heart. The loss of Mason City weighs heavily on all of us, and the loss of so many has left the certainty of our cause in doubt. Many of the resistance had relocated to Mason City in anticipation of the protection and freedom to live openly with our children that Omaha's plasma field offered. Besides Omaha, none of the other Council members were within the city limits when the shield was activated, as they had chosen a more defendable location for a capitol city: a city built in secret behind camouflaging holograms called Hoffen City. A plasma field has been constructed beneath its foundation as well, but after what happened to Mason City, who can guess if that option will ever be available to us? My father, General Knenne, has little hope that our campaign will be successful against the Ex Natu without the shields. Holograms will not stop an attack, and time is no longer on our side. If the Ex Natu were unaware of our presence before, we have certainly garnered their attention by detonating an entire city.

Our one hope is the Dikaió, and even that may fail us since the Omahas' Dominus bracelets were lost in the explosion. Without them, we are completely reliant on the christening system, which Omaha had not yet completed.

My mother was appointed Matriarch and a Dikaió Syntec, so she has the permissions necessary to assign the roles that Omaha had finished. Thankfully, one of those roles was the Dikaió Administrator, so at least some of the small-arms and sprite-centered military applications of the Dikaió are available to us. The Council called on my father to take that responsibility, but he refused. He has never trusted the Dikaió and prefers his own two hands and the familiarity of a gun or knife for battle. I, however, have trained in the art of Dikaió warfare my whole life, and now that my daughter Raza is weaned, I was the logical choice to wear the mantle.

My first task is to prepare a defense against Ex Natu retaliation. All of our sources suggest that they are not entirely sure what happened. Thanks to Omaha's brilliance and my father's tactical knowledge, our resistance has managed to remain hidden for nearly thirty years. However, they are connecting the dots quickly. All the news outlets have switched from calling the explosion an unfortunate accident to an act of terrorism by an unknown group. While we cannot stop the Ex Natu from examining the scene of the explosion and piecing together what clues they can from that site, my father is convinced that the underground bunker in Clarington Station was protected from the explosion—though we have not been able to establish contact with survivors, if they exist. It would have been simple to use the secret tracks connecting Clarington Station to our forces in Hoffen City, but the explosion collapsed the tunnel. The underground tracks were going to be the only entrance to Mason city after the field was activated.

As it stands, we'll have to travel above ground to get to the city. I've put together a team to find possible survivors and remove any evidence of our existence before the Ex Natu find either. If Omaha and my father have taught me anything, it's that the best way to defend against the Ex Natu is to withhold as much information from them as possible for as long as possible. Our ground team consists of myself, my father General Knenne, Omaha's son Abraham christened a Dikaió Atheno, and six Dikaió Choruses as support. My husband Jacob Nelson wanted to join the party as well, but he's the only other person left that understands anything about the holographic shield generators. He's been assigned to research what went wrong and fix that issue in Hoffen City before the shields are activated. Plus, one of us needs to be with our little Raza. Besides, I have my own reasons for wanting to go on this mission. While I do expect that my father is right that some of our resistance members survived the explosion in the bunker, my secret hope is that we'll find at least one of Omaha's Dominus bracelets hidden in his offices there. At least with them, we'll have a hope of winning this war.

I reread the above entry and cannot believe how naïve we were in thinking we could just walk in under the Ex Natu's noses. I don't know if they knew we were coming, or if they discovered us after we were there, but there's no hiding the war any longer. The good news is that the Dikaió has proven to be everything Omaha had hoped it would be and more.

We arrived at Mason City after dark. The forest on the outskirts of the city were on fire; well, it was not quite fire. The flames were an eerie pink that looked almost like pulsating, glowing bubblegum. We had to skirt quite a ways North to find a way through the forest fire. If we had been on foot, it would have been nearly impossible, but my father had the foresight to bring flying sprites, rather than the slower but more conspicuous cycle sprites. The flying sprites did not have the range of cycle sprites, but they made up for it in speed and stealth. We covered the distance fairly quickly, though not nearly as quickly as we would have flying in open sky. Instead, we hovered at ground level, weaving between trees and stones.

Normally, I quite enjoy riding a flying sprite and the way the wind feels in my hair. I have quite a few fond childhood memories of the experience; though as a teenager, I realized these outings were just training exercises with my father. I suppose learning how to accurately fire a rocket launcher from the hip while executing a loop-de-loop should have been a clue regarding the purpose of our father-daughter dates. When I made that realization, I started using the Dikaió, to fire several weapons simultaneously with an accuracy my father could not match. After that, the exercises stopped. I guess my training was complete. But still, every time I fly a sprite I think fondly of those days, and some small part of me wishes we could go back to the simplicity of a father, his little girl, and a precision rocket hitting its target. I felt suddenly very aware of the weight of the several weapons strapped to my body. They made it difficult to sit comfortably on the sprite.

But those stray thoughts of days long gone were quickly disregarded as we rode around Mason City looking for a way through the fire. It was difficult to think of anything other than the burning pink trees, which seemed to blaze without being consumed. Out of curiosity, I pulled back on the sprite's arms and braked, then bent down and picked up a stick, and threw it at one of the burning-but-not-burning trees. The stick turned to a puff of smoke when it touched the fire, completely incinerated, but the tree inside the blaze still stood there in all its fiery glory. "How?" I muttered out loud.

"They're holograms," Abraham called. He had pulled up beside me and stopped. "The trees are gone. All that's left is a holographic plasma forest. The holograms were supposed to hide the city."

"It's downright eerie," I said. "I don't think the Ex Natu would have been fooled."

"Well, the collapse of the plasma field has ruined the effect of the hologram. This isn't what my father planned for it to look like." He looked away from the trees and his voice broke. "None of this was the plan."

I touched his arm gently and got back on my sprite. I felt selfish thinking about missing my childhood with my father. At least he was still here. Abraham was still unmarried, and he had lost his whole family in the explosion. Abraham was just a couple of years younger than me, and we had been friends as long as I could remember. In the early years, we had often been left to play together while our parents planned and plotted the survival of our people and way of life. I smiled at my dearest friend, "C,mon, let's see what we can salvage of your father's dream." He nodded, and we flew quickly forward to rejoin the group.

Omaha's plasma field was supposed to envelope the entire city, and the field had completely surrounded the rim of the perimeter, but rather than forming the bubble it was designed to create, the integrity of the field had failed. Essentially, the bubble popped, coating the city in holographic plasma. It was impossible to know what the interior of the city looked like unless we could get around or through the fiery forest. We made it all the way to the bluffs without finding a single opening at ground level into Mason City. "We could go over." I pointed toward the tops of the trees and the clear sky above them.

"No. That's almost certainly the way the Ex Natu inspectors entered the city. They'll be watching the skies. We'll have to go around to the Aiworth bridge and track back up the tunnel that way," my father said, already leading the party up the bluffs on his way to the Missouri River.

Abraham wondered out loud, "How are we going to get survivors out if the Aiworth is our only exit? We didn't bring enough sprites for that sort of evacuation."

"We didn't bring enough sprites to do any sort of evacuation. We won't be able to plan any kind of logistics until we've confirmed survivors," the General replied. "This is a scouting mission, not a rescue mission."

"But if there are survivors, maybe my mother and father…" Abraham trailed off.

None of us responded. It was an empty hope at best. The Omahas were both integral to the design of the plasma field. They would have been onsite below the Capitol Building when it was activated. The survivors in the bunker would be non-essential personnel that were prepping the move from the underground headquarters to the Capitol Building once the city was subdued.

The bluffs rose about two-hundred feet above the Aiworth bridge and the opening to the tracks leading to Clarington Station. Below us were the raging waters of the Missouri River. My heart wrenched wildly in my chest as we shot off the top of the bluff and hovered over the waters, slowly descending toward the bridge. In my head, I knew that the sprites' gyroscopes and stabilizers were not going to dump us into the waters below, but for better or worse, my body never seemed to listen to my head, and right then, it was pumping me full of adrenaline. It took all my will power not to clamp down hard on the throttle and rocket back to the safety of the tops of the cliffs. Instead, I slowed my breathing as all the children of the resistance learned early in their life. "Mari, you're always only one deep breath away from bravery," the memory of my father's voice said. Somehow, he was right. He was always right.

As we entered the tunnel, the adrenaline had all but passed. "Line up fifty yards apart," I yelled. "Maintain quiet radio contact. If there's a surprise ahead, there's no point in all of us running into it."

My father nodded his approval. "I'll take point," he said just before I could. Then his sprite sped into the tunnel before I could argue with him.

The man had no Dikaió to protect him, yet he was always so foolhardily running into danger. Maybe foolhardy is not quite the right term. I mean, he seemed to come through the danger unscathed every time, but he was getting older, slower. One day his luck was going to run out. I should have been on point, but now, as the next highest level of the command, I was stuck bringing up the rear to lead the retreat if we needed it.

Honestly, the ride through the tunnel was one hundred times more dangerous than the jump off the cliff at the entrance. At the speed the flying sprites moved, one wrong turn could cause any one of us to hit the walls like bugs on a windshield, and yet, my adrenaline did not seem to mind speeding through the tunnel at all. Even the turns felt like little more than a Sunday stroll in the park with my parents. Of course, the speed of the sprites also meant that we made it to our old underground headquarters very quickly. My father was standing by his flying sprite, keeping watch while Abraham used the Dikaió to open the door.

The security room inside looked just the same as it always did, except there was no one at the desk, and the monitors were displaying nothing but static and fuzz. The inner door was still shut. The hairs on my neck raised, and I pulled my weapons from their holsters. I looked to my father, and he also had his weapons ready. The Choruses followed suit and pulled out their weapons, training them on the door. My father's eyes met mine, and he nodded toward the door to the tunnel. I bristled. He wanted me to take up the rear again. The old man was pushing his luck. I was the Administrator. I should have been taking point. I could protect everyone with the Dikaió, but he still outranked me, and I obediently dropped back to cover the door to the tunnel.

My father nodded to Abraham.

"Dikaió, open," Abraham called to the inner door and then presented his identity. "Abraham Omaha, Atheno." The secret door slid open.

Several guns greeted us.

"Stand down!" My father yelled. The sounds of weapons being lowered and sighs of relief echoed through the room and the bunker beyond.

"General Knenne!" A familiar voice called. Governor Aiworth rushed up and clasped my father's hand. "I'm so glad it's you."

The Library

"Hold on. Hold on," Mallory interrupted. "How is there a Governor Aiworth, but Abraham Omaha is the Dikaió Atheno? I thought the Governors were Athenos."

Alex nodded. "I wondered that too. It turns out that the idea of Governorship was around before the Dikaió. This Governor Aiworth was the Governor of Mason City and can't even use the Dikaió at all."

Caleb smiled, "Yeah, but later in Hoffen City he gets the Dikaió because—"

Alex shouted, interrupting him, "Just wait your turn. I haven't even got to the important part yet."

Caleb shrugged. "The only important part of the Mason City rescue was getting my ancestors out." He wrapped his arms around Mallory. "Our ancestors and our children's ancestors."

Mallory blushed, and she touched his arm tenderly.

"Well, maybe." Alex looked down at the table.

Caleb pulled away from Mallory. "What do you mean by that? Are you saying that Governor Aiworth in the Chronicles isn't my ancestor?"

"No," Alex shook her head. "He is, but there's something mentioned in my book that night that means—well, it might mean—" She began to fiddle with the ends of her gloves.

"What is it, Alex?" Mallory felt anxiety rising up like bile in the pit of her stomach.

Alex's voice grew soft, nearly a whisper. "It's about the Ex Natu and the nano sprites."

"Is that the important part you haven't got to yet?" Caleb asked.

"No—well it wasn't, but I guess it's important—at least for you and Mallory." She squirmed in her chair.

"Alex," Caleb coaxed, his demeanor suddenly shifting to the politician mode that the Archivist had laughed at earlier. "Just keep telling the story. We'll figure it out."

Alex sighed in relief, took a deep breath, and then started where she had left off.

The Chronicles of Humanity's Administrators (continued)

"Keep watch at the door, Mari," my father ordered as he patted the Governor's shoulder and walked inside the underground bunker with him, Abraham, and the Choruses.

Keep watch at the door? That was not why I had come along on the mission. I wanted to search Omaha's office for the other bracelets, but I did not argue. I just nodded in silent acquiescence. The General still outranked me, and he was still my father.

I stepped back out into the relative darkness of the tunnel and looked off in the direction of Mason City. There was nothing but silence down that long blackness. I doubted trains would ever run down these tracks again. For all we knew, the entrance at Clarington station had been obliterated in the blast, and there was not even a way the Ex Natu could get into the tunnels. And even if they could, why would they come down here searching for survivors? It did not make any sense to stand here doing nothing. It did not help our cause at all. Not the way the Dikaió would anyway—and what use was the Dikaió if we could not unlock its full potential with a Dominus bracelet?

I looked back into the little room that separated the tunnel and the underground bunker. The secret panel was still open, and I could see people bustling around in the bunker, packing and preparing to evacuate. Cardboard boxes were being tossed into incinerators to destroy any evidence that there was ever a resistance in this space. What would happen if they threw Omaha's belongings haphazardly into one of those boxes? They might incinerate the one thing we could use to win this war. That settled it; I ran through the doors into the bunker. I needed to find those bracelets.

Maybe events would have gone differently if I had stayed at my post.

12

The Chronicles of Humanity's Administrators (continued) *

I wove in and out of people hell bent on leaving nothing incriminating behind. Men, women, children: None of them acknowledged me as I ran past them. Fear was palpable in their expressions; their faces looked white, and it was not just the stark Dikaió lights. Despite years of training with my father, none of these people were ready for a war. It was all just theoretical. They had never been in a real fight, and if the Ex Natu came for us, I wondered if any of us would make it out of here alive. My momentum was fading, drained by the terror in the room, and I could feel my run slowing to a walk. I closed my eyes and took a deep breath. Bravery is always just one deep breath away. When I exhaled, I was running again, lost in purpose.

Omaha's office was just to the left of the main hall. The door was open, and I could see stray papers laying on the floor through the doorway. As I ran inside, I cursed. Filing cabinets stood with their drawers open and empty. His desk had been ransacked and emptied as well. My shoulders slumped. I walked slowly around the desk and pulled the drawers open as far as they would go to see if anything had been missed. The cleaners had been thorough. I lowered myself slowly into his chair and sighed. "Where did you hide them, Omaha?" I whispered. Then on a whim, I called out, "Dikaió, open."

CLICK!

The sound had come from behind me. I spun around in the chair, and my mouth dropped open. A panel in the wall had opened slightly, just like the one in the security room that led to the underground bunker. Omaha loved his cloak and dagger secrets. Behind the pane was a dark staircase leading farther underground. "So, that's where you hid them." I mused to myself and slipped behind the panel into the darkness, closing it quietly behind me. "Dikaió, lights on," I said, and white Dikaió lights sprang to life. I descended into whatever secrets Omaha had hewn into the bluffs beyond the bunker. At the end of the staircase was another door, which opened with a Dikaió command. When I walked through it into the room, Dikaió torches sprang to life, lighting up the space without a command. The room was stark and small with wood paneling and several wooden benches lined the walls. The only other thing in the room beyond the benches and the torches was another small wooden door on the far side that was bolted shut. I smiled. If Omaha had installed a door in a hidden room, then he intended it to be opened. I crossed the room and unbolted the door.

The Library

Mallory slapped the table and interrupted. "It's sounds just like the room that was under City Hall!"

Alex nodded. "Yes, I thought so, too."

"The one where Alex hid during the fire?" Caleb asked.

"I didn't hide in it during the fire, Caleb. I was there before the fire started." Alex crossed her gloved arms.

Mallory bit her lip and tilted her head slightly. "But it does sound exactly like the one under City Hall, with the benches and all."

Alex uncrossed her arms and smiled "And it gets weirder."

Mallory put her elbows on the table and leaned forward, resting her chin in her hands, and stared intently at her friend. "Really? Do tell."

Caleb laughed and leaned backward in his chair. "I don't think anything can be weirder than hiding in a burning building."

"Aiworth! I swear one of these days…" Alex growled finishing her threat under her breath.

Caleb roared with laughter.

"Shush, Caleb," Mallory turned her head slightly toward her husband without taking her chin out of her hands or moving her eyes off Alex. "I want to hear about the room."

"Didn't that room just lead to the beam-and-pillars that made up the foundation of the building?" Caleb ignored his wife.

Alex shrugged, "Maybe. Maybe more if the *Chronicles* are correct."

"More?" Mallory's leg began to dance in anticipation.

"Like a hiding place for fires?" Caleb chuckled.

"I'm going to my room." Alex stood up from the table and started to walk away.

Mallory slapped her hands on the table again and sat up straight. "No, Alex! Tell us what's behind the door." She coaxed her husband. "Please be nice, Caleb. I want to know."

"Okay, okay! I'll stop!" He laughed and rolled his hand in a "please-continue" fashion toward Alex, but neither his smile, nor the mischievous twinkle in his eyes faded.

Alex sat back down and restarted Mari's story where she had left off:

The Chronicles of Humanity's Administrators (continued)

The door swung open grudgingly on old metal hinges. There was only darkness on the other side of the door.

"Dikaió, lights on," I called but nothing happened.

I reached into a pocket of my flak jacket and pulled a small portable Dikaió torch out. "Dikaió, torch on," I said, and it sprung to light, though it did not illuminate much. Inside the room was what looked like a natural cave. I could definitely hear water dripping somewhere inside. I stepped into the darkness and shone my torch around. The rock-hewn chamber was high enough that I couldn't see the top, and it extended into unknown darkness. Several medium-sized cycle sprites were lined up in rows facing away from the stairs into the darkness. I walked over to the nearest one and said, "Dikaió sprite, acknowledge Mari Nelson: Administrator."

The sprite floated about six inches off the ground, small white lights flashed on the top of it, and its headlight illuminated the sprites in front of it. Suddenly all of the other sprites came to life and floated off the ground as well, with all of their headlights pointing ahead. Apparently, they were all linked.

"What is your destination?" I asked. The sprite was silent. Omaha had not given these sprites verbal capabilities. It did not matter. I knew where the sprites were headed: the only place they would be: Hoffen City. Omaha had created an evacuation route through a natural system of caves. I peered into the cave ahead, lit up by the sprites' headlights. There were hundreds of openings. Some were natural, some had clearly been hewn with sprite tools. Omaha was a clever one. It would be impossible to know with certainty, which opening to take. Only these sprites knew where to go, and only a Dikaió user could operate them, which meant the Ex Natu would never find the way. The two cities under the protection of the lights, and the train system connecting them, would have made this subterranean subterfuge unnecessary, but I was glad Omaha hadn't retired these sprites and the tunnels in the surety of his plasma field plans.

Suddenly, a dull rumble sounded above me, and the room shook. Dust and rocks dropped in a haze from the ceiling of the cave.

Surely it could not be a train. With the explosion in Mason City, there was no way the tracks were in use. Then the source of the rumble dawned on me. My eyes went wide, and I ran up the stairs as fast as my feet would carry me. I flew through the little room with the benches and out of the secret panel in Omaha's office. I was met with the sounds of gunshots and screaming. I looked out the office windows down the hallway and could see tear gas swirling around the room. Passing through the smoke like wraiths, Ex Natu soldiers moved with lethal precision. They were dressed in black flak jackets, black masks, and black helmets, swarming into the room, firing assault weapons as they came. No one in the bunker was using the Dikaió. Despite all their training, they were panicked by an actual battle. I knew they had not been ready.

I threw the office door open and ran down the hallway, screaming as I went, "Dikaió sprites, protect me and the civilians!"

Sprites came to life all around the bunker, and their impenetrable silver steel dove in front of the people hunkered around the room. The Ex Natu paused their firing, clearly surprised by the sprites' actions. Using civilian sprites in warfare was forbidden by international treaties and consid- ered an act of terrorism, but those were the same treaties the Ex Natu had used to exterminate billions around the world. Omaha was right that the Ex Natu called everything that did not suit their agenda "terrorism." He refused to be bound by the conventions of modern warfare; a trait my father never liked. My father was sure that honor in warfare would save civilians' lives, but where was the Ex Natu's honor in bursting into a room and firing on unarmed people?

I could see out of the corner of my eye that many of the people who had been so busily moving around earlier were laying on the floor unmoving: more Ex Natu casualties—no, not Ex Natu casualties; they were my casualties—people I had let die by not listening to my father. And then, as if my thoughts had summoned him, my father was beside me. He moved so fast, a gun in one hand and a knife in the other. Like a striking snake, he darted in and out of the shield of sprites flying around me, shooting and slashing at the Ex Natu. Every attack he made was lethal. He never missed; he could not. If he gave the Ex Natu a moment of reprieve, their nano sprites would instantly heal every wound inflicted. Clangs and zings sounded all about us as bullets were deflected by the shield of sprites whirling around the room, while father and daughter moved steadily forward.

I knew my father was trying to protect me just like the sprites, and I could tell by his furtive glances that he was worried about what I was planning. Every glance was a concerned command. "Fight, Mari. Fight!" I ignored him. I could have worked with my father and fought the traditional way. My gun had found its way to my hand by instinct, but my guilt and anger pushed me forward with an alternate plan. An alternate plan that Omaha had devised, not my father. Omaha's plan led me through the Ex Natu soldiers until I was as close to the center of their throngs as I could get. I spread my feet into a battle stance, and I pushed them hard into the floor. I took a deep breath. Then I screamed into the room, "Dikaió alert alpha! Target all Ex Natu. Attack!"

Omaha had spread the Dikaió through everything in the underground bunker. Coffee pots and pencils flung themselves off desks at the Ex Natu. Chairs slipped behind them and tripped them as they floundered backwards before the unexpected attack. Staplers fired their pointed contents at the soldiers. Even pieces of paper were flapping about around them. Desks and ceiling lamps swung wildly at the intruders, and sprites whipped and slashed at them haphazardly. Much of the Ex Natu's own gear had been infused with the Dikaió. The soldiers' guns ripped free from their hands and turned on them. Their clothing and helmets twisted and turned their bodies about like helpless marionettes, dancing themselves to death. The scene might have been comical if it was not so grotesque. It was as if a hurricane were moving through the room, but those of us who were naturally born stood in the center of its eye, completely untouched by the destructive winds of Omaha's magic. But we were equally helpless to look away from the horrors of it: No matter how far from humanity they had turned, the Ex Natu were still men and women behind those masks, and their wanton destruction before a force they had no way to fight back against was hard to watch. Abruptly, just as quickly as it started; everything dropped to the ground, amidst piles of Ex Natu soldiers: all dead.

My father stood by my side panting, his eyes rolling in his head as he looked around the room. He looked like he was going to be sick. Then he threw his gun and knife on the floor and wretched. His voice quavered weakly, "And what of honor, Mari?"

I felt my own stomach swirling in the aftermath of what had just happened. I closed my eyes and breathed deeply. I thought about all the people the Ex Natu had just killed. The Dikaió was horrible, but it was the only weapon we would be able to use to beat a nigh invulnerable enemy. Calm warmth spread slowly through my body: just one breath away from bravery. I touched my father's arm. "It's not about honor. It's about survival," I said quietly.

He shook loose and spun around, towering over me. The veins in his forehead throbbed. "Is that why you deserted your post? Because you don't care about honor?" He pointed at all the death around us. "And without honor where is the survival for all of these? Acting honorably would have avoided all of this. Where were you?"

Normally, I would have looked at the ground and withered before the rage of my progenitor, but this time I met my father's eyes in defiance. "Looking for the Dominus bracelets." I also pointed at the mess in the bunker. "This is only a taste of the Dikaió's power, and it's spreading ever farther into everything and everywhere. If we have those bracelets, we can win this war."

"And you'll be no better than them." My father spat again. He softened. "Mari, we've had this conversation—we've had this conversation with Omaha when he was alive. What you want isn't right. We're not terrorists." He closed his eyes and shook his head. "We're not gods. That future isn't any better than the one they're chasing after." He kicked at a twisted boot of an Ex Natu soldier. "You want to give up your humanity. The Ex Natu, Omaha, you—all suffering from god complexes."

"What are you talking about? You think I want power? It's simpler than that, father. I want to live. I want them to live." I pointed at the rest of the people in the room who were timidly exiting their hiding places. The sounds of mourning began to mount as they discovered who had been lost in the Ex Natu attack. "I want my children to live: your grandchildren! That's why we started this war, isn't it?" I turned away from him, not wanting him to see my angry tears and mistake them for weakness.

"Mari…" He touched my shoulder tenderly.

I sniffed hard and wiped my eyes with the back of my sleeve. As my arm moved across my face, I realized I was still holding my gun. I tossed it away just as my father had. He was right on that account; I was never going to need to use it to fight again. I spoke without turning back to face him. "There's a fleet of cycle sprites below the bunker for evacuation. Get Abraham, and round these people up. We should go."

I expected a reprimand about the chain of command and not giving him orders, but a conflict with the General would have been preferable to what my father said next. "Abraham's dead."

The angry tears I had just wiped away were replaced with sadness, as rebellion became regret. "No!" I stammered, and my knees buckled slightly. I fell towards my father.

He held me up and pulled me in close to his chest. "He

thought you were at the door and ran to protect you when they blew the outer panel."

"No!" I said again. "Dikaió, no!" I yelled into my father's chest. Nothing happened. I cringed as my father tensed. He was right again. Apparently, there was a part of me that thought of the Dikaió as god-like power, but the magic had no more power over life and death then the nano sprites crawling through the dead Ex Natu at our feet.

My father held me for awhile, but he began to fidget uncomfortably. Tender moments were never something a warrior took easily, but for all his faults, he was a loving father. He always let me pull back when I was ready and never pushed me away. I stepped back and wiped away my tears. He changed the subject. "You said there's a way out below?"

I nodded. "Yes, a fleet of cycle sprites below Omaha's office. I don't know if it's enough for everyone, but there's a secret waiting room for people if we need to take multiple trips. How much time do you think we have?"

"Minutes at most." He was already moving toward the office barking orders. "I know it's hard but leave the dead. More soldiers are on the way: many, many more with war sprites." Some people reacted immediately in fear, looking around in panic. Others seemed to not hear him. These were not soldiers. My father bent down and retrieved his gun. He raised it in the air and fired a single shot. Some screamed, some cried, but all eyes turned to him. "Everyone line up here single file!" He barked. An orderly file formed immediately. "Administrator, please show these people the way out," he said to me stiffly.

I slipped by him into the hallway. "This way," I called. The people followed me wordlessly down the stairs into the dark cavern below. When every sprite but one had a rider, I yelled to the crowd. "The rest of you wait in the room with the benches." I could see my father starting to head back to the room with the group that was staying behind. "Father—I mean, General," I called after him.

He paused and looked back at me, and I gestured toward the empty sprite. His eyes narrowed, and he made his way slowly toward me. He lowered his voice to a whisper. "I should stay here with the ones being left behind. They'll need protection."

I whispered in response, "The Dikaió is here. I can protect them." He started to protest, but I cut him off and pointed into the darkness. "I doubt the Dikaió is in there. This group will need you more than the one with me."

His shoulders slumped. He could see the wisdom in what I was saying. "How do I send the sprites back for you when I don't have the Dikaió?"

"There are plenty of christened people in Hoffen City who will be able to send them back." I gestured to the sprite again, and he reluctantly climbed on. "Dikaió sprites, activate," I called out, and the sprites' lights came on as they floated up off the ground. "Take these people to Hoffen City." The sprites shot off into the caves en masse, splitting up into different tunnels. I wondered where they would meet up or if they would all get to Hoffen City using different routes. I tracked them for a short time by the lights reflecting off the caverns, but soon I was standing in darkness and had to pull my Dikaió torch out to find my way back to the waiting room.

We left the door to the caverns open, so we could watch for the returning light of the sprites, but the panel to Omaha's office had a lock on the inside, which I engaged. I stood by the panel for a long time listening for the Ex Natu, and I thought I heard scuffling and voices outside, but it was impossible to be sure. The room was sound-proofed, and no doubt temperature-regulated to scuttle infra-red as well. Omaha thought of everything. Most of the people there, men and women with no children, sat on the benches staring at the floor, but there were some that kept glancing at me nervously. I wanted to believe they were afraid of the Ex Natu soldiers on the other side of the door, but they were not looking at the door. They were looking at me, and when they saw me looking back, they quickly turned away, but slowly their eyes would return to me: wide and apprehensive.

The tension in the room made time stretch unnaturally. I kept checking my watch, expecting hours to have passed, only to find minutes instead. I smiled a bit. If my mother were here, she would be clawing at the walls with her claustro-phobia. I never had that issue, having been stuck indoors in small rooms for nearly the entirety of my childhood, hiding from the Ex Natu. If anything, wide open spaces gave me the willies. I still remember the first time I was old enough to fit in with the never-aging Ex Natu in society; I felt like a rabbit on a wide-open prairie full of hawks. Maybe that is why flying always made me a little jumpy, just little old me in the wide-open sky. The small, enclosed waiting room felt safe to me.

As I studied the wooden walls, I could not help but admire the craftsmanship. The wood in the room ran horizontally to the floor and ceiling, all the way around the room, and it looked almost seamless as if the paneling had been grown together rather than hewn and fitted with human hand. I walked slowly around the room, trying not to trip over the fearful people in my charge, but also very curious all of a sudden about where the middle plank ended, and the next piece began. Then I saw it: a super-fine seam between the two planks. I looked at the beams above and below that one. The top one was about six inches behind it, and the bottom was about six inches in front of it, creating a sort of diagonal line of seams. As my eyes traveled down the line, I found the diagonal line ended and started back at a matching diagonal line of seams toward the ceiling. I traveled around the room again and could not find any other seams in the walls. Even the corners were solid pieces of wood that had been bent at a severe angle. It was the strangest piece of construction I had ever seen.

A commotion in the room disrupted my fascination with the wooden paneling. I tensed and turned toward the door leading to Omaha's office; readying myself for battle with the Ex Natu undoubtedly rummaging on the other side. The door was sealed, and after a moment, I realized that all the faces in the room were turned in the other direction. I slowly turned around and saw the stairway leading to the cave flashing with steadily brightening lights. The sprites had returned. "Okay everyone," I whispered, "let's go. But keep it orderly. There should be room for everyone here."

The people stood quickly and filed down the stairs eagerly. When I reached the bottom, I found my father helping everyone find a sprite. He saw me and walked over. "You were right. The sprites took us straight to Hoffen City."

"Is there a risk of being followed if the door is breached?" I asked looking back up the stairs.

He shook his head. "I don't see how. There are hundreds, maybe thousands of tunnels along the route; I don't think I could find my way back without the sprites, and my memory and navigation skills are pretty good. It would take lifetimes to find the path."

I mounted a sprite and looked at him grimly. "They have that."

"True," he said climbing onto a sprite next to me. "But generations from now, we'll be more than a match for them."

I shrugged and acquiesced the point. The part that made me most uneasy was not that the Ex Natu might eventually find Hoffen City; it was that I had not found the Dominus bracelets. I felt sure Omaha had left them in the bunker somewhere. If the Ex Natu were to find them and unlock the secret of the Dikaió, all would be lost.

The Library

Mallory screamed, "The bracelets are in the paneling!" She straightened her hands like spears and touched the tips of her fingers together moving her elbows apart. "The seams make an arrow, like this." She jutted her chin to the point of her spear.

Caleb swiveled in his chair. "Do you think so?"

"Oh, she's quite correct." The Archivist interjected.

All three teens jumped. The Archivist was sitting in her chair with her feet up on the table. She was tearing small pieces of bread off a roll and nibbling at them. "At least one of them was. That's where I found this." She held up her arm and jangled the bracelet about.

Alex leaned in. "It was just the one?"

"Yes, just the one, but that's all I needed." The Archivist shrugged.

"Did you try to call the sprites to get back to Hoffen City?" Mallory asked.

"Of course." The Archivist scowled. "I wouldn't have had to build that bucket of bolts to go find a Chorus for me if it were as easy as hopping on a cycle sprite and scooting off through the underground tunnels." She threw the leftover roll at the clockwork sprite. It bounced off its head in several pieces, but the bronze sprite did not even flinch. A house sprite appeared quickly and swept up the roll and the crumbs and vanished again. The Archivist sighed and turned back to the group. "It might have saved me years of isolation and helped immensely with the work here." Her face seemed to age before them, as she started to fall back into memories of her past.

Ever the diplomat, Caleb spoke quietly to distract, "Mari probably destroyed the other bracelets."

The Archivist snapped out of her stupor and nodded. "Perhaps, but I doubt she ever found them. She would have used them to take down the Ex Natu rather than use the tactic she chose."

"What did she choose?" Mallory asked.

Caleb did not let the Archivist answer. "The only thing I don't get is how you came to have the *Chronicles* at all? I mean either they were outside the city, and there would have been no record of Mari after the fact, or they were inside the city, and no one here would know about what happened."

"Well, that's a very binary thought process," the Archivist dismissed him, "but I guess I can't expect too much from the generation that got rid of all the books."

"It wasn't us," Mallory defended him.

The Archivist waved away her comments. "That's neither here nor there. Dikaió sprite, bring me an empty book, and a pen and ink." The clockwork sprite whirred away quickly and returned with a small leather-bound book. When the Archivist opened it, Mallory could see that the pages inside were blank white. "Dikaió pen, copy the first page of the *Governors' Chronicles* in this book." The pen sprang off the table, dipped itself in the bottle of ink, and then began to write an exact replica of the *Governors' Chronicles* in a neat font .

"Are all the books here made with the Dikaió?" Mallory was nearly crawling on the table to get a better view.

"Not all. Some, like the one your neanderthal of a husband drooled on, are original non-Dikaió books, but they could be copied just like this if the need arose." The Archivist held up her hand, "Dikaió, cease. Erase the copy from this book." The pen hovered over the book it had been writing in, and the ink on the page floated up from the page, returning to the pen, which soon rested in the ink bottle.

Mallory gasped. "Could all the copies here be erased so easily?"

"No!" The Archivist looked like Mallory had struck her. "Thankfully, no. Once the ink is dry, it would require a chemical process to separate it from the page.

"Oh!" Mallory sank quickly back into her chair. "That's good."

Alex rapped her knuckles on the table for attention. "That's all very interesting, but what did Mari do, Aiworth? We've told you what we read. It's your turn."

Caleb looked at the Archivist as if to ask if she wanted to tell the story. She was probably much more familiar with it than they were, having read all of the *Chronicles*. She just smiled and opened her palms signaling that he should go ahead. Caleb turned to the girls. "Well, the *Governors' Chronicles* begin in Hoffen City when Mari is an old woman…around the time when the old Chorus that your grandparents knew was still a child."

"So, you know where his parents went?" Mallory gasped.

"Well sort of…I know why they left, and why they never returned," Caleb smiled. "Where they went after the fact, who knows?"

The Archivist leaned in toward the three heirs. "I can fill in those details when you're done, young Governor."

"Really? This I have to hear." Caleb turned to the Archivist smiling.

Mallory screamed, "Caleb, please!"

He laughed, "Alright! Alright! Me first." He leaned back in his chair and began.

13

The Chronicles of Humanity's Governors

My name is Jeremy Aiworth, the first official Governor of Hoffen City. My father was the Governor of Mason City and filled that role here as well, though he was never officially affirmed by the Council. His leadership of the city was just a fact that no one even seemed to question, even after he was christened a Dikaió Athenos. Our city has adopted a sort of nepotism in its desire to elevate the idea of family. The Council insisted that I also be christened a Dikaió Athenos and follow my father as Governor when he was ready to retire or in the event of his death. I write these words in celebration of his retirement, thankfully, not the latter. Though I do wonder if I'll be able to fill the shoes of the Governorship that my father carved out for himself here. While the Athenos christening made him much less proficient in the use of the Dikaió than the Matriarch or the Administrator; the christening included a hodgepodge of Dikaió abilities, which included both military and civilian applications, mixed with my father's charismatic personality—not to mention how much the city flourished under his governorship—giving him the support of the magistrates and the guilds. However, my father said they never completely trusted him, and believing that he, Eva Knenne, and Mari Nelson were all too old to keep leading the city. Considering even Mari has grandchildren at this point, I will go on record saying I agree with their sentiment.

We are not Ex Natu, and we should not live as if we are un-aging immortals. Each generation ought to train up the next. With that goal in mind, the City Council established what they're calling the Triad of Governorship, giving the Governor equal status in the government as a check on the Matriarch and the Administrator. Below them on the Council will be the guild leaders. In addition, the Council will include a rotating set of four citizens that are elected democratically, charged with enforcing a smooth rotation of the leadership.

My father had worked a long time to overcome the stigma of his christening, so he championed much of the Council's plan for years. However, the mandatory retirement for the current leaders left him without a place on the Council, and he was outraged at the Council for adopting the policy over his objections. "What am I going to do in retirement?" He yelled at them. "Travel? Like this?" He tugged at his white hair and traced the wrinkles around his eyes. "How long has it been since the Ex Natu have seen an old man, do you think? Almost sixty years, I imagine. Wouldn't that be a surprise?"

"Governor Aiworth, you're ninety-three years old," the City Services Manager pleaded. "You have to pass the mantle of leadership in an orderly fashion. If you died without training in a replacement, think about how the city would fair."

"What would that matter to me? I'd be dead." My father was never a reasonable man.

Mari Nelson, the Administrator, jumped in then. "And what of the Ex Natu? We're the only ones who have ever faced them. If we step down, then what?"

"Administrator Nelson, surely you've trained your son to use the Dikaió to defend our people as well as you." Bud Hages, the Sprite Master threw his hands in the air. "We must adhere to our generational mandate. The decision of this Council is not up for debate."

The Administrator's eyes narrowed, and she leaned over in her seat toward the Sprite Master. "Don't think I couldn't make you see things my way."

"Mother!" Her son Alexander yelled, standing from his seat in front of the Council and taking a step toward her. "Don't."

"And why shouldn't I? We've only survived as long as we have because of the leadership they're trying to force out."

"Think of Caroline's future. What kind of legacy would

you be leaving her if there were a civil war in our city?" he asked pleadingly.

She sat back in her chair upon hearing the name of her granddaughter invoked. Then she waved her hand dismissively. "She thinks the Ex Natu are a bogeyman that hides under the bed at night, and so do you." She stood up abruptly. "They've wiped entire nations off the map without batting an eye. What are you going to do about them when they come without us to lead?"

"Mother, the day is going to come when you're not here. You need to teach us how to defend the city if we need to." He turned to the Governor and the Matriarch. "You need to teach us how to continue what you've started."

Eva slammed her cane on the ground and blue streaks of lightning sparked out from the bottom of it. The Dikaió lights in the room flashed and sparked with blue lightning as well. The old Syntec spoke with more force than her frail frame suggested she could, "Silence!"

The room obeyed.

Even her daughter rolled her eyes and sat down in a huff.

"The Council has ruled. The time for discussion has come to an end." The Matriarch turned toward the rest of the heirs, and spoke to her son, Mari's younger brother. "Adam, since you cannot be Matriarch, the torch is passed to your daughter. Evelyn, come take my seat with my blessing."

Evelyn stood and walked meekly to her grandmother. The old woman smiled and rubbed the young woman's cheek. "Come child, sit at the table of your birthright." Then Eva turned to the room and waved her hand high above her head. "I never imagined my love of my beautiful Mari would lead to all this." She lowered her raised hand onto the Administrator's shoulder and smiled widely, her cheerful mouth and eyes settling into wrinkles created from years of this very expression. "My beautiful girl's life was all I thought about in those early days, but it's been my life's pleasure to see all of your children grow—to christen them with the gifts of the Dikaió. Whatever the future holds for them, let's pursue it together in peace and love."

The Governor laughed out loud. "What a bunch of malarkey, Eva! Peace? Love? For decades I've sat at this table with you. Your tongue's sharper than any of your husband's knives; may he rest in peace. Good riddance, if you choose to leave, you old witch, but I'll not be gotten rid of so easily."

Mari moved quickly from her seat and put her knife at the Governor's throat. "I could make you leave, right now."

The Governor laughed harder, though he was careful not to move too close to the knife. "And how many times have you put that same knife to my throat, Mari? I don't see you calling on your successor."

Mari growled then slammed her knife on the table in front of her chair. "Alexander Nelson, my son, this knife and this seat are yours. I will accept the Council's decision."

My father looked at me then. "I suppose you want me to hand you my seat, eh?"

I knew my father well enough to know if I said, "yes," he'd just dig his heels in, so instead I said, "You're my father. My loyalty is to you and our family. If the Council forcibly removes you, then they'll make an enemy of the new

Governor too."

My father's shoulders straightened, and he stood taller. I saw pride in his eyes. He sighed heavily, and his old frame deflated. "No. They're right. It wouldn't do to have a city at war with itself, especially when there's a bigger threat outside our borders. Far be it from me to let my son give his loyalty to a villain. I submit to the Council's decision. Come on Jeremy, I give my seat willingly."

I walked quickly to the old man's side and embraced him. "I will honor your legacy."

He patted my shoulder, and I swear there was a tear in his eye. "If you don't, you'll have trouble sitting in this seat." He slapped his hand repeatedly on my backside, as if paddling a young child.

The whole room erupted in laughter as the humorous remark let the tension out of the room in a flood of goodwill. Then the laughter was slowly replaced by unease. There was a shrill noise coming from the walls. It was muffled, but it sounded almost as if someone were scraping a piece of metal across concrete.

CRASH!

The windows exploded inward, covering us with glass and a wave of heat. My father shouted something, but I could not hear anything he was saying. All I could hear was that whining noise, like metal scraping on metal, much louder now without the windows to muffle its screaming whine. I saw Mari leap over the table, moving faster than I thought her elderly frame could carry her. Her son, Alexander, was running after her toward the door, and strangely, furniture and other random objects were flying toward them—including the chair I had been sitting on before the explosion. The objects started to circle around them like meridian bands around a globe. Then someone yelled the words I had spent my whole life dreading: "It's the Ex Natu!"

I didn't have the training the Administrators and the magistrates had, but the Athenos christening included some defensive military privileges, and I knew there were people outside that needed protection. "Dikaió, protect!" I yelled as I leapt over the table and headed toward the door. Another unoccupied chair, the coffee pot, and some floorboards broke loose and began to circle around me like Mari and Alexander.

I'm not sure what I expected to see outside. Millions of Ex Natu soldiers crawling over buildings. Flying sprites the size of cities blocking out the sun. Instead, I walked out into a relatively peaceful spring day. The sky was blue, the sun was shining, and birds were calmly flying overhead. The only thing that was really different was that there was a large sprite standing in the street with giant barrels on its back. Its arms had funnels for hands, and there was fire dripping from the funnels. I turned around and looked at City Hall, which I had just exited. The roof was ablaze.

I did not think but ran back inside. The Council and the rest of the group that had been at the proceedings were exactly as I had left them—sitting and crawling on the ground. Most were looking somewhat stunned, though a few were at the windows looking out into the street. "The building's on fire!" I yelled. "You all need to get out!"

Pandemonium broke out as they all rushed toward the

door at once. I stepped backwards out into the street and felt a wave of heat surround me. Turning quickly, I almost knocked over Mari. She was standing with her feet spread apart, and her arms at her sides. A large rectangle of sheet metal hovered in the air in front of her, glowing red with flames blasting around the sides. "Get those people out of here!" She screamed. Then she stepped forward and yelled, "Dikaió, attack!" Bricks shimmied themselves loose from the building and flew around the sheet metal. I could not see what happened, but I heard loud clanks in the direction of the attacking sprite, and the flames around the metal shield disappeared. The sheet metal flipped horizontally and flung itself at the sprite. I watched, mesmerized, as the red-hot projectile found its mark in one of the sprite's tanks.

The explosion was immense. The sprite spun into the air, end over end, landing in a flaming heap in the middle of the street. The force blew Mari backwards into me. In turn, I flew back into the throng trying to escape the burning building. Thankfully, the flying objects the Dikaió had summoned to protect us stopped the most lethal debris from doing any damage. In the commotion, I could barely hear Adam Carpenter, the City Services Manager calling out: "Dikaió hydrant sprites, to me!"

I pushed myself out of the mix of arms and legs flailing about and was suddenly doused with a stream of cold water. I coughed and sputtered out of the blast of liquid to find several silver hydrant sprites, dutifully spraying water at the building. I stumbled forward and found some composure. "Enough!" I yelled. The sprawling mass of people paused and looked at me in confusion. "Come through orderly. Let the elderly out first, then the women. The danger has passed for the moment." My father and Eva walked out first and began directing the rest while the hydrant sprites worked on the fire.

I turned to look at the fiery hulk laying in the street. Mari and Alexander were standing over the sprite, conferring. I walked toward them, and I was just about to ask what it was when Alexander turned toward me. "It's already sent out a signal telling the Ex Natu that it's found something here. We need to direct their attention away from the city."

"What about the plasma field?" Adam Carpenter's voice sounded from behind me. "My wife says its ready."

I turned around and saw that the City Hall fire was already extinguished, and Adam and the rest of the Council were standing nearby.

My father scoffed: "And if it's not? We could be another Mason City."

I nodded. "The field is a last resort. Unless the Ex Natu are in the city, I don't think we should use it."

Alexander shook his head and pointed at the burning sprite. "The Ex Natu are in the city. What good are divergence plans? Won't they come looking in the last place this one signaled from?"

The new Matriarch, Evelyn, who was always a quiet woman, spoke, "What if we did both? Some of us can go out and distract the Ex Natu, but meanwhile, those who remain in the city should be ready to activate the plasma field if needed. We can always get back via the sprites in the Mason caves if necessary."

Adam shrugged. "That seems reasonable. Who's going and who's staying?"

Mari shook her head. "The only people who can fit in with the Ex Natu are going. That's everyone between 25 and 45. Infiltrate the Ex Natu cities. We don't know how far the Dikaió has spread, but it should be integrated enough to keep them occupied. The goal is to make them forget the signal this sprite sent because they're too busy with war on their own turf. The older and younger people here will move this sprite out of the city and prepare for the worst."

I looked around to see what my father thought, but he had slipped away from the group. I sighed. It was just as well. If I was the Governor, I needed to make my own decisions now. "The Council is still assembled," I said. "We'll vote on it and go from there. All those in favor of Mari Nelson's battle plan?"

"Aye!" The Council was unanimous.

The Library

Mallory slapped the table again causing everyone to jump. "And that's what happened to the Chorus's parents."

Caleb nodded. "Yes, but I wish you'd quit doing that every time you figure something out." He slapped the table irritably mimicking his wife. "Besides if you'd let me finish, you'd know why."

Alex held up the copy of the *Administrator's Chronicles* that she had apparently left at some point to collect. "I already know why. I read ahead while you were talking."

Mallory turned to her. "Alex!"

"What?" Alex shrugged and pointed at the book Caleb was holding. "The Governors have always been such boring storytellers. Honestly, I don't know how you can sit there and listen to him drone on like that."

The Archivist rolled her eyes, but nodded. "That's true."

"Hey!" Caleb yelled. "Don't pick on my family like that!"

"Yeah!" Mallory chimed in. "Don't pick on our family like that."

Caleb's frown turned into a sheepish grin when Mallory called the Governors "our family," and he hugged her.

Alex smirked and put her boots on the table. "Oh c'mon, Mallory. You're more a Matriarch than a Governor's wife. Sounds like the Athenoses were the weakest part of the Triad anyway."

Now, Caleb slapped the table for real and stood up. "Well, we're both Choruses now, Nelson. I'll take you down right here, right now."

Alex pulled her boots quickly off the table and stood up. "Anytime, Aiworth!"

"Dikaió, sit!" Commanded the Archivist, and their chairs slid forward, hitting them in the back of the legs. Their knees buckled and the pair collapsed into their chairs in a huff. They looked at her like hurt puppies.

"Ow!" Caleb whined.

"Good grief! I can't believe this is what's left of our people." The Archivist sighed.

Mallory touched Caleb's arm tenderly, concerned about her husband's pain, but then her brow furrowed. "Hey!" She turned to Alex. "If you looked ahead, that means I'm the only one that doesn't know what happened."

The Archivist chuckled. "Isn't that ironic. It's the *Matriarch's Chronicles* that have the best version of events too." She half swiveled in her chair. "Dikaió Library, bring us the *Matriarchs' Chronicles.*" Seconds later a small silver house sprite appeared carrying the large book and handed it to the Archivist. She offered the book to Mallory. "Sadly, it's the final day's entry."

Mallory took the book, turned to the final entry, which looked to still be in Eva Knenne's hand, and began to read aloud.

The Chronicles of the Matriarchs

What shall I write in the *Chronicles* now? The Matriarch is lost. My dear granddaughter Evelyn is taken from us before she had a chance to live. Our great society ended by my own daughter's hand. If my dear Kirk were here, he would have fought someone. And what good would it have been, when the betrayer of our people was the very one we'd committed our lives to protecting? Instead, I'm forced to pass the mantle of Matriarch to Mari's granddaughter, Nicolette. She's the only female in our family left with the christening of Dikaió Syntec. I know I don't have enough years left to pass on all that I know of the Dikaió, and I fear I've written far too little in these pages to be of much use to the girl.

Why does my daughter have to be so heartless?

The whole thing began in the yard of the Matriarch's house. I love that house. Omaha had let us design our homes in the Governorship District any way we wished. I selected a picturesque shingle-style cottage out of a collection of photographs he had shown us. It had open-air verandas on the second floor that wrapped almost all the way around the house. I particularly liked the picture windows, one on each side of the home. A stone mason had cut gray-and-brown cobblestones and intricately stacked them about midway up the house. My favorite feature, though, was the periwinkle wooden siding that ran midway up the deep-black shingles covering the roof, which offset the royal red door in the front. The Culture Guild had planted matching rose bushes throughout the landscaping, drawing the eye from every perspective. They had also planted two oak trees in the yard, and I could imagine what they would look like in the future, tall and grandiose.

Mari stood between the two young oaks, looking wild and caged. "Mother, they've been gone for weeks. We have to accept the possibility that they've been captured or worse."

"Mari," I patted her hand. "They have the Dikaió. They'll be fine."

"What if the Ex Natu figured out how to counter the Dikaió? What if it didn't work?" She shifted from foot to foot. "If they lead them here, we won't have the firepower even with the Dikaió to ward off a full-fledged Ex Natu attack."

I shook my head. "We've lived here for so long without a peep from the Ex Natu. It's fine."

"Fine? Mother, that's naïve. The whole reason we sent people to war was because a fire sprite set fire to City Hall. They already know we're here." She pointed in the direction of City Hall. "There have been reports of rumblings of other fire sprites in the woods. It's just a matter of time before they're here setting fire to your house too." Her pointing finger moved toward my lovely cottage. "The only option is to turn on the light before they actually show up. The holograph will disguise us, and the plasma field will ward off any attack they can muster."

I was horrified. "But Mason City—"

She cut me off. "Sally Carpenter fixed that. She said the containment magnets were out of line. She assured me before she left that the light would work if we needed it."

"You think Sally Carpenter is smarter than Omaha?" The idea that the City Manager's young wife was smarter than the man who had designed the Dikaió and the light was unbelievable at the time, though I'd give much to have that intelligence back among our ranks now.

"I'm doing it, Mother!" Mari turned on her heel and began walking down the road toward City Hall.

"Mari!" I hobbled after her. I don't mean to malign the decisions we made in having a family over eternal youth, but getting old is a curse. Maybe if I had been younger, I could have stopped her, but I was only halfway to City Hall before she entered the building. I was about ten feet from the door when an eerie pink light surrounded the city. It was low to the ground, like fog on a misty night, swirling and dancing about amongst the tall grass of the pastureland.

I stopped and leaned on my cane, breathing heavily. "Oh no! Mari. No, no, no…"

Then the pink light slowly began to rise. I waited for the

explosive collapse, and my inevitable exit into the life beyond life, but it never came. Within a few minutes, the pink light topped out in the sky and formed a dome. Then it disappeared, and all I could see was blue sky. I hobbled to the edge of City Hall and looked down the road. It was the oddest thing: Instead of the pastureland running to the edge of the forest, all I could see were infinite fields trailing off into the horizon. There was nary a tree to be seen, but there were piles of burning branches where the plasma field had taken them off the trees on the other side.

"It worked," I whispered.

"It worked; didn't it?" I jumped as Mari's voice sounded behind me. She sounded happy like a great weight had been lifted off her shoulders. I don't know that I'd heard her so carefree since she was a child.

I smiled, too. "You were right. I guess our people will have to come back through the tunnels after all."

Her smile faded. "I didn't think that would be wise."

My heart sunk. "What? What did you do, Mari?"

"What needed to be done to protect our people." She pointed toward the foundation of City Hall. "I sealed the passage and deactivated the sprites in the tunnels. There's no way the Ex Natu will be able to use our people to find us now. We're free!"

The Library

"And that's why the Chorus's parents never returned," Mallory shook her head and closed the book, not wanting to read anymore. It was hard to believe someone in her family had done such an evil thing.

"They did return," the Archivist corrected. "But the plasma field sealed them out, and they were forever stuck outside the city."

"It's a terrible thing to do," Mallory whispered.

"Administrator Mari wasn't wrong though," the Archivist shrugged. She pulled a small blue book from her pocket and waved it in the air. "These are the *Chronicles of the Lost*: a record of those who were stuck outside the city. It begins on the day your people and mine went their separate ways so to speak."

The teens all leaned in eagerly, expecting the Archivist to start reading and continue the story, but her face grew hard, and she pushed her chair away from the table. "But I'm not ready to revisit those stories." She slid the book back into her pocket.

Mallory dropped her head on top of the *Chronicles of the Matriarch* and groaned, "Really?"

The Archivist's eyebrows arched angrily, and then she softened and shook her head. "I know youth has an insatiable curiosity, but some of these stories—" she tapped her shirt and struggled to find the words to continue. Her next words were choked with emotion. "Well, I've spent years collecting books here to escape those memories. Besides, I'm old. My afternoons are meant for napping."

"Afternoon?" Caleb looked at the windows. "Did we miss lunch?"

The Archivist nodded. "Oh yes, I had mine while you were all so enraptured in the storytelling. That's why I'm ready for a nap."

Mallory's stomach roiled, and her curiosity about the Archivist's book was suddenly replaced by ravenous hunger. "Can we have some?"

"Sure, just call a sprite to make you some. I'm going to bed." The Archivist started to walk away.

"Wait!" Mallory called.

"What is it now?" The Archivist snapped her head back toward her, real anger in her voice this time.

"I'm sorry," Mallory stumbled. "But the sprites won't listen to us. We don't have the Dikaió. We're just Choruses, you know." Mallory made her point by calling to the sprite that brought the *Chronicles of the Lost*. "Dikaió sprite, bring me a sandwich." The sprite's eyes did not even flicker in acknowledgement of her request.

The Archivist sighed. "Oh yes, you're all quite helpless without a christening, aren't you? Fine. Fine." She held the bracelet on her hand closer to her mouth. "Mallory Aiworth, Caleb Aiworth, and Alex Nelson are christened Dikaió Archivists." She waved her hands dramatically. "Happy now?" Then she turned in a huff and left the dining room.

"Archivist?" Alex spat. "I'm a Dikaió Administrator."

Caleb also looked disappointed. "Yeah, and I'm an Athenos."

However, Mallory's eyes were wide with wonder. "Sprite," she called, and the house sprite's eyes flickered, turning toward her.

She giggled in excitement. "Jump up and down," she ordered.

The sprite did not really have legs, but it began to bob up and down as best it could.

Mallory laughed out loud. She jumped out of her chair and ran to the doorway, stopped, and turned around wild-eyed. "Sprite," she called. "Bring me the *Chronicles of the Matriarchs*."

The sprite quickly went to the table, grabbed the large book, and carried it to Mallory, handing it up to her. Mallory clutched the book to her chest and began to spin in circles around the Library; her thick curls bounding about her head like brown clouds. She began to hum one of the old, wordless hymns of her parents, but slowly the humming was replaced with lyrics:

> "Oh, wondrous day,
> The curse is broken!
> Wherever I go
> I have the Dikaió"

Caleb laughed. "I'm happy for you, lovely wife, but a poet you are not!" He turned his attention to the sprite. "Sprite, bring us two loaves of bread, two pounds of roasted chicken, mayonnaise, lettuce, tomatoes, carrot sticks, celery, ranch dressing, a gallon of milk, plates, glasses and cutlery—and make it snappy." He snapped his fingers for emphasis.

The house sprite did not move.

Caleb's eyebrows lowered. "Dikaió sprite, acknowledge me!"

Still the sprite did not move.

Mallory stopped dancing and looked bewildered. "Why isn't it responding?"

Alex shook her head. "It's the nano sprites, remember? Omaha made the Dikaió in a way so that it would never be able to be controlled by someone with nano sprites to keep the Ex Natu from using it."

Caleb's eyebrows furrowed further. "That can't be right. Archivist?" He turned to find their old host, but she had left to find her afternoon rest. He turned back to the girls and snapped his fingers impatiently. "Alex, you try it."

Alex shrugged. "Sprite, do a somersault."

The sprite rolled end-over-end in obedience to her command.

"Sprite do another somersault!" Caleb yelled.

The sprite ignored him.

Caleb leapt up, knocking his chair over. He kicked it skidding across the floor in irritation. "You're kidding me! It's not bad enough being the only man here, but now I'm stuck being a worthless Chorus in a world full of Dikaió users?"

Mallory ran to her husband. "Oh Caleb, I'm so sorry. I know how frustrating that is."

"What would you know about it?" Caleb snapped.

Mallory's eyes went wide. "Really? I mean—Really?"

Caleb looked at his wife and seemed to realize what he said. "Well, I suppose you would understand part of it, but she doesn't." He pointed at Alex.

"It's worse than you think," Alex said.

Caleb sulked. "What could be worse than having to rely on a bunch of women for everything?"

"I was trying to tell you earlier, when my story got interrupted." Alex looked at them both sadly. "Mari said that the

Ex Natu made the nano sprites to keep them young, keep them from getting disease, rapid healing—but as part of the plan to keep the world from getting overpopulated with undying humans, the nano sprites also made them infertile."

Caleb looked at her in confusion. "Infertile?" Then his eyes widened as the definition floated to the surface of his memory. "You mean we won't be able to have children?"

"If the Dikaió doesn't work for you, I think it's likely," Alex looked like she was going to cry, but her voice was like steel.

Mallory had heard a lot of bad news in her life, but nothing quite prepared her for Alex's words. She had always *wished* she would be able to use the Dikaió, but she had always *known* that she would be a mother. She could see her future children's faces in her mind's eye: A beautiful mixture of her and Caleb's features: his eyes and nose, her hair and mouth—now those children were fading into impossibility. On top of that, they had just discovered that the reason for their very existence was parenthood. And because a sprite injected her husband without his permission, their connection to that heritage was broken—replaced by the ability to order lunch from a silver hunk of metal. It was unbearable. Mallory's stomach churned, and she felt like she was about to be sick. Her legs buckled, and she sank to the floor. Caleb dropped down beside her and pulled her into his arms.

"It can't be true," he whispered. "It can't be. It can't be."

The couple's tears quietly mingled as they clung to each other in the deepest sorrow either had ever known.

Mallory was having trouble holding on to coherent thoughts, and she could not remember when she had broken away from Caleb, or if it was him who had left her side—but at some point, they were separated to process their grief alone. She ambled through the Library, at first walking through the narrow shelves of books then up the stairs. Floor after floor, wonder after wonder, she passed by without noticing. She would give up the books, the Dikaió, all of it, to have children—but now that possibility had been torn away from her. She eventually made her way back to their room. Caleb was not there. She spotted her backpack in the corner next to her hiking boots and knelt down. She needed to take her mind off their bleak future.

Mallory pulled out the culture sprite heart she had taken from the Ex Natu fields. The heart's little red light was still dark, and the tentacles that connected it to the sprite hung limply out of her hand, tiny bits of copper wire frayed from their ends where she had ripped it free. She turned it this way and that. Turning to a small vanity in the corner of the room with a chair, she sat down and set the heart in front of her. Small screws held it together, and she wished she had her tools from the shed behind her house. Then Mallory remembered that she could use the Dikaió now, so she decided to try it out. "Dikaió, bring me a screwdriver that will fit these screws." She tapped the screws on the heart. She really was not sure that it would work. How could the Dikaió know what she wanted? On the other hand, she had seen her people use the Dikaió for many such trivialities back home, and it worked fine for them.

Only seconds later, the small door for the house sprites opened, and a sprite hovered into the room holding a small screwdriver. It came toward Mallory holding the tool out to her. While the sprite had no eyes, it seemed to sense what was on the vanity and stopped short about three feet from her. It dropped the screwdriver on the plush carpet floor and then quickly retreated from the room. Mallory smiled. Word must be spreading among the sprites. "That's right. Beware the Sprite Slayer!" She called after the sprite, then she walked over and picked up the screwdriver. The screws came out easily enough, but she had to pry the sections of the heart open with some force even after they were out. The heart was lined with green wood that had slivers of metal pressed into it, and in the center, there was a mesh of wiring surrounding a glowing blue metal ball. She touched the glowing ball with her screwdriver and flew backwards out of her chair. It felt like she had been hit with a Dikaió cart. Her muscles, even her heart, twitched erratically as her hair stood on end.

Eventually, her body calmed itself down, and she was able to get off the floor. The little blue ball must be the sprite's power source. She had never seen one up close, and for the first time she wished that Sprite Master Reddy Lamarr were around to ask about it. Instead, she called out again. "Dikaió, bring me a book about power sources for sprites." The little door opened again, and the timid house sprite came in carrying a spiral-bound book. It hesitated just inside the room, not approaching Mallory. She smiled. "Dikaió, come, little sprite. I won't hurt you." She held out her hand, and the sprite rolled over quickly, handing her the book. She felt the urge to pet it as if it were an animal, but when she raised her hand, the sprite retreated quickly across the room and into the little door.

Mallory opened the book and scanned the table of contents. The book was very technical with way more detail than the sprite book had been back home. There were electrical diagrams that looked like mazes full of symbols she did not understand, but she did find a picture that looked similar to the sprite heart she was dissecting. As she studied the image, she traced a line from the power source that led to a switch labeled on and off. She returned to the actual heart on the vanity, and found several wires coiled around the power source, leading off in several different directions, but one of them led to a tiny switch. She used her small screwdriver to flip the switch, and suddenly the blue glowing ball turned dull gray.

Mallory's eyebrows arched. "But how?" She asked the empty room. She braced herself, and then reached in with her tiny screwdriver to touch the ball again. Nothing happened. Then she flipped the small switch again. The orb began to glow in the middle, and Mallory watched for about a minute as the glow slowly filled the ball until it was as strong as it was when she first started. Then she reached in and flicked the switch off again.

She studied the diagrams some more and began disassembling the heart, piece by piece. Minutes or hours passed, she had no idea how long, and then she was holding the small gray ball in her hand. It was roughly the size of a marble. So much power in such a tiny item. She slipped the ball and the tiny screwdriver into the pocket of her blue jumper. Then she stood up and stretched. She looked at the cozy bed in their room, and her thoughts again turned to Caleb and the possibility that they would never have children. She was sure that he was still hurting as much as she was, and she wanted to be with him to comfort each other. She went to the door and looked for his square symbol. He was upstairs somewhere, so she headed toward the staircase and started climbing.

She should be happy that her husband was not dead. But there was another fear nagging her about her husband becoming what the clockwork sprite referred to as "the enemy." Given the Ex Natu's perpetual youth and nigh immortality, she could not help but wonder if Caleb would still love her when she was old and gray, and he was still young and vital. There was more to marriage and love than just having children. Sickness, aging, dying: Love thrives in an environment of human trial. Without difficulties, would it grow cold and die, just like she would long before her husband? And he would not even have his children and grandchildren and great grandchildren there as companions.

Her heart wrenched when she thought of Caleb young and alone, haunting the halls of this Library forever.

As her heart ached, her stomach churned, and she felt like she needed to throw up. She looked around and realized she had no idea where anything was on this floor. "Dikaió sprite!" she called out, and immediately a house sprite rolled up to her. This one did not seem to be afraid of her like the last one was—maybe because she was not holding a sprite heart in her hand while she talked to it. "Take me to the nearest restroom—fast."

The sprite whirred and zoomed away from her, and Mallory stumbled quickly after it, trying to keep the contents of her stomach where they were until they got to a toilet. The sprite opened a door that was almost hidden in the paneling of the walls, and Mallory brushed quickly by it. The door led to a large room full of paintings and statuary, but Mallory saw the only sculpture she was interested in through a door to the left. She ran through the room into the attached restroom and knelt before the porcelain commode. There was not a lot left from breakfast to come up, and with Alex's revelation, she had not felt like eating lunch, so she dry-heaved a lot. The sick feeling in her stomach abated after a few failed heaves, and she pulled herself up to the small sink to wash the sickness off her face.

There was an oval mirror on the wall, and she grimaced at her disheveled appearance. Her hair was still standing on end from the electric shock from the sprite heart. Tears pooled in her eyes, and it was difficult to tell if they were from being sick or from sorrow. Snot bubbles inflated and deflated in her nostrils, and she pulled some paper from the roll beside the toilet to clear out her nose. This restroom had not been used in a long time, and the paper was covered in dust. It puffed up into her face as she tried to clean herself, which made her eyes water more, and then she sneezed, blowing the contents of her nose all over the mirror. She moaned in frustration, pulling more paper from the roll, turned on the faucet to wet the paper, and began washing up herself and the restroom.

As she cleaned, she tilted her head and bit her lip. She had not really thought about it much, but it was amazing how quickly they had fallen back into the habits of civilized life. Just a short time ago, she was all excited about seeing a river after running out of water, but here she was pulling water from a pipe with just the twist of a knob as if by magic, and she was taking it for granted. She wondered about all the things that she took for granted in the city and the Library that were missing during their brief life in the wilderness. Without the magic of the Dikaió at her beck and call, she had always been the one that had to work a little harder—but the wilderness had been bereft of the old magic too, bereft of elevators and running water. Yet, all of this had been invented and built by human beings. She wondered about the things humans had not created, the primal magic of nature: rain, wind, lightning, rivers, trees. Who or what had invented those? And if human beings were part of nature, were they invented too, like some sprite made from flesh and blood, answering the calls of a Dikaió beyond their comprehension?

She tossed the wad of paper in the trash and exited the restroom. She froze. The artwork in the room seemed to make that last question about how humans had come to be reverberate in her mind. One painting particularly drew her attention. A woman with a blue and white satin dress shimmered in light. She was perched on a stool with one arm resting on an open book on a tall table, the other hand clutched at her breast. One of her feet was set firmly on a spoke of the stool; the other balanced atop a white and brown globe on the floor: Her upright position forever frozen in a tenuous grapple with gravity. The woman's eyes rolled up toward the ceiling, as if her father had just told a really bad joke.

Mallory smiled, thinking of her father telling one of his favorite jokes. "Mallory, what's the opposite of a sprite?"

Mallory would pause and feel perplexed. Even though she had heard the joke a thousand times, she kept forgetting the answer.

Her father bounced back and forth, left to right, in anticipation of the punchline desperate to bubble out of him. When Mallory finally shrugged, he would giggle and say, "A sp-left!" Then his hands would start to roll as he waited for the pun to find its mark. "A sp-left, Mallory! Get it? A sp-left!"

Mallory thought the woman in the painting knew the

pain of a punchline like that, but the more she studied the picture, the more she realized there was something beyond this woman painted in light. Behind the woman in the light, another painting hung in the background draped in shadow. In that painting, a woman in a black dress mimicked the woman painted in light, hands on her breast, looking up into the air, but this woman was stricken with sorrow. Her gaze fixated on a man without a shirt, hanging on to a wooden beam with his arms outstretched. His head was looking down at the woman, their eyes forever locked. The man's face was clouded in shadows, too. She wanted to know who it was hanging there. She felt like she should know him, maybe even could know him.

Mallory stepped closer to the painting, but the details of the man's face were no more clear than from a distance. Her eyes moved away from the man's face, and they drifted around the painting, following the lines of the angles created by the background details: the yellow swirl of a tapestry, the angle of a chair's legs, the flow of the lines in the checkerboard floor, and then she gasped. She jumped back from the painting. At the bottom, a snake reached out toward her: mouth open, fangs protruding. But it was trapped under the corner of a square stone. Blood streaked across the floor all around the snake. The cornerstone had crushed it.

Mallory shook her head in confusion and stepped further back. The center of the room had a small, gilded table with four chairs with plush cushions, and Mallory sat down to rest. Her eyes drifted around the room looking at the rest of the art and sculptures there, but none of them gripped her quite like the dad-joke girl and the mysterious man behind her. She wished that she knew the story of the person who painted it. What message did they intend to share through the ages? Was it about the Ex Natu? Was it about her people? Was it from a time before there was a division between the two? Or had the Archivist painted it?

That last question made Mallory think about the book the Archivist had taken with her. She called it the *Chronicles of the Lost*. Her eyes dropped to the floor. Those were her people now: the Lost. And she felt the pain of the separation succinctly. Again, she found herself wishing to be back with her mother and father, just to sit between them on the couch in silence would be enough to still the turmoil in her mind, but she had no one here to turn to. Her husband was all but taken from her, and Alex, her best friend, had become distant and cold since leaving the city. The only thing that seemed to give her purpose was the oath she had made to care for their children, but now that sacred duty had been stolen from her as well. Both she and Alex were like the Archivist now, lost. She wanted to know more about her people.

Mallory sat up straight and turned about to look around the room. The house sprite was waiting patiently by the door to the gallery, and Mallory called out to it. "Dikaió sprite, bring me a blank book and a Dikaió pen to write with."

The sprite did not hesitate; it backed quickly out of the door, but it was not gone more than a minute before it reappeared carrying a leather-bound book full of blank pages, a quill pen, and a bottle of ink. It laid the items on the table and backed away quickly to the door in case she needed further assistance. Mallory opened the book and tried to remember the words the Archivist had used. She was not sure how exact she needed to be in using the Dikaió. Her mother's wording as the Matriarch giving christenings to the people of the city had to be exact, or someone might end up like Mallory without the ability to use the Dikaió. In fact, everyone in the city was so afraid of saying something wrong that very few stray words were uttered. She thought about what Mari had done to the Ex Natu with just her words and shuddered. It's no wonder they had indoctrinated them in a culture of measured speech. They did not even know what power they were sitting on in the city—or Hoffen City—it was going to take some time to get used to calling it that.

She sighed and remembered that the command had not been too complicated. "Dikaió pen, copy the *Chronicles of the Lost.*"

The pen leapt from the table and began to write:

The Chronicles of the Lost

While it was many years ago, these *Chronicles* would hardly be complete without an account of the day we lost Hoffen City. It breaks my heart to remember it, but it is forever seared in my mind. So much has changed since that day, and the war has only gotten worse. Who would have known when our parents chose to live apart from the Ex Natu that their choice would have led to so much death? I suppose I should be thankful to be alive, and that my husband is alive with me, that we have children now, but so many of our friends died in the battle in the woods outside Hoffen

City.

Or at least where I think Hoffen City was.

It is hard to know precisely because when we returned to the city, all we found was endless forest, and that's when we panicked. The holographic plasma shield had been activated. It had not blown up everything around it, which was somewhat reassuring since our people were safe, but we thought the triggering of the field also meant the Ex Natu had found the city. And if that were the case, it was likely they were in the woods with us right now. Our leadership was divided over what to do next. The young Governor Aiworth said that we should go to the bunker in Mason City and use the sprites to return. The new Matriarch Knenne said that doing so might lead the Ex Natu to the city, and that we should return to the major cities. We were still young enough to pass as Ex Natu. That's why we were chosen for this mission in the first place. Alexander Nelson the new administrator wanted to stay in the woods and fight. In the end, the Ex Natu cast the deciding vote. Whether they had tracked the initial fire sprite or followed us after our Dikaió "distractions" in the cities, the enemies came out of nowhere.

A terrible screeching of metal on metal sounded all around us, and suddenly the woods were on fire. People started running in every direction to avoid the fire. The Administrator yelled, "Dikaió, protect us!" The few sprites we had spread out to protect the crowd jumped to attention and surrounded us, but the Dikaió did not seem to inhabit living things like the trees or brush in the forest. Once the trees were cut down and had their life extinguished, the

Dikaió might seep into it, but as long as it was still alive; it was worthless to us. The Administrator pulled his weapons and called out, "Dikaió sprite, to me." A silver cycle sprite slid up behind him, and he expertly flipped a leg over it. He bent down as if about to fly forward and fight our foes. But before he could move, a giant blur of fur took him off his sprite.

Snarling teeth and razor-sharp claws silenced him before he could command the Dikaió to fight back or fire a weapon. The brown creature turned toward me with the Administrator's blood dripping from its mouth. It looked like a wolf but was probably twice the size of any I had ever seen. The Ex Natu called them the "wilding wolves." They created them to get rid of natural humans like us—to "rewild the planet," turning the wild places back to nature. They were genetically engineered to survive for years without eating, but their appetites were insatiable. The Ex Natu also gave them larger brains, specifically designed for outwitting and hunting people. As with most things human beings do, the wilding wolves turned out to be a horrible miscalculation. The beasts reproduce very quickly, and they are killing machines. The new broods not only hunted people; they hunted everything. Sure, they've killed many of us over the years, but the world will soon be empty of any living animal at the rate they're going. These days, the Ex Natu spend a great deal of time and resources trying to remove the scourge of the wilding wolves, and also trying to preserve other species within heavily forti-fied preserves built to keep the wolves out.

Of course, I had no idea what the beasts were on that day in the woods. All I knew right then was that I did not have any sort of military Dikaió privileges to fight the thing that had just killed the Administrator. Maybe I should have run, but instead I dropped to the ground, curled into a ball, and closed my eyes. I felt the creature's hot breath on my eyelids and prepared myself for death. There was a thud and a squishy crunching noise, but death never came.

"Get up! We need to go now!" A familiar voice yelled. I looked up and saw my husband holding out a hand to me. He was also holding a huge branch like a club in his other hand. The wilding wolf's blood trickled down the branch. Being careful to avoid both the creature and the blood, I reached up, and he yanked me to my feet. He jumped on the cycle sprite the Administrator had called, and I climbed on behind him. We shot forward through the chaos of wilding wolves and fire sprites, and soon the battle was behind us. My husband had no intention of fighting.

I was bereft. "The others!"

"If they survive, we'll regroup, but we can't win this fight here. We need to be in a place where we can use the Dikaió," he called back.

The rest of that day was a blur. I don't know how my husband managed to get us out of the woods, but we flew through the night and did not stop until we were inside the Davis metroplex, the capital city of our region. The Davis metroplex was massive. Even on a cycle sprite going at its maximum speed, it would take an hour to span its borders. There were glimpses of the old world in the city's architecture, spanning the centuries before the Ex Natu: a cathedral here, a library there. But most of the houses and the buildings had been torn down and replaced with Ex Natu aesthetics, and immortality had done nothing for their taste in architecture. There was a certain utilitarian drabness about the city: black boxes stacked atop black boxes. Red, white, and blue lights flashed at different places among the buildings, but even those served little more than a technical purpose, warning sprite riders to avoid the buildings and stay in their lanes.

We made our way to a safe house our people had quietly maintained ownership of on the south side of the metroplex, being careful to not attract attention to ourselves. It was as drab on the exterior as the rest. I walked quickly to the door and leaned in as if unlocking it, but I had no key. "Dikaió, unlock," I whispered, and several locks disengaged. The inside of the house was little better than the outside, only containing the most utilitarian features. There was a couch, a recliner, a flat screen, a table with two chairs, a small stove, and a refrigerator. Dust covered everything. Several fresh trails had been tracked across the counter, tiny paw prints leading to the cabinets. I paused and shivered, blocking the doorway. "Rats."

My husband brushed past me, nearly knocking me over. "Better than the Ex Natu."

"Says you," I closed the door behind me.

He turned and smiled. "Dikaió, lock down." The door locks all engaged, and the windows rattled as the steel shutters rotated completely closed. He nodded and asked into the quiet home. "Dikaió house sprite?" A small door slid open, and a house sprite rushed into the room. "Pest removal, please."

The sprite spun slowly in a circle, and then shot backward

into the walls. For a moment everything was quiet, and then the home was full of scratching noises in the walls and tiny squeaks. The door to one of the cupboards was slightly ajar, and a hoard of cockroaches fell out of it fleeing. I felt like throwing up, and then several red streams of light strobed from the vent in the kitchen. As the lights touched each cockroach, they stopped moving, dead in their tracks. When all was quiet again, the house droid reappeared and vacuumed up the remains of the roaches on the counter, and then opened a cupboard and removed three rat corpses. It sprayed a foam over the hole that they had opened in the back of the cabinet, which quickly hardened, sealing up their den. Then the sprite ran past us back into its own den in the wall, and the door shut behind it.

"Well, we're finally alone," my husband laughed.

I started to cry.

Everything I'd ever known was gone, and now, we were stuck in a life we would never be able to enjoy. There would never be peace for us here. Refugee spies in an enemy city. My husband did not comfort me; he just went around the house checking supplies. When my tears finally ran out, I picked myself up and joined my husband to see what he had found. There were three Dikaió suits in the closet that self-fitted to our size. There were some old rations in the house, which theoretically would never expire, but in reality, tasted like polystyrene foam and would never last. We were going to need to get work and food.

We were still young enough that none of the Ex Natu would recognize us as being different than them; that was the whole point of our excursions outside of Hoffen City after all. My husband worked in city management, so it was not hard for him to find work in the Ex Natu Internal Works division, doing maintenance on city machinery—though it was difficult not using the Dikaió, and he risked exposure if he were ever injured. Still, he stayed under the radar by saying very little and kept busy fixing things. My skills as an Archivist almost entirely relied on the Dikaió and the ethereal collection of knowledge in Dikaió records and books, which meant that I was mostly stuck in the house. I tried to venture out to stores and restaurants like normal people, but fashion among the Ex Natu was changing rapidly. Men and women had begun to dress very similarly, and the dark gray jumpsuits they favored were as drab as the architecture. Our colorful Dikaió suits were standing out more and more, and I refused to change to fit in. I felt like I had so little left of our identity as it was. Besides that, clothes weren't the only fashion issue. Probably half of the city, men and women both, had shaved their heads and were getting nano-tattoos, images that looked alive and moved about their bodies, continuously thwarting their nano sprites' attempts to heal them. Every time I went out, more and more of them were adapting to this style. Before long, I felt like every Ex Natu eye was on me when I left the house, and I just quit going out.

My husband did not have that choice. He needed to fit in. One day he came home with all his lovely brown locks chopped off, and his head clean shaven.

"That's it!" I screamed, pointing at his head and then falling heavily into a chair at the kitchen table. "We have to leave."

He was taken aback, but then a wry smile curled his lips. "You don't like it? It's all the rage you know." He rubbed his hand on his waxy head.

I shook my head. "No. It's all the Ex Natu rage. You're not one of them. Never will be. You've gotten too comfortable here. We need to leave."

He sighed. "Let's stick to the plan. We just need to lay low until we can connect with the others."

"It's been six months. There are no others. We need to leave." I stood up and pulled a packed suitcase out from under the table.

"Be reasonable; it's just a haircut." He crossed the room and reached out to embrace me.

I took a step back. "It's not just a haircut. It's a choice, and you'll have to make it now." I sighed deeply and touched my stomach tenderly. "Your family or the Ex Natu."

His head tilted slowly toward my stomach and recognition spread across his face. "My family?" His eyes shifted up to meet mine. "My family? Mrs. Carpenter are you—are we pregnant?"

I blinked back tears. "We?"

He put his hands on both sides of my face. "Of course, 'we.' I'll always choose you, Emilia. I'll start packing right away."

Tears flowed freely down my cheeks now. "Adam—" My words were taken away by sobs, but he seemed to know my meaning, as he pulled me to him and kissed me deeply.

The Library

Mallory sat up straight and pushed the book away in disgust. The pen scratched a long black line as the book moved away. It floated awkwardly in the air above where the book used to be, and then it slowly moved back to the book and started to write again. Mallory's brow furrowed. "Dikaió, pause." The pen stopped writing in the book. She stood up and stretched her back. The Carpenters' pregnancy was just another thorn in her side, and it was more than she could bear. She knew it was all in the past, and they had passed into the life after life long ago. She was sure their history would be fraught with danger, bringing a life into the world of the Ex Natu, but at least they could. She'd fight a hundred Ex Natu to bear a child, to be like Emilia and Adam Carpenter.

Her head tilted to the side, and she began to chew the corner of her mouth. All her self pity vanished behind a connection her brain was trying to make. Her mind batted about like a blind person in a dark room, trying to understand. Everything seemed so foggy to her lately. Her mind, which was usually so quick to make connections and see the big picture, felt like mushed peas. Her stomach growled then churned violently. For a moment she thought she was going to be sick again, and she remembered that she had not had anything to eat in a while. She shook her head and tried to focus on the name: Carpenter. She thought of Jake Carpenter, the City Services Manager back home. Adam Carpenter also worked in City Services, then he worked in city maintenance; maybe he was an ancestor of Jake's: a distant cousin. That's what the Archivist had said about her husband. Adam

Carpenter must have been the ancestor of the Archivist's husband, but then where did the Archivist come from? Did they find other survivors from the city?

Suddenly, the lights in the room dimmed and a red light above the door began flashing. She could hear a soft clanging sound, though if it were an alarm, it was totally ineffectual. It sounded like it was echoing through the building from a long distance away. She strained her ears to try and pinpoint the sound. Then without warning, the Archivist's voice filled the room, and Mallory nearly fell off her chair in surprise. "Attention, the Library is under attack. Seek shelter. Attention, the Library is under attack. Seek shelter." The Archivist repeated the phrase over and over in an urgent but calmly authoritative tone. Mallory jumped up from the chair and ran out of the gallery. She was in a circular hallway just over the interior chamber with the stain-glassed memorial of the Archivist's husband and sons. She looked up at the man captured in the stain glass, and the importance of his image flitted about in her memory, but the Archivist's insistence that the Library was under attack made it seem unimportant to fixate on at the moment.

Just ahead of her was a banister, over which was the empty space of the interior chamber. Mallory ran forward and leaned over the banister. She was expecting to see Ex Natu and lethal sprites waving whip-like tentacles and swarming into the Library space, but what she saw instead perplexed her. She was six stories up, and the figures below were tiny, but she recognized the copper toned metal and the blond mop of hair immediately: it was the clockwork sprite and Caleb. And Caleb had something long and metal that he was using to pound on the clockwork sprite, which was where the soft clanging noise was coming from. "What are you doing, Caleb?" she thought to herself as she rushed along the banister toward the stairs and descended as quickly as she could.

She ran through the carved double doors of the dining room, and then squeezed through the tight rows of books. When she exited the shelves, Caleb's words laced with heavy sobs stopped her short.

"You stole my family," he repeated over and over while he smashed the clockwork sprite with what Mallory could now tell was a heavy flagpole. The flag, whose pattern she did not recognize, draped unceremoniously on the ground, while the metal pole smashed against the sprite. It was not even leaving a dent. Mallory remembered the city's reaction to the loss of the Dikaió and how everyone had gone slightly crazy, beating the sprites that no longer responded to them. Caleb had led that charge in her own house alongside his father to much the same effect as what he was having on the clockwork sprite: none.

She moved toward the pair. "Caleb," she called.

The clockwork sprite's eyes flashed, and it moved quickly away from them both. Its rush caused books to fall from the shelves and loose leaves of paper fluttered into the air around it. Its arms quickly lengthened into whips, moving in a defensive pattern about it. "Sprite Slayer. The male would have died without the injection. You must understand."

Mallory had once wondered if the sprite could feel fear,

but now she was certain of it. She stepped cautiously toward Caleb, keeping her tone and movements even. "I'm no danger to you, sprite. You may leave without harm."

Caleb turned to face her; the flagpole he was holding just barely missing her head. "Mallory, it's responsible. It took away…It took everything!" He threw the flagpole down in disgust.

The Archivist and Alex stepped into the inner chamber. They were both holding weapons and had several more strapped all over their bodies. They were ready for a fight. "What is going on?" The Archivist yelled.

The clockwork sprite answered. "The male Chorus attacked me, and I sounded the Library's alarm."

"Seriously?" The Archivist holstered her weapons angrily. "Well, Governor, you're certainly more trouble than you're worth. Care to explain?"

Caleb looked at her forlorn but silent.

Mallory took his hand. "The sprite gave him an injection to save his life when he was injured in the ruins of Mason City."

Alex holstered her weapons and nodded. "Mallory shot him."

The Archivist's eyes widened. "Shot him?"

"It was an accident." Mallory waved her hands, trying to wipe away that detail from the conversation. "Anyway…the injection had nano sprites in it."

The Archivist stiffened. She stared at Mallory without saying anything. Her gaze drifted up to the stained glass image of her husband and sons above them. Slowly, her head tilted to the side. "That's terrible."

"You're telling me," Caleb bellowed. "That monstrosity turned me into an Ex Natu!" He pointed a finger at the clockwork sprite, which still had its tentacles partially extended and was eyeing Mallory warily.

"No," the Archivist waved her hands, still staring at her family's portrait. "It's terrible because she's pregnant, and now, it's just a matter of time."

C aleb spun around and bounded toward Mallory. "Is it true? Are we having a family?"

Mallory stepped backwards away from him and put her hands protectively on her belly. Her head bent down trying to see her stomach. She stared at her torso, wide-eyed and blinking. "I—I don't know."

Alex spun on the Archivist. "Is it true? How could you possibly know that?"

The Archivist did not answer. She just stood there looking at her family image above them. A smile spread across her face, and then she spun on her heel and disappeared into the rows of books screaming, "Dikaió, shut off that infernal alarm!"

"Where are you going?" Alex called after her, but it was to no avail. Alex sighed and addressed the copper sprite. "Sprite can you tell if what the Archivist said is true, like the way you could tell how to help Caleb when he was hurt? Is Mallory pregnant?"

The sprite's eyes flashed. "Yes, Archivist. My scans show that the Sprite Slayer is carrying a human child in her womb." The clockwork sprite completely retracted its tentacle-whips, ascertaining the danger to itself had passed.

Alex grunted and pounded her fist on the nearest bookshelf.

But Caleb and Mallory barely noticed. Caleb knelt down in front of his wife and reached his hand toward her belly. Mallory took another step away from him, still holding her stomach protectively. He looked up at her sadly. The anguish in his eyes was almost unbearable. Yet when Mallory looked down at his yellow locks, she was not sure who she was looking at: her husband or the enemy. Caleb was an Ex Natu now, and the Ex Natu were immortal. She again found herself afraid of what that would mean for their marriage, for this child. "Mal," his voice choked on her name. "Please, don't look at me like that. I love you, and we're having a baby. A family, Mal—our family."

Mallory took a deep breath and breathed out slowly.

Caleb was still her husband, enemy or not. And this was not a future he had chosen against her or against their people. She was not sure how their love would survive what he had become. The heart-racing attraction she felt toward him was definitely lacking, and she was not sure how to get it back.

But she grew up as the heir of the Matriarch; she knew what duty was, and she had a duty to him and to their child. Even though it was hard not to think about the Ex Natu thing, when she considered him from a purely aesthetic level, he was still ridiculously handsome with his new beard, and she knew he would never betray her. He had already proven that. She took one step forward and enveloped his outstretched hand in both of hers. "Yes, Caleb." Then she took another step forward and moved his hand on to her belly. "You're going to be a father."

"And you're going to be a mother," he smiled up at her. "Parents; just like we were always meant to be."

Alex shuffled uncomfortably beside the books. "This complicates our plans to go back to the city."

Caleb nodded as he kissed Mallory's belly. "Agreed. Our duty is here; our future is here."

Alex nearly spit. "You'll trade one life for tens of thousands, then?"

Caleb stood up and stared her down. "You swore a duty to our children, Alex Nelson. Did you not?"

Alex sneered up at him. "Don't talk to me of duty. You are the heir of the Governorship. What of your duty to your people?"

Caleb looked at Mallory: a mixture of sadness and joy contorting his face. "I was the heir. But that life is over. Until a moment ago, I didn't know what I was. A Chorus? An Ex Natu? A curse to my wife and my friend. And I may still be all those things." His countenance fell again on Mallory's stomach. "But at least I can say with certainty I am a father."

Alex huffed and disappeared into the rows of books.

Caleb looked angrily after her and said to himself, Mallory, and his growing child, "I'm your father." He touched Mallory's stomach, and then lifted his hand to her cheek. "And your husband. The Library is our home now. It's where we'll be safe."

Mallory knew it should be a joyous moment, but she could not help but feel a sense of foreboding. She tilted her head up and looked at the stained glass image above them. The sun was setting and the light in the image was starting to fade; soon the Dikaió light would ignite to replace the sun's radiation, but in the moment, the faces above were dim and fading. The Archivist's dead husband and two sons looked down at them from the life after life. She thought again how much they all looked like Jake Carpenter back home. Then she stroked Caleb's hair and said, "Maybe."

Caleb's body stiffened. "What do you mean 'maybe'?"

Mallory ignored his question. Her head tipped slightly while she stared at the image above, "Sprite, may I ask you a question?"

The clockwork sprite's eyes flashed, but it came no nearer to her. "Of course, Sprite Slayer."

Mallory's eyes did not leave the dying light in the eyes of the memorial above her. "What's the Archivist's given name?"

"The Archivist is named Emilia Carpenter." The sprite said without hesitation.

Mallory's gaze slowly descended to Caleb's eyes. "And she has nano sprites like this Chorus?"

"Of course, Sprite Slayer." The clockwork sprite said

matter-of-factly. "Without nano sprites the Archivist's body would have failed centuries ago."

Caleb nearly fell over trying to turn around and face the clockwork sprite. "She's an Ex Natu? How is that possible? She can use the Dikaió."

Mallory shrugged. "The Dominus bracelet, obviously."

Caleb's eyes went wide. "The Dominus bracelet can give an Ex Natu the Dikaió?"

Mallory shrugged. "It makes sense. Omaha developed the bracelets before adding the safeguard to the Dikaió to discount those with nano sprites. If the Archivist has a Dominus bracelet, she controls every part of the Dikaió. Is that correct, sprite?"

"No, Sprite Slayer, the Library's Archivist has not achieved access to all the secrets of the Dikaió," the sprite answered.

"Even with all these books?" Mallory motioned around the Library. "Didn't Omaha write some directions somewhere? Can't she just tell the Dikaió to copy Omaha's instructions into a book?"

"Yes, Sprite Slayer. The Library has a collection of the writings of the man who went by the name Omaha on the third floor. The Archivist has collected those volumes in the fashion you suggest. However, Omaha added security codes to many of the references to the Dikaió, and much is missing from those records," the sprite said.

"Still, maybe they have some clues about where the other Dominus bracelets are." Caleb mused. "Sprite, take us to them immediately."

The sprite did not move.

"Mal?" Caleb whined. "Would you?" He motioned to the sprite and waved his hand as if to say, "Make it move, please?"

Mallory smiled and shook her head. "No."

"What? Why not?" Caleb was shocked.

"I'm starving." Mallory put her hands on her stomach protectively. "And no wonder. Whatever is coming down the line here in this place, I need to make sure our baby is getting fed. Let's get some food first, then we'll go sleuthing."

Caleb's shoulders slumped even as his stomach growled. He straightened. "I could eat," he said smiling.

Despite all the revelations of the day, good and bad, Mallory was exhilarated when six house sprites rolled into the inner chamber carrying platters of cheese, fruit, luncheon meats, fresh bread, milk, juice, dill pickles, and ice cream: all at her command with the Dikaió. She grabbed a pickle and a bowl of vanilla ice cream and dipped the pickle in with vigor. Caleb, who was happily loading a sandwich with the bread, cheese, and meat, blanched as Mallory shoved a huge bite of pickled ice cream in her mouth. "Ewww! Mal, that's disgusting."

"I know, but I can't help it." She shoved in another creamy bite. "It's all I can think about eating right now."

Caleb watched her dip another pickle and set his sandwich back on the tray the house sprite was carrying without taking a bite. "I think I'll wait until she's done," he said and patted the sprite on the head.

Mallory laughed, "It's sweet and sour, like candy. You should try some." She held out half a pickle with melted cream running down her hand.

Caleb turned the color of the pickle. "Please, stop."

Mallory laughed more and shoved the rest of the pickle in her mouth. "Your loss," she mumbled as she chewed.

When the pickles were gone, she grabbed Caleb's sandwich and was four bites in before he realized what was happening. "Mal, that's mine!"

She patted her belly and shrugged. "It's for your baby, Handsome. You understand."

"But there's plenty of food; you could have just made your own." Caleb started loading up another sandwich, watching her suspiciously.

"Baby doesn't want to wait," Mallory shrugged some more. "He says he wants food now."

Caleb perked up. "Is it a boy? Do women know things like that?"

Mallory laughed. "I hope so. How else can we explain the little guy's appetite?"

Caleb's eyes narrowed as he cradled his sandwich protectively. "I don't think it works that way." Then he took a giant bite.

Mallory finished off Caleb's first sandwich and then poured herself a glass of milk, then a glass of juice to wash it down with. "Ugh," she sighed. "I'm stuffed."

Caleb was also slowing down. "Yeah, I'm getting there, too. Should we go see Omaha's writings?"

Mallory nodded and said, "we're finished, sprites. Please take away the food." The house sprites scurried away with the food, and another one showed up to vacuum up the crumbs that had fallen out of their sandwiches. Then Mallory addressed the clockwork sprite: "Would you please take us to the Omaha collection?"

The clockwork sprite began to move away from them. "Of course, Sprite Slayer, this way."

"The stairs are back that way," Caleb corrected.

"Yes, Chorus, but the Sprite Slayer's condition requires an elevator, so that she does not exert herself beyond what is physically reasonable. The elevator is this way," the clockwork sprite replied.

"An elevator?" Mallory shouted. "The Library has an elevator?"

"Of course," the Clockwork sprite answered. "The building's design is a perfect replica of The Globe Library in the Davis City Metroplex, complete with four elevators."

"The Ex Natu capitol city?" Mallory marveled.

"Correct," the sprite affirmed.

Caleb looked confused. "The what?"

"Davis City is the Ex Natu capitol city. It's where the Archivist and her husband went when Mari locked them out of Hoffen City," Mallory said as if it was common knowledge.

The three of them paused outside a silver sliding door, and the sprite pressed a circular button with an up arrow on it. Caleb crossed his arms. "That doesn't tell me what a capitol city is, but it does bring up another thing that's had me confused. How did you know about the Archivist's past? It wasn't in any of the *Chronicles* we read."

Mallory glanced at the clockwork sprite and said, "I'll tell you that part later."

Caleb looked at the sprite and seemed to understand the signal Mallory was sending him. "Okay then, what's a capitol city?"

The door to the elevator opened, and the clockwork sprite entered then turned to hold the door for them. "A capitol city is where the seat of government resides, Chorus."

"Like City Hall?" Caleb let Mallory go in first and then followed her into the elevator.

The clockwork sprite's eyes flashed as it pushed the button marked with a number six. "No, Chorus. Not at all like a city hall. A city hall is a building. A capitol city is a city."

Mallory laughed and slapped her husband's arm. "Exactly. Don't be silly, Caleb."

When the elevator doors opened on the sixth floor, Caleb was still arguing with the sprite. "You're saying that the seat of government of the Ex Natu resides in a capitol city, but City Hall is where the seat of government of our city was as well. Why are they not the same thing?"

"As I have explained two times before, a capitol city is a city, and a city hall is a building." The clockwork sprite led them around the edge of the inner chamber's railing to the shelves of books on this floor. "Would you like me to explain the difference between a building and a city?"

"Of course not," Caleb moaned, and then under his breath he whispered, "I'm right, anyway."

The clockwork sprite spoke without looking back. "My hearing is able to process sounds a thousand times quieter than a human can utter, Chorus. And you are not correct."

Caleb started looking about wildly—no doubt, for

something to hit the sprite with out of irritation, but before he could find anything that would deliver a sufficient blow, the sprite stopped. "This is the Omaha collection," it said. "There are four known volumes, though one is missing from the shelves."

Mallory looked at the books on the shelves. They were marked with roman numerals: I, III, and IV. "Do any of these volumes describe the abilities of an Archivist with the Dikaió?"

The sprite's eyes blinked slowly. "Volume one has simple descriptions of various Dikaió roles, including that of the Archivist, but as I have indicated, the full capabilities and limitations of the Dikaió are unknown."

Mallory bent down and pulled the first volume off the shelf and handed it to Caleb to carry. He seemed about to protest, but Mallory put her hand on her belly and made a pouty face. Caleb squinted his eyes suspiciously at her but tucked the large volume dutifully under his arm. Mallory smiled at him and then turned again to the clockwork sprite. "Do you have any way of knowing where the second volume is?"

The Sprite's eyes blinked. "While I have no direct way to track the book's whereabouts, the Library records suggest that the last person to request access to this set of books was the new Archivist, Alex Nelson."

"Alex?" Caleb looked surprised. "When?"

The clockwork sprite's eyes blinked again. "Shortly before you attacked me, Chorus."

Mallory tilted her head to the side, bit her lip, and

wondered what Alex was after. "Can you give a summary of the contents of the book Archivist Nelson took?"

"Volume two of the *Omaha Chronicles* contains his notes on defensive measures, holographic plasma fields, city-management schematics, aquaponic gardening, general horticultural applications…"

Mallory cut off the sprite. "Go back! Holographic plasma fields? Like the one over the Library?"

"Correct, Sprite Slayer," the clockwork sprite answered.

Caleb's eyes went wide. "Can an Archivist turn off the generators?"

The sprite did not blink before replying. "Not with the Dikaió, but physically, anyone with access to the generator could potentially shut down the plasma fields if the power coupling is removed."

Caleb looked up at the symbols on the wall that showed all of their locations in the Library. The circle that tracked Alex was moving near them with a "B" beside the symbol. "Are the generators in the basement?"

"Yes, Chorus, that is a very good guess," the sprite replied.

Mallory and Caleb exchanged worried glances, and then the Dikaió lights in the entire building dimmed, and red lights started flashing. The Archivist's voice began to boom throughout the Library again: "Attention, the Library is under attack. Seek shelter. Attention, the Library is under attack. Seek shelter."

"Alex! No!" Mallory yelled.

Caleb looked at the clockwork sprite. "Is the plasma field still up outside, sprite?"

The clockwork sprite turned slowly in a circle; its eyes blinking rapidly. "Negative, Chorus. The plasma field has been shut down."

"We need to get to the basement, now!" Mallory started running to the elevator with Caleb by her side. The clockwork sprite floated to the banister overlooking the inner chamber and flung itself over the top.

The elevator ride was excruciatingly slow as the pair descended to the basement of the Library. Mallory had imagined the nether regions of the Library would look like the basement of City Hall. Cold linoleum floors, old shelves, and filing cabinets full of unnecessary, ancient paperwork. But the basement was nothing of the sort. The walls and floors were a lot more like the waiting room under City Hall than the functional basement. Seamless wooden paneling covered the floor, walls, and ceiling. There were shelves down there, but rather than being full of boxes and old paperwork, they were full of countless old artifacts and works of art: sculptures, paintings, musical instruments, weapons, et cetera. Mallory was nearly overcome with a curious need to explore, and if not for the imminent danger they were in without the protection of the Library's light, she would have spent hours down there uncovering the secrets of history. But right now they needed to find Alex.

She looked up at the tracker decorations on the wall just in time to see Alex's circle with a one beside it disappear. "She's already out of the building," Mallory yelled.

"Nelson, you're going to get us all killed," Caleb roared. "I'll go after her. You see if there's anything you can do with the plasma field."

Mallory bit her lip. "I don't even know where to look for it."

If Caleb heard her protest, he did not acknowledge it, and the doors of the elevator were closing behind him. Mallory looked back up at the tracker. A triangle was moving toward her rapidly. Mallory looked in the direction of the triangle and saw the flowing rainbow flash of the Archivist run by. Mallory hurried after her. The Archivist moved unnaturally fast. It was hard to keep up with her, but Mallory followed the triangle tracking her motions. Then she turned past a shelf with a beautifully decorated spear in a glass case and saw an open door with flashes of light emanating out of it. Mallory walked into the room and was met with a horrific site.

The Archivist was holding a severed live wire with her bare hand. The skin on her hand was black and smoldering, but she barely seemed to notice. She pulled the wire over to a large spherical machine that was half sunk into the floor. "I should have known better than to trust them," she hissed as she pushed the electrical wire back into place. "Dikaió welding torch!" She yelled, and what looked like a nozzle attached to a stick floated toward her. Mallory thought it looked very familiar to the system used by the hydrant and fire sprites. When the Archivist clicked a button, a narrow blue flame shot out, and she began welding the wire back into place.

"Can I help?" Mallory called from her place in the doorway.

The Archivist spun on her with an evil looking sneer on her face. "Haven't you done enough?" Her eyes drifted down to Mallory's belly, and the sneer softened, but then her face turned to emotionless stone. "Why don't you start by telling me what happened."

"It's Alex," Mallory started. "She wants to go home and warn our people."

The Archivist let go of the live wire and held up her charred hand. New skin immediately swallowed up the burns, and the Archivist's hand looked normal, confirming what the sprite had told them about her being an Ex Natu. "I thought you didn't know the way back to Hoffen City."

"We don't—I don't know what she's thinking." Mallory threw up her hands.

"Whatever she's thinking, the fool is going to get us all killed," the Archivist yelled. "Dikaió, bring me some wide electrical tape." She snapped her fingers in irritation. A house sprite rolled in carrying a roll of black tape that was roughly the same size of the electrical wire that the Archivist had just attached. The Archivist spun the tape around the wire, covering the electrical leads.

"Is it fixed then? Is the light back up?" Mallory asked hopefully.

"The light? No, the plasma field is not back up. Your friend has taken the regulator." The Archivist pointed to a section of the machine that seemed slightly less dusty than the rest and had a few disconnected nodes dangling out of it. "If we turned it on now—" the Archivist made an explosion motion with her hands. "It looks like my sprite already has her though," she smiled and pointed at the tracker in the decorations. Alex's circle had reappeared on the board, but just as quickly as it appeared, it disappeared again. The Archivist frowned. "I better get up there and see what's going on." She hesitated and looked suspiciously at Mallory. "*WE* had better get up there. This room is officially off limits for all of you." She pointed toward the door, and Mallory quietly acquiesced.

The Archivist walked with Mallory quickly to the elevator, but Mallory could tell she wanted to move faster. There was a nervousness about her that made Mallory wonder if she was afraid. "If the Ex Natu came, your Dominus bracelet could defend us, right?"

The Archivist looked at her as if she were stupid and shook her head. "Maybe for a time, but even with the bracelet, I'm no army. But I have plans for every eventuality, even you and your friends. Still, things would go better for the Library if I could get that field back up."

The elevator stopped and the doors opened. Mallory wanted to ask how she had come to be an Ex Natu, how she ended up with the nano sprites. Was she horribly hurt like Caleb? The founders of their people were willing to die rather than become Ex Natu. What had changed for Emilia Carpenter? But she did not get the chance to ask because the Archivist shot out of the elevator with more speed and vitality than any woman her age had any right to have. Mallory walked quickly after and was surprised when she found the clockwork sprite laying on the foyer floor; it's eyes dark. The Archivist did not stop to check the sprite; instead, she ran out the door on the hunt for Alex.

A blast of cold air hit Mallory from outside the open door, and she could see the trees beyond the Library's light had started to shed their autumn leaves. Winter was growing ever nearer. Mallory knelt down on the cold floor and looked at the sprite. Its arms were partly extended, coiled in heaps on the floor, and she could see blood splattered on them. It must have lassoed Alex and pulled her into its grip. Mallory tilted her head to the side and bit her lip. There was still a chunk of metal missing from where the Ex Natu's culture sprite had sliced the copper clockwork sprite, and around its sharp edges, there were bits of shredded leather.

Mallory bent down further and looked inside the sprite. She saw the problem immediately. Alex had picked up her trick on turning a sprite off. The sprite's heart had a hole in it, and the flashing red light was dark. Mallory made her hand as small as she could and reached inside the sprite. She carefully began to unplug the tendrils of the heart using her fingers like tweezers. When all the tendrils were loose, she extracted the heart through the hull. She looked inside the hull and could see that a magistrate's projectile was lodged inside, flattening the small energy ball.

Mallory patted at her pockets and found the tiny screwdriver and the silver ball. She quickly pulled the sprite's heart apart and pulled the projectile and ball loose. She put the undamaged ball in its place and moved the wire coils back into position around it. A small blue glow began to emanate from the center of the ball, and Mallory closed the heart and repositioned it inside the sprite. Then she began reconnecting the tendrils in the order she had detached them. When the last one snapped into place, the clockwork sprite's eyes slowly began to glow, blinking on and off in strange patterns. Its arms began to retract inside its body, and Mallory pulled her hand out of its torso quickly, so as not to get it torn off when the sprite stood up. She hoped that the energy source was just that and did not turn this sprite into an Ex Natu weapon.

The sprite righted itself, and then looked at Mallory blinking. "You repaired me?"

Mallory nodded.

The sprite slowly reached up to the hole in its chest. "Thank you, Sprite Master."

Mallory blinked. "Sprite Master?"

"Only a Sprite Master could make such a difficult repair," the clockwork sprite intoned. "I will go and stop the other Archivist now. But I will be careful not to let her get too close." Its arms began to extend into whips as it turned toward the door.

Mallory hated being called by Reddy Lamarr's title, but she didn't have time to correct the clockwork sprite. Right then, she needed it to obey her and not question her authority. She yelled after the sprite, "Dikaió, wait!"

The Sprite paused.

"Do not kill her," Mallory ordered.

The Sprite turned toward her. "She is a threat to the Library and to the Archivists. She must be stopped."

"Dikaió sprite, do not kill Alex Nelson," Mallory ordered again. "Hold on!" Mallory looked around the room. She shrugged and grabbed a random book off the nearest shelf then wedged it inside the gap in the sprite's torso. "She won't be able to shoot through that before you restrain her arms. Now, go bring her back, but do not kill her."

The sprite's eyes blinked, and then it disappeared in a sonic blast out the door.

Mallory was alone in the Library: the very unprotected Library. There was a plush chair in the foyer with blue, striped upholstery, and she sat down in it with a huff. She wondered how Caleb was faring in trying to get ahold of Alex. In a physical altercation, Caleb could probably overpower her, but with her magistrate weapons, Caleb would never get close. Mallory hoped that her friend would not kill the father of her children in her misplaced notion of getting back to their city. The three of them were supposed to be a family. On the other hand, Caleb was Ex Natu now. He would be hard to kill just like the Archivist. Would the Archivist kill Alex? None of them knew what she was capable of if she were pushed. She had lived alone in this library a long, long time.

Mallory looked up at the stained glass windows with the Triad of Government in the foyer. The sprite had said that the Library was a near replica of the Globe Library in the Ex Natu capitol. She wondered what the Ex Natu stained glass windows in this room had depicted in their pictures. She assumed it was not the governmental structure of their sworn enemy. What would the immortal immortalize in art? She thought about the *Chronicles of the Lost* that she had left partially written in the art room upstairs. The Ex Natu were not that interested in art anymore. The Archivist had written that their aesthetics were shabby drab, and Mallory could imagine it after seeing the citadel by Aiworth bridge. It had been just a bunch of giant black blocks stacked on top of one another with a flashing red light on top. She tried to picture an entire city made of buildings like that, and for some reason when she pictured it in her mind's eye, it was a dark and stormy scene with rain and lightning.

Her imagination even filled in the thunder—or did it? The hairs on her neck raised when there was another crash in the Library. Someone or something had broken some glass somewhere in the building. There was a crunching noise: boots coming down hard on the broken glass. Why would any of her friends or the Archivist have broken a window and climbed into the Library? She looked up at the tracker in the molding above the shelves. She saw her star, but there was a new symbol on the board: The library had recognized a new patron, and a pentagon shape had appeared. The pentagon was on the move. Mallory grabbed the sides of her chair and looked in the direction of the noise. Somewhere in the stacks of books behind her, a stranger was coming her way.

16

Mallory was frozen in fear. Her eyes flicked back and forth between the pentagon in the decorative borders of the walls and the stacks of shelves, where the new symbol suggested the stranger was coming her way. For a moment, she wondered if an Ex Natu sprite had made it into the Library to kill them. She had never seen any of the sprites represented in the tracking system. The four symbols she had seen were just her star, Caleb's square, Alex's circle, and the Archivist's triangle. It was not much to go on, but Mallory assumed the Library only tracked people, which meant that the pentagon had to be a person and not a sprite. Was it an Ex Natu? If it were, then she was in serious danger. On the other hand, she had never seen one of them up close.

Her fear was replaced with curiosity. She glanced around the room, looking for cover. There was a large plant in the corner of the room with orange and purple flowers. The flowers looked a little like birds' heads with orange plumes, but the massive green leaves were roughly the size of her face: perfect for hiding behind. She ran to the plant and tried to pull it quietly away from the wall. The ceramic pot the plant lived in was massive and heavy. It scraped loudly along the floor, and Mallory grimaced at the noise. She looked to see if the pentagon had changed speed. Nothing had changed, so she ducked behind the plant and pulled her arms and legs as near to her body as she could.

Mallory reached up to the leaves and pulled them just slightly back, so she could see the rest of the room. Moments later a figure walked out from the bookshelves. It was a person, a woman. She was dressed in a coat made from wilding wolf fur, including a hood that obscured her features. Mallory tilted her head slightly to the side. Under the coat, she was wearing a pair of brown pants and dark brown boots. A long sheath hung from her belt, holding a sword of some sort. A magistrate's weapon was holstered on the other side of her belt. Mallory wondered if she had made the coat herself. She thought back to the Ex Natu she had seen in Mason City. They had killed a ton of wilding wolves on their flying sprites, so killing the wolves was certainly something the Ex Natu did. But those animals had all been consumed in an inferno. The furs on the woman did not look like they had been scorched by fire. It looked like she had killed the wilding wolves for sport and wore their skins like a trophy. Whoever this woman was, she was a very dangerous person.

The wolf woman moved quickly with determination as if she knew exactly where she was going. Then she paused and looked up at the markings above Mallory's hiding place. "You might as well come out," the woman shouted. "I know you're there."

Mallory looked at the wall above her and cursed under her breath. Her star hovered in the decorative molding above her like an omen in the sky. She measured the distance from the plant to the front door. There was no way she would make it there before the wolf woman overtook her. There was nothing to do but hope that the woman was peaceful, and if not, to hope the others would return before this stranger attacked. Mallory slowly stood up and stepped timidly out from behind the bush. "My friends will be back any minute." She intended the words to be threatening, but the choked squeak that accompanied them gave away her fear.

The woman smiled. "I'm counting on it, Mallory."

Mallory stepped backward and again looked toward the exit. Not only did she know the secrets of the Library, but she knew her name. "Who are you?" Mallory asked, her fear rising. The woman smiled and removed her hood. A bob of bright red, shoulder-length hair spilled out, and her features were suddenly clear. "Miss Lamarr?" Mallory stammered in disbelief.

"Yes, Mallory. It's me," the Sprite Master smirked.

Mallory's forehead wrinkled. Something was wrong, horribly wrong. She wondered if she were stuck in a dream: some nightmare where her husband was an Ex Natu, she was carrying his baby, Alex had disabled the Library's defenses, and now the older woman who Caleb had been so enamored with back home had somehow come to ruin her marriage on top of it all. She shook her head, as much in disbelief as to try and clear away the confusion. "How can you be here?"

"How did I find you?" Reddy pulled off her backpack and took off the wolfskin coat. "That part was easy. I put a tracker in the rope I gave you during the exiling ceremony. Much like the one in this building." She pointed at the molding. "But with global positioning rather than just a local matrix." She pulled a small black box about the size of a playing card from her pocket. One side of it glowed white, and Reddy Lamarr waved it at Mallory as if to suggest she should know exactly what it was.

Mallory bit the side of her lip. "The metal wiring?" she asked.

Lamarr shrugged. "Well, that was more to act as an antenna for sending the signal, but more or less. Getting inside to you was much more difficult with the plasma field and all."

"Plasma field?" Mallory asked in a daze.

"Oh, I mean, the Library's light," the Sprite Master corrected.

Mallory nodded, but the hairs on her neck were standing straight up. She needed a moment to process what was happening. Nothing about the Sprite Master's arrival was right. It could not be Reddy Lamarr. Who was this person? She took a step toward the door, but her escape was stalled by a question she could not help but ask. "Why were you wearing the wolf skins?"

The Sprite Master held up the coat and smiled. "It smells like them. They'll ignore you if you smell like them." She lowered the coat slowly. Her smile faded, and she muttered to herself. "Oh, Reddy. That was clumsy."

Mallory took another step toward the door. "How do you know about the wolves? How do you know the light is called a plasma field?"

The Sprite Master shook her head. "You always were a clever one, Mallory Knenne: Dangerously so."

Mallory still did not understand what was happening, but she recognized the threat in Reddy Lamarr's voice. Mallory darted for the door. Her hand was on the handle when Reddy called behind her. "Dikaió, stop her!"

The bolts on the door locked, and Mallory felt the clothes she was wearing begin to tighten and harden around her. She strained against them, but they slowly pulled her to the ground. Mallory was sure this was a dream now. One of those dreams where you try to run from danger, but you go nowhere—except the Dikaió clothing the Archivist had provided her was biting into her skin, and it hurt. She screamed, "Help!" But the word barely escaped her lips before Reddy Lamarr was on top of her, shoving a scrap of wolf fur in her mouth. "Hold that in," she commanded the fabric of Mallory's clothing, and a ribbon of fabric unwove itself and crawled snake like up her bodice, wrapping itself around her mouth, holding the fur securely in place.

"Now, let's not give away the surprise, shall we?" Lamarr grinned wickedly at her.

The animal fur in Mallory's mouth tasted awful, like dirt and blood. It smelled even worse: pungent like mushrooms and sulfur, with just enough hint of sweetness that it made her want to throw up. The tiny tendrils of fur tickling the inside of her mouth occasionally licked the back of her throat as she batted at them with her tongue, adding a gag reflux to the nausea. Her stomach lurched, and bile came halfway up her esophagus, burning inside her chest. She closed her eyes and tried to relax. She was not sure Reddy Lamarr would save her if she choked on her own vomit. She tried to think of more pleasant circumstances: her youth, her parents, Caleb, but in every memory, Reddy Lamarr's presence lurked like a shadow. Mallory could not remember a time that she had not been the Sprite Master as part of the City Council. While she never really got to know the woman, the Sprite Master was as much a part of the city as the Matriarch, the Governor, and the Administrator.

Lamarr had even helped save the city when Mallory and Alex had deactivated the Dikaió by helping make parts in the Sprite Rookery for the Chorus carts. The sprite husks from the Rookery that could not be activated without the Dikaió were what they had used to beat the fire sprites by dropping them off buildings. Without Reddy Lamarr, the city and all its inhabitants would have been destroyed. Yet here she was, in a Library outside the city, which she could not possibly know existed. And she understood its tracking system. But even more perplexing, she was using the Dikaió. Had the Dikaió been restored to Hoffen City? She could not imagine how.

Mallory looked at Lamarr closely, since there was little else she could do, and she was again amazed about how really young she looked for her age. She had to be older than Mallory's mother, but she did not look much older than Mallory or Alex. Nary a wrinkle had touched her face. Suddenly, Mallory wondered how old the woman really was? Was her youth and beauty aided by nano sprites. Mallory scanned down Lamarr's arms, and she saw it: a Dominus bracelet just like the Archivist's. It could not be. There had been an Ex Natu in Hoffen City this whole time. Not just this whole time—she must have been there since before the light was activated. How else could she explain it? But how did an Ex Natu get hold of a Dominus bracelet?

The ancient woman walked to the door and ordered, "Dikaió, open!" The door unbolted itself and swung open. "Culture sprites, defend me!" She yelled and stepped back inside the Library's foyer.

Mallory's eyes widened as the Archivist's culture sprites entered the room, their arms lengthening into the lethal whips Mallory had seen do so much damage. There were six of them, and they circled the Sprite Master facing outward. Mallory squirmed and squealed on the floor, but it was no use. She could not move or say anything. Reddy Lamarr looked down at her and smirked again. "Don't worry, Mallory. Your friends aren't who I'm after." Her eyes narrowed. "I'm here for our people's betrayer."

Now Mallory was really confused. What did Lamarr mean by "our people": the Ex Natu or the people of Hoffen City? A cramp in her thigh muscles interrupted her questioning thoughts. The fabric was so tight she could not even flex her leg to try and work it out. Sharp pains pulsated up her body like electricity. If she could have screamed, it might have helped, but all she could do was cry. The tears streaming down her face mingled with the fur in her mouth, and as it got wet, the smell of the wilding wolves intensified. If Reddy Lamarr had offered to untie her and ungag her in that moment, she would have done anything for her.

A voice deep inside her, that sounded a lot like her own, warned, "Not anything, Mal. You're a mother and wife."

Yes, a mother and a wife. No amount of suffering would make her betray her love and duty. She concentrated on her spasming leg. "Enough!" She shouted at the rebellious limb in her mind, and somehow her leg acquiesced somewhat. The sharp pangs receded into a dull throb. Her limbs were bound tight, so she used her core muscles to pull herself into a slight V shape, and then when she expanded, she found she had moved slightly closer to the door. She repeated the motion twice more before the Sprite Master noticed her.

"Determined as always, Mallory." The Sprite Master sighed. "Dikaió, secure her to the chair." One of the culture sprites broke formation and used its whip like a tentacle to scoop her off the floor, carried her across the foyer, and dropped her roughly into the blue-upholstered chair. The fabric of her clothing loosened its grip on her slightly as bits of it tore into strands and began to weave themselves into the fabric of the chair. She used the brief loosening to squirm violently to try and escape, but her clothing was still tight enough to keep her in place. Soon she was sewn into the chair and found herself unable to move again. The struggle had at least worked the cramp out of her leg, and the chair was much more comfortable than being hog-tied on the floor, so there were some things to be thankful for. She could also see out the door from this new position, and she hoped that anyone approaching the Library would see her, too.

Just then a crunching noise sounded in the bookshelves behind her. Someone was stepping on the broken glass the Sprite Master had left on the floor when she broke the window. The Sprite Master called out. "I know you're there. You might as well make yourself known."

Caleb's voice called from the depths. "Reddy, is that really you?"

The Sprite Master sighed. "Is she with you, Caleb?"

"Alex ran away." Caleb walked into the foyer.

She shook her head. "Not her, the other one."

"The Archivist?" Caleb scratched his head in confusion.

She nodded. "If that's what you call her."

"She's looking for Alex." Caleb tilted his head in confusion. "How are you here, Reddy?"

"I'm here for the betrayer." The Sprite Master's lip curled. "The one you call the Archivist, and I intend to kill her."

Caleb ran his hand through his hair and glanced at Mallory sewn into the chair, and he shrugged at her before looking at the Sprite Master with an innocent expression. "What?"

"Dikaió, securc him," the Sprite Master shouted, and Caleb's clothing began to contract around him.

"Hey!" he screamed. "What's happening?" One of the

culture sprites dragged another upholstered chair into the foyer and pushed Caleb into it. His clothes began to weave themselves into the upholstery just like Mallory's had. "Reddy?" Caleb called, just before she shoved a clump of wolf fur in his mouth, too. Caleb squirmed wildly then he stopped and inhaled some of the odor from the wolf fur in his mouth. His eyes crossed and rolled in their sockets. He pushed hard with the tips of his feet and tipped his chair backward.

The clatter of Caleb hitting the ground made the Sprite Master jump. She walked over to him and looked down at him disdainfully. "To think I had even considered you a potential match."

Mallory's brows furrowed. Considered him a match? Ex Natu or not, that was her husband that horrible woman was talking about. She squirmed and moaned violently, trying to get loose. She was going to claw Reddy Lamarr's eyes out. She pressed hard with her toes like Caleb had done and found her chair tipping to the side in Caleb's direction. She landed hard on his stomach, and Caleb inhaled sharply, and then made sobbing noises as the stench of the wolf fur again filled his nose. Mallory inhaled as well, and choked back her own tears, again trying not to vomit.

Reddy Lamarr had stepped back when Mallory fell, but then she started laughing. "And this is exactly why I had to destroy the plasma field in Hoffen City." She waved her hands at the pair squirming in their bindings on the floor. "Our people had completely forgotten the threat to their existence, and with every generation they were growing increasingly idiotic and incompetent. Can you imagine if you two had taken over the Triad?"

Mallory stopped squirming and rolled her eyes up toward the Sprite Master, glaring at her.

"Oh yes, little Miss Knenne. While you and the Nelson girl were resetting everyone's christening, I took down the light. The remote charges I planted on the generators sat there for decades waiting for the right moment to save our people from their slow descent into obsolescence, and your bungling offered just the chance I needed," the Sprite Master nodded. "Your expulsion from the city also offered me the best chance I was ever going to get to take down the only woman who could stop me from leading our people to a decisive victory: the one Caleb here called the Archivist. I'm going to kill—"

Her rant was cut short as a copper-colored tentacle shot through the doorway and wrapped around the Sprite Master's mouth, dragging her outside. The six culture sprites immediately spun around and followed her out into the Library's courtyard. Mallory could almost see what was happening, but her view of the action was framed by the doorway, as if she were watching a screen. Loud metallic clanging sounded as the culture sprites unleashed their whips on the copper sprite. It dropped the Sprite Master, just as the Archivist yelled from somewhere outside Mallory's frame of vision, "Dikaió, cease defense." The clanging stopped, but Mallory watched as the Sprite Master pulled a magistrate weapon from her belt and fired in the direction of the Archivist. Mallory half expected the copper sprite to lunge in the direction of the projectile and save her, but when she heard the Archivist scream, she realized that her order to cease defense affected her own defense as well.

Mallory wanted to do something to help the Archivist, and she squirmed on Caleb's abdomen. Caleb moaned and muttered, probably telling her to stop. Mallory sighed and held still. Her squirming was not getting her anywhere anyway. Then there was more crunching noise in the Library behind her. Mallory looked up at the moulding near the ceiling. A triangle had appeared. It was Alex. Moments later, Alex's voice sounded in the room: "Dikaió, release Mallory and Caleb."

Mallory felt her clothes go limp and one side of them released from the chair, as did Caleb's. She reached up and pulled the wolf fur from her mouth, spitting pieces of hair everywhere as she did. Caleb ripped his wolf fur out as well, joining Mallory's spit fest. Mallory started to stand up, but Alex cleared her throat, making her pause. The other side of her clothing was still sewn into the chair. If she pushed her way up her clothing would stay there, and she would be naked. "Dikaió, dress me, please," she said embarrassedly. While her clothing untangled itself from the chair, and the ribbons crawled over her body reforming clothing, Mallory could not help but think how silly it was to feel embarrassed in the midst of such a deadly situation. She had no idea who would win the fight outdoors, or what would happen to them if they did, but she knew that whatever happened, she would feel better about the results fully clothed. When she was appropriately covered, she stood up. "C'mon, Caleb," she said. "Get up. We've got to do something."

"There are now four women in my life that can use the Dikaió," Caleb pouted, "and I can't even dress myself without it."

Mallory looked down at him and chuckled. He was holding the ribbons of his clothing over his body and looking up at Alex and Mallory with flushed cheeks.

Mallory giggled. "What do you say, Alex? Should we leave him as is?"

Caleb looked up at her and pleaded, "C'mon, Mal."

"Dikaió, dress Caleb," Alex said rolling her eyes. "What's wrong with you, Mallory? Look what's happening out there. This isn't a time for jokes."

Caleb squirmed as the fabric crawled over him, resewing his clothing. "Gah! It tickles," he squealed.

Alex growled in irritation. "I shouldn't have come back."

Mallory's teeth clinched in rage. "Why did you? If you hate us so much, why didn't you just stay gone?" She waved her hands in circles emphatically. "Go back to the city. No one's stopping you."

Alex looked Mallory in the eyes, and then her steely gaze dropped to her stomach. Her eyes softened, tears forming in the corners. "I don't hate you, Mallory. You're my only friend. I'd do anything to protect you, but I want to protect our people too—I came back because I saw that one coming." She pointed toward the door. "I thought the Ex Natu had found us. I couldn't leave, especially after—"

Mallory tried not to scream. "After you took the regulator off the generators. She was only able to get in because of you."

Alex winced but did not argue. "She?"

"It's Reddy Lamarr," Caleb climbed to his feet fully dressed.

"The Sprite Master from the city? How can that be?" Alex blinked.

"She's Ex Natu," Mallory ran to the door.

"What?" Caleb's face twisted in disgust. He had not been there for that part of the revelation.

Mallory chose to ignore whatever Caleb's look meant, but she made a mental note to ask him about it later. "She's been in the city for ages; she's the one who destroyed the light, not us." She nodded toward Alex.

Alex shook her head. "But she was on the Council. She could use the Dikaió. I've seen her birth sprites at the Rookery."

Mallory pulled herself flat against the door jamb, then leaned her head out to get a better look. Before she could see anything useful, a magistrate projectile splintered the wood just above her head, and she pulled her head back inside quickly.

"Mal!" Caleb yelled running to her side.

"I'm fine. I'm fine." She shook Caleb off. "She has a Dominus bracelet."

Alex's eyes blinked several times. "You're sure?"

"That makes sense," Caleb mused. "How else do you explain an Ex Natu using the Dikaió?"

"Also, I saw it on her wrist," Mallory held up her left hand to demonstrate.

Alex's eyes narrowed, and she ran past Caleb and Mallory, drawing her magistrate weapons with both hands as she ran.

"Dikaió, defend me," she yelled. She jumped and kicked off the door jamb out into the courtyard, landing in a somersault, both guns blazing in the direction of the Sprite Master. Every projectile hit its target, but the Sprite Master didn't drop. She turned on Alex and fired at her. A silver-steeled sprite jumped in front of Alex saving her life, and Alex ducked down behind it, firing two more shots into the Sprite Master's shoulder and abdomen.

The Sprite Master dropped to her knees and whispered, "Dikaió, attack Alex Nelson."

The silver culture sprite that had just saved Alex spun on her and hit her hard with blunt force. Alex flew backwards several feet and rolled across the ground.

The Archivist came running to her aid, yelling, "Dikaió, cease attack." She spun in the air and kicked the Sprite Master in the head, sending her crashing back into the wall of the Library.

"Alex!" Mallory screamed and tried to run out and check on her friend, but Caleb grabbed her arm and pulled her back away from the door.

"Mallory, no!" he yelled. She struggled to escape his grasp, but he held tight.

"Alex is hurt!" Mallory clawed at him.

Caleb held tighter. "Mallory, remember the baby! She's protecting your baby! You have to, too!"

Mallory stopped struggling and nodded, touching Caleb's face gently. "You're right! But we have to do something to help them."

Caleb released her and held his hands up. "Okay. Ask the

house sprites if there are weapons here that we can use."

Mallory nodded. "Dikaió sprite?" she called to the Library. A small panel nearby opened, and a house sprite quickly approached them. "Does the Library have any weapons for Archivists to use?" The house sprite turned and rolled into the bookshelves, and Mallory and Caleb hustled after it. It led them past the elevator, and into a narrow back hallway that was made even more narrow by tables stacked full of old books. Many of them had spines that were starting to deteriorate. Some of them were just stacks of pages, nearly unbound completely. A dusty mustiness permeated the air, and Mallory was surprised at how pungent old books could smell.

Following the sprite down the narrow path made Mallory feel like she was back in the underground passages below Mason City. She closed her eyes and breathed slowly. This was no time for claustrophobia. Caleb bumped into her and whispered, "it's okay, Mal. You can do this." Then he nudged her softly forward. The sprite led them about thirty feet down the hallway then took a sharp left into another hallway, narrower and darker than the previous. Mallory's breaths grew more shallow and rapid, but then the sprite stopped at double doors made of steel that were tightly bolted shut.

Mallory leaned near the door and said quietly, "Dikaió, open." A large groaning noise sounded on the other side of the doors, and then there was a loud clank, and the doors shuddered, slowly swinging open. The room was almost pitch black. "Dikaió, lights," Mallory said. The lights in the room flickered on, and she could not help but feel a smile creep across her lips. It still felt good after so many years of deprivation to have the Dikaió respond to her voice, but her smile quickly faded when she saw what was in the room.

The space was nearly as big as the Rookery and held as many shelves: There were rows and rows of various weapons. Some looked familiar, variations of the magistrate weapons in the city. Some were completely unrecognizable. There were weapons that looked similar to the cubical sprite that had followed them into the woods, and weapons that looked like the big tube that the Archivist had used to defeat it. Mallory stepped into the room and gasped. On either side of the door, two fire sprites stood guarding the entrance, their dark hulking forms with their two large tanks full of accelerant attached to large nozzles. The scars in her feet began to ache, as she stared up into the same empty eyes that had spewed glass into the building, wounding her feet on that awful day when the fire sprites attacked the city.

"She really is Ex Natu," Caleb whispered; his mouth tensing with disgust.

Mallory nodded but shook her head. "Yes, but she wasn't always. Something happened. Something Reddy Lamarr knows about. Something that changed her."

Caleb's eyebrows furrowed. "Reddy called her a traitor."

Mallory gasped. "You're really going to go back to calling her by her first name? Even after she shoved all that fur in your mouth and left you tied to a chair?"

Caleb smiled. "You're still cute when you're jealous, Mal."

Mallory gave her husband a look that assured him he was going to pay a heavy price for that comment soon, but before she could say anything, their conversation was interrupted.

"Verify security clearance," the Archivist's voice suddenly sounded in the room. "You have five seconds."

Mallory looked back at Caleb in a panic. "Name and Dikaió christening," he urged. "Like in the *Chronicles*."

"Five…"

Mallory's mind went blank. What was her name again?

"Four…"

"Mal," Caleb urged.

Oh, that was right. Her name was Mal. No, it was longer than that.

"Three…"

"Mallory Knenne," she said. "Dikaió Syntec."

"Unrecognized security access," the voice responded. "Two…"

"Archivist!" Caleb shouted. "Archivist."

"Oh right! Right!" Mallory was stuttering now.

"One…" The metal plates inside the fire sprites began to slowly scrape together, creating sparks they would use to ignite the fuel in their tanks.

"Mallory…" she looked at Caleb, and he grabbed her hand, nodding reassuringly. She continued, "Mallory Aiworth, Dikaió Archivist."

"Security recognition acknowledged," the Archivist's voice said, and the screeching metal of the fire sprites slowly spun to a stop.

Caleb sighed heavily and squeezed her shoulder. "You're going to be the death of me yet, Mal."

"Just wait until you meet our baby," Mallory patted her

belly. "She's going to drive you crazy."

"She? I thought his appetite meant he was going to be a boy," Caleb laughed.

"I'm pretty sure things don't work that way," Mallory chided. "Let's find something to help Alex with." Mallory walked into the room and picked up a long magistrate weapon. "Whoa! This one looks like it could do some damage." She pointed it at one of the fire sprites and playfully pulled the trigger.

The resulting explosion knocked both of them off their feet. Mallory pulled herself up off the floor and stared in disbelief. One of the tanks of accelerant on the fire sprites was gone, and flames were everywhere. The door frame was on fire. The piles of old books in the hallway were on fire as well, and the flames were spreading fast. The Archivist's voice started shouting through the building again: ""Attention, the Library is under attack. Seek shelter. Attention, the Library is under attack. Seek shelter."

"Mallory!" Caleb yelled. "What did you do?"

Mallory held up the weapon as an offering of proof to Caleb. "How could I have known it was loaded?"

Caleb grabbed as many weapons as he could carry and yelled, "grab what you can, and let's get out of here."

Mallory followed suit, and the two ran to the door to make their escape. They leapt through the flames eating away at the door frame and dove out into the narrow hallway with the old books, but there was no way they were getting out that way. The old books seemed more flammable than the accelerant in the fire sprite's tanks. The hallway was an inferno. Caleb pushed Mallory back into the room with all the weapons. They scanned the room quickly looking for another exit, and there were none readily apparent.

"We're trapped," Mallory whimpered.

The fire did not seem to be spreading through the weapons room very quickly. The floor and walls were made of marble instead of the carpet and wood decoration the rest of the Library boasted, but Mallory knew that the thousands of books on the other side of the narrow hallway would turn the building into an inferno that would eventually consume this room, too. "We have to do something, Caleb. All those books."

Caleb held her close. "We'll figure out something, Mal. What I wouldn't give for a hydrant sprite."

Mallory bit her lip and tilted her head. She called out, "Dikaió hydrant sprites, to us, please."

Nothing happened.

Caleb shook his head. "I can't believe the Archivist would have all these books, and not have some sort of fire-suppression system. She seemed like such a smart lady and with so many years of experience, too."

Mallory tilted her head the other way. "Dikaió, start Library fire suppression system," she said uncertainly.

Small tubes set on swivels descended from the ceiling and aimed at the flaming sprite at the entrance to the weapons room. It fired a small ball at the fire, and when the ball was within a foot of the center of the flames, it exploded in a cloud of white foam. The fire disappeared instantly as if all the oxygen had been sucked out of it.

"Whoa!" Caleb exhaled.

Mallory smiled. "That was awesome!" She shook loose of Caleb's arms and ran to the hallway. The once flaming books were all covered in white foam. All traces of the fire were gone. Even the intensity of the heated air had been replaced by a cold, wet humidity. She reached out and touched the foam. "What is this stuff?"

"We don't have time for curiosity, Mal." Caleb pushed past her holding as many weapons as he could carry. "I'm going to see if I can help Alex and the Archivist. You stay in there." He nodded toward the weapons room. "Use whatever you can to stay alive if I don't come back."

"If you don't come back?" Mallory grabbed his arm. "You mean, until you come back."

He smiled and pulled his wife into his arms, kissing her deeply. "Until I come back." He winked and then ran down the narrow hallway, his sandals splashing through piles of white foam as he went.

Mallory did not like being left alone. Certainly not with her husband and friend fighting an unknown force. She tilted her head and thought about the battle outside. Three Ex Natu, two Dominus bracelets, and then there was Alex, just a mortal, but who might be the most dangerous of them all. She smiled at that thought. Back in the city, she knew Alex had been trained as a magistrate and knew how to fight and how to shoot, but mostly, she knew her friend as the one who always wanted to help her. When Mallory was the only Chorus in the city, Alex always wanted to use the Dikaió to do things for her. Even when they broke everyone's christening, it was just Alex trying to help. And Alex had seemed so helpless without the Dikaió. Mallory almost laughed at the memory of Alex that night, small and frightened. Since then, she had seen her shoot the ear off a guy about to kill her, drop a fire sprite by crushing it with the husk of another sprite, kill countless wilding wolves, and now she was battling an Ex Natu with a Dominus bracelet.

A rage-filled scream in the hallway outside the weapons room interrupted her thoughts. Mallory ran into the shelter of the shelves of weapons, filling her arms with as many things off the shelves as she could carry. She had no idea what most of them did, but she hoped something there would protect her from Reddy Lamarr. She bunkered down between two medium-sized, very dangerous looking sprites. They both had what appeared to be abdominal muscles covered in spikes. "Dikaió, protect me," she whispered. The sprites' eyes lit up, and the spike-covered muscles extended out, revealing themselves to be balls attached to chains. The sprites moved into defensive positions around her, and Mallory picked one of the weapons she was holding to start the fight with, one with red fins on the back of a long white cylinder with a triangular red cone on the front. There didn't appear to be a trigger, but she held it menacingly and hoped that when the time came, it would do something helpful.

"Mallory Aiworth!" A familiar voice called. "You burned my books! When I find you, I'll, I'll…"

The Archivist! Mallory jumped out of her hiding place and ran toward the entrance of the weapons room. When she burst out of the shelves, she saw Caleb and the Archivist standing together. Caleb smiled, and the Archivist's angry expression turned to one of horror.

"Stop!" She screamed.

Mallory slowed but kept walking toward them.

"I said, 'Stop!'" The Archivist screamed again.

Mallory could tell she meant it and stopped dead in her tracks.

The Archivist held out her hand and said, "slowly put the missile on the ground."

The missile? Mallory realized she was still holding the long cylindrical weapon in her arms. "This?" She held it up inquisitively.

The Archivist winced. "Yes, that. Very slowly, place it on the ground."

Mallory slowly bent down and set the missile on the ground. "Okay. Okay. I'm putting it down."

When the missile was on the ground, the Archivist

began muttering. "It isn't enough they break my plasma field, they destroy my books; now, they're trying to blow us all to kingdom come." She sighed heavily and then said, "Dikaió, clean this place up. Put it all back in order." Several compartments in the walls opened, and house sprites poured into the room. Two gently picked up the missile at Mallory's feet. "Careful!" the Archivist yelled. Mallory stepped out of their way as they headed off into the shelving. Another two began plucking smaller weapons out of her pockets, putting them away as well. Others started vacuuming up the foam that had extinguished the fire, and still others began to load up burned books and carried them off in bundles into the walls of the Library.

"Take those to the conservatory, and we'll see if we can salvage them," the Archivist yelled after them. Then she turned to Mallory and Caleb. "Before these savages do any more damage."

Mallory bounced from foot to foot completely oblivious to the Archivist's biting remarks. "So? What happened?"

Caleb started to mimic her, bouncing from foot to foot as well. "It was amazing."

The Archivist looked at them both with disgust and started hopping from foot to foot and spinning in circles while tapping at her armpits. "Amazing!" she sang then stopped and pointed at Caleb incredulously. "An assassin tried to kill me, and this monkey says it's amazing."

Caleb stopped hopping and spread his arms wide, flashing his goofy grin that Mallory found irresistible. She grinned back to match and ran over to him. With her hand on his broad chest, she looked up into his blue eyes. "Tell me," she cooed.

"It was Alex. She lay there like she was dead until Reddy was inches from her and distracted by the Archivist. Then WHOOP!" he dropped to the floor and windmilled his legs awkwardly. "She tripped her like this."

Mallory laughed. "Just like that?"

Caleb lay on the floor breathing heavily with wide eyes. "Yes, just like that." He pulled himself up to one knee and mimed grabbing something. "Then she slipped off her Dominus bracelet just as slick as you please—it was AMAZING!"

The Archivist sighed and rolled her eyes. "No wonder your friend was so desperate to leave." She gazed around at the mess left behind by the fire. "Sprite!" she yelled, and the clockwork sprite zoomed into the room. Mallory inhaled sharply. The bronze-colored sprite was missing one of its eyes. A tangle of wires hung from the socket the eye once occupied. Parts of its body were crumpled in long dents. A loose tentacle stuttered back and forth as it kept trying to retract and failed. The culture sprites that Reddy Lamarr had co-opted had nearly destroyed the poor thing in her attempt to kill the traitor, whatever that meant. "You're a mess," the Archivist said matter of factly.

"Yes, Archivist," the sprite said. Its voice was low and metallic sounding.

"Are your sensors working well enough to scan the walls for structural damage?" The Archivist pointed.

The sprite's one eye blinked. "Yes, Archivist." It turned

around and paused for a moment staring at the walls of the weapons room and then moved to the door to scan the hallway. "Neither wall is load bearing, but there is fire damage to the wooden studs. They will need to be replaced."

"Well, I guess I don't have to worry about whether a construction project would leave the plasma field down too long." The Archivist shrugged.

"Doesn't Alex have the regulator? Can't we just replace it?" Mallory asked.

Caleb's enthusiastic demeanor disappeared. "Alex is gone."

"Gone?" Mallory shook her head. "But she came back."

"Well, she's gone again," the Archivist spit.

"What about the Sprite Master?" Mallory asked.

The Archivist's eyebrows shot up. "Sprite Master? You mean the assassin?"

Caleb nodded. "She was the Sprite Master in Hoffen City."

"And an Ex Natu," Mallory added.

The Archivist's mouth opened and closed, and then her face looked frightened. "And we left her laying up there?" She turned and ran out of the weapons room. "With me, sprite. Dikaió, defend me." The clockwork sprite rushed after her.

"C'mon, Mallory!" Caleb yelled, running after the Archivist.

Mallory sighed. She still wanted to know what happened, but if Reddy Lamarr was still out there, she did not want to go unarmed. She walked back to the shelving and picked up the long weapon that she had accidentally started the fire with. It had a strap, and she looped it over her shoulder. She practiced pulling into a firing position a few times, being careful not to aim it anywhere near the other fire sprite at the doorway. Confident she could use it if she needed, she started to head toward the door, but she was stopped as a red-headed figure limped into the room.

"Mallory, help me." Reddy Lamarr stood there facing her. She was covered in blood that seemed to have once poured out of now healed wounds.

Mallory did not hesitate. She shouldered her weapon and shot the Sprite Master. The woman flew backward out the door like a child's rag doll tossed across the room, her limbs flailing behind her as she sailed. A loud thud sounded as she hit the wall in the hallway. Mallory walked cautiously forward to check to see if she was dead this time. Reddy Lamarr lay on the ground in the hallway covered in soot and white foam from the fire. A tiny trickle of blood ran from the large wound in her chest that Mallory's weapon had created.

"Please," the Sprite Master, who was not even close to dead, moaned. "The one you call the Archivist. She's in league with the Ex Natu. She's going to kill you and our people in Hoffen City."

Mallory shouldered her weapon again and aimed it at Reddy Lamarr's head. "And why should I believe the Ex Natu that's lived among us for how long? Centuries? The one who tracked us here? Tied Caleb and I to chairs?"

The Sprite Master coughed, and a large misshapen lump of metal popped out of the hole in her chest. Skin started to knit itself into existence from the outside inward, closing up the hole, as if it were little more than a sweater. "You're right to be suspicious, but I can prove it. I just need a pen and paper. Dikaió, bring me a pen and paper," she called out.

Nothing happened.

She looked down at her wrist, and her head drooped.

Mallory followed her gaze. "So, it's true. You can't use the Dikaió without the bracelet?" She pointed with her weapon at the Sprite Master's bare arm.

Reddy Lamarr nodded and pulled herself to a sitting position. She leaned back heavily against the wall. "If the Ex Natu get hold of a Dominus bracelet, it will be the end of us."

Mallory lowered her weapon and tilted her head. "Well, that just goes to show you, the Archivist can't be in league with the Ex Natu. She has a Dominus bracelet and hasn't given it to them."

"Oh, she is," Reddy Lamarr sighed. "I could prove it if Alex hadn't taken mine. But without the Dikaió, I'm just like you."

Mallory smiled. "Dikaió, bring me a pen and paper," she said. When a house sprite appeared carrying a pen and paper, she could not help but gloat over Reddy Lamarr. "Not just like me," Mallory handed the paper and pen to the Sprite Master.

The Sprite Master looked up at her in bewilderment. "She christened you?"

Mallory shrugged. "Yes, I'm an Archivist, now!"

"An Archivist in training, more of a beginning apprentice really." the Archivist's voice called out from farther down the hall. "But I have half a mind to revoke your christening after what you did to my Library, little Matriarch. Speaking of which, how is it that you have a rifle again? I thought I had that put away. Dikaió, put Mrs. Aiworth's rifle away!"

The house sprite that handed Mallory the pen and paper reached up for Mallory's weapon. Mallory ducked under the strap and handed the rifle to the sprite, which quickly zipped back into the weapons room to shelve it. There was not much point in arguing when the Archivist had a Dominus bracelet and Reddy Lamarr no longer did, though she would have been happy to shoot the Sprite Master again if she made any sudden movements. And in her anger, she did not really register the Archivist's threat about revoking her christening. Instead, she peered angrily down at the red-headed woman on the floor. "Well? You have your pen and paper. You were going to prove something?"

Reddy Lamarr held the pen and paper back up to Mallory. "Use the Dikaió and tell it to copy the ninety-seventh page of the Chronicles of the Lost: her diary." She motioned at the Archivist.

The Archivist stopped walking down the hall toward them. "How could you possibly know about that book and have come from Hoffen City? The plasma field was up long before I began keeping it."

Mallory tilted her head, bit her lip, and looked at Reddy Lamarr. She was not about to volunteer that she had already read parts of the Archivist's Chronicles, but the Archivist was right. Something was off about what the Sprite Master was saying.

"That's neither here nor there," the Sprite Master spit back at the Archivist interrupting Mallory's thoughts. "You're a traitor! You betrayed your own people, your own family, and you wrote it all down like you were proud of it."

Caleb interrupted, "Wait, wait. Go back, Reddy."

Mallory grimaced at him and rolled her eyes. She hated the way he called her by her first name, and he knew it.

Caleb caught her look and half-smiled at her, "I mean, 'Go back, Miss Lamarr.' The Archivist has a valid point: How exactly did you get inside Hoffen City after the plasma field was activated?"

She shook her head. "Write the page first." She motioned her head toward the paper and pen.

Mallory held the pen and paper lightly in her hands like she was testing their weight. She tilted her head to the side and bit her lip. Finally, she looked at Reddy Lamarr and said, "let's say you're right, and the Archivist is a traitor in league with the Ex Natu. What exactly would we do about it at this point? She has a Dominus bracelet. We don't. Alex was the only one proficient enough with weapons to stand a fighting chance, and she's gone—again. So, what are you hoping we'll do if you're right?"

The Archivist smiled and walked the few feet to join Mallory and Caleb looking down at the Sprite Master. "Little Matriarch, I take it back. You may make a decent Archivist yet. That was a very well-reasoned response."

The Sprite Master sprang from the floor faster than Mallory thought possible. She clamped her hand over the Archivist's mouth and grabbed for her wrist, reaching for the Dominus bracelet. Caleb clasped her by the shoulder, but the Sprite Master expertly twisted her torso, spinning in the air, throwing the Archivist and Caleb both to the floor, but landing on her feet without loosening her grip on the Archivist's mouth or the Dominus bracelet. Mallory took a step back. Adrenaline rushed through her, and her body tensed to run, but her voice came out sounding much calmer than she expected. "Dikaió, detain Reddy Lamarr." The clockwork sprite spun around the corner at the far end of the hall and burst across the length of it to their location at sonic speed, throwing half-burnt books behind its wake like droplets from a wave. Its half-functioning tendrils lashed out and knocked the Sprite Master off the Archivist. She flipped again: end-over-end this time, crashing hard into one of the tables. It fell over on top of her.

Mallory gasped. The Sprite Master's hand was sticking out from under the table, and it held the Archivist's Dominus bracelet. The Sprite Master was momentarily stunned, but Mallory knew that the Ex Natu did not stay down long. Mallory dove at the bracelet, trying not to jostle her baby too much, and plucked it out of Reddy Lamarr's hand before the ancient woman recovered. She stood up holding the bracelet and looked at it thoughtfully. A million scenarios flooded her mind. With this bracelet, she could become the most powerful Dikaió user: a just ending to the girl once cursed to be a Chorus. She could give it to Caleb and restore her husband's ability to use the Dikaió, and he could give her a more powerful christening. They could return to the city with Alex and restore the power of the Triad, ruling as Dikaió Dominuses. They could restore the city's light. And surely, they would be powerful enough to stave off any attack from the Ex Natu. Not only that, but Mallory could bring back books to the city by having the Dikaió copy all the books here in the Library. She started to slip the bracelet over her hand.

"Mal?" Caleb's voice sounded far away even though he was almost next to her. He looked at the Archivist, who looked weak and feeble all of a sudden, and then back to her.

Mallory's gray eyes drifted toward his. The clear blue in his calmed the storm in hers like they always did. He was her husband. She pulled the bracelet away from her hand and touched her stomach. This was their home now, for better or worse, and in the end, she wanted to stay. She handed the bracelet to a very surprised Archivist. "I have what I need," she said quietly and reached for Caleb's hand.

The Archivist held the bracelet tightly in her hand, her mouth agape. Then she nodded at Mallory and Caleb before quickly sliding the bracelet back onto her arm.

Reddy Lamarr regained her composure and tried to get out from under the table quickly, but the clockwork sprite had wrapped one of its tendrils around her arms and one around her legs, securing her just as Mallory had commanded. "You're a fool, Mallory Knenne," the Sprite Master shouted. "She'll betray you, too."

The Archivist spun around on her. "I don't know what you think you know, but I assure you that you can't understand what I've been through or why I've made the choices I made."

"Spare me your sob story, traitor," Lamarr answered. "I've been through worse than you and didn't betray my people."

"You turned our light off and made us vulnerable to the Ex Natu," Caleb said. "If that's not betrayal, I don't know what is."

The Sprite Master looked at him with hurt in her eyes. "I did what I had to do. You would understand if you would read the book! Our people deserve vengeance."

Mallory suddenly felt ravenous. "This is clearly going nowhere, and I'm hungry."

The Archivist laughed out loud. "For heaven's sake! You turn on a dime! One moment you're wise beyond your years, and the next your driven by the slightest whim of carnal need."

Caleb laughed. "I suggest dinner and a story—two stories—perhaps. We want to know how you ended up in our city." He pointed at the Sprite Master. "And I'd like to know what all this traitor business is." He pointed at the Archivist.

The Archivist's cheer turned sour. "Careful, young Governor. I won't be called a traitor in my own home, not by the likes of her, nor by you."

"Apologies," Caleb backtracked. "But she acts like she knows you, and if it's all a misunderstanding then I'd like to clear it up."

The Archivist shook her head. "It's no misunderstanding. I know exactly what she's on about, but what I did wasn't a betrayal, it was diplomacy. I was betrayed by the Ex Natu: one Ex Natu in particular."

"You're a liar!" The Sprite Master yelled, squirming in the arms of the clockwork sprite. "You killed them all." She stopped struggling and started to sob. "You killed them—not just your family, but mine too. Their blood cries out from the ground for vengeance, and you blamed it all on a man long dead."

Mallory started walking away. "This is maddening. We've been going back and forth forever, and I still have no idea what either of you two are talking about. I'm going to go to the dining room and eat. Dikaió sprite, bring Reddy Lamarr to accompany me but keep her secure."

The sprite fell in line behind her, dragging the Sprite Master down the hall. "Yes, Sprite Master," its broken voice wobbled.

Reddy Lamarr laughed. "Sprite Master? You'd take my title, too?"

Mallory's eye twitched. She paused and then added with a smile, "Coming husband?"

Caleb walked quickly and caught up with his wife. He glanced back at the Archivist who did not follow. She just glared at the young and very old as they disappeared around the corner of the hallway heading toward the dining room. "I hope giving back the Dominus bracelet was the right thing to do," Caleb said softly to Mallory.

Mallory's eyes widened. "I thought that's what you wanted me to do."

"What?" Caleb yelled. "Why would you think that?"

"You looked right at me and said 'Mal' then nodded at the Archivist while she was laying there all pitiful on the floor." Mallory waved her hands in circles. "What were you trying to say if not 'give her back the bracelet?'"

Caleb shook his head and lifted the palms of his hands in exasperation. "I was saying watch out. She was edging toward you slowly. I thought she was going to attack you." He shook his head.

The Sprite Master laughed. "You two are idiots. She's going to kill us all. You should have never given her back the Dominus bracelet."

Caleb shook his head again then sighed. "It doesn't matter. What's done is done."

Mallory tilted her head and thought about that for a while. "The Archivist has forgotten more about the Dikaió then we'll ever know, Caleb. Besides, I think she's sincere in wanting someone to take over the Library for her. I see a desperation in her sometimes—like she's trapped here and would do anything to leave. Whatever the Sprite Master has been going on about is part of it, I'm sure."

Back in the Dining Room, Mallory motioned to one of the chairs with armrests. "Dikaió, secure Reddy Lamarr to that chair." The clockwork sprite haphazardly dropped the Sprite Master into the chair, and then just like what had happened to Caleb and Mallory, Lamarr's chair began to weave itself into the fabric of her clothing. "Now, how about breakfast for dinner? Dikaió, bring us fruit, eggs, bacon, toast with butter, and ice cream."

Caleb laughed. "Should we wait and have the ice cream after?"

"No," Mallory shook her head. "We should have it first."

The Sprite Master squirmed in her chair. "Just kill me now!"

Mallory frowned. "She complains more than Alex ever did. Maybe we should get some of that wolf fur out in the hallway and see how she likes the taste of it?"

Caleb shook his head. "But who would provide us a story during our dinner, Mal? I mean we went through all the trouble of tying her up."

Mallory saw house sprites coming from the kitchen with trays of food and waved her hand in concession. "It's too late now anyhow. Okay, Ms. Lamarr, tell us who you are…really."

The Sprite Master snarled at her. "You're in league with the traitor. Why would I tell you anything?"

Caleb sighed. "Oh, come now, Reddy. We have only been here a short time. You've known us all our lives. I thought I knew you too, and then you show up here with these accusations, tie us up, try to kill our host, and tell us you put our people in danger from a threat we've only just discovered exists. Maybe if you tell us why, we might trust you."

"Write the page from the book," the Sprite Master said. "You'll know why."

Mallory had not waited to start eating, but she took a breath and called. "Dikaió, bring me the copy of The Chronicles of the Lost I started earlier today and a pen."

Caleb shouted, "Mal! You started it before the Archivist said it was okay?"

"You know me better than that, Caleb." Mallory laughed. "I'm not the most patient woman in the world. And speaking of which…" She waved her fork at Reddy Lamarr. "While we wait for the book, you tell us who you are. Deal?"

The Sprite Master glared at her and squirmed, testing the strength of her bonds.

Caleb laughed, "Even if you could, you really don't want to break out of those. It doesn't leave much to the imagination if you know what I mean." Then he looked at Mallory. "Maybe she's just cranky because she's hungry? It's a long journey from the city after all. And when those nano sprites heal you up, it leaves you with a hole in your stomach." He held the toast up to the Sprite Master's mouth.

The Sprite Master looked at him with loathing, but she leaned forward and took a bite anyway. She barely chewed before swallowing and took another huge bite nearly taking off Caleb's fingers with it. Caleb pulled his hand away. "Mallory, maybe you could have a sprite do this?"

Mallory shrugged, "Dikaió, feed Reddy Lamarr—without letting her loose," she added quickly, not quite sure how literal she needed to be with the Dikaió. A plate floated up from the table, and a house sprite whirred in, filling it with food from the table. Then it fed the Sprite Master as if she were a baby. Another sprite appeared at the side of the table holding the book with the fragment of the Chronicles of the Lost that Mallory had started earlier and a pen. It placed them on the table. "Dikaió, resume copying," Mallory ordered. The pen sprang up and started writing.

Mallory waved at the book. "It's going to be awhile before it gets to page ninety-seven, Ms. Lamarr, and you know me well enough to know I'll lose interest long before it gets there if I'm not entertained. How about a story? Tell us who you are."

Color was flushing up through the Sprite Master's cheeks. She rolled her eyes, but she signaled acquiescence and began to tell her story between bites. "Years ago, I worked for a man named Omaha."

Mallory and Caleb nearly choked on their food. Caleb leaned forward. "You worked for Omaha? Like in the underground resistance?"

Reddy Lamarr nodded. "You've been reading, Caleb. That's good." She took another big bite of food, chewed, and then began to speak.

"I grew up in the bunker below Mason City. I did not even see sunlight until I was old enough to pass for an Ex Natu, and even then, it was a rare occasion, running messages to and from Omaha at the field generators under City Hall. By that time, he had grown too paranoid to use normal communication channels like radio or satellite relay. 'Reddy,' he'd say, 'the Ex Natu have eyes and ears everywhere.' Once

I pointed out that if that were true, they had just heard him say that, and he laughed as if I were joking. I was not. The Ex Natu terrified me. They terrified all of the children of the resistance. They were the real-life bogeymen. Though, you would never know it walking among them in the cities. They look through you as if you do not exist; even when they're talking to you directly.

"But after enough trips back and forth through the city relaying messages, I kind of understood why they were the way they were. In the bunker, everyone knew everyone. There were so few children that we were all very close. Up in the city, there were so many Ex Natu, it would be impossible for them to know everyone, even with centuries of living together. We spent our childhood learning to blend in with them, memorizing where the safe houses of the various cities were located, where to shop, who to talk to, what to say.

"But going up to the city was full of danger. While we were packing up the bunker in anticipation of moving to Hoffen City, Governor Aiworth told me to run to City Hall and tell Omaha that he needed his help with a Dikaió bug he'd found. Omaha had created the Dikaió to be intuitive and learning, almost like it can read your mind. You know this; at least in terms of use, if not the underlying mechanics of it. When Mallory commanded the Dikaió to feed me, the sprite came to put the food in my mouth, just as she imagined it. But in those early days, it had not learned nearly as much as it has now. And sometimes those little bugs became huge issues. If someone's temper flared, they could seriously hurt others with just a wrong word. And if the words weren't just so, a person could mix up the command. The sprite could have tried to feed me to the plate instead of the other way around. The first Governor's issue wasn't nearly as ridiculous as that, but he had managed to turn off all the sprites in the bunker with a careless word, and no one could figure out exactly how to turn them back on.

"So, he sent me to go fetch Omaha to fix the issue. I took the secret path to the surface and started the long track to City Hall. I was full of trepidation, not about bothering Omaha, mind you, he was the best of us. In all the years I knew him, I never remember him so much as frowning. He always had a smile for you no matter what the situation was. No, I was anxious about walking among the Ex Natu, and you really did have to walk among them: throngs of them all around you. I was halfway to City Hall when someone on a flying sprite lost control and accidentally ran it into the pack of pedestrians I was walking among. Shoulders and elbows hit me from every direction, and for a moment I lost all sense of who I was. It was like the world slowed down, and I was watching everything happen to someone else. Then I was flung to the ground. There was a mass of people that went with me, tangled together in some giant web of humanity. We all sat there for a moment in a bloody, stunned silence, and then their wounds began to heal. Cuts sewed themselves up, twisted limbs set themselves right, and people started standing up all around me dusting off the dirt and blood. But I could feel that my arm was sprained if not broken. And even worse, my temple had scraped across the ground. My own blood was dripping into my eye, and it was not stopping.

"Panic welled up. This was the moment all of us born in the resistance dreaded. The only people old enough to not be Ex Natu were much older. I did not have any wrinkles. There wasn't a speck of gray in my red hair. But my wounds were not going to heal. And now, I had to run the gauntlet, hoping none of them would notice. I stood gingerly to my feet, testing if there were injuries to my legs. They seemed okay. I imitated the Ex Natu around me dusting off dirt, and wiping at the blood pouring from my forehead as if it didn't hurt. The pain in my arm made me dizzy, but passing out would be a dead giveaway. I stopped moving my arm and jammed my hand in my pocket to try and stabilize it a little. The world swam as I turned, trying to find the direction of City Hall. When I had my bearings, I couldn't decide if I was any closer to it than going back to the bunker, but the last thing I wanted to do was lead a bunch of Ex Natu back to the families underground. Protecting family was the whole point.

"So instead, I kept my head down. All I could think about was the blood trickling down my forehead. The slow crawl down my skin was impossible to ignore like a spider crawling on your ear. All I wanted to do was wipe it away, but I was terrified that if I touched it, everyone around me would look at what I was reaching for and wonder why my hand was smeared with red. And some of the Ex Natu did look at me just a bit too long, but I made it to City Hall without being stopped. The building was a lot like the one in Hoffen City, though much larger. The generators that powered the plasma field were a massive project being installed underneath the building. Omaha and his wife were just on the precipice of being too old to be Ex Natu, so operating out in the open was nearly as dangerous for him as the cut on my head. But the Mason City's mayor's three children were living in the bunker with us, and it would not be much longer before he was too old to avoid discovery, as well.

"I walked into the construction area and found Omaha and his wife standing over a generator, arguing about the specifications of the regulator. 'I'm sorry to interrupt, sir,' I said softly.

"His frown turned into the warm smile that made Omaha so beloved in our community. 'Reddy, no need to be sorry. What is it?'

"'The sprites are no longer responding to Dikaió commands. The Governor ordered them to do something new, and now they're just not doing anything.' I held up my hands in supplication. 'He sent me to get you to do something.'

"Melody Omaha looked around worriedly, and then back to me. 'Reddy, dear. Did you cut your head?'

"I nodded touching my hair. My fingers were immediately covered in blood. The cut had not stopped bleeding, and the sight of the red on my fingers made me swoon slightly. 'There was an accident. A flying sprite hit us on the sidewalk.'

"Omaha shook his head. 'Any casualties?'

"'No, they all seemed fine. Except me,' I brushed at the wound again. More blood.

"'Okay, dear.' Melody said with anxiety in her voice. She reached into Omaha's back pocket and pulled out his hand-kerchief. 'Is this clean?'

"Omaha looked at it in surprise. 'How'd that get in there?'

"'I'll assume that's a yes,' Melody took off her construction helmet and tucked the handkerchief inside then placed the helmet gingerly on my head. I winced in pain, and she grabbed my hand quickly. 'Not here. I need you to be strong.'

"I nodded.

"'I'm afraid we don't have much time left,' Omaha was looking around at his crew, who had stopped working to see what their boss was up to.

"I saw the gaze of the crew and asked, 'do you have Ex Natu working here with you?'

"Omaha smiled. 'Of course. It would be awfully suspicious to bring in all my own people instead of using the city's construction crews.'

"My stomach rolled. 'About the sprites…'

"'There's an automatic update scheduled for tonight that should clear out that bug of the Dikaió,' Omaha said matter-of-factly. 'For now, they just need a hard reset command.' He looked at his watch and grimaced. 'I could do it, but we're so close here. Melody?'

"She folded her arms. 'I'm staying here with you. I still don't think you've got this regulator quite calibrated to the proper magnetic harmonics.'

"'Melody! We've been over this a hundred times.' Omaha's cheerful disposition disappeared. 'It's going to work.'

"'Not if I leave to go fix the sprites' problem, it won't,' she countered. She rolled up her sleeve, revealing a Dominus bracelet. 'Here, Reddy. Take this, reset the sprites, get your head cleaned up, and come straight back. Okay?'

"I took the bracelet from her, slid it over my hand, and then I almost screamed.

"One of the Ex Natu workers was standing next to us. He was a large man, maybe a foot taller than Omaha. He had a black goatee and eyes that seemed too small for his head. Those eyes were trained on me like a cat tracking a bird. 'Why is her head not healing?' he asked pointing at my helmet. Behind him, a crowd of curious onlookers were slowly moving closer to us. The construction worker turned and gestured toward the crowd. 'We saw you put a bandage on her. Why would she need a bandage?'

"Omaha laughed nervously. 'There was an accident. It's not her blood. Everyone's fine.'

"The worker's eyes narrowed, and he studied me carefully. 'But why not just wipe it off? Why keep the bandage under the helmet?'

"Melody spoke then, 'Reddy, take my cycle sprite and go finish that job we need you to do.' Then she turned to the construction worker. 'We're not paying you to ask questions about our office assistant, Greg.' She raised her voice. 'We're not paying you to stand around either. None of you! Everyone get back to work!'

"Greg did not seem interested in getting back to work, but he did not stop me from getting on Melody's cycle sprite either. As I started forward, he spoke brusquely, 'Something's not right. I'm going to call the Investigators.'

"Omaha shook his head. 'Come on, Greg. We don't need the authorities involved. They'll delay our project for years.'

"'Years are all we've got now,' Greg said. 'What's

your hurry? I've never liked you or your pushy wife here. Something's not right, and we need to figure it out before we do anymore work. Yeah, I'm calling the investigators.'

"Melody looked at me earnestly and waved me away. 'Go,' she mouthed, and I did.

"I hit the sprite's accelerator full throttle. I needed to get back to the bunker and get the sprites back into working order. If the Ex Natu were getting suspicious, we were going to need them for more than menial tasks; we were going to need them for weapons of war. I ducked through alleys and stopped and started frequently, double-checking for tails as the General had trained us to do, and I arrived at the train depot without being followed. I left the cycle sprite outside and slipped into the newspaper stand taking the secret elevator into the tunnels. I was halfway to the bunker when the tunnel began to shake. I tried to grab the wall to stay standing, but it seemed to physically move away from my hand. Then rocks rained down on my head. For the second time that day, I found myself flailing to the ground. My injured arm twisted under me, and I was sure it was broken now. If I had not been wearing Melody's construction helmet, I would have been killed for certain. As it was, my bloody head was not the only injury openly bleeding now. I pulled myself slowly up and again tested my legs. There were some cuts and bruises, but they seemed relatively unscathed. What I thought had been a collapse did not appear too major when I looked around. Scattered about the tunnel, rocks had fallen here and there, but the tunnel appeared stable. Had it been an earthquake? Was everyone okay? I started running toward the bunker.

"It wasn't until I got there and found the entire community in disarray that I heard what happened. The field generator had been activated and exploded. Omaha, Melody, everyone was dead. Melody had been right. The calibration had been wrong. Omaha was never known for his patience when it came to testing new technology, but he was never known for second-guessing his wife when it came to numbers either. The two were an indomitable pair. Her cold calculating pragmatism, and his unbridled genius. I could not help but think the workers' questions about my injuries had caused the Omahas' premature ignition of the plasma field. What had the Ex Natu done to get them to activate it? Had the Investigators pushed the issue? Had our cover been blown? Whatever the case, there was no doubt now. The Ex Natu were coming for us. An explosion like that would attract their attention from all over the world. It was just a matter of time before they found this bunker too.

"I saw a bunch of people pulling paper from boxes, tearing it to pieces with their bare hands. The paper shredding sprites beside them were dark and inactive. I touched Melody's Dominus bracelet on my arm. Well, if this were the end of my life, I could do my part to keep Hoffen City safe. 'Dikaió hard reset, all sprites.' I whispered then I rolled my shirt sleeve down over the bracelet. There was no point getting anyone's hopes up over that. No one left in the bunker knew how to use the Dikaió better than I did. I had quite a bit of battle training, and even if I was no Mari Knenne, I knew I could hold my own against the Ex Natu. I was sure the Governor would have demanded the bracelet if he knew I had it. The man was anything if not a megalomaniac, but his control of the Dikaió as an Atheno was wanting when it came to civil defense. I walked over and took several sheaves of paper from the people ripping it and fed the sheets to the paper shredder sprites. The workers looked up at me gratefully and started shredding documents in earnest using the sprites.

"All the communication lines with Hoffen City were disconnected. The train tunnel we were going to use to get there had collapsed, making it essentially unusable. For untold hours, maybe days, we just kept packing as if we were still going to Hoffen City, while destroying every record of our existence. And then the doorbell rang, so to speak. It was General Knenne along with a team who had come to rescue us. I looked at the team, hoping to see the Administrator. If anyone could use the Dominus bracelet to rescue us, it would be her, but I did not see her with the group. Omaha's son Alexander was there, and I considered giving him the bracelet. It was his birthright after all, even if, like the Governor, he was just an Athenos.

"Then Mari came through the door. She was moving quickly, silently in the shadows. I tried to push through the crowd in the main room of the bunker to give the bracelet to her, but I did not make it far before the Governor caught sight of me and called me over to the team that had just come in. 'Reddy was the last one to talk to Omaha. Maybe she can answer your questions.' I grimaced and joined the small group.

"'What happened up there?' General Knenne was never one to mince words.

"'I'm not sure,' I shook my head. 'When I left, the Ex Natu construction workers were asking questions. Dangerous questions.' I did not feel like elaborating that the questions were about me, but General Knenne was not going to let me off that easy.

"'What kinds of questions? About the generator? About our people?' he prodded.

"I tried to look past him to see where Mari had disappeared. I could not see her. 'About me. About this.' I moved my hair to show him the injury on my forehead.

"'You went into the city with that?' the Governor said way too loudly.

"'Clearly not. You were the one who sent me, Your Governorship.' I glared at him. 'There was an accident while I was up there. Everyone else healed, of course, but the workers noticed that I didn't.'

"General Knenne sighed and raised his hand. 'So, Omaha sent you back here and activated the plasma field?'

"'I know the first part of that is true. I'm not sure what happened to the plasma field or Mason City," I shrugged my shoulders. 'I don't think Omaha would have activated it without more testing if there weren't an emergency though.'

"The General nearly spat. 'I wouldn't put it past him. Still, we're going to need to evacuate everyone here as soon as possible. Zero footprint.'

"'What do you mean as soon as possible?' the Governor demanded. 'We need immediate evacuation.'

"The General shook his head. 'We didn't bring enough resources for that, Governor. And with the amount of Ex Natu activity up there, I can't recommend a mass evacuation. We'll have to take people out a few at a time and take the long way to Hoffen City."

"Multiple loud explosions sounded in the room all around us, and a blinding light dazed me. All I could see was white. Then there was a sound like someone playing a snare drum underwater, and I could hear a crowd screaming far away, as if they were on the far side of a long hallway. Fire ripped through my shoulder, my stomach, and my cheek. I felt my body lifted off the floor, caught in the talons of a fiery bird intent on taking me into the life after life. I hit the ground with a dull thud for the third time that day, and slowly my senses returned. Smoke had filled the room, and I could see swarms of men dressed in black. Beams of light flashed about from their hands, and then I realized those lights were mounted on weapons. They were shooting everyone. The Ex Natu were here.

"The places where the fire had struck me were cooling into a dull pain, and I could feel that they were sticky wet too. I'd been hit, and I was bleeding—a lot. I tried to move, and the room swam out of focus as pain racked my body, so I laid still again, and the blurriness subsided somewhat. Then sprites and bits of furniture began to fly at the soldiers. I saw the Administrator, armored in office junk, launch herself into the crowd of Ex Natu, and then the room began to swirl again, and everything went dark.

"I don't know how long I was unconscious for, but when I

finally did wake up, the only people in the room were bodies: our people and Ex Natu. The room looked like a tornado had gone through and torn the place apart. No one was moving. I again tried to get up, and again I felt like I was going to pass out, but this time I pushed myself into a sitting position. The wound in my stomach began to bleed profusely, and I could feel myself starting to fade with it. It felt like, if I wanted to, I could just step out of my body. I was going to die there with the rest, but I was still somehow all alone. I looked down at my wrist. The Dominus bracelet was still there, but there was nothing the Dikaió could do to save me. I looked around the room, and that's when I saw it.

"An Ex Natu near me had a backpack with a red cross on it. I wondered what an Ex Natu would need with a first aid kit. But I also wondered if there was anything in there that could help me. I crawled over to the soldier, all but willing myself not to die in the process. I opened the medic kit and found an injectable bandage. I'd had basic field training with General Knenne and knew how to inject the polymer into others to stop their bleeding, but I'd never done it to myself. I knocked the cap off the syringe, and gingerly pulled up my blood-saturated shirt. I felt along my torso until I felt the place where the projectile had gone in, and then turned the syringe on myself. The polymer felt cold like ice at first, and then the nerves in the wound began to burn in protest. But the bleeding stopped. I kept it together to inject polymer into my shoulder wound as well, but the wound on my face was going to have to wait. I was exhausted.

"I laid down and fell asleep again.

"When I woke up, it took me a moment to remember where I was and what had happened. I stood up, and the memory of the day's events flooded over me. I reached down to the wound in my abdomen and was surprised to find the hole had healed completely. The same thing had happened to my shoulder. I reached up to the place where I had been shot in my cheek and was surprised to find that it had healed as well. I moved my arm and found that the bones had knitted themselves back together too. Even the scrape on my head was gone. I looked down and found the bloody syringe on the ground. There was no writing on it indicating that the polymer was full of nano sprites, but apparently it was. I felt strong: younger than I had before I had been shot, and yet I felt sick. I was infested.

"Where would I go now? To one of the other Ex Natu cities? Join them? I would never know the joy of having children. Love? Why bother now? As far as anyone knew, I died in that bunker. No one even bothered to look for me anyway. I needed to sit down. 'Dikaió chair,' I ordered and then thought better of it. Ex Natu couldn't use the Dikaió. To my surprise a chair bumped into the back of my legs. I sat down and felt the Dominus bracelet bounce on my wrist. I lifted it up and looked it over. No, I could not go to an Ex Natu city with this. If they got access to the Dikaió, we'd all be doomed.

"Nano sprites or not, I needed to get to Hoffen City. And I needed to get there fast. There would almost certainly be reinforcements coming when these soldiers did not report. Standing up quickly, I walked among the dead and did not see the Administrator or the General among them. 'Dikaió sprite,' I shouted to no sprite in particular. 'Show me where Administrator Mari went.' A house sprite sprang up and headed toward Omaha's office. It stopped in front of a large wall. 'Dikaió open,' I ordered. The wall shuttered, but it did not open. I thought about it for moment and then said, 'Dikaió unlock and open.' There was a metallic clink on the other side of the wall, and then it opened to a small room with a stairway that descended into cave tunnels below. The sprite went down the stairs. I paused then relocked the door and followed the sprite down into the darkness.

The tunnels were pitch black, and the sprite was not equipped with lights. "Dikaió stop!" I called. The sprite paused, and I tore the sleeves off my shirt then tore them into long strips. I worked as quickly as I could tying the strips together, fashioning a long leash, which I then attached to the sprite. "Okay, Dikaió, take me to Administrator Mari." The sprite headed into the tunnels, and I clung to the leash. We were in the tunnels for weeks. The hunger and thirst were unbearable, but the nano sprites kept my body alive, just like they keep the wilding wolves alive even though they can't find animals to eat in the wild anymore. Eventually, I stumbled on the cycle sprites and the stairway that led to the City Hall of Hoffen City."

The Sprite Master paused her story and looked at them like there was nothing left to tell.

Mallory shifted in her chair. "So, you were there before Mari activated the light?"

Reddy Lamarr looked at her like she was stupid. "Yes, of course, several years before. Mari was a young woman when the city exploded; she was quite old when she used the Dikaió to fill in the stairway leading down to the tunnels." The Sprite Master nodded her head toward the table. "May I have a drink now?"

Mallory flushed with embarrassment both by her question and her lack of manners. "Oh yes, of course. Sprite, give Reddy Lamarr a drink."

The Sprite Master drank deeply from the glass the sprite offered her.

Mallory tilted her head and bit her lip. "I thought all the middle-aged adults went out to distract the Ex Natu. How did you stay behind? You don't look old, but you're not a child either."

The Sprite Master shook her head. "The same way I stayed in the city without my curse being discovered. I had to look like I was aging like everyone else, so I spent hours every day applying makeup to make myself look older."

Caleb laughed. "That's funny! Most women do that to make themselves look younger."

The Sprite Master grinned at him. "Well, I had to do that as well. Constantly reinventing myself as a younger me."

"But the christening records kept track of the births," Mallory quizzed. "How could you reinvent yourself without being born?"

The older woman's face darkened. "People are terrible at telling strangers apart, and red heads look like other red heads for the most part."

Mallory's lip curled in disgust. "What did you do with the girls you looked like?"

The Sprite Master rolled her eyes away from the pair. "Nothing like that. I'm no killer, Mallory."

"Then how?" Mallory sighed deeply.

"Making myself look older worked at first." the Sprite Master nodded. "But after a while, people were going to start asking questions, and I realized I would end up dead or spending eternity in prison if I stayed alive forever as the same person, so I used the Dikaió to add new birth christenings to the Matriarch's records, and each time, I just took off the makeup. No one questioned me. How could someone new possibly get into the city?"

"So how did you become the Sprite Master?" Caleb asked. "That role is handed down through families."

"I honestly didn't intend to. I married an older Sprite Master when his wife died. He had children already, and I was using makeup again to appear past the time of childbirth. His grandson was killed when the boys built the fire sprite. The boy's father was killed in the fires during the attack. I altered the records again and created a fictional sister with a Talos christening, faked my death in the fire, and assumed that role." The Sprite Master paused and looked at them thoughtfully. "It would have been roughly around the time that your grandparents were children."

"I always thought you looked younger than you were," Mallory mused. "But you weren't wearing makeup to make yourself look older then."

The Sprite Master squirmed in her bonds trying to get comfortable then shrugged. "By that time, all the books had been destroyed, and there was no record of the Ex Natu. Who was going to be suspicious? But you see that's what made me worried. If the Ex Natu came, what chance would we have against them? That's when I decided to use the Dikaió to check for news outside the plasma field, and that was when I stumbled across the traitor here. It's when I knew I had to get out and stop her before she brought them to us." She nodded toward the book. "Has it finished copying her story yet?"

"There's no need," the Archivist spoke quietly from the other side of the doors to the dining room. There was no way to know how long she had been standing there listening to the Sprite Master's tale. "I'll tell you what happened. It's better if you hear it from me anyway."

19

The Archivist began to pace. "She calls me a traitor, but I wasn't the one who betrayed our people. That happened long before I was born. Omaha was the one who pushed us into a forever war with the Ex Natu." She paused and looked at Reddy with irritation. "And if you worked for him, you're as much responsible for it as he was."

"How dare you!" the Sprite Master screamed, gnashing her teeth and rocking in her chair. "You aren't fit to utter his name!"

"You don't even know what the Dikaió is!" The Archivist yelled back. "Walking around using a Dominus bracelet to hide in the shadows and make sprites....and you certainly don't know what Omaha did before he became the de facto leader of the underground."

The Sprite Master screamed, "if you dare sully his memory with your lies, I'll kill you."

The Archivist laughed. "Oh, I think you've made your intentions clear since you arrived. But I won't have my actions, and the memory of my family, dishonored by a member of the Omaha cult. He is an Ex Natu weapons designer, and we're just a sick form of job security." She waved absently at everyone at the table.

"Lies!" The Sprite Master knocked her chair over and bit her lip. Blood trickled down her chin mixed with sprays of spittle. "Lies!"

"Enough! Dikaió, shut her up!" A strip of fabric from the shoulder of the Sprite Master's shirt unraveled and wrapped itself around her head, stuffing itself in her mouth and pulling the gag tight. "As I was saying—Omaha designed the Dikaió to finish off the inhabitants of the Southeastern Asian Islands for the Ex Natu." The Archivist crouched over the Sprite Master, who stared at her with murderous hate, and whispered. "Men, women, children, multi-generational families—he fully intended to kill them all. When he gave the Dikaió to Eva Knenne, it wasn't to save her and Mari. He intended to assassinate them."

Mallory held up her hand. "Hold on! What about the Chronicles of the Matriarch? None of this was mentioned in Eva's writing."

The Archivist stood up and waved away her question. "Well, it would hardly be a decent assassination attempt if she knew about it. The Dikaió is invisible, after all." She lifted her arm and jangled her Dominus bracelet then opened her hand slowly, spinning in a slow circle. "And it's like a virus, infecting everything. It could kill any one of us with a word, including the Ex Natu, and it could be something as innocuous as a…a…" she paused and looked at the table, picking up a silver spoon off a plate. "…a dirty spoon jumping off your plate." She made a motion like she was stabbing herself with the silverware.

Caleb leaned forward in his chair and said, "Assuming that was true, Omaha didn't assassinate Eva. Something must have changed."

The Archivist nodded. "Omaha was scheduled to get injected with nano sprites just like the General and Eva Knenne, but his wife got pregnant. Suddenly the problem was at his doorstep, and he shifted from being our people's enemy to being our savior. When he dug through the assassination files, he came across the Knennes on the hit list and thought the General would be a good recruit to protect his child, but he never intended to go live in Hoffen City with the rest of us."

Mallory tilted her head. "What are you saying exactly?"

The Archivist looked suddenly old and haggard. "His plan was to hide Alexander there, have them activate the plasma shield, and then rejoin the Ex Natu. The whole thing would be his little secret, and if the people having families were stuck in a little ball of invisible fire they couldn't escape from, they wouldn't jeopardize the Ex Natu's plans to limit overpopulation."

"But he died in the Mason City accident," Caleb added.

The Archivist walked to the table where the pen was busy copying her Chronicles of the Lost. "Dikaió, stop writing," she ordered. She picked up the book, flipped backward a few pages, and handed it to Caleb. "Read it out loud, starting here at the top."

The Chronicles of the Lost (continued)

I wondered if Adam and the boys were still looking for me or if they had given me up for dead yet? I tried to escape the cold little room with the mirrored walls and ceiling so many times. The loud music with the disharmonic tones made it too hard to concentrate. I tried to use the Dikaió to free myself, but the words that made it work always seemed just out of reach. The distraction also made it impossible to keep time. I also thought of trying to mark it by the frequency of beatings or the timing of the food and water deliveries, but immortality had left the Ex Natu without the need to track time and seasons, and very little need of food and water, so my needs were only met sporadically. Whenever they came to my room, I did not know if they were going to beat me or feed me. Then one day the door opened, and something was different: Instead of being dragged right to the interrogation room, I was dragged into an elevator. I was too disoriented to know if we went up or down, but the doors opened on a hallway which led to a much more comfortable room with red carpet, a large mahogany desk, and plush chairs. There were no windows, and a small stained glass table lamp was the only light in the room. I remember it vividly because it had the dragonfly of the Matriarch in the glass. A dark-skinned man with piercing blue eyes and a noble jaw sat on the other side of the desk. He smiled at me and waved away the men that had brought me to the room. They left, closing the door behind them.

"Hello, Emilia," he looked me over and then followed my gaze to the lamp. "You recognize it?"

I shifted my gaze to his eyes and said nothing.

He touched the lamp. "The sign of the Matriarch, yes?"

My muscles all tensed. How could he know that?

"Well, not originally, mind you," he continued. "This one is from an age long forgotten: one of only a few surviving art pieces from Clara Driscoll. She was the lead designer for the Tiffany girls back in the early 20th century. Louis Tiffany did most of the big artwork of course, but Clara knew what the public wanted. And it's her designs that survive even all these centuries later." He leaned back in his chair and folded his hands. "The Tiffany girls weren't allowed to marry, you know. They had to give up the hope of family for their career. Clara eventually left the work for love and married a man named Edward Booth, though she never did have children. Still, her work with unions and women's rights were pretty instrumental in building the civilized world; the very one that led to the creation of immortality." He leaned forward and touched the lamp again. "Giving someone called "The Matriarch," whose sole existence is to propagate families, Driscoll's dragonfly as a symbol is delightfully ironic, don't you think? Driscoll had to forsake family to have a life, and Eva Knenne had to forsake her life to have a family."

I had no idea what he was talking about, but sitting in

this office was better than getting beaten, so I tried to draw out the conversation. "How do you know about Eva Knenne?"

"Has it been so long that you don't recognize me, Emilia?" He looked hurt.

"Your face is familiar," I said. "Were you one of the brutes who tortured me. There were so many, I can't remember?"

"Torture?" He shook his head. "I've never been one for torture."

My mind was starting to clear a bit without the cold, the mirrors, and the music playing. There was a letter opener on the desk next to the lamp, and I wondered if the Dikaió was here. I decided to distract the man more—get him talking before making my move. "Why was I tortured then?"

He shook his head sadly. "I'm truly sorry. It was necessary to make sure you weren't able to, or weren't going to, give up the location of Hoffen City. Your resolve needed to be tested."

"Give it up?" I was confused.

He picked up a sheaf of papers. "You said that you didn't know where it was. That 'we lost it.' How did you come to lose an entire city, Emilia? Who all is the "we" with you?" The man shifted in his seat, and his blue eyes stared intensely at me. "Is Alexander outside the city?"

What was he talking about? "Alexander?"

The man dropped the papers on the desk and leaned forward quickly. "My son!"

Then I recognized him; I was only a child when I saw him last. "Omaha?"

He smiled broadly. "The one and only."

"But how? You died in the Mason City explosion." My

voice was barely a whisper.

"That was an unfortunate ruse. The Ex Natu had become suspicious. It would have been nice for Alexander, but the plans for Mason City had to be discarded. The day of the explosion I was detained by the Ex Natu investigators and taken to the Davis City Metroplex to be questioned about exactly what I was building under City Hall in Mason City. I told them it was a new energy source that could power the city indefinitely" He paused and looked like he was about to cry, but he did not. "They called Melody over video and told her to activate it—to demonstrate that it wasn't dangerous. I objected. She said the calibrations weren't quite right, that it wouldn't prove anything because it could be dangerous if it were activated without the adjustments. But they made her do it." He stopped and picked up a pen out of its holder, clicking the button on it absently over and over. "Turns out an uncalibrated plasma field generator makes an excellent bomb." He stopped talking and looked at his pen in silence for a time. I shifted in my chair and waited for him to continue. Soon enough he did. "They liked it so much, they put me back in charge of weapons development—said I should stay where my talent was."

"That was decades ago. You look younger than you should, Omaha, at least if…" I didn't finish the sentence.

"If I weren't an Ex Natu?" He laughed. "Well, you found me out—us out I suppose. Melody and I got our nano sprites shortly after Alexander was born. But they couldn't save her, not from a plasma explosion." He again looked like he was going to cry, but he pulled himself together quickly. "But a part of her survived in Alexander. Your people, the Dikaió, Hoffen City, it was all because I wanted a life for him, a life he couldn't have roaming about freely in the world. Contained within a plasma field, hidden from the Ex Natu, a piece of history could exist where humans lived as they always had: living, dying, generations, families."

"But why not in the open?" I demanded. "Why not at peace?"

He shook his head. "There could never be peace, Emilia. The mission of the Ex Natu is a necessary one. Eventually your kind would desire immortality, too; maybe not your generation, but the next or the next. Our planet could never sustain a growing population of immortals. There just wouldn't be enough resources to go around, not to mention the devastating effect we would have on the environment." He shook his head. "It would have been unconscionable to continue replicating the species without the check and balance of death."

"But you convinced General Knenne to help you fight the Ex Natu," I exclaimed. "Why would you do that if you believed in their mission?"

"General Knenne believed in the Ex Natu as much as I did! He was responsible for wiping out the pro-family forces in the Southeast Asian Islands. He was little more than an Ex Natu weapon. They could point him and his troops in the right direction, and he would pull the trigger. He would have killed Alexander, you, me, everyone—without batting an eye. I simply pointed the weapon in a different direction: a defensive direction—one that would allow Alexander to survive." He chuckled. "Knenne's wife having a baby; that was providential. She wasn't nearly so clever as she thought she was at keeping Mari a secret. Their neighbors reported the girl's crying almost daily, but General Knenne was a powerful person, which made dealing with the treasonous act of his wife a delicate matter. The Dikaió was fresh out of the laboratory at the time, and my superiors commissioned me to kill her and her baby with it—make it look like an accident. But Melody was pregnant already, and I was in the process of building the underground movement and getting my son clear from the Ex Natu threat, so I decided to recruit them instead. General Knenne wasn't easy to convince, but he decided to go along with it when I took the Dikaió away from the Ex Natu with the christening protocol. The man was brilliant; I'll give him that. In retrospect, I'm glad that without the nano sprites, he would grow old and die. That sort of strategist would never be satisfied in the boring world of the Ex Natu or the simple world I imagined in Hoffen City." Omaha smiled broadly as if his cleverness should be perfectly clear.

I needed to clarify something he said. "So some of the Ex Natu know about the Dikaió?"

"No, no." He shook his head. "I gave the general a list of everyone who knew about the project and they, along with the records of its existence, were erased. Besides, the Dikaió is far too dangerous for the Ex Natu. They'd chosen to give up the ability to reproduce for a form of immortality, and while they were free from age, disease, and most injury, they could still die. The Dikaió is a terrible weapon. It could easily have led to the extinction of our entire species if a civil war were to break out between the Ex Natu. It's much more suited to caring for the mortals of Hoffen City."

I shook my head unable to process what I was being told. "What does erased mean?"

He waved his hand. "I'm sure you understand my meaning, Emilia." Then he slapped the arms of his chair. "Anyway! Enough about my past. What happened at Hoffen City? Why are you here instead of there?"

I lowered my head in the memory of it all. "A fire sprite attacked. Those of us who were of the age to hide in the Ex Natu cities left to distract them and keep them from finding Hoffen City; the generator was activated while we were outside the city. The tunnels were sealed. There's no way back."

"Hmmm…and that brings me back to my earlier question. Did Alexander leave the city with you? Is he safe?" he asked earnestly.

I paused. His son seemed to be the only reason he had helped our people at all. The man would be as old as Mari now with grandchildren if he had survived. But I was afraid of what would happen if I were to tell Omaha that his son was dead. It was possible he might help us if I told him the Ex Natu killed him just after the Mason City explosion, but that would just lead to more war—or even worse, he could bring the war to Hoffen City in full force. He had built the plasma field generator; he might know how to take it down. And I had come here to stop the war. I just wanted to live in peace—no more fighting. But I could give him an honest answer without revealing my misgivings. "No, your son was not with us."

Omaha sat back in his chair and nodded. He casually reached over to the side of his desk and pressed what I presumed was a button underneath it. "Bring it in." The door opened, and one of the Ex Natu guards walked in carrying a small case. Omaha stood up and took it from the guard. "Thank you. You can go." The guard retreated and closed the door behind him. Locks engaged in loud clicks somewhere inside the door. Omaha turned to me. "Dikaió, bind her to the chair." Before I had a chance to move, the chair's fabric opened around me and wove into my own clothes, securing me to the chair. Omaha placed the small case on his desk and opened it, but I could not see what was inside. "Thank you for putting my fears to rest, Emilia. Do you have children?"

"Two sons," I said squirming against the bonds. "And they're the reason I came here. I want the war to end. I had hoped to negotiate peace."

He turned to me. "Then you understand the anxiety that I've felt about Alexander's well-being." He held up a syringe and tapped the glass tube, while depressing the stopper. White fluid squirted from the needle. "I wish that I could do the same for you, but a battalion of soldiers has been dispatched to root out your friends and family hiding in the caves across the river from Mason City."

"And then what? Bring them here? They don't know where Hoffen City is either. Just leave them in peace," I pleaded.

He looked sad again. "I'm afraid that's out of my hands, but I can do something kind for you in exchange for the peace you've given me. I can give you something that I have found heals the pain of loss." He lowered the syringe toward me. "I can give you the gift of time."

I realized he intended to inject me with nano sprites. I looked again at the letter opener on the table and yelled desperately, "Dikaió, kill him and free me!" My bonds immediately fell slack, and the letter opener leapt from the table, slashing at his neck. He fell forward trying to avoid the blade, and I felt the needle enter my shoulder and a warm surge spread up from there. "Dikaió, defend me," I yelled, but nothing happened. Out of the corner of my eye, I could see the yellowish-green coloring of old bruises washing away. It was too late. I was one of them. The loss was palpable; I would never have the Dikaió again. I couldn't let that stop me. I needed to save my family. I tried to shove Omaha's body away from me, but he was quite heavy, and he was still moving.

The letter opener was continuing its attack at his neck, and it was not going to stop until he was dead. His eyes were looking into my mine the whole time: wide, panicked, and full of confusion. Then his confusion turned to rage. He whispered, "Dikaió, cease." The blade clattered to the floor, and the wounds on Omaha's neck immediately began to close.

I was stupefied. How did he have the Dikaió? But there was not time to indulge such thoughts. He was healing quickly, but for the moment, he was still weakened and laying heavily on me. I needed to move fast if I was going to survive. I pushed hard with my legs and toppled the chair; both of us sprawling onto the floor. And that's when I saw his secret.

He was wearing a Dominus bracelet. I rolled on top of him, pinning his arms with my knees. I needed to buy myself more time, so I drove the fingernails of my left hand into the wound in his neck caused by the letter opener. I pulled hard, tearing it back open. Omaha screamed and thrashed beneath me. With my right hand, I tried to slip off the Dominus bracelet. He immediately understood what I was after and balled up his fist to keep me from pulling the bracelet off. I looked around quickly. The letter opener was just within reach, so I twisted my hand hard in his wound. He closed his eyes and screamed, and I grabbed the knife then slashed at his fist. His hand sprang open, and I pulled the bracelet free.

I rolled off him and slipped on the bracelet. "Dikaió, defend me!" Suddenly the office was a flurry of flying debris.

Omaha took a submissive position on the floor, kneeling with his hands over his neck and the back of his head. I thought about erasing him, as he called it, but I needed to get to my family. I turned to the door of the room. "Dikaió, open!" The locks clicked, and the door swung open. Two Ex Natu guards turned around surprised. I stepped toward them. "Dikaió, remove these two from the building," I said, and immediately, debris from the room flew at them. Their clothing twisted quickly, binding their arms and legs, and the debris knocked them off balance. The invisible hands of the Dikaió dragged them down the long hall, and I followed. Doors opened here and there, and the two Ex Natu guards were dragged through them. Then we entered what appeared to be a recreational room. A panel in the wall slid open, revealing the blue sky of a beautifully clear day. The two guards were flung outside the building. Unfortunately for them we were on the top floor of the observation tower. I could see the tops of the trees and, just a little ways off in the distance, the Aiworth bridge crossing the Missouri river. There was no way down from there, but with the Dominus bracelet, that was not going to be a problem. "Dikaió, bring me a flying sprite."

"You're not going anywhere!" a voice behind me screamed. I turned to see Omaha covered in blood standing in the doorway of the room. He was breathing hard and holding a weapon. "I'm going to need that bracelet back."

I touched the bracelet. "Call off the attack on my family, and I'll consider it."

He shook his head. "You don't understand what's at stake: what we've done for our species and our planet. You're one of us now, Emilia. You'll appreciate this gift in time."

I heard a familiar whining noise behind me, so I yelled "I'll never be one of you!" And I stepped backwards out the window onto a flying sprite. I spun quickly into a riding position and said, "Dikaió, take me to Adam."

The sprite started to fly away, but I heard a noise behind me like someone was beating a stick on a large sheet of metal. Fire seared through my shoulder and then across my chest. I looked down, and saw several spots of red seeping from my core. Omaha was shooting me. "Dikaió, evasive maneuvers," I yelled. The flying sprite ducked and weaved, and I nearly lost my grip falling to my death far below, but I was determined to rescue my family. I gripped harder on the sprite's handles. Then I heard a little click followed by a sickening pain in each of the holes where the projectiles had entered. They were spinning inside me. Omaha had designed a weapon to kill an immortal Ex Natu, causing maximum destruction to the body—faster than the nano sprites could heal. "Dikaió, stop!" I screamed. It was a plea more than a command, but the spinning pain immediately ended. "Dikaió, out of me, now!" That one was a command. Four tiny metal stars burst out of my shoulder and chest and hovered in front of me, matching the speed of the flying sprite.

"Owww!" I screamed. "You couldn't have gone back the way you came? Dikaió, return to your sender." The tiny stars flew around me and back the way they had come. The holes in my skin began to heal immediately, and the pain in my chest became a dull ache. The nano sprite healing was incredibly itchy, but I couldn't very well scratch inside myself. I decided to ignore it and focus on saving my family.

The flying sprite brought me to the unfinished fortress we were building. My heart sank. There were hundreds of Ex Natu soldiers and sprites converging on the building. Building materials were flying around battering the Ex Natu forces, but there were too many of them, and I could see in the distance that in minutes Ex Natu reinforcements would be there. But maybe with the Dominus bracelet I could do something about it. "Dikaió, take me in through that opening in the roof!" I yelled.

I swooped down through the large circular opening in the center of the roof right into the middle of a fire fight. Ex Natu were hovering in the room on flying sprites, firing at the lost. I saw a mop of hair hiding behind some shelving. It looked like the color of my son's hair. Panic swelled inside me, more painful than the Ex Natu stars had been. "Dikaió, turn the Ex Natu weapons against themselves," I said.

The Ex Natu's expression turned to surprise as their weapons leapt out of their hands and turned on them. The flying sprites flew into one another and fell in fiery explosions. I thought of the nearly finished plasma generator in the basement of the building and looked at the Dominus bracelet. I was not sure what a Dominus bracelet was capable of, but I decided to go all out. "Dikaió, complete the plasma field generator; set it to the same specifications as those at Hoffen City. When complete, turn it on." Nothing happened.

"Mommy!"

Every mother can recognize her child's voice, and the fear and desperation I heard in my son's cry drove away every thought of the plasma field generator. I looked about frantically and saw a group of Ex Natu chasing a child through a doorway. "Dikaió, take me there!" I pointed. "Quickly!" The flying sprite swooped quickly down, and I leapt off. Running through the doorway into what would one day be the dining room and kitchen area. I got there just in time to see Adam catch my son in his arms and spin him around to shield the Ex Natu's fire with his body. Our other son lay dead just a few feet away.

Horror. Rage. Intense loss. It all hit me at once. "Dikaió, kill them all!" I screamed. "Every Ex Natu!"

I rushed past the Ex Natu soldiers, now dangling in the air by the force of the Dikaió and fell on top of the bloody body of my husband. "Adam!" I screamed tugging at him.

"Dikaió, let him live! Let my boys live!"

That command was beyond the Dominus bracelet's power.

The pink fire of the plasma field bathed the room in an ethereal glow as I lay there amidst the loss of all that I loved. I was the only thing left alive within the plasma field.

I was alone.

I was the Lost.

The Library

Caleb stopped reading and looked up. Mallory was holding the Archivist in an awkward embrace, wiping tears away. "You poor thing!" she sobbed.

The Archivist looked solemn and patted Mallory's arm. "It was a long, long time ago. I've cried all the tears I have for those I've lost. But you can understand why this one riding in here with these accusations is upsetting."

Mallory nodded, "Reddy Lamarr has always been an awful person—hasn't she, Caleb?"

Caleb sighed and looked at the Sprite Master, raising his eyebrows at her. Her nose wrinkled in disgust, and she mumbled beneath her gag. "Yes, I mean, I'm usually a pretty good judge of character, but I guess you were right about her, Mal." The Sprite Master rolled her eyes and sighed heavily. "The question is what do we do now?"

The Archivist straightened her back and tried to get out of Mallory's embrace. "We need to get your other friend back before she does something foolish. If that Dominus bracelet winds up in the hands of the Ex Natu, it could mean the end of all of us, and my family's fate will be your family's as well, including all of Hoffen City."

Caleb shrugged. "We don't even know what her plan is."

Mallory, still clinging to the Archivist, said, "she took the book with Omaha's writings about the plasma generator from the shelves upstairs. Could she fix Hoffen City's light with that and the Dominus bracelet, like you did here?"

The Archivist nodded. "We built several backup generators and fail safes for the plasma field generator in Hoffen City. It's possible with a Dominus bracelet and the regulator she took from my generator here."

Caleb put his hands on the table. "Meaning if we don't catch her, and she gets past the Ex Natu, she could actually protect the city with the regulator and the Dominus bracelet you took from Omaha?"

Mallory froze. She tilted her head, bit her lip, and then quickly pulled away from the Archivist. "Hold on! I thought you said you found your Dominus bracelet in the paneling of the bunker." She looked at Caleb for confirmation.

Caleb blinked in confusion, registering that something was off.

Reddy Lamarr squirmed in her restraints, a muffled scream sounding through the binding over her mouth.

The Archivist's eyes narrowed, and she stood up quickly raising her wrist to speak into the Dominus bracelet. "Dikaió, secure Mall—"

KABOOM!

An explosion interrupted the Archivist's command, and Mallory felt herself flying weightlessly through the air. She tumbled like a rag doll casually thrown by a child, until her back slapped hard against a pillar, and she spun around, rolling to the ground. The Archivist landed several feet away from her. Mallory's vision swam, but she was surprised to see blue sky swimming beneath dark murky waves where the dining room wall used to be. Several flying sprites hovered in the sky with Ex Natu riders atop them. Panic began to override the pain of her collision. She pulled herself up onto her elbows and looked desperately around for Caleb. He was lying face down under the table, which had also flown several feet across the room.

A thick black boot landed on the table just above his head. Mallory's eyes slowly trailed up the body to its owner, and she found herself looking into the face of a dark-skinned man with blue eyes. His head was shaved, and he was grinning—ear to ear. Dark Ex Natu tattoos moved about haphazardly under the skin of his neck and face. He jumped down from the table and walked slowly over to where the Archivist was laying. "How many decades has it been, Emilia? I came as soon as you called."

The man walked casually across the rubble to the fallen woman. He was wearing a military uniform, and Mallory was struck by the insignia on it: a heater shield with a W shape on top and stripes leading to a point at the bottom. The same symbol she had seen in different reliefs around the Library. The same symbol Reddy Lamarr had used as her family crest. This must be Omaha, and it looked like the Archivist was in trouble. She could only imagine what would happen if he retrieved the Dominus bracelet she was wearing. Mallory tried to move toward her, but when she did, severe pain shot through her side. Her ribs might be broken. Her attention turned from the Archivist to her stomach. She clutched at the bump growing there and nearly panicked at the thought that the blast might have harmed her child.

Caleb lifted his head, and when he saw her holding her stomach, he yelled across the room. "Mal, are you okay?"

She looked back at him, tears blurring her vision. "I don't know."

Omaha bent down to the Archivist and touched her arm tenderly. "It would have been easier if you'd lowered the plasma field earlier. That was annoying. But I'd call us even." He pointed at the rubble behind him and shrugged. Then his attention turned to Mallory. "Is this the one you called me about? The fruit of our little experiment?"

The Archivist moaned a little and looked up from the floor. A long gash was quickly healing across her forehead. "Your little experiment, you mean."

He shrugged again. "Fine. My little experiment. Is this her?"

The Archivist rolled off her back and breathed heavily. "Yes, that's her, and her husband was injected with your sprites."

Omaha stood up and beamed. "And she's pregnant?"

Mallory grabbed her stomach defensively and tried to scoot backwards, but the pain in her side kept her from moving quickly.

"Yes," the Archivist said quietly. Then she began to shout, but Mallory realized it was not her; it was her voice sounding throughout the Library. "Attention, the Library is under attack. Seek shelter. Attention, the Library is under attack. Seek shelter."

Omaha froze for a moment looking around in confusion,

but quickly his face relaxed, and he chuckled heartily. "Bit of a delay in your alarm, Emilia."

"It gave me all the distraction I needed." The Archivist had jumped up and was running across the room. "Dikaió, defend me and get that table off Caleb Aiworth!" She yelled. The table flew off of Caleb, and dinnerware and bits of rubble from the ruined outer wall began to swirl around her. She looked at Caleb. "Get Mallory and the baby out of here!"

Omaha's mirth turned sour. "Come now, Emilia. I'm sorry I blew up your wall. It was for effect. Don't be mad. You're barely even scratched." He shifted his weight to his other foot. "We had an agreement."

"It's not the wall, Omaha. Do you really think I would ever deal with you," she shouted through gritted teeth, "after what you did to my family?"

He waved his hand dismissively. "I thought we had put that unpleasant business behind us. How did you put it? 'Without forgiveness immortality would be hell.'" He pointed to the inside of the Library. "We left you alone. Gave you all of this just like you asked…for the benefit of humanity. I even let you keep a Dominus bracelet to help you pass the time. The only stipulation was that you find us a fertile Chorus." He pointed at Mallory and Caleb. "And you've brought us two, one of them already pregnant! Those were the terms, Emilia."

"Well, the terms have changed. They're under my protection, now," she spat.

"Changed? Your protection?" Omaha looked genuinely surprised. He waved his hand grandly toward the armies outside. "You called me, and now the whole world is watching, Emilia. Would you protect them from us all?"

"If I must," the Archivist called back. "Caleb, go!" She ordered.

Caleb reached down and gently picked up Mallory. "I've got you, Mal."

"Careful of my side. I don't want to hurt the baby." Mallory winced.

"I don't understand," Omaha shifted his weight to his other foot.

"I've spent the last few decades in the hell of delayed vengeance," the Archivist crouched into a defensive stance. "But since I finally had an excuse to call you over for a visit, this seems like as good a time as any to kill you."

Omaha looked disappointed. He reached up and touched his ear. "The mission is a scrub. Erase every sign of its existence." Mallory looked outside and saw Ex Natu soldiers trampling the beautiful gardens. They started gathering the animals and birds into cages. Several fire sprites were circled at the edge of the woods that marked the plasma field's former perimeter, and they started spraying liquid fire at the trees.

What was happening?

The Archivist smiled. "I think not. Dikaió sprites, to me: battle mode." Wall panels all around the Library sprang open and thousands of house sprites began to pour out. They were armed with weapons of every shape and size. The bookshelves spilled their precious contents into piles on the floor, and the shelves transformed into flying sprites, swooping down from every floor of the Library. Electricity arced from the book-ends now attached to the tips of the long boards which had become wings. The walls in the back of the building crumbled apart as several fire sprites from the armory trudged toward them, the sound of metal scraping against metal reverberating off the walls. The Archivist jumped atop the clockwork sprite, which had somehow combined with two house sprites into a type of chariot with whips and cannons.

Omaha's eyebrows went up. "Oh? You've been a very naughty girl, Emilia. You've stolen all my weapon designs. What fun!" He giggled like a child and spun around, leaping over rubble to scramble outside. "To war!" He screamed. Then Omaha ran toward the Ex Natu, and Mallory could have sworn she heard him yell, "Dikaió, defend me!"

The Archivist's chariot raced after him, firing cannons and whipping furiously, but somehow the man out ran it all. Flying sprites and their surprised Ex Natu riders flew through the air into the path of the whips and artillery, exploding everywhere but keeping Omaha safe. He *was* using the Dikaió then. There were multiple Dominus bracelets on the field of battle, and the two people bearing them were both masters of the Dikaió with armies at their command. Mallory was not sure where Omaha was heading, until a large hovering ship appeared over the tree line. Several silver flying sprites aligned themselves like a floating stair way, and Omaha leaped up them, landing in the cockpit of the ship. As soon as he was in the ship, it launched several missiles rocketing toward the Archivist. The Library's flying shelves flew in front of them spewing lightning, and the tubes exploded before getting anywhere near to the Archivist, but one of the bookshelves came hurtling through the missing wall, crashing near where Caleb and Mallory stood.

Caleb's attention had been frozen, until the flaming shelf sprite woke him from his daze. He held Mallory tightly and carried her back through the path that the fire sprites had cleared to the armory. Mallory grimaced from the pain in her side but squeaked out, "We can't just leave her. We have to help!"

"Don't start that again, Mal." Caleb yelled. "We're way out of our league here, and you know it."

She sighed and held tightly to his broad shoulders, in too much pain to argue anyway.

Outside of the armory, all the burnt walls in the hallway were gone. Only piles of books indicated they ever existed; the tables had apparently dumped them and headed out to fight the Ex Natu. Caleb shook his head. "All that huss and fuss over her books, and this is how she treats them?"

Mallory winced as he stepped over a pile on the floor. It was not just the pain in her side that caused the reaction either. She wanted to read everything here, to know all that there was to know, and now she feared she would never have the chance. She did not even know if these books would survive the war waging outside the Library.

Caleb set her down gently near a pile of books and ran back to grab all the weapons he could find. "It's not that I want to take all your fun away, Mal," he called. "It's just that I want to keep the baby safe. Besides, you can still see all the way outside from here." He was right. The armory's walls were also gone. The fire sprites had destroyed them, on their way to defend the Library and the Archivist. The building shook and the lights in the room flickered. Dust sprinkled down from a newly formed crack in the ceiling. Mallory looked back the way they had come, and she gasped. The outdoors was nothing but small blasts and smoke. The sound of the battle was likely deafening outside, but here in the armory it sounded like soft crackles in static. There must be some sort of noise canceling in the room. Caleb came back with his hands full. He handed her the weapon she had used to blow up the fire sprite that used to guard the entryway of the Armory. "Here you go. I found your favorite."

They both startled when another voice sounded in the room. "Do you see what I mean now?"

Mallory pulled the weapon to her shoulder, and pain racked her side. If her finger had been on the trigger, Reddy Lamarr would have been vaporized.

Caleb pushed her weapon down. "What is going on, Reddy?"

The Sprite Master held up the copy of the *Chronicles of the Lost* that had been blown out of Caleb's hands in the dining room and shook it at them. "She interrupted the writing and wasn't ever going to let you get to page 84. The part when she cut a deal with the Ex Natu. They let her live here in isolation in return for using the Dikaió to help them track down anyone that was evading the anti-reproduction laws. Not that it's any consolation to be right, now that they're here for you."

"A deal with Omaha," Caleb corrected.

The Sprite Master shook her head. "I refuse to believe

that part of the story. Omaha died in the Mason City explosion."

Mallory tilted her head and examined her with some empathy. "How do you explain the Ex Natu claiming to be Omaha? The one she's fighting with out there, right now. He has a shield on the sleeve of his arm, just like the one that you used to mark your sprites with."

Reddy Lamarr was taken aback. "A shield is a common mark, Miss Knenne."

Mallory shook her head. "It's Mrs. Aiworth, and it is exactly like the one you used; stripes and all. It's Omaha's family crest, isn't it?"

The Sprite Master nodded. "When the memory of his great work faded, I adopted his crest in his honor. There needed to be some record of him. It wasn't right that history should forget him. And it's not right that there's some Ex Natu out there wearing his mark. But I refuse to believe Omaha is still alive, or that he is a willing enemy of our people."

The building shook again, and this time the overhead lights went out all the way. Along with the lights, whatever had been canceling the noise outside disappeared as well. The roar of multiple explosions and the shrieks of flying sprites above echoed in the room. It was unbearably loud. All three of them dropped their weapons and put their hands over their ears. The lights sprang back to life and the barrage of noise disappeared again. Mallory looked across the Library and groaned, "he's coming!"

Ex Natu troops and culture sprites were climbing over the

rubble into the building.

The Sprite Master started to protest again. "It's not Omaha…" She trailed off when the dark-skinned man stepped through the opening into the Library with the troops. "It can't be him."

"We have to get out of here," Caleb said earnestly. He picked up Mallory as gingerly as he could. "Ask the Dikaió for a way out, Mal!"

"Dikaió, where's the nearest exit on this side of the Library?" Her voice was a whisper. Even with the adrenaline surge, the pain in her side was excruciating. She swore to herself and everything she held dear, if anything happened to her baby, she would kill the man called Omaha. No house sprites came to show them the way. Mallory grew worried. "They all went to fight."

Something clattered across the room. The Sprite Master pointed and said, "Look!" Some of the weapons had fallen on the floor in the shape of an arrow.

Caleb nodded. "Let's go."

As they passed over the arrow, more weapons fell off their shelves ahead of them. Mallory whispered through her pain, "Dikaió, clean up behind us. Distract the invaders and lead them away from us." The weapons they had passed sprung up off the floor and flew back onto their shelves as if they had never moved. There was a clanging noise somewhere in the Library like a metal door being opened and closed several times.

Distantly a voice called, "it came from over there!"

At the far end of the armory, two poles and a broom had

created an arrow leading along the back wall toward the east side of the building. Mallory clung to Caleb, but she felt herself getting weaker. Something inside her was wrong. She felt something in the back of her throat, like she had taken too big of a bite and had not chewed as well as she should have. Her throat spasmed, and she started to cough. Caleb stopped and looked at her with genuine fright as blood splattered his shoulder. "Mal!" he whispered. Then he turned around and started walking back toward the Ex Natu.

"What are you doing?" the Sprite Master whispered frantically.

"She's not going to make it." Caleb shook his head. "Something's really wrong, and she's pregnant. I'm going to ask them for mercy."

Mallory wanted to scream at him. "No! Don't do it." The clockwork sprite said death would be better than what the Ex Natu would do to them. But all that came out were more bloody coughs. She wanted to fight him. Get away from him and the danger coming. But she was too weak. Her grip on his neck was slipping already, and the world was getting dimmer at the edges of her vision. She was scared and about to pass out.

The Sprite Master yelled from behind them. "The Ex Natu don't do mercy, Caleb Aiworth. You're a fool." She reached out and grabbed his shoulder. "Leave her. Come with me. I promise we can be happy together, and we'll have eternity."

Mallory's vision swam back into focus, and she squirmed in Caleb's arms. "I don't care how quickly she heals; I'm going to rip her arms off!"

Caleb held her close to himself. His muscles felt like iron beneath his clothing, but there was genuine mirth in his voice. "You'd better run, Reddy! I don't know how much longer I can hold her back! The Ex Natu will be the least of your worries if she gets loose."

"You're both fools; the last gasp of a city of fools!" the Sprite Master hissed. And then she ran along the back wall toward the east and the exit.

Mallory's body slumped, and her threats dissolved into violent coughing. Caleb's smirk turned into concerned worry. "C'mon, Mal. Hold it together, Beautiful." He walked through the gap in the back hallway created by the fire sprites and called into the Library. "We're here! We're here! Someone, please help us!"

He dropped to his knees just inside the Library's once perfect rows. Piles of books were everywhere, left unceremoniously where the sprite bookshelves had dumped them. The sound of metal scraping metal echoed through every floor of the Library, and several Ex Natu stood around supervising fire sprites as they burned the books. Mallory's chest burned, and she started to cry. So much knowledge, and they only got a taste of it while they here—and now it was gone. In the dining room, Mallory saw a woman on her knees in chains. The Archivist was also crying as her books burned. It was the deepest sadness Mallory had ever seen. The older woman's teary eyes met Mallory's gaze, and if it were possible, the woman's face fell further, shifting from sadness to despair.

Caleb hollered again. "Someone, please help us. She's

hurt."

"Of course, Caleb Aiworth," Omaha's voice sounded from their left. "That's the whole reason we came. To help you."

"Sir, at this point, I don't know who to trust," Caleb replied. "But my wife is pregnant, and she's hurt. The baby... please don't let them die."

Omaha knelt down in front of Caleb and Mallory. "I wouldn't dream of it. Our friend over there thinks this baby is special. And we need to know if it is. Tell me. Is it true that you were injected with nano sprites?"

Caleb nodded. "Yes, sir. Before we even knew what those were. Or anything about the Ex Natu. It wasn't my fault."

"No, no. Of course not. People get accidentally injected with nano sprites all the time," Omaha looked back at the Archivist and rolled his eyes. Then he waved his hand dismissively. "Now, think very hard about this next question. When did your wife get pregnant?"

Mallory was barely conscious, but she whispered, "we don't know."

Caleb nodded in agreement. "One minute, we're being told I will never have children because of the nano sprites, and the next, Mallory is miraculously pregnant. It was the best news of my life, and I can't lose them. Please, help us."

"So, you don't know if it happened before or after the injection?" Omaha asked.

"I don't know." Caleb's voice trembled. "Please, my wife and child."

"Of course, of course." Omaha nodded and stood up. "I'm taking all of them with me. Bring two paramedic sprites and take them to my facilities in Davis City." Several Ex Natu soldiers ran out of the Library. He reached down and squeezed Caleb's shoulder, and Mallory's eyes widened. She gasped and started coughing. He was wearing a Dominus bracelet on each wrist. She looked toward the Archivist and saw that hers had been removed. The *Chronicles* of their people said Omaha made four of them. Alex had the one Reddy Lamarr had brought. The Archivist had the one she found in the underground bunker, or was it the one she had taken from Omaha in their fight in the Ex Natu tower? It was hard to know. Were those the two he now wore? On the other hand, Omaha said he gave her one to use in her research. What was true?

Mallory looked at the Archivist still in chains across the room. Her tears had dried up now, and she was looking at Omaha with murderous intention. Was anything she had told them true? Was Reddy Lamarr right that the Archivist was a traitor to her people? Caleb had said it best, she did not know who to trust anymore; except for Caleb. She clung to him even harder. Ex Natu or not, he was the only one who had never betrayed her, ever.

Two pairs of gloved hands grabbed hold of her and began to pull her away from him. "Caleb! No, Caleb!"

Caleb began to cry. "Hold still, Mal. They're going to help you." He turned to Omaha. "I have your word they're going to help her?"

"Of course, of course," Omaha said absently. He was holding a holographic screen and using his finger to move glowing dots around on a green matrix.

An Ex Natu soldier clamped an iron band around Caleb's neck. "Ow!" Caleb screamed, and the soldier kicked him hard in the back of the leg just behind his knee. Caleb fell forward hard on his face as a bloody tooth scattered across the floor. Another soldier clamped shackles on his ankles and wrists.

Mallory tried to scream, but she suddenly felt like she was floating in warm sludge. Her eyes slowly drifted down to her arm where a soldier was withdrawing an empty syringe. The world became a tunnel, and then she slumped back onto a stretcher floating behind her. There was no longer any pain in her side, but she could not feel her teeth anymore either. In fact, she could not feel anything. She tried to lift her hand to slap the Ex Natu with the needle, but her hand was far too heavy to do anything like that. Instead, she stuck out her tongue at him. The reflection of her face in his shiny helmet just showed a woozy-looking girl distorted by the curves of the man's head. "I feel just like that girl," Mallory thought to herself. The paramedics strapped her to a bed and moved her into an ambulance. Her last thought as the doors closed was "I hope that girl's baby is okay."

The Chief Magistrate waved his weapon toward the pastureland. "There aren't enough culture sprites! They're flanking on the south. Sarai, this isn't going to work. We need to initiate Plan B. Take the women and children to the skyscrapers downtown. Block the doors to the staircases!"

"I won't leave you, Roger!" The Matriarch held her own weapon awkwardly, watching as the beasts from the dark forest flooded past the sprites, which were whipping at them wildly. Sprays of blood flew with every strike, but it was impossible for the sprites to hit the same creature twice or with much effectiveness. There were thousands of the snarling beasts pouring out from the trees. It looked like a river of fur overflowing its banks in waves of bloody death. The cattle and sheep were all slaughtered, and the beasts were on their way toward the city.

The Matriarch's husband grabbed her and kissed her hard. "I love you, Mrs. Knenne, but this is no time to argue. Go, now!" He pulled away from her and fired into the swarm as it crashed into the Administrator's first line of defense, a mixture of armed magistrates and common men with clubs and sharpened bits of sprite steel. Between the men and the sprites, the wave of beasts broke—their bodies piling high. It was clear from the sheer numbers that the defense was doomed to fail. Even if the whole city fought the beasts as they had originally planned, it would just be a matter of time before they were all dead. That much was clear. Now, the only hope was for some of them to take shelter at the top of the skyscrapers and use the staircases as a bottleneck to keep the beasts at bay.

There was no point in arguing that fact, and she had a duty to the people of the city, and her daughter. The Matriarch grimaced, squeezed her husband's hand for what might be the last time, and picked up the small girl crying beside her. Her daughter had only just learned to walk, and there was not time to wait for her to waddle to safety. Then she called for the other women and children to follow her. They ran, even the smallest children capable of brandishing at least a kitchen knife without hurting themselves were armed to fight the beasts if it came down to it. They had all been so valiant coming out to fight, but she could see the terror in their eyes as they turned to run with her. They passed by the mound where City Hall had once stood. Piles of broken glass, metal, stone, and blackened wood were all that was left of the building. The dream was to build a new one. That dream seemed impossible now.

Suddenly, the junk pile exploded into the air, nearly knocking the entire crowd of women and children over. The Matriarch steadied herself and swung her weapon toward the source of the blast; she pulled the trigger.

The projectile never reached its target.

It bounced off a rusty sprite husk floating in the air. A dirty boot stood on top of the husk, its leather partner floating on another husk beside it. The boots belonged to a figure standing erect twenty-five feet in the air. The figure did not even look down at the Matriarch or even seem to notice that a projectile had just been fired. The sprite rider surveyed the battlefield in the pastureland while a hundred more rusty husks floated in the air all around them. Then the rider, a woman, spoke in a commanding voice: "Dikaió, code red, authorization Dikaió Dominus. Backup generators activate; emergency plasma field activate."

All the women and children gasped in unison as a loud grinding noise sounded in the ground below them. It sounded like metal scraping against metal, and the Matriarch feared that fire sprites might follow after the horrible noise. Instead, a ring of pink fire encircled the city. Howls from the dark-forest beasts rang out as those on the perimeter burst into flames. The fire began to rise, burning through branches from the dark trees that had grown past the original boundary of the light. Huge bits of burning trees fell on the river of beasts, crushing some and igniting others. The

Matriarch's eyes widened. The light was returning.

When it was about one hundred feet up, the pink fire wavered and started to fall back toward the ground. Crashing from that height, it would certainly kill all the beasts, but it would kill a lot of the citizens of the city as well. The Matriarch looked questioningly toward the figure in the sky. She flinched slightly and clinched her fists. "Dikaió, match the frequency of the regulator for the plasma field of the Library and compensate for the size of Hoffen City." The wavering light started climbing again, and very quickly, it coalesced into a familiar dome above the city. Citizens began to cheer, but when the Matriarch looked back to the field of battle, she knew those cheers were premature. Hundreds of the beasts weren't on fire, and were ravaging their defenses, totally oblivious to the return of the light.

The figure then commanded, "Dikaió, defend Hoffen City and its citizens—100% mortality of the wilding wolves."

The Matriarch watched in fascination as all the remains of City Hall jumped off the ground and joined the figure in the air. Thousands of pieces of debris hovered there with her, searching for targets in the pastureland, and then a multitude of small sonic booms sounded as the debris shot forward faster than any projectile fired from a magistrate's weapon. As the debris hit the beasts of the dark forest, their bodies flew about in a macabre dance. The sound of their yelps and howls joined together in a cacophony of death, and then the air was quiet.

It took a moment to register the victory on the pasture-land, but then cheers from the men who survived the waves of beasts joined the women and children.

The Matriarch stayed silent and walked toward the floating figure. Who was this Dikaió-wielding stranger? The rider looked down at her, and the Matriarch froze mid-step. "Alex? Alex Nelson?"

"Dikaió down." Alex floated toward the Matriarch and stumbled off the rusted sprite husk she was riding. Her black leather gloves were torn and tattered, as were her clothes. Dried blood had stained her blue shirt in rusty splotches. Her black hair was long and matted, her face was gaunt, and her eyes sunk deep in her skull. Her lips were dried and chapped. She looked like she had not slept or had anything to eat or drink in days. Alex took a clumsy step toward the Matriarch and collapsed into her arms.

"The Ex Natu are coming," she whispered.

Acknowledgements

We thank God for calling us to finish this project: We owe sincere gratitude to You not only for providing constant inspiration and real joy in the process, but also for hounding us with conviction when we were distracted, discouraged, and ready to quit. We are thankful that You gave us this idea, that You turned our hearts toward our children and their needs, that You blessed our marriage with times of creative bonding, while guarding our words so that we would not mislead or cause harm in the process.

To our parents, thanks for helping us obtain library cards and supporting our creativity. Thanks to Stephen's father, Dale Porter, for exhilarating overnight adventures at the TV studio and encouraging his education. Thanks to Stephen's mother, Terry Porter, for providing his first dictionary and encyclopedia sets. Thanks to Gayle's father, John Gustafson, for trips to the library and teaching her how to operate the microfiche machine and use the Dewey decimal system. Thanks to Gayle's mother, Marjorie Gustafson, for teaching her that girls can learn anything if they are willing to work hard. Thanks to all our parents for giving us a good sense of humor, and for showing us beautiful places to remind us that God is the creative genius who made this vast, gorgeous world.

To our dear friends, Brad and Joy Kroes, and Ken and Donna Stucki, thank you for encouraging us and never telling us that we were making a huge mistake to become writers. We are grateful for your faithful friendship, for laughter and good food, and for your indelible patience with our incessant puns and sarcasm.

We also thank August, Anne, William and Abigail Thurmer;

Brandon and Kaylee Gustafson; and our church family for patiently cheering us on during this endeavor.

Finally, thank you to our readers who give purpose and fresh perspective to our writing. May you be inspired by our words, as you have inspired us to write.

www.ingramcontent.com/pod-product-compliance
Lightning Source LLC
Chambersburg PA
CBHW060727190726
48285CB00001B/104